Praise for Alexa Martin

"With so much conflict around them, Martin's characters find their strength in the abundant warmth of their connection."

—*New York Times*

"Alexa Martin's books are like sitting with a friend at a bar, drink in hand, while you laugh uproariously all night. I love everything she writes."

—Ali Rosen, author of *Recipe for Second Chances* and *Unlikely Story*

"Alexa Martin's romances never fail to deliver perfectly paced swoons, charming humor, and profound questions. *Better than Fiction* delights with bookish rom-com joy on every page, with a wonderfully relatable heroine whose connection to the man she's learning to love underlies her moving journey back to herself. This is a romance for the reader and the dreamer in everyone."

—Emily Wibberley and Austin Siegemund-Broka, authors of *The Roughest Draft*

"Alexa Martin is a powerhouse! In *Better Than Fiction* she delivers another one of her signature stories—clever, relatable, flirty, and warm. Between these pages is a loving tribute to independent bookstores and the people who find home and community among their stacks. Don't miss this unputdownable story about what it means to be truly loved in more ways than one."

—Rosie Danan, author of *The Roommate*

"*Better Than Fiction* is a charming, heartfelt rom-com, filled with great characters, laugh-out-loud banter, and some very cheeky seniors. It's also a sensitive portrayal of grief and a timely reminder of the vital role books and bookshops play in bringing people together. I loved it."

—Freya Sampson, author of *The Last Chance Library*

"Even at its most tender and aching moments, *Better Than Fiction* is charming and honey-sweet to its core."

—NPR

"Martin is an incredible storyteller and has a unique ability to blend fiction with real-life situations in the sports world."

—*New York Times* bestselling author La La Anthony

"The writing is snappy, the pacing is quick, the romance is sublime, and the humor is off the charts. Alexa Martin delivers a stellar love story, and I can't wait to see what she writes next."

—*USA Today* on *Intercepted*

"Martin scores a touchdown of a debut with *Intercepted*, a witty rom-com set in the world of professional football players and their wives."

—*Entertainment Weekly*

"Alexa Martin's books are the ultimate reading escape, filled with fabulous characters; witty, dazzling prose; and swoon-worthy romances."

—*New York Times* bestselling author Chanel Cleeton on *Mom Jeans and Other Mistakes*

"Alexa Martin is so good at this; I'm so impressed by how nuanced and thoughtful this book is, while still being hilarious and sexy!"

—*New York Times* bestselling author Jasmine Guillory on *Fumbled*

"Alexa Martin is an auto-buy author for me. *Mom Jeans and Other Mistakes* is a celebration of the strength, joy, and complications of female friendships that span our lifetimes. I will read anything Alexa Martin writes!"

—*USA Today* bestselling author Lyssa Kay Adams

TITLES BY ALEXA MARTIN

Mom Jeans and Other Mistakes

Better Than Fiction

Next-Door Nemesis

How to Sell a Romance

By the Bootstraps

THE PLAYBOOK SERIES

Intercepted

Fumbled

Blitz

Snapped

By the Bootstraps

ALEXA MARTIN

BERKLEY ROMANCE
NEW YORK

BERKLEY ROMANCE
Published by Berkley
An imprint of Penguin Random House LLC
1745 Broadway, New York, NY 10019
penguinrandomhouse.com

ISBN: 9780593816370

An application to register this book for cataloging has been submitted to the Library of Congress.

First Edition: May 2026

Printed in the United States of America
1st Printing

The authorized representative in the EU for product safety and compliance is Penguin Random House Ireland, Morrison Chambers, 32 Nassau Street, Dublin D02 YH68, Ireland, https://eu-contact.penguin.ie.

To anyone who's fallen off their horse and climbed back on no matter how hard it felt. Keep going, we've got this.

To Lindsay and Maxym, thank you for our cult of three and for being the community I thought I could only dream up in books with fictional towns.

By the Bootstraps

Chapter 1

Once upon a time, a great prophet proclaimed that in order to save a horse, one must ride a cowboy. I haven't been known to heed advice easily or often, but as a lover of horses and cowboys, it's advice I've decided to take seriously.

Too seriously, some might say.

"I still can't believe you're doing this, Luna." Gabby's frazzled voice fills the few empty crevices of my overstuffed car. "Maybe you should turn around."

"The time to change my mind was approximately twelve hours ago. Though a case could be made for a month ago." I accidentally stumbled across the small town of Celestial, Texas, during one of my many disassociation internet spirals, and it felt like fate. My name *is* Luna Starr, for goodness' sake. Moving to a town named Celestial, selling nearly all my possessions, and buying a house sight unseen seemed like a reasonable, if not inspired, idea. "I'm almost here. There's no turning back now."

Despite being surrounded by open fields that stretch far beyond what the eye can see, my navigation is saying I'm only thirty minutes away from my new home. The sun sits in the west of the cloudless, bright blue sky. Its relenting rays pound against the Texas terrain, the triple-digit temperature putting my car's air-conditioning to the test.

"You're a pain in my ass, but fine." Gabby snaps my attention back to her. I can practically see her beautiful face twisting into a frown. "I need you to understand that just because you abandoned me physically doesn't mean you get to leave me emotionally. I require at least two to fifteen phone calls daily, and if you ever leave my text messages on read, let it be known that I will be booking the first flight to Texas so I can scream at you in person. Got it?"

"Gabby, please be for real." I take my eyes away from the empty road in front of me and glance at the number ticking away on my phone. "We've been talking for the last three hours and forty-six minutes. There's no version of reality where I don't call you multiple times a day, every day."

"You say that now—" She cuts herself off, but the unspoken fear hangs heavy in the silence.

"It's never going to happen." The conviction in my voice drowns out the guilt I've been too selfish to let myself feel. "You're my family, and unfortunately for you, that means you're stuck with me for the long haul. Whether you like it or not."

Family is something I'm in serious need of as of late. This is not a declaration I can afford to take lightly.

"Good." She clears her throat, and just like she's done for me over the last year, I pretend I don't know she's crying. "As long as we're clear on the ground rules, I guess I'll let you finish your drive in peace. I told Frankie I'd cover for her class tonight. If I'm late, the Pilates moms will have my head."

"What are you waiting for?" A shiver runs down my spine at the thought of my best friend being the target of their ire. Gabby is a middle school teacher by day, a Pilates teacher by night—and summer—and I still don't know what's more terrifying, angry teens or moms. "Go make those women sweat and shake!"

It sounds naughtier than I intended. This happens more often than not thanks to my former life as an avid romance reader and professional romance novel pusher.

Luckily, Gabby has been my best friend for long enough that my unintentional innuendo doesn't faze her. Something I doubt will hold true for the good people of Celestial.

"Always do!" she says. "Send me pictures of your place once you've settled in."

She's seen the pictures the Realtor sent me approximately a million and one times. The fact that she's even remotely interested in looking at this house anymore is a testament to her love for me.

"You know I will!"

We hang up and the narrator from the cowboy romance audiobook I've been listening to starts right back where I forgot she left off. Her calm, beautiful voice pours from the speakers as the main character confronts the handsome hero who knows his way around a horse and, even though we haven't made it to that part of the book yet, I can safely assume, the bedroom. It's the eighth cowboy romance I've read since I made the decision to move.

The words meld with the scenery. Never-ending fields meet bright blue skies, and if I look closely enough, I can almost see my happily ever after playing out right alongside the book.

Or at least I hope so. It would suck if my story ended up being a horror novel.

I shake my fears out of my head and fall back into the story. I laugh at the author's jokes, and my breath hitches just so when they kiss for the first time. The safety and comfort of another romance novel wraps around me until I can finally relax my grip on the steering wheel and lose track of time.

Not that it matters.

When it comes to a schedule, I'm always on one. Thanks to my immaculate road trip planning, I knew when I left my house this morning that I'd be rolling into my new town by six o'clock p.m. Maybe earlier, but not a second later, and not even the brush with Dallas traffic could change it. It's 5:45 when the billboard announcing I've arrived finally rises from the horizon.

Welcome to Celestial, Texas.
Where the only thing brighter
than the stars are
the people.

The knot my stomach's been tied in loosens for the first time in months, and the relief I was convinced I'd never feel again pours through my veins like whiskey. My head swims and my foot tingles on the gas pedal. I almost pull over, but the winking lights over the scenic downtown streets beckon me farther.

My entire life, I've always known what comes next. For as long as I can remember, I didn't just have my next move planned, but the three—or fifty—that followed. I was the kid in middle school who could tell you what college I'd attend and knew that by the time I was twenty-one, I'd have it all figured out. Every little thing was accounted for, except, of course, life itself. And no amount of planning could've prepared me for the unimaginable or the fact that now, at the ripe old age of thirty, I'm starting over.

I never truly understood the term fight or flight until I decided to move to Celestial. It was like instinct and survival took hold of my nervous system and didn't release the controls until I had signed on the dotted line for my new house. It was the most rash, spontaneous, exhilarating thing I've done in my entire life.

It happened at the speed of lightning, and the adrenaline made it easy for me to bolster a confidence I wasn't sure I felt. After the way everything in my life had gone over the last few months—or one could argue, years—it was impossible to block out the quiet whisper in my brain telling me this town was too good to be true. That this was one more thing to add to a seemingly never-ending list of unshakable devastation and massive mistakes.

But as I get my first look at my new neighbors, goose bumps trail up my arms and hope blossoms deep in my belly. Bright smiles greet me as they wave hello to me as if I'm not some stranger driving through their town but instead like I've been here all my life. Their unhurried strides and comfortable gaits hint at lives where they've never had to run from anything, least of all the grief of losing the life you thought you were meant for. And for the first time, it really hits me. Maybe this is the first right decision I've made in a long time.

Maybe this is the fresh start I need.

In your face, therapist who told me that running from my problems wouldn't solve anything!

Unlike escaping the crisscross one-way streets hidden in the valleys of skyscrapers in downtown Denver, a residential neighborhood chases away downtown Celestial before I can even process the change of scenery. Bikes and scooters litter the chalk art–decorated driveways. My heart nearly explodes as I drive past an elderly couple sitting side by side on their front porch drinking what I can only hope are glasses of ice-cold sweet tea. Families crowd the sidewalks as they take their furry friends on walks now that evening is approaching and the temperature is falling from unfathomably hot to extremely uncomfortable. It's like a Hallmark movie come to life, and I don't know if I'll fit in, but *god* do I want to.

I pass the high school at the edge of town, and when I hit the open road again, I feel like I'm flying. I roll down my windows and the hot evening air that rushes inside hits me like a shot of espresso.

I turn off the audiobook and scan the radio until it finally lands on a station that is more music than static. Faith Hill's crisp voice explodes from my speakers, and I squeal before singing along with her about a man who knows how to love her right. Wide-open spaces surround me as I speed closer and closer to my very own slice of heaven. Cows lift their heads with little interest as I drive by, and I search for the houses belonging to the mailboxes posted alongside the empty highway. A quiet peacefulness swirls with effervescent excitement simmering just beneath my skin, and by the time my navigation tells me to turn left, I'm ready to explode.

I left Denver before the sun came up this morning, and

after what feels like an eternity fueled by extreme coffee consumption, I'm here.

Or at least I think I am.

The driveway is so unassuming, I drive past it three times before I finally spot the unmarked gravel road. Overgrown grass and a worn-down fence with rusted wire act as the welcome to my new house. My tires send pebbles flying, and the sound of them pelting my car can be heard over the radio. Dust billows around my car, but I can't be bothered to close my windows. I want to smell the Texas air, feel the heat of the waning day, taste the dirt that sneaks into my mouth because I can't stop smiling. I want to speed through what's left of the drive, but I dig deep to find the self-control I've had such a loose grip on so I can savor what's left of this new beginning.

As I draw nearer, the two-story farmhouse leaps out like the castle in every fairy tale I lost myself in as a child. The wraparound porch goes on forever, just like the open fields encasing it. Windows line the walls, and black shutters wave to me as they move with the evening breeze. It doesn't look exactly as I remember it looking in the pictures. The white paint is dull, and hints of brown wink at me from where it's chipped. Wood is warped in places I either ignored or overlooked, and the gutters look like they're liable to crash to the ground at any moment. But as I pull into the empty space in front of the detached garage, none of that matters.

When I first reached out to the lone real estate agency I was able to find in Celestial, I was only half-serious. Things had devolved into a mess of astronomical proportions, and there was so much on my plate that the thought of walking away from it all never seemed like an actual option.

And then I opened the email with the listing for this house.

I might be a pretty practical person most of the time—I budget wisely, drink my recommended water intake daily, and bought a modest Honda instead of the Audi the salesman tried to talk me into—but an even bigger part of me loves to lean into big dreams and happily ever afters. I was the top romance salesperson at the Book Nook for two years and promoted to the director of events and communication for a reason. I know people think they're insulting me when they call me delusional, but I wear it like a badge of honor. People act like being grounded is so important, when really, it's so much easier to see the big picture when you allow yourself to venture into the clouds. And this farmhouse, in this town, hundreds of miles from the only place I've ever lived, is the first piece of my big picture.

My engine rattles and makes a sound I don't love when I turn off the car. It's the first break it's had since I stopped at a gas station called Buc-ee's, a magical land with approximately a million bathrooms and a never-ending supply of coffee, and it's clear my car is as relieved as I am to have finally made it.

I reach for my door handle, but before I can open it, my hand freezes and my heart hammers inside my chest. Without any warning, the nerves I should've felt before I sent the sizable down payment for a house I've never set foot in make a very sudden and very unwelcome appearance. Alongside the fear that no matter where I live, I'll never have a real home again.

"Oh no. Absolutely not." My loud voice is a stark contrast to the peaceful quiet of my new front yard as I scold myself. "Good things only from here on out, Starr. You deserve this."

Gabby might've wanted to beat me to death with the self-help books I've relied on for the last few months, and I can admit to going a little overboard with the positive affirmation sticky notes I plastered in every nook and corner of my apartment. It's just that when you feel like you're dangling by a thread to survive, you'll latch on to anything if it means you might not fall. The power of positive thinking might seem flimsy to others, but it's been a lifeline for me, and it's all I know to ensure nothing taints what I plan on building here.

In my new home, enveloped in possibility and wonder, there's no room for negativity.

No room for fear.

Not even in my mind.

I close my eyes and draw in a deep, even breath. Focusing on pushing the nerves away and clinging to the relief I felt not thirty minutes ago, I allow my head to drift into the vast, open skies above. I push away the past and envision the future that, for the first time in a long time, I'm in charge of, until it does the trick.

Thank the lucky stars.

Before I can lose my courage, I hop out of the car and pull my suitcases out of the jam-packed trunk. Naive excitement chases the fear away and propels me up the unpaved walkway I already have big plans for. Ignoring the precariously wobbly steps and the way the wood planks bow from the weight of my suitcase, I throw open the squeaky screen door and grab the lockbox hanging on my front door. I memorized the code days ago, but my hands are so shaky that it takes me five times before I get it right. When the box clicks open and the key falls into my hand, I nearly weep.

This is it. My perfect chance at a fresh start.

And maybe, if I'm really lucky, a happily ever after of my very own.

Chapter 2

After weeks of anticipation, I push open my front door and cross the threshold of my new home for the very first time. I draw in a deep breath like one does when sitting in a brand-new car, only to quickly discover that that's one sensation that does not transfer to old, in-need-of-love houses.

The sharp, biting odor the previous owners left behind hits me like one of the crumbling bricks on the fireplace, and my eyes water while my senses struggle to adjust. The floor groans beneath my feet as I walk deeper into the room, like it's an old house's way of saying hello. Sunlight spills in through the open blinds lining the far wall and the falling dust looks more like confetti than the culprit behind my itchy sinuses.

I wasn't under the impression that I was getting a turnkey-ready home when I sent in the down payment for this house. Houses in rural Texas might seem like a steal compared to the prices in metro Denver, but even I knew landing a three-bedroom house on five acres for just over one hundred thousand dollars meant there'd be plenty of work. It's just that now, seeing everything in person, I can't help but notice the way the scratches marring the original hardwood floors are a little deeper and the need for new paint on the chipped walls is a little more dire than I'd anticipated. And those are just the cosmetic things.

This should probably scare me, but instead, it does the opposite.

From its bones to mine, I can feel down to the studs that this is where I'm meant to be. It might be more work than I anticipated, but every project will turn this forgotten old house into something that nobody will be able to deny is worthy and loved. It's my opportunity to create the home I never thought I'd find.

I abandon my suitcases in the middle of the floor and wander from room to room. The house might not be a mansion by any stretch of the imagination, but it feels like one to me. At a whopping 2,200 square feet, it's more than three times bigger than the one-room apartment I left in Denver. I feel every square inch as I twirl around in the open kitchen and skip up and down the narrow staircase until my lungs burn. There isn't a single room that doesn't need at least a coat of paint, and my fingers itch to turn my Pinterest board dreams into reality.

It takes me more trips than I hoped to unpack my car. By the time I finish setting up the blow-up mattress in my new bedroom, the honeyed, amber glow of the golden hour pours through the open window overlooking the back of my house. When the caffeine-fueled determination begins to fade and my stomach starts to growl, I'm faced with two options:

1) Eat a leftover protein bar from the road and soak in the claw-foot tub I've been dreaming of since the moment I saw it.

2) Freshen up, venture into town, and celebrate my arrival with a cocktail and a hot meal.

As a lover of both lazy nights in and craft cocktails, this choice isn't one I take lightly. But after careful consideration and a directive from my stomach that anything less than a meal simply won't do after a day of fast food, going into town is the clear option. This is, after all, the first night of the rest of my life. If I want to immerse myself into my new community, there's no time like the present.

After donating nearly all my winter clothes, I was able to fit almost my entire wardrobe—footwear excluded—in my suitcases. I unzip them both and flip through everything until I spot one of the sundresses I unearthed while I was cleaning out my closet. The dress might be at least four years old, but the tags are still firmly in place . . . just like on the other seven dresses I forgot I bought for the vacation I never took. It's lavender with little red flowers scattered all over and, miraculously, still fits me like a glove. It's perfect for my Celestial debut.

The sun begins to set as I rush through my makeup and hair routine. I quickly draw on the cat eyeliner I perfected during the early days of lockdown and coat my lashes with mascara. I spritz my curls with water, cover them with mousse, and cross my fingers that it will rid them of the frizz that built up over the drive and unpacking the car. It's not much, but hopefully it's enough to make it look like I've tried.

I slip my feet into the sexy metallic sandals Gabby gave me as a going-away present. They cost a fortune and I tried to tell her no, but she insisted that my well-worn sneakers were no way to walk into my new life. I wish I had a full-length mirror to see how right she was. Instead, I carefully apply my favorite red lipstick before leaning into a small mirror haphazardly hanging on the wall and whisper to my reflection, "You got this, Starr. Everyone is going to love you."

And if they don't? Who cares? I only sold my childhood home, quit my job, and uprooted my life to be here.

Dear god.

Please let them like me.

WISPY CLOUDS DANCE above me as a pink-and-purple sunset chases the blue out of the vast Texas sky while I drive back into town. The beauty is almost enough to distract me from the twinge of sadness that creeps in as the sun sets below a mountain-free horizon. My fingers itch to leave the steering wheel and snap a picture to send to my mom. Our text messages are filled with snapshots of the sky. She'd love this.

Or at least she would have.

There are more people out now than when I drove through town earlier, and the small town is buzzing with untapped energy. Beneath the darkening skies and twinkling lights zigzagging over Main Street, the quaint downtown buildings look even more magical now than they did hours ago. I didn't think it was possible, but it's even better than I imagined.

Unlike the nightmare that is finding parking in downtown Denver, I find an open spot right away. I check my rearview mirror one last time, take a deep breath, and join the strangers I hope will soon become friends on the sidewalk. Some offer smiles, while others wave. A small few don't seem to notice me at all. It's like the first day of school all over again, and the endless possibilities are as enticing as they are terrifying.

Pleasant conversation fills the air, but despite my propensity to eavesdrop when the opportunity arises, I can't focus. As soon as I told anyone I was moving to Texas, they would warn me about the heat. Colorado may have a reputation for snow, but any native knows that the summers get hot. I'd spent enough time hiking trails on summer days that even though I knew it would be bad, I figured I was prepared.

News flash. Nothing could prepare me for this.

The cool breeze I'm accustomed to is nowhere to be found, and instead, humidity lingers heavy in the night air. Even with the sun out of the picture, heat still clings to my skin as beads of sweat fall beneath the mass of curls covering my neck. It's so distracting that I don't even realize I've followed the crowd away from Main Street until a little town square only accessible by foot appears in front of me.

It's like I've stepped out of the real world and onto the set of a Hallmark movie. Tiny shops and restaurants with different color doors and awnings enclose the space. Baskets overflowing with flowers hang from every streetlight, and music plays from speakers embedded in the pavement. Peals of laughter and elated shrieks of joy echo off the buildings as kids sprint through the water fountains at the center of the square. Water shoots up from the ground with impeccable timing as toddlers and teens alike try to anticipate where it will come from next. Benches dot the space, filled with grateful parents who watch the aquatic babysitter wear out their little ones. If it weren't for the persistent growl of my stomach, I'd sit down and join them.

I wander around the square, my meandering steps in direct opposition to my empty stomach, and take my time to look into all the adorable storefronts. I peek through the window of the closed flower shop and steal a glance at the vases stuffed with blooms. A chalkboard sign sits outside a coffee shop, the seasonal drinks sprawled across it in perfect penmanship, and I make a note to swing by tomorrow to try the iced blueberry vanilla latte. The bell above the door of Joanie's Ice Cream rings over and over again as crowds file in and out holding cones piled high with different flavors.

For such small town, Celestial has an impressive number of restaurants. I'm on the verge of being overwhelmed by choices when a large group of women files out of the door to my left and their boisterous voices draw the attention of almost everyone around me. Crumb and Crust is written in bold, white script letters on a turquoise-and-yellow awning hanging above the door. I have no idea what kind of food they serve inside, but thanks to the women who just left, I don't care. Nobody leaves a restaurant as happy as they were unless they've had their fair share of good food and, likely, better drinks.

Which happens to be exactly what I'm in the market for.

The noise of the square falls away as soon as the window-plated door closes behind me. It smells like heaven and carbs inside, and my stomach cramps in anticipation. Customers fill every booth, and mountains of food cover the tables. If the women outside didn't already have me convinced, one look around the cozy space would have.

"Welcome to Crumb and Crust." A young girl greets me from behind a hostess table. Glossy chestnut hair tumbles past her shoulders, and her warm smile seems more genuine than out of paid obligation. "How many tonight?"

"Just me," I say.

It's funny how when I was a teenager, the thought of eating dinner alone was the saddest, scariest scenario I could think of, and now it's one of the rituals I look forward to most. Thank goodness, since for now, eating alone is my only option.

"Wonderful." She scans the paper in front of her and scratches in a number with the pink pen she's holding. "If you want a table, we're looking at a twenty- to thirty-minute wait. But if you're okay with it, the bar is first come, first serve, and a large party just left, so there are a lot of open seats."

Not only am I too hungry to wait thirty more minutes, but sitting at the bar feels like the thing someone who just moved to town and is interested in meeting new people would do.

"The bar is perfect, thank you."

"You're welcome," she says, before lowering her voice and leaning across the table separating us. "By the way, I love your dress and your shoes . . . and your hair. You look so hot."

As someone who identifies strongly as a girl's girl, you will never, ever catch me dressing for male validation. You think the care I put into my curls, the four different shades of red lipstick I own, and the carefully chosen color story of my wardrobe is all for a *man*? Ew. Yuck. Absolutely not. I'm doing it all for the girls.

"Oh my god. Thank you so much!" I'm convinced my feet are no longer on the ground. I stick my hands into the hidden slits sewn into the skirt to give her the only acceptable response. "It has pockets!"

I'm not supposed to admit this, but even though getting a compliment from another woman will always make my day, the exact same words always mean more coming from the mouth of a teenage girl. And it's not that I'm ageist, because

I'm not! It's that I'm still traumatized from my high school years of not being one of the cool kids.

Fitting in with the youths? Be still my tender heart, it's like achieving the super platinum level of winning.

Her grin widens. "Adorable!"

Honestly, I could go home right now because I'm going to dine on this for the next three to five business days. The urge to tell her the long, sordid story about when and where I ordered the dress and ask what leave-in conditioner she uses is almost too strong to overcome. But I know that in order to fall asleep basking in the glow of a compliment, not ruminating on the way I embarrassed myself, I must fight my natural inclination to be cringe. It's not easy and takes more effort than I'd care to admit, but I manage to walk to the bar leaving her—and her perfect hair—behind me.

Not long before I moved, Gabby convinced me to try a new bar near my apartment. Every square inch of the place was designed with Instagram in mind, and the influencers with their phones glued to their hands were eating it up. Neon signs with popular sayings hung on gold leaf–covered wallpaper. Velvet barstools sat in front of marble countertops. The food looked more presentable than edible, and every cocktail came garnished with floral ice cubes and glitter rims.

This bar is not that.

It's not a dive bar by any stretch of the imagination, but it's clear to anyone who enters that interior design came second to the items they are serving. Priorities that I, for one, very much appreciate. The heavy wood bar top is reminiscent of the one I used to see when my mom and I watched *Cheers* together. Glasses hang from overhead as the busy bartenders hustle back and forth, pulling from the beer tap handles and grabbing bottles of alcohol from the stacked shelves lining the wall behind them.

My hostess with great hair didn't lie; other than a few men wearing cowboy hats and talking to the TV instead of one another, almost all the seats are open. I should sit closer to the other diners, but before I can tell myself otherwise, I veer toward the empty seats in the corner of the bar. I'm still tucking my sundress beneath me on the leather-upholstered stool when a bartender appears in front of me with two menus in his hands.

"Evening, ma'am," he says, and his thick Texas drawl is the only thing that can distract me from the sting of being referred to as *ma'am* by someone this close to my age. "Are we eating, drinking, or both tonight?"

"Both, please." I smile gratefully when he hands me the menus.

"Good choice." He smiles back, not lacking the Southern hospitality Celestial's official town Instagram boasted about. "Take all the time you need. If you need anything or have any questions, my name's Nolan. Just give me a call."

"Thank you, but I'm starving," I say, and as if on cue, my stomach starts to growl. "I'm sure I'll be ready to order in a minute."

Spoiler alert: I need much longer than a minute to look everything over.

I'm so hungry that all of the food on the Southern-inspired menu looks divine. There are at least three things I need and five more that I want. And that's just the food! The drink menu is equally loaded, but unlike the food where I can, and likely will, order at least one extra meal to go, I can only have one cocktail.

"Ugh." I toss the menu on the bar, unable to deal with my own bullshit at the moment. Curse my indecisiveness! I know I said I like eating alone, but in moments like this, it would be really nice if I had someone to split things with.

"Can't make up your mind?" The smooth, deep voice catches me by surprise, and I damn near jolt off my seat.

I was so focused on the menu, I didn't even realize someone sat in the empty seat next to me. Thankfully, the stealthy stranger also has catlike reflexes and his large hand in the middle of my back steadies me before I go flying off the stool.

Way to play it cool, Luna.

There goes my plan for not ruminating on my cringey behavior tonight.

"Oh my god!" My laughter carries over the country music playing on the speakers overhead and the murmur of sports talk from the TVs behind the bar as I try, and fail, to play off my mortifying little snafu. "I'm so sorry."

"No, I'm sorry," he says. "I didn't mean to startle you."

"Trust me, it's not you. I—"

I turn to apologize, to explain my long history of overreacting to the barest hint of a threat, but when I face the stranger beside me, I not only forget what I was going to say, but my knowledge of the English language altogether. In my defense, I'd imagine most people would also be rendered speechless if they, too, were to come face-to-face with someone who is perhaps the most beautiful human walking planet earth . . . and likely all the other planets too.

I don't think I can be blamed for this.

I don't think anybody could be blamed for this.

His flawless, dark brown skin looks as if silk has been poured across the sharp angles of his high cheekbones and chiseled jawline. A neatly trimmed beard that my fingers itch to touch frames his full, deceptively soft lips. Onyx eyes so dark and mysterious stare back at me, and even though I've been in his presence for mere seconds, something tells me that if it meant I could know even a fraction of the secrets they're hiding, I would gladly spend the rest of my life gazing into them. Sinewy arms corded with muscles are at direct odds with the gentle touch of his hand on my back. And as if all this wasn't already too much hotness for one person, the mass of long, perfectly twisted locs piled into a messy bun at the top of his stunning head is the cherry on top of an already decadent sundae.

Hard yet soft.

Strong yet gentle.

Wild yet controlled.

His beauty is a living, breathing contradiction, and I don't know how to look away. Or if I want to.

"Ma'am?" He pulls his hand off my back like it's on fire, and his apologetic gaze turns wary as he begins to shift uncomfortably on his stool, and that awful word sounds even worse coming from his hot mouth. "Are you alright?"

My first night out in Celestial and I've been called *ma'am* twice and officially turned into a creep.

Lovely.

"I'm fine and, really, I should be the one apologizing." I rush out the words and attempt to shake myself free of whatever horny spell his face put me under. "I startle really easily. Always have, but you're a stranger, so how would you know? I actually got banned from a haunted house in high school because of how overboard I was. My mom used to startle me all the time and she was my literal mom. It's one of the things that drove her most insane about me. I've tried to get over it, I even went to a hypnotist once, but I can't figure it out. Clearly."

I don't know what I expected to happen when my brain finally took control of my mouth and told me to shut the hell up, but absolute silence from the man next to me was not it.

This poor man probably just wanted a drink, and instead, some random-ass stranger—me!—not only openly ogled him, but word-vomited all over him too. Heat detonates across my face, and I send a silent prayer of gratefulness up to my parents. It's in small, horrifying moments like this that I'm reminded how lucky I am that my mom fell in love with a Black man. Of course I wish he could've taught me to ride a bike or read, but if I couldn't get memories, at least I can always count on the melanin he passed down to prevent my face from lighting up like a neon sign, proclaiming to all who look my way that I, Luna Starr, have embarrassed myself.

Again.

I pull out my phone, ready to email my Realtor to inform them that despite my recent arrival, it's already time for me to move, when the weirdest thing happens.

I don't know if it's a trick of the light or if I'm still lightheaded from giving him my entire life story without taking a single breath, but I'm pretty sure the corner of his mouth turns up into something that resembles a smile.

"What's one of the other things?"

Am I hallucinating?

"What's one of what things?" I don't know if it's because I can only focus on the rich, smooth tenor of his voice and the way his full lips move when he speaks, but I'm not following.

"What's one of the other things that drove your mom insane?"

It's the last thing I expect him to say, but for some reason, instead of my veins turning to ice like they're wont to do when someone mentions my mom, an unfamiliar warmth flows through me like honey.

"I know it's hard to believe because I seem so put together and perfect, but she wasn't short on pet peeves when it came to me," I say, turning my body so I'm facing him head-on. "Though, I guess if I had to pick just one thing going off the very brief amount of time I've spent with you, it might be my tendency to ramble and overshare when I'm nervous or embarrassed."

A burst of laughter slips through his full lips, and the whisper of a smile from earlier transforms into a full-blown grin. I try not to repeat my earlier mistake and stare at how bright his perfect teeth look against his skin, but I can't help myself. I can't pretend to know this man, but something tells me that witnessing the way his eyes crinkle in the corners and a small dimple appears on his left cheek is a gift I should cherish.

"You are talking very fast." Remnants of his smile linger in his eyes even as it fades from his mouth. "Are you embarrassed?"

I feel like most men would use this as an easy opening to try to pick me up, but to my complete disappointment and dismay, there's only unassuming curiosity in his words.

"You know, shouting at a stranger in the middle of a restaurant would leave me embarrassed any day, but it doesn't help that I just moved into town and this is my first night in Celestial." I fidget with my hands, wishing more than anything I had a cocktail to hold and alcohol to ease my nerves. "I've been talking a big game and telling anyone who asked that I didn't have any second thoughts about moving here, but I guess I'm a little nervous that I won't fit in. It's scary not knowing anyone."

I regret the words as soon as I say them. It's almost as if by saying my fears out loud, I've invited them in and given them permission to come true. I don't know what it is about this man, but I can't seem to stop myself from saying the first thing on my mind when I'm with him.

"If it makes you feel better, I've lived here my entire life and I don't think you need to worry about fitting in. But trust me"—he leans in and his voice drops to a whisper—"fitting in around here is overrated."

Goose bumps snake down my spine as the warmth of his breath dances along the shell of my ear. His proximity knocks me completely off-balance, and I struggle to keep my slow, measured breaths from turning ragged. I know it's been a month or twelve since I've had sex, but this is absurd. There's no reason to be turned on by a literal whisper.

Before I can do something stupid like tell him about the time my mom banned me from the stairs after I fell and put a hole through the wall, or worse, invite him back to my place for the night, Nolan reappears holding a paper bag. The man, *the stranger*, leans back and I get an up-close view as the last bits of his smile flee and shutters fall over his eyes. It's devastating and I would do anything to put another smile on his face.

"Your usual." Nolan slides the to-go bag across the bar, completely oblivious to the huge loss I just suffered. "Dan told me to let you know he put the extra ranch in the box on the bottom this time."

"Appreciate it, Nolan." The man beside me takes his food,

only looking back to me after he unfolds his long body from his stool. "Good luck in Celestial. I hope you like it here."

Panic hits me like lightning. Heat blazes from my head down to my toes when I realize that after all that, I don't even know his name. He turns to leave, and like the rest of the time we've spent together, I act before I can think better of it.

I jump off the barstool and wrap my fingers around his wrist.

"Luna! I'm Luna," I shout, repeating myself when his questioning gaze meets mine. "You didn't tell me your name."

It sounds more like an accusation than a question, but our earlier interaction must have softened him to my antics, because he doesn't seem fazed at all.

"Tate." He turns his palm over and shakes my hand with his strong, calloused one. "Nice meeting you, Luna."

I've never loved my name more.

"Nice to meet you too, Tate." I return the sentiment and let go of my grip on his hand, knowing that *nice* doesn't come close to describing what meeting him felt like. "See you around again someday?"

"Maybe." *Maybe* sounds a lot like *no* the way he says it. "It's a pretty small town."

My smile only wavers a little bit. "I think I'll take that as a yes."

A quick nod is his only response and then he's gone. The bar feels a lot bigger and the air-conditioning is cooler without him here. I replay the interaction in my head, the details simultaneously as fuzzy as they are clear, but no matter how many times I go over it, I'm unsure if I should feel more hopeful or foolish.

"Don't take it personally," Nolan says with a careful, gentle tone that dances the line to pity. "Tate's like that with everyone."

Foolish.

I should definitely feel more foolish.

"I guess that means I'm fitting in just fine." I try to hide my disappointment behind forced enthusiasm. "Now that it's just us, I'm going to need you to tell me what to order. Everything looks amazing and I can't make up my mind."

"That I can help you with." He points to the menu and I return his smile.

I nod along as he lists his favorite items on the menu and agree to his suggestions without hearing a single word he says, too busy trying to remember a man I might not ever see again to focus on something unimportant like food.

I know I came to Celestial hoping for a cowboy romance, but maybe, just maybe a brooding hero with onyx eyes and a reserved smile is what I really need.

Chapter 3

Road trips are so sneaky.

Maybe there was magic in the margarita I couldn't even finish and the hot honey chicken sandwich that was the size of my head—I absolutely managed to finish that—but you'd think after hours and hours of sitting in the car, I'd be left with more energy than I'd know what to do with. I haven't had a night with more than five hours of sleep since my mom died, since her body couldn't handle the alcohol she was so sure she needed, and I knew last night would be no different. I had big plans to stay up all night going over my to-do list while I prepared for the movers to arrive in the morning. So color me shocked when I lay on the air mattress and only thought about Tate for a few minutes before I was out like a light.

THE TEXAS HEAT kisses my face and pulls me from my dreamless sleep. I squint against the bright, unrelenting sunshine creeping through the window and rub the sleep out of my eyes. I reach for my phone so I can move "order and install blackout curtains" to the top of my to-do list.

"Shit!" I scream when my vision clears and my screen comes into focus. Not only is it after ten, I slept through five missed calls and two texts from Gabby, one missed call from my uncle, and worse, I have three missed calls and two voicemails from my movers.

I delete the voicemail from my uncle without bothering to listen, and I roll off the half-deflated mattress. I run down my stairs, praying I won't be greeted with all my belongings stacked in my front yard.

For the first time in years, luck is on my side.

Not only are my boxes nowhere to be found, neither is the giant moving truck or the grumpy driver I'm determined to win over before our time together comes to an end. I hit the number on my phone without listening to their messages. The phone rings in my ear as I make my way back into my practically empty room and somehow manage to slam my toe into the corner of my suitcase.

"Holy owwww! Mother fu—" I cry out at the same time a man's voice comes through my phone, because if I have anything at all, it's horrible timing.

"Hello?" He sounds like he's not sure if he should be angry, concerned, or annoyed.

"Brian? This is Luna," I force through gritted teeth, trying to ignore the way the pain in my toe is radiating up my entire leg. "I missed your calls earlier."

"Did you listen to the voicemails?" His tone settles on annoyed, and unfortunately, I can't fault him for it. "I left two."

"You did? I'm so sorry. I didn't see them." I feign ignorance, and thanks to years of experience, I do it very well. "The service here isn't great."

I'm definitely going to have to up their tip.

"The first message was to inform you of some truck trouble we were experiencing and letting you know your delivery might be delayed until tomorrow." He pauses and I try not to react. I have a feeling I'm already working this man's last nerve, and since he, quite literally, holds all my possessions, I don't want to make things worse than they already are. "The second message was to tell you we figured everything out and although there will still be a delay, it won't be by much."

I exhale a sigh of relief and collapse back onto the air mattress.

"What the heck, Brian? Was it necessary to scare me like that? I thought we were friends." I ordered in when they were loading the moving truck, and not just pizza either. I got the good stuff! "We had falafel together!"

Is nothing sacred anymore?

"You know we like you, girl." He sounds so exasperated with me that I can't ask him not to call me *girl*. "We're about two hours out. Keep your phone on you until we get there, will ya?"

"Ten-four, captain." I salute even though he can't see me, and I know he's rolling his eyes despite me not being able to see him either. "Also, if you stop by a Buc-ee's, can you grab me the biggest cup of coffee that they offer and some tacos? Oh! And fudge!"

"Bye." He hangs up and I stare at my phone for longer than I should. *Was that a yes or no?*

"Rude," I whisper to an empty room. "But understandable."

Now that I have two hours instead of the two minutes I

was afraid I had, I'm not really sure what to do with my time. Back in Colorado, my mornings were run like a tight ship. From my coffee, to my shower, to my workout, everything had a precise time and I didn't stray from it—not even on my days off—until I strayed so far, I ended up unemployed on an air mattress in a small Texas town.

My to-do list is a million and one miles long, but until the moving truck gets here, there's not much I can do. Without the constant go, go, go of my old life insistently nagging at the back of my brain, I don't have anything to do other than letting the peace and calm of my new reality wash over me like the shower I should be taking.

I tuck my legs beneath me and stare out my window into the crystal-clear blue skies looming over the never-ending pastures surrounding my new home. The possibilities of what I can create here feel endless, and that somehow feels almost as scary as having no possibilities at all. It's as if nothing counted until this very moment and now it's up to me, and me alone, to make sure I turn my life into something worth living for.

My farmhouse sits on a modest five acres, but the property next to me goes on for miles. The houses—multiple—sitting in the distance are only specks on the horizon as I search for horses and cattle like my own personal version of *Where's Waldo?*

Below my window, the empty chicken coop I'm determined to fill with the best, most loved chickens is sandwiched between the house I can't wait to explore despite my tragically black green thumb and a finished shed that will soon become my craft space. Before this move, my biggest home project was installing a ceiling fan in my bedroom.

I ended up hiring a Taskrabbit.

That's not going to happen this time. This time I'm prepared. I took every class Home Depot had leading up to this move, and I'm pretty sure I'm working toward my PhD from YouTube University and HGTV-U. Plus, thanks to being unemployed—woof—and the windfall of money I've received from selling my childhood home and my mom's life insurance—double woof—I have enough money to focus on the house before I worry about finding a new job.

Rainbow to every dark night of the soul and all that jazz.

Counting cows is as effective as counting sheep, and I almost fall back asleep. But as tempting as a nap sounds, I force myself into the shower instead. Poor Brian has dealt with enough from me. The least I can do is greet him with clean hair and brushed teeth.

Unlike my ultramodern bathroom in my apartment back in Denver, what my new bathroom lacks in size and outlet options, it makes up for in charm. Sun pours through the giant stained-glass window above the claw-foot tub, and delicate flowers decorate the square tiles lining the bottom half of the chipped-paint walls. The Realtor told me the pedestal sink is original to the house, and even though it's adorable, it has to go. I don't have a lot of makeup, but as a curly girl with more hair products than I'd care to admit, I had to order a vanity with plenty of storage space. It should be arriving in the next few days, and it's one of the first renovation projects on my list.

I lather up my loofah and make quick work of washing off the remaining scent of fast food clinging to my skin, thanks to the time I spent in the car yesterday. When the inspection for this house came back, the water heater was on the list of suggested replacements. It still works, but the days of long, lazy showers are a thing of the past until I reach that section of my checklist. The hot water begins to fade as I rinse the last bits of conditioner from my hair. It might have been short, but that magical, brand-new feeling a shower gives you still hits me as I step onto the tile floors.

I tuck a towel tight around my body before venturing back into the bedroom. Cold air whirs from the vent, and goose bumps chase the drops of water falling from curls down my back. I carefully approach the suitcases still sitting haphazardly in the middle of my room and pull out another dress with the tags still on. This one is yellow and it slips right over my head. The soft linen skims my freshly lotioned skin, and not for the first time, I thank god that the generous boob genetics that plagued my mom's side of my family tree skipped over me and I can go braless.

A knock sounds at my door just before the doorbell rings right as I finish running curl cream through my hair.

Perfect timing!

This never happens.

"Here I come!" I don't bother to give myself a once-over before running to meet Brian and the rest of his talented, strong, wonderful motley moving crew. "Did you bring me coffee?"

The clownish size of my smile preemptively makes up for the scowl Brian wears so well, except when I swing open the front door, it's not Brian's grumpy face that I see.

No.

Not even close.

It's not that Brian isn't a handsome man, he is. He's just not . . . this man.

And by *man*, what I mean is perhaps the most handsome

man I've ever seen in my entire life—only coming in second to maybe Tate, and I'd have to stand them next to each other to decide—and he's standing on my front porch with gifts and a cowboy hat.

I've heard the term *sun-kissed* before, but up until this moment, I'm not sure I ever knew what it meant. His brown skin sparkles even in the shade, flecks of gold winking at me as if the sun poured down from the sky and deemed him—and him alone—the recipient of all its beauty. Smile lines crease at the corners of honey eyes framed by the thickest lashes I've ever seen. I clench my fists in order to not reach out and trace them with my fingertips and bite my tongue to stop myself from asking about the stories behind every line on his gorgeous face.

Have I died and gone to heaven? Because for such a small town, Celestial sure does seem to have an abundance of fine-ass men. And to think, up until this very moment, the only luck I thought I had was the bad kind.

"I didn't bring coffee, but I did bring gifts." He holds up a glass bottle of milk and a canvas bag filled with what looks like a cornucopia of fruits and vegetables. "If you want a coffee, though, I'm sure I can make that happen."

"I'm so sorry!" My face heats, but I can't be sure if it's from embarrassment, the rush of hot air as I opened the door, or, and let's be honest here, lust. "I thought you were someone else."

"Damn, and here I was hoping I'd be the first one showing up at your doorstep." The deep timbre of his voice pulls my attention away from the fabric straining against his impressive arms and back to his even more impressive face. "Though, seeing you, it makes sense that I'm not."

Oh . . . wow.

"The movers! I thought you were the movers," I rush out, and the flush that covers my face this time is definitely not weather related. "You're the first person to come by."

His full lips curve into a kind, unassuming smile. If he notices how flustered he's making me, he's polite enough to pretend not to notice. It only makes me like him more.

"Lucky me, then." He stretches out his empty hand and introduces himself. "I'm Silas Jacobs. Nice to meet you."

Other than Nolan and Tate from last night, the only other name I know in Celestial is Patricia, the Realtor who helped me with my move. But for some reason the name triggers recognition in the recesses of my brain.

"Of course, Jacobs! My neighbor!" I shout the answer to a question that hasn't been asked. "I'm Luna. It's so nice to finally meet you. Patricia told me all about you."

"Oh no." A grimace chases away his smile. It makes me want to weep. "Patricia has a way with words. I hope she didn't say anything too bad."

"Not at all." I tell him the god's honest truth. "She was trying to sell me a house, so everything was quite complimentary."

As soon as I told Patricia I was hoping to find a house out of the city and on a little bit of land, she started regaling me with tales about the family who owned the legendary Starlight Ridge Ranch that bordered what would become my very own slice of heaven. She told me how the Jacobs family has been a staple of the Celestial community since their family first landed there in the late 1800s. She regaled me about their history and how what began as a modest working farm exploded into the nearly ten-thousand-acre cattle ranch it is today, thanks to generations of determined and hardworking

Jacobses. She went on and on about the longhorn cattle that roam the land and the fresh produce from their gigantic garden that keeps the farmers market stocked.

She told me everything about Starlight Ridge Ranch, it seems, except for the fact that Silas Jacobs is hot. Really hot. Like a nineties-fine, stars-in-a-Janet-Jackson-video kind of hot.

And now he's living next door.

Just like the start of every cowboy romance I've ever read.

"I was worried she might've filled you in on the wild tractor tales of my younger years." Quiet laughter spurred on by the memories of stories I'm already desperate to hear falls from his mouth. "You never know the stories you'll get around here."

"I can't tell you what she's telling the people she's not making a commission off of, but she gave me a glowing review." I open the screen door a little wider. "Do you want to come in?"

I probably should have led with that, but it's easy to forget things when a tall, dark, and handsome man with huge biceps and broad shoulders appears on your foot porch.

"You know what?" He glances at the very expensive-looking watch on his wrist. "I have a few minutes to spare, so sure. Why not?"

Before he steps inside, he pulls off his cowboy hat and holds it to his chest. It's like he's unwrapping a gift and each reveal is more wonderful than the one before. His fresh fade is lined so sharp, it's only outdone by the sharp cut of his jaw. Once he's inside, he toes off the well-loved cowboy boots it's clear he wears out of necessity, not fashion. There is something so familiar and comfortable about seeing this man standing in my living room in his socks. His presence fills every single nook and cranny.

"Welcome to my humble abode." The gentle hum of the air conditioner buzzes over the sound of my pulse in my ears. "I'd offer you a place to sit, but like I said, you beat the movers."

"Wow." He looks around the space with wide-eyed wonder. "The last time I was here, Mrs. Monroe had every inch of this place filled with tchotchkes and floral lace. It doesn't even look like the same place."

"I bet." Patricia told me the former owners lived here for over fifty years. If the amount of junk I acquired over the last two years is any indicator, I can only imagine all the things they packed in this house. "It's wild to see how what makes a home has less to do with the house itself than the people living in it."

It's the reason I sold my house in Colorado. I knew I could keep it and not change a thing, but at the end of the day, without my mom or grandma there, it would never feel the same again. I'd rather live in a town of strangers than a house filled with ghosts.

"Truly." He smirks and mischief swirls like whiskey in his hypnotic eyes. "Though I have a feeling the cats they had over the years will make it harder than not to forget about them."

So that's what that smell is!

"Patricia forgot to mention the cats when sending me information about the house."

"I'm sure she did." His raspy laughter winds through the room like tendrils of smoke. "This was a packed house. The Monroes had as many cats as they had dogs and kids."

The veins in his arms pull my attention when he readjusts his grip on the bag he's holding, and I remember my manners in my pitiful attempt not to stare.

"Let me take that." I don't wait for an answer, and my eyes go wide when I take it from him. Judging by how heavy it is, he must've given me enough to feed a family of four. "This is unbelievably thoughtful of you. I don't know how I'm going to be able to go through it all."

He avoids my gaze almost as if he's embarrassed . . . which can't be right.

"I may have gone a little overboard." He shoves his hand in his pocket and shifts on his feet. "It's just some produce from our garden and milk from our cows. And don't worry, it's pasteurized."

"Thank you," I say. "I'm excited to get in touch with the simple, natural things in life, but I'd prefer to skip the salmonella and listeria part. I haven't made it to the grocery store yet, so it will be put to very good use."

"Happy to hear it." His warm smile turns shy. "We haven't had a new neighbor around here in a while. My sister had to tell me what to bring to make a good impression. She'll be happy to hear I listened to her . . . and happier that she was right."

My cold, only-child heart warms hearing the obvious fondness in his voice when he mentions his sister. A man this gorgeous shouldn't be allowed to be sweet too.

"This is the best first impression." Although, he could've just shown up and smiled at me and I would've felt the same way. "Now I'll have to figure out a way to return the favor. I don't want to be all take and no give."

"No." He shakes his head, and a devilish glint lights his gorgeous eyes. "We wouldn't want that."

In a blink, I'm twelve again, running away after the cutest boy in school looked my way. I spin on bare feet and hurry to the kitchen, the blush I'm beginning to think might be a permanent fixture burning my face.

"I'm going to put these away," I call over my shoulder, unable to look back as the sound of his heavy footsteps follow behind me. "I wish I could get you something, but I don't even have cups to offer you a glass of water."

I pull open the old white refrigerator NeNe Leakes would think was dreadful and busy myself with unloading the groceries he brought. I only get the milk in before strong hands take the bag from me and Silas takes over.

"No need," he says, like he has no idea of the effect he has over me. "Meeting you was more than enough. I'm just glad to know you're right next door."

"If by 'right next door,' you mean miles away," I try to joke, but it falls flat. It's hard to land a punch line when you can barely speak.

"Practically nothing," he says, and I don't have to wonder if that lazy grin works on all the girls. I know it does. "So, what brought you to Celestial?"

The truth dances on the tip of my tongue, but I catch myself before I let it slip. Trauma dumping would be no way to thank him for his kindness.

"I was just ready for a change." The palatable, socially acceptable answer is an easy lie. "I lived in Denver my entire life, and as much as I loved it, I wanted to get out of the city. Try my luck at something new. I could never have afforded a house on this much land there, and even though I love an occasional snowstorm, I was tired of the snow."

He visibly recoils at the word *snow*, and I bite back my smile, realizing that anything cold-related is probably akin to a curse word to these warm-blooded Texans.

"You had me at 'snow.' I hope you're ready for the heat though. These summer months get a little . . ." He pauses, searching for the right word. "Intense."

"So I've been told." Gabby emailed me every single heat record in Celestial going back to 1987. "But I heard there's a lake close by that sounds nice, and if it doesn't do the trick, I figure I can always rely on air-conditioning to get me to the other side."

"Sounding like a true Texan already," he says, and for a reason I don't understand, I bask in his easy acceptance. "Lucky for you, if the worst happens and something goes wrong with your AC, I have an in with the best handyman in town."

"Oh really?" I bite back my laughter. Having an in with the local handyman feels about as small-town as you can get. "What's the in?"

"He's my brother. Sometimes that makes him harder to deal with though."

The room swims as my mind runs rampant trying to imagine two Silas Jacobses wrecking havoc and breaking hearts throughout Celestial. "You have a brother?"

"Yeah." He nods once before adding on what could very well be my ending. "Twin brother. And before you ask, no, we're not identical."

I was going to ask.

My mouth opens and shuts while my brain misfires as I try to comprehend what a trio of Jacobs siblings could look like. Could they all be as hot as Silas? What if they're hotter? No! I cut off that line of thinking before I can even dream it. That can't be true. If that were the case, the town would have to issue a public service warning or something. It definitely would've had to be disclosed in the paperwork before I closed on the house.

Warning: Hot neighbors abound. In rare cases, deaths related to unsatisfied horniness may occur.

Thankfully, before I can do something stupid like asking to see a family picture or requesting an invitation to their next family dinner, Silas's phone buzzes.

He sighs as he reads whatever's written on his phone before returning it to his back pocket. Lucky phone.

A rueful smile at odds with the hesitation in his eyes twists across his handsome face as he takes a step away from me. "Business calls."

"I meant what I said earlier. You'll have to come over once I've settled in a little bit." I walk with him back to the front door, watching with abject fascination as he slips his well-worn boots back on. "Maybe I can make you dinner . . . use some of the goods you brought me."

"I'd like that. My number is in the bag and you know where I live." His eyes warm when he looks me over. My stomach twists into knots. "You're more than welcome to stop by whenever you want. I'd love to get you on a horse and show you Starlight Ridge."

"That'd be good." It's almost impossible to choke the understatement of the century out over the excitement clogging my throat.

"Can't wait." His gaze lingers on me for a moment longer, and the scorching air feels like a cool breeze compared to the intensity of it. It's almost like he's going to lean in at any—

Buzzzzzz

His phone sounds again, breaking the moment with startling effectiveness.

"Gotta go," he says, and I don't think I'm imagining the disappointment in his voice.

He puts his cowboy hat on and jogs down my wobbly front steps and uneven pathway to his red pickup truck that's so big, it makes my poor Honda look like a toy car.

If I had even a little decorum or at least a modicum of self-respect, I'd close the door. I'd walk away and hope I'd have the chance to watch him another day.

But why wait for tomorrow when it's happening today?

I lean against the rickety doorframe, ignoring the bite of splinters pushing into my bare shoulder. I watch intently, seeing the way his Levi's tighten around his thighs as he climbs into his truck with the ease only someone over six feet tall could accomplish.

His engine rumbles to life, and just as I begin to straighten, disappointment that the show's over weighing down my limbs, he rolls down his window and sends my mundane world into a tailspin.

"Welcome to Celestial, Luna." His Southern drawl turns my name into a song, and I sway on my feet. "Try to take it easy on us, will you? I don't know what it is, but I have a feeling you're going to turn this town upside down."

Then, not even giving me a chance to respond, he hits the gas and sends his tires spinning. He waves his hand out the window as kicked-up rocks and a cloud of dirt chase him down my driveway until he's long gone . . . but his words remain.

If he knew anything about me, he'd know that I've never

turned anything upside down in my entire life, and there's no way he could be right.

Unless he is.

And while I try my hardest to never agree with a man, for Silas Jacobs? I might make an exception.

After all, I did come to Celestial for a fresh start, and maybe, just maybe, that means shaking things up a little bit.

Chapter 4

Sweat drips down my back, my hair is frizzy, and my sundress might be ruined, but I'm all moved in.

Not long after Silas left, Brian and his crew arrived like knights in a shining U-Haul with a truck full of my belongings and, in the second most beautiful sight of the day, a large plastic cup filled with iced coffee.

They lugged in all my furniture and brought all my boxes to their designated rooms before spending an extra three hours assembling my new furniture and hooking up the sparkling new washer and dryer I purchased before the move.

"I know you're going to miss me," I say to Brian as he starts the engine of the truck. "You don't have to rush out. There's still time for me to order dinner."

"Yeah right, girl." He rolls his eyes, but it doesn't distract from the quiet affection in his voice. "You were crazy moving to Texas in August. It felt like I drove this truck straight into hell. I need to get back to Colorado yesterday."

"Fine," I agree, but only because he's blaming his desire to leave on the weather and not disagreeing that he's going to miss me . . . which he will, obviously. And not just because I tipped them more than triple the amount the internet suggested either. "Thank you again for everything, and safe travels back through the seven circles."

"Will do." His quick huff of laughter is the last thing I hear before he rolls up the window and down my driveway.

I lock the door behind me and take in the living room with all my stuff in it. Boxes are stacked in the corner of almost every room. The walls are still white(ish) and empty, but it's already starting to feel like home.

Something I haven't felt in the last three months. It feels as terrifying as it does good.

I'm deciding between unpacking a box, taking another shower, or calling Gabby to fill her in on the not one, but two gorgeous men I've already met when Gabby's name on the screen makes the decision for me.

"Good evening, Gabrielle Owens." I collapse onto the pink couch I ordered leading up to the move. "How's your day going?"

"Oh, you know." She sighs dreamily into the phone. "Just pondering my existence now that my best friend has abandoned me for Texas and already forgotten to call me."

"Really, Gabby?" I should have known the calm, peaceful lilt in her voice was a trap. "The movers left not even ten minutes ago, and I was literally just getting ready to call you."

"How convenient. You know, if you're going to lie, you should at least make it believable."

"First of all, you know I've never lied to you." Not once. Not when she asked about getting bangs or when she asked what I thought of her last boyfriend. Not even when I lied to everyone else about my mom. Not ever. "Second, do you want to keep having this fight or do you want me to tell you about my neighbor who stopped by earlier today and the even hotter guy I met at the bar last night?"

"You have my attention," she says in the way she does when she knows the gossip is going to be good. "Start with the neighbor."

"He was wearing cowboy boots, a cowboy hat, and drives a pickup truck that only makes sense if someone lives and works on a ranch." I give her the highlight reel. "He brought me milk *from his cows* and a bag of vegetables *from his garden*."

"Okay." The giddiness I'm feeling is reflected in her voice, and I momentarily regret not FaceTiming her so I could see her reaction. "Say more . . ."

"The T-shirt he had on hugged his biceps with such precision it looked like he ordered it custom. He has a lazy smile, and you can tell from only meeting him once that it comes easy and often." I pause and take a breath as I remember his words from this morning. "Before he left, he told me to come over. That he'd love to get me on a horse and show me his ranch. And—"

"There's more?" She cuts me off. "How could there possibly be any more?"

"He has a brother . . . a twin brother." I pause to make room for her gasp. "They aren't identical, but he lives in Celestial too. He's a handyman, and after seeing Silas, I think it's safe to assume he's also hot."

Silence hangs loud and heavy between us as I let the gravity of my words sink in. And then, even though we're thirty-year-old adult women with more baggage than my new house could ever contain, we scream.

Because at the end of the day, despite all the garbage life has thrown at me, when faced with the possibility of my cowboy dreams coming true, only one thing stands true: I'm just a girl.

And as someone wise once said, girls will be girls.

"Hot twin cowboy neighbors?" she asks once we've stopped screeching like tween girls at a boy band concert.

"One hot cowboy neighbor, one likely hot handyman," I correct her before adding on, "and one even hotter man from the bar who told me his name and nothing else. He had locs, flawless brown skin, and eyes so dark I almost started speaking in sonnets."

"What the hell?" she screams through the phone. "I thought this place had a population of, like, ten? How in the fuck are there this many hot guys there?"

"I don't know and I don't care." After the last few months—no, years—that I've had? A little eye candy is the least that I deserve. "I'm just grateful for the view."

"Yeah, screw the mountains. I want to look at asses. Actually, you know what?" She stops talking, and I can hear her slippers shuffling around on her always spotless hardwood floors. "Fuck it."

I wait for her to explain further, but no explanation comes. Gabby is the most responsible person I've ever met. I don't think I've heard her say *fuck it* to anything. Ever.

"Wait . . . what's happening?"

I knew I should've FaceTimed her!

"I'm booking my ticket. I was going to let you get settled and come down for Christmas break, but now I'm bumping it up to fall break. Twin neighbors and a hot mystery townie change everything." She says this like it's the most obvious thing in the world and she can't understand why I'm asking. "What airport should I fly into?"

"I just got here yesterday. I have no idea. Hold, please." I switch her over to speaker and search "airport" in my maps app. "Looks like Dallas is your best bet, but it's still going to be a pretty far drive to Celestial."

Two to three hours to be exact, but at least I'll have an excuse to stop at Buc-ee's on the way to and from.

"Even better. You know I love a road trip."

I absolutely do not know that she loves a road trip.

"Since when?" I ask incredulously. "You wouldn't even drive to the mountains with me, and you spent the last month complaining about my drive here, which, might I add, you didn't even go on."

"Semantics." She brushes me off as her fingers click away on her keyboard. "Woo! It's booked and official! I arrive in Dallas on October 15th at 12:20 p.m. I want to come before school starts, but I have that stupid wedding in freaking Connecticut."

"The wedding with the dress?"

"Yes, *that* wedding." She practically growls, and I feel bad asking for clarification. "But the money I'm making from it is covering the ticket, so I guess it worked out in the end."

Gabby agreed to be a bridesmaid in her cousin's wedding, but did so before she knew that the dress was not only hideous, it was also six hundred dollars. Before alterations. It took me and her mom two hours to talk her off the ledge, and I'm still not sure we could be considered successful. The only reason she didn't tell her cousin where to shove the chartreuse nightmare is because her dad intervened and promised to reimburse her for the entire cost of the dress plus twenty percent if she went along with it. The only catch was he wouldn't pay her until the day after the wedding, and she had to smile for all the pictures.

"I need you to know that since your sacrifice is now directly benefitting me, I deeply appreciate it." I look over the stack of boxes at the darkening sky through the curtainless windows. "So please keep that in mind when I tell you what I have to say next—"

"You're hanging up on me, aren't you?" She reads my mind.

"I don't want to." I say it like I mean it, because I do. Yapping with Gabby is my favorite pastime. "But it's getting late, and I have to start unpacking now if I want my house to be ready for guests by October."

"Since this sacrifice will directly benefit me, I'll allow it." She echoes my earlier sentiment. "But when you're preparing for me, remember that I want wallpaper in my room and just because you moved into a farmhouse, doesn't mean your decor style can morph into a beige-and-white girlie."

"Excuse me? How dare you!" If I sound offended, it's because I am. "I showed you the Pinterest board for your room before I left. You know I'd never be a beige decor stan."

Don't get me wrong, if someone loves beige and white, I'd never yuck their yum. It's just that their yum will never influence or override mine. And my yum is a pink couch and more wallpaper than a house can handle.

"I know, it's just so easy to get you worked up." Her twinkly giggle floats through the speaker. "Call me tomorrow if you have time, but send me pictures and videos of your house no matter what."

"I'll do both," I promise and make good on half of it the second we hang up by spamming her with pictures of the new furniture Brian assembled and selfies of me with my washer and dryer.

Like the best friend that she is, she dutifully adds a heart to every picture and peppers in the occasional compliment. She sends a screenshot with all of her travel details, and I respond with an ungodly number of crying emojis.

I add the dates into my calendar before tapping back into my project management skills and opening up my to-do list. In no time, it's transformed into the detailed spreadsheet of my dreams, complete with start and finish dates for each item.

Beginning with unpacking my kitchen before bed tonight.

Sure, starting over at square one isn't where I imagined I'd be, but as I listen to the cowboy romance while I go through the boxes, the reality of my life blends seamlessly with the fantasy of fiction. I can't help but start to believe that maybe, just maybe, my dreams can come true too.

No matter how dirty they might be.

Chapter 5

I hate to be the bearer of bad news, but the experts are right. Exercise and a good night's sleep can do wonders for your mental health. It's even worse news, then, that despite the brand-new mattress I covered in brand-new sheets, a brand-new down comforter, and more pillows than I've ever seen outside of an advertisement, sleep has evaded me yet again. So it's terrible, awful, *horrendous* news that exercise is not only great for my cardiovascular health, but the best option for my mental well-being too.

Boo.

Thanks to my unreliable sleep schedule, early-morning boxing classes were a staple to my morning routine. Other than Gabby—and easy access to wacky tobacky on occasion—my boxing gym is the only thing I think I'm going to miss from my life in Colorado. Not only was I obsessed with every single instructor, there's something very therapeutic about punching your worries away. And although I'll never admit to anything, I'm pretty sure I can credit those heavy bags for keeping me out of prison a time or two . . . or three.

The cool breeze I was hoping for when I left my house early this morning is nowhere to be found, and I'm starting to think it will never come. It's too early for anyone in Colorado to be up, let alone texting me, but that doesn't stop my uncle's name from popping up on my phone as I pull into an empty parking spot. I avoid the preview of what he has to say and delete it without reading. I refuse to let him ruin my day before it even begins.

The sun shines bright in the cloudless blue sky as I navigate through the crowded parking lot to the high school stadium. The air is thick with humidity from the rain that's supposed to come later in the day. My workout hasn't even begun and sweat is already falling down the back of my neck. I miss my air-conditioned gym even more.

It's not that the Celestial High School stadium isn't nice. Outside of college and professional ones, it's the nicest stadium I've ever seen. Nothing in Denver compares. Fresh paint lines the turf, and a huge scoreboard looms over the end zone. The sun glares off the glass of the press box sitting high atop the silver bleachers that seem to grow larger with every step I take. Tall lights surround the field like a promise for many exciting Friday nights to come. It would probably be the best workout destination ever if they added some shade . . . and removed the football team.

The few times I've driven past the stadium, it was completely empty, but this morning bodies crowd the field and spectators fill the stands. Part of me wants to go home—I much prefer simple torture over working out in front of a large group of strangers—but I force myself to stay and find a seat in the empty row at the bottom of the bleachers instead.

Chaos ricochets around me. Whistles echo throughout the air. Coaches yell from the sidelines, and parents scream in opposite directions from behind me. Cameras snap and shutter, and drones buzz as they hover above the field attempting to capture the seriousness of Texas football.

The temperature is steadily rising. I know I need to get my run in before it's too hot, but I somehow manage to get caught up watching the impressive practice alongside the rest of the crowd.

What should be a shit show, with at least a hundred kids—and curiously, a bulldog—running around, moves like a well-oiled machine. Small groups are scattered all across the field, everyone working in tandem at their respective stations doing different drills. They work as one, even stopping to help teammates who are struggling as they move from location to location. It's so mesmerizing that by the time I tuck my headphones in my ears, I've almost forgotten why I came here in the first place.

Almost.

I tighten my shoelaces and walk to the track. Logically, I know everyone here is watching the football practice, but it still feels like all eyes are on me. Anxiety prickles at the base of my neck. I rush through my stretches, not giving proper time to my hamstrings, which have been tighter than normal since my move, and start to jog. Beyoncé blares in my ears, and before long, my feet fall into a familiar rhythm and the rest of the world drifts away. All thoughts of projects, to-do lists, and the niggling worries always itching the back of my brain disappear as my muscles relax and my pace picks up.

Maybe it's because I'm outrunning them with the well-timed efficiency of an adult girl boss who is running away from her feelings, but much to the surprise of the insecure, anxiety-riddled teenage girl always lurking in the back of my mind, I don't even notice when the hordes of teenage boys start running on the track with me. I round the curve of the track for my third mile, and the only thing on my mind is keeping my breathing even with the ever-increasing burn in my muscles. I'm so in the zone that nothing could distract me.

Nothing.

Except a pair of onyx eyes that somehow managed to haunt the few hours of sleep I had last night.

I pull out my headphones and slow to a walk as I approach him on the side of the field.

"It's you," I say. "I guess you were right about this being a small town."

"Lived here almost my entire life." His voice is as quiet among the rowdy boys as it was in the bar. I have to strain my ears to hear him. "Trust me, there's no hiding from anyone here."

"You were hiding from me? Maybe that's why I almost didn't recognize you," I tease, and a spark of pleasure twists my stomach when the lips that have taunted my memories curve into a whisper of a smile. I'll figure out why this practical stranger's smile lives in my mind rent-free another day.

Or never.

"It's this." He points to the navy floppy bucket hat he's wearing. "Nobody knows it's me when they don't see the locs."

He's not wrong—the bucket hat hiding his locs and shielding his face does make him hard to spot—but that's not why he looks so different today. He's as stoic as he was the other night and his eyes are just as dark, but there's a lightness about him that wasn't there before. The hardness to his jaw is softened, and the lines around his eyes look suspiciously like smile lines. I don't know this man from Adam, but he looks . . . happy.

"That must be it," I lie. "I didn't take you as a monogrammed polo and khaki shorts kind of guy."

Not that I have room to talk about clothes right now. Other than the mint I spend on keeping my running shoes in tip-top condition, I think I may be one of the few women in the world who doesn't see the appeal of a matching workout set. I got the shirt I'm wearing now at a soccer tournament in tenth grade and my shorts on clearance at the Nike outlet five years ago. Something I've never regretted until this very moment.

"I'm not," he reassures me, and a happy thrill zaps through my veins knowing I was right. "I only wear this for football. I'll change before I leave."

"Don't let him trick you. This is his favorite outfit." A kid with an impish grin that promises as much fun as it does trouble appears next to Tate. "He has a closet full of khakis, don't you, Coach?"

"You're supposed to be running laps, so why are you talking to us, Aiden?" Tate's deadpan voice cuts through the noise, but instead of seeming alarmed, the kid, Aiden, seems amused.

"I'm trying to help you out in front of your lady friend. Girls like it when guys dress good." He drapes a sweat-covered arm over Tate's shoulder and turns his attention to me. "Right?"

"Well—"

"Don't answer that." Tate shakes his head, and his hard gaze cuts from me to the jokester beside him. "If you're not running in five seconds, I'm adding four sets of barrel rolls for you and two laps for everyone else."

"Dang, Coach T! I know you didn't act like this when you

were all big, playing college ball. Why you gotta be like that?" Aiden clutches his heart, and I bite back my laughter at his dramatics. "I was trying to run, but your lady friend here was embarrassing the rest of us with how she was lapping us."

"Aiden." Tate points to the track. "Go."

"Fine, fine. I see how it is." Aiden throws his arms in the air and starts to jog away backward with a smirk that says he absolutely does *not* see how it is. "Showing out in front of the hot new girl in town. I thought you had more game than that."

Nobody is braver than a child without a fully developed prefrontal cortex. If Tate was looking at me the way he's looking at Aiden, I'd be shaking out of fear, not laughter. But going off the roar of laughter that breaks out all around us, I'm the only one.

"Five sets of barrel rolls!" Tate shouts to Aiden's back as he sprints away. "And the next person who says anything can join him."

"Don't worry, Coach T," another kid says as he jogs by. "We all know your game is as good off the field as it is on it."

"Dammit, Josh." Tate shakes his head. "You threw up the last time you did barrel rolls. Don't make me have you rolling across the field with him."

"I would never." Josh holds up his hands in surrender. "But you should know Coach Linc promised to send twenty dollars to the person who gets you the most worked up in front of your friend."

Tate spins around, and I follow his gaze to the redheaded man waving from the end zone, his shit-eating grin visible from fifty yards away.

"Children." Tate shakes his head as he turns to face me,

and even though I can tell he's trying not to break, it's impossible to miss the amusement dancing in his eyes. "Even the adults I work with are children."

"They seem like fun though." I wave back to another group of kids as they run past us.

Or at least, I try.

"Don't encourage them." Tate's large hand wraps around mine and pulls it down to my side. "It's like being at the zoo when they say you can't feed the animals. Except they're the animals and they feed off attention."

I try to pay attention. I really, really do. It's just hard to do when he puts his hands back in his pockets but his touch manages to stick around. Sparks crackle and pop, the feeling burning into my skin.

"Got it. Don't feed the kids." I nod, knowing damn well that I do not have it and will most likely wave at the next person who looks my way. It's called manners, for goodness' sake. Look it up. It's also called a nervous tic, but maybe don't look that one up.

"Attention!" he adds on quickly, panic and humor lacing his voice. Before this moment, I didn't think it was possible for a man like Tate to look flustered, and it's as adorable as it is shocking. "Don't feed the kids attention. We feed them food. Often."

"Very important distinction," I say. Part of me wants to tease him about it a little more, but I'm not sure he's a teasing kind of guy, so I have mercy and change the topic instead. "So you played college football and now you're a high school coach?"

It's more of a statement than a question, thanks to the kids calling him Coach T, his embroidered polo, and the fact that he's standing on the football field before eight o'clock in the morning. They're small details of what I'm sure is a big life, and I'm surprised by how much I want to learn more.

"Yeah, I—" he starts but doesn't finish.

"He isn't just *a* high school football coach, he's *the* head football coach of the Celestial Astros." An adult, not a kid this time, answers for Tate. He's wearing a polo that matches Tate's, but his is embroidered with "Coach Matt" instead. He has scruffy brown hair, bright red cheeks, and kind eyes. I like him immediately. "And he's going to lead us to the state championship for the first time since he was a student here and led the team to victory as the quarterback before heading down to Austin. Ain't that right, Coach?"

Head coach? The quarterback? Austin? I wish Tate was the one telling me this, but I'll take what I can get. I grab on to each morsel of information about this tall, dark, and gorgeous man and tuck it away somewhere deep in the back of my mind. Someplace so deep, it will probably come up when I fall asleep tonight, just like his smile.

"Christ, Matt," Tate groans. "I already gave you the damn job. There's no need to lay it on so thick."

"I'm not laying it on, just telling her the god's honest truth." Matt waves Tate off before turning his attention to me and extending his hand. "Matt Holmes. Nice to meet you."

"Luna Starr." I shake his hand. "Nice to meet you too."

"Nice." Matt's eyes go wide and his smile doubles in size. "Luna Starr of Celestial. What a stellar name."

I've heard a lot about locker room talk over the years, and almost all of it was bad. I'd be lying if I said I didn't have preconceived notions when I pictured what high school football coaches, especially in Texas, would be like. But I can say, with one hundred percent certainty, in no uncertain terms, never did I ever think one would use the word *stellar* in casual conversation.

I was right. Matt Holmes is a good one.

"Thank you for noticing." I smile back. "I think it's pretty stellar too."

"You're both stellar," Tate says, but the words sound clunky coming out of his mouth. "But you know what would be even more stellar, Matt? If you got the guys organized so we could knock out a quick scrimmage before it gets too hot."

"Stellar scrimmage, got it." Matt winks at me before blowing into the whistle hanging around his neck and running down the field. "Get some more water, boys! It's time to scrimmage."

I watch as the kids break out into a flurry of activity and excitement. They showed up for practice, but scrimmaging is what they came for. They all scatter in different directions and line up at the water hose contraptions spread out around the field while Matt huddles up with a couple of other people wearing matching polos.

"Matt seems fun," I tell Tate, something I'm sure he already knows, even if he doesn't want to admit it.

"Yeah." He fidgets with the whistle around his neck and shifts from side to side. "We have a good group of guys here, the players and coaches. I got lucky."

I've had my fair share of toxic jobs, and I know healthy work environments start from the top.

"I don't think that's luck," I say. "It sounds like good leadership to me."

"Thanks, but . . ." He looks away, and just when I think he's about to brush off my compliment, something catches his eye and I get to watch as his face transforms right in front of me. He crouches down to the ground, and the English bulldog I saw earlier runs into his arms, his entire little potato body wiggling and shaking with so much excitement, he almost knocks Tate over.

"Whoa! Calm down." Tate laughs and the rest of the world falls silent. His bucket hat falls off and the sun shines directly upon him, as if summoned by the power of his rare, and oh-so-beautiful, smile. "Are you almost ready to go home?"

The dog's tongue falls out of his mouth as he grunts and snorts his answer, leaning into Tate's touch as he scratches him behind the ear.

Lucky puppy.

"So, what?" I squat down next to him and hold my hands out for the dog to sniff. "Matt you'll introduce me to, but you keep this guy all to yourself?"

"If you remember correctly, Matt introduced himself. Trust me, I have no control over who that man talks to. But I mean, look at this face." He cups his hands around his dog's wrinkly face and scrunches up the folds even more. "Who'd want to share this guy?"

It's almost as if the man I've talked to up until now has been replaced by Tate's goofy, dog-loving twin. His dazzling—yes, dazzling—smile fits so seamlessly on his face, his dimple popping and his white teeth shining against his dark skin, it's unfathomable to think he'd ever frown.

"Nobody in their right mind, that's for sure." I rub my hand across the dog's silky fur and he wiggles his way out of Tate's grip and comes straight to me. "Well, hello! Are you the best puppy in the world? I think you are!"

I don't mean for my voice to jump three octaves, but laws

are laws and I can't not use this voice when I talk to dogs. Especially ones as cuddly and lovey as this one.

"Sorry." Tate apologizes as the dog tries to drown me in slobber. "If you meet Duke at his level, he's going to aim for the face every time."

He has a bulldog named Duke and is capable of smiling. I tuck two more nuggets back with the rest of my scant, but important, knowledge of Tate.

"He's just a lover, not a fighter." I laugh as I attempt, and fail, to dodge his wet tongue. "Right, Duke?"

"Duke, chill. Here—" Tate's strong hands come around my waist. I lose the ability to breathe, and his fingers burn through my threadbare T-shirt as he lifts me off the ground. "He'll still let you pet him, but he's not as intense with the licking when you're standing up."

"Thanks," I say. The track doesn't feel solid beneath my feet as he takes a step back, his touch still lingering at my waist. "Drowning in dog slobber at a football practice is not how I want to go out."

"I don't know," Tate says. "There are worse ways to go out than being loved to death by Duke."

I open my mouth to agree with him, but before I can, whistles start to blare from across the field, and a chorus of deep voices chants while the rest of the group clap in unison.

"Astros on three, Astros on three," they shout. "One, two, three, Astros!"

Applause breaks out and the kids disperse to their spots either on the field or the sideline.

"Aye, Coach T!" one of the players yells, but there are too many kids around to even guess who's talking. "You still trying to spit game or are you going to come back to practice now?"

"Okay, Coach T!" someone else from somewhere else yells. "We see that rizz!"

Spit game? Rizz? Kids really say this stuff?? I thought it was just a joke on the internet.

Holy shit.

How old am I?

Also, and more importantly, is that what was going on here?

"Christ," he hisses beneath his breath, aiming a glare at the masses of laughing teens across the field. "I'm so sorry. I swear they live to give me a hard time."

"No apologies necessary. I've never worked with teenagers, but as a former teen myself, I remember messing with my coaches and teachers. It's a rite of passage."

I used to drive my soccer coach nuts. If he was as hot as Tate, I can only imagine how insufferable I would've been.

"That's nice of you to say." A rueful grin tugs on the corner of his mouth, and if I wasn't already melting from the sun, I'm pretty sure that look would do the trick. "I'll let them know you defended them when I'm making everyone run extra ladders at the end of practice."

"Ladders?" I ask, sounding only half as horrified as I really am. "In this weather?"

If you've never done a ladder before, first of all, congratulations. Second of all, let me explain. A ladder is where you're made to stand at the baseline on a field and then sprint to the next line, then back, then the next one, and repeat again. So on a football field, you'd stand at the back of the end zone, run to the ten-yard line, back to the end zone, then to the twenty-yard line, back to the end zone, and repeat until you've made it all the way across the field and back. It's torture in the form of conditioning, and honestly? Waterboard me. I don't want it.

"What can I say? That's Texas football for you." He shrugs, and all of a sudden, his grin looks evil. "Enjoy the rest of your workout. Feel free to join them on the ladders if you want."

"Oh yeah. About that . . ." I look at my watch. "I have literally anywhere else to be, but maybe I'll see you around again sometime."

I think back to our farewell from our night in the bar.

"Maybe," he says. "It's a pretty small town."

He repeats what he said to me that night, and although I've been known to find meaning where there isn't any, I can't help the way the butterflies that are flying rampant since my arrival in Celestial take flight again.

Unlike when he left the bar, this time when Tate leaves, I watch him go, but this go around I get the added bonus of watching Duke chase after him on his little legs and my new friend Matt waving to me down the sideline.

"Bye, Luna! See ya—"

"Later, Luna!" A symphony of teen boys drowns out the end of Matt's sentence. "Bye, Moon Girl!"

Moon Girl? I was teased almost my entire life for my name so I probably shouldn't love this as much as I do, but what can I say? I'm kind of obsessed. It's just too bad for the team that Tate, on the other hand, isn't impressed at all.

"Have you all lost your minds? I know your parents taught you better than that. When you're talking to her, it's Miss Starr or ma'am," Tate bellows, and I swear the base in his voice causes the ground to tremor. "Now try it again."

He lifts a hand in the air and raises one finger at a time.

"Goodbye, Miss Starr!" they chant in unison when he gets to three, and it's so loud, I'm pretty sure the entire town of Celestial can hear them.

"Goodbye, Astro football players and coaches." I laugh as I wave back to everyone. "Stay hydrated, don't get hurt, and play good!"

As far as pep talks go, it's not my best work, but it will have to do.

"What can I add on to that?" Tate turns back to his team with a very excited Duke sitting right at his feet. "That's advice for the ages, boys."

I consider running another lap for approximately 2.5 seconds before I think better of it and grab my stuff from the bleachers instead. I might not have gotten my full workout in, but I did get to see Tate, and with the way he makes my heart flutter, who's to say which is better for my cardiovascular health?

Chapter 6

There are a multitude of reasons I should head home the second I leave the football field. Not only have I likely peaked for the day, but I have boxes to unpack and DIY projects to accomplish. Also, I'm sweaty, gross, and I might stink. Nobody deserves to cross my path in this condition. It's an easy decision, really.

But where's the fun in *easy*?

I turn the radio up when the first chords of my favorite song from the Chicks begins to play on the only station that doesn't turn to static between my house and town. It's too hot outside, but I roll the windows down anyway. I pretend to be unbothered by the oppressive heat and sing at the top of my lungs as I drive deeper into town.

I need to run errands at nearly every store in town. There are a million and one things on my to-do list that will probably cost me a million and two dollars at the hardware store alone. Don't even get me started on groceries. Those would be the responsible stops to make. But as an adult, I have the God-given right to make as many bad decisions as possible.

It's still early and the temperature is already creeping toward triple digits. Only the bravest souls are out as I pull into the empty space in front of the building with a for-sale sign in the window next to the craft store I knew I needed to visit the first time I drove past it.

"The Artist Alchemy" is scrolled whimsically across the storefront window in loopy handwriting and again on the sign hanging above it. A purple wooden bench covered with hundreds of hand-painted stars sits on the sidewalk outside the front door. Two embroidered pillows nuzzled in each corner remind me to buy an embroidery kit inside.

I pull open the heavy glass door and a bell rings overhead. A burst of cold air and the smell of acrylic paint ushers me inside. The playful design outside continues inside with rainbow color-coded shelves jam-packed with paints, yarn, and more craft supplies than I dreamt of finding in this tiny town. There aren't many other customers here now, but between the many indented seat cushions and giant corkboard covered with art, it's obvious how well loved this store is.

"Welcome in!" a friendly voice shouts from somewhere deep in the store. "I'm grabbing some yarn for the knitting group tonight, but I'll be out in a minute."

"Take your time," I call back to the unknown voice. "I'm just looking around."

It's nice knowing help is close by, but I welcome having some time to explore by myself. I haven't been in a store like this in years. The familiar scents and sights cause memories I haven't thought about in forever to come rushing back with such ferocity, it damn near knocks the breath out of me.

I can almost hear my grandma's voice, so patient and kind, explaining every item to me as she held my hand while we perused aisles much like these. She was a very serious crafter, and by proxy, so was I. My favorite childhood memories are sitting with her at the table, trying to keep up with whatever new project she was working on at the moment. She was always finding local craft fairs to sell her bounty of goods, and I'd be right by her side through it all, hustling my little butt off to get her as many sales as possible.

I tried to keep it up over the years, but work, the general messiness of life, and the lack of space in my one-bedroom apartment made it difficult to do as much as I wanted. But now, with an abundance of space and time, I find myself in the very privileged position to fill my life with passions over obligations. Because my new house was a steal and the price of real estate in Denver is at an all-time high, my savings account has more money in it than I ever thought possible. Add in my mom's life insurance, and I have enough of a cushion to update my house, take a work sabbatical, and stock up on plenty of crafts to keep my mind and hands busy.

They say money can't buy you happiness, but it can buy you distractions.

And I need a lot of them.

I grab one of the little baskets stacked up inside the front door. My hands itch with the need to buy everything I see. Other than the diamond art and friendship bracelet supplies stashed in one of the many boxes I have yet to unpack, I'm building my crafty arsenal from scratch. I start in the paint aisle, tossing in sets of acrylic, water, and oil paints with abandon before grabbing multiple sets of paintbrushes. By the time I get to the paper pads and canvases, my basket is already overflowing.

"Holy sh— I mean, crap!" the voice from earlier yells just as a pixie of a woman comes barreling toward me. I don't even have time to react before she yanks the basket out of my hands with a strength I'm not sure someone her size should possess. "Let me help you."

Standing at a very average five feet, five inches, I still tower over the woman in front of me. The pink-and-purple hair flowing down her back is the only thing brighter than her blue eyes. She has porcelain skin that's paler than I thought possible living in a Texas town that boasts its outdoorsy appeal. She aims a wide, welcoming smile my way, but there's a hint of mischief that gives me the very distinct feeling she's one of a kind in Celestial.

I follow her to the front of the store and take the new basket she hands me from behind the counter.

"Thank you," I say. "I want everything in here! I'm not sure I have the self-control to stop myself."

Her blue eyes crinkle at the corners, and her delicate laughter fills the entire store.

"You and me both," she says. "My living room looks like a miniature version of the store, and I'm not even the least bit sorry about it."

"Money well spent." Stranger or not, now I need an invite to her house. "I think my entire paycheck would go right back to the owner if I worked here."

It's what happened when I worked at the Book Nook. You can now find the majority of my former paychecks in the countless romance novels that will soon be lining the bookshelves I have yet to purchase.

"That's exactly why I opened this store!" she squeals. "Well, that and an excuse to knit during work hours."

My jaw drops and the words tumble out of my mouth before I can stop them. "This is your store?"

I don't mean to sound so surprised—and therefore rude—but when I imagine the person who owns a craft store, I picture an older woman with an affinity for printed maxi skirts, embroidered sweatshirts, and beaded jewelry. The woman in front of me doesn't look a day over twenty-five and is wearing baggy jeans and a cropped tee that showcases the colorful tattoo snaking down her side.

"It is." She pulls the items out of my basket, and her already bright smile widens with what I can only assume is pride. "I took my art degree and opened it straight out of college. My parents thought I lost my mind, but our five-year anniversary is this September, so look who's laughing now."

She doesn't seem offended by my question, and the knot forming in my stomach starts to loosen. I don't want any enemies in Celestial, least of all one with unlimited access to knitting hooks and paper cutters.

"That's amazing," I say. "I can't wait to give you all my money and help you keep proving them wrong."

Investing in women who encourage my self-interests is the most fun way to do feminism.

"I can't wait either," she says, extending her hand across the front desk. "I'm Millicent Dean, but all my friends call me Millie."

I shake her hand, not caring at all that enthusiasm gives away my borderline desperate desire to fit in around here. "Nice to meet you, Millie. I'm—"

"Luna Starr," she finishes for me. "The proud new owner of the Monroe farmhouse and Celestial's newest resident."

"Ummm . . ." I struggle to find the words, not sure if I should feel honored or terrified that this stranger knows my name and where I live. "How did you—"

She cuts me off again, but with the added flourish of a dismissive wave of her hand.

"Don't worry," she says. "I'm not a stalker."

"Are you sure?" I ask. "Because that sounds exactly like something a stalker would say."

I couldn't be more serious, but she laughs like I just told the world's funniest joke.

"This might come as a surprise to you, but people aren't moving to Celestial in droves. So when someone new comes along, word gets around really fast." She takes the last set of paintbrushes out of the basket and studies me with curious eyes. "Especially when said new person is cuddled up with Tate on the sidelines at morning football practice."

My breath catches in my throat.

"Wait. What? But that was—we weren't . . ." I stumble over my words, trying to sort through the barrage of thoughts bombarding my brain. "How'd you hear that? I just—"

"I work hard, but the Celestial Whisper Network works harder," she says as if that explains everything. "If you're going to survive here, you have to understand that secrets don't exist in Celestial. Half the town heard about you and Tate before you left the field."

"Me and Tate?" My head is spinning. She's telling me about my own freaking life and I still can't keep up! "There is no me and Tate . . . like, at all."

"Yeah," she says with a wink and an exaggerated nod that sends her pink-and-purple hair flying. "*Sure* there's not."

"There's not." Did I move to Celestial or the Twilight Zone?

"I've only met him twice, and he's seemed more annoyed than anything the two times we have talked."

"Oh yes," she says. I don't like the way her shoulders shimmy and her eyes light up. "The infamous bar meeting."

My jaw hits the floor. "You know about that too?"

"Duh," she says like I'm stupid. "Like I said, the Celestial Whisper Network doesn't miss."

I tuck an imaginary stray curl behind my ear, flustered at the thought of people already talking about me.

"I don't know if I should be worried or flattered. I haven't been the topic of gossip since middle school." And to be honest, it wasn't great for me.

Hannah, my middle school nemesis, started a rumor that me and my mom were witches. I'm sure it doesn't come as a shock with a name like Luna Starr, but my mom was obsessed with the moon, planets, and all things astrology. I think the proper term for her style is eclectic, but back in the day, people just thought she was a freak. Think Stevie Nicks meets *Hocus Pocus* and you've got her. She had long, wavy brown hair that went down to her butt and she never left the house without being draped in silver and a crystal or five wrapped around her neck. If my mom remembered back-to-school night, it only took one appearance for all the birthday invites to be magically rescinded. Gabby was the only person who stuck up for me, and I never let her go.

I'd like to say that when I look back on it now at my big age, I'm grateful for the character building it gave me, but fuck that. It was awful and I still wish Hannah nothing but the absolute worst. So please forgive me, but being the center of gossip doesn't exactly send a thrill down my spine.

"Yapping is the unofficial pastime of Celestial. People gossip about anything and everything around here. So normally I'd say don't think anything of it at all. But in this case . . ." She drops her voice and leans in closer despite no one being around us. "I'd say be flattered since people are only talking about how the hot new girl—that's you—has Tate, the town's unflappable hottie, in a tizzy."

I'd love to bask in the compliment of a town calling me 'hot' for a little longer, but I can't let this go on.

Damn my moral compass and hatred of misinformation.

"I'm so sorry, but 'a tizzy'?" I try not to laugh at the absurdity of it all. "This would be fun if true, but the Whisper Network got it wrong this time."

"So Tate didn't sit next to you?" She looks like I kicked her puppy, and I waver on telling her the truth.

Is it really misinformation if it can't sway elections?

How bad would it really be if people think the hot football coach is attracted to me?

"He did, but that was it. He just had the misfortune of finding the open seat next to me and being forced to listen as I rambled." I cave like the truthful loser I am, but instead of having the sad puppy-dog eyes when I told her the real story, her fairylike features light with glee and her smile triples in size. "What? Why are you making that face?"

"Because," she says, bouncing up and down behind the counter. "Tate sat next to you! The Whisper Network is still batting one thousand!"

"No," I try to explain, not understanding where the disconnect is. "He literally just sat next to me. That's it. I'm not even sure he smiled, and I barely got him to tell me his name."

"Well, yeah. Grumpy, annoyed, and quiet are Tate's manufacturer settings," she says before hopping onto the counter and swinging her legs toward me. "You're new here, so you're missing the bigger picture. Tate always orders to-go, but he always stands at the end of the bar and waits for his order. I don't think I've ever seen him sit down."

"Oh."

"Yeah. 'Oh,'" she mocks with a teasing smile. "Tate only talks to his football team and maybe the players' parents if they're lucky. The fact that he said anything at all to you is huge, but it's even bigger given that he had to know you're the new owner of the Monroe farmhouse and he talked to you anyway. He avoids anything that even comes close to Starlight Ridge Ranch."

"Wait." My brain can't process a universe where someone like Tate might possibly be interested in me, but I perk up instantaneously at the newest piece of gossip she's brought to my attention. "Why would he avoid Starlight Ridge Ranch?"

Her head snaps back and her big eyes grow even wider. "You don't know?"

"I haven't signed up for the Whisper Network yet and I live outside of town. You're pretty much the first person I've talked to, and therefore, the first person to loop me in to the Celestial inner workings." I watched enough Hallmark movies before coming that I figured the small-town gossip trope had to have some truth behind it, but I wasn't convinced enough to start digging around as soon as I landed. "Does Tate have an issue with Silas or something?"

"You know Silas?" A giddy smile chases the shock straight off her face. "Tell me everything!"

"There's not much to tell," I say. "He came over yesterday with a little welcome gift and introduced himself."

"He brought you a gift?" she breathes out, inferring much more from what I told her than intended. "Do you think Tate knows?"

"It was nothing big, some milk and produce from the ranch. He said his sister told him to do it. I think he was just being a good neighbor." I keep the details light. I have a feeling the town will know every word of this conversation the moment I leave the store . . . maybe even before, and I'm not ready to feed the machine just yet. "I have no idea if Tate knows. Why would he?"

"I don't know. Let's just say those two have a lot of . . ." She looks to the ceiling and searches for the right word. "History."

They're both still strangers to me, but it's hard to believe either of them could have a problem with anyone, let alone each other. Tate barely speaks and Silas was nothing but kind. But I guess Matt did say Tate went to high school here, and they look around the same age. Maybe they had some high school beef that turned into small-town lore? If I'm still carrying my hatred of Hannah, who I haven't seen since eighth grade continuation, it could be possible for them to hold a grudge in the same town.

I wait for Millie to expand on said "history," but she sits quietly, returning my stare without saying another word.

"You know"—I narrow my eyes at the pixie sitting on the counter—"you're very tight-lipped for someone who was so excited to spill the tea a few moments ago."

"What can I say?" She shrugs. "I can't give you all the good stuff now."

Call me greedy, but I think she can.

It's not like I have anyone else I can ask. I basically had to pry Tate's name out of him, and the last thing I'm going to do is show up at my neighbor's house asking him to elaborate on the vague gossip I've heard.

"Why not?"

"Because." She hops off the counter. "Then we won't have anything to talk about the next time you come to the store."

I couldn't bite back my smile if I tried—which I don't.

"We wouldn't want that."

"Exactly." She claps her hands together and skips across the store to grab a basket of her own. "Now let's get you everything you need. You're going to love the 'new friend discount' I offer."

I follow her into the scrapbooking aisle and stock up on glitter paper and grab one of every washi tape she has in stock. "*Discount* is actually one of my favorite words."

Funny enough, the other two are *new* and *friend*.

Who would've guessed?

"What a coincidence!" she throws over her shoulder as she rummages through the stickers and calligraphy pens. "That's one of mine too."

I've only been here for a couple of days, but these small-town perks are already stacking up, and for the first time in months—maybe even years—I'm excited to see what will happen next. I knew Celestial was the place for me, but not even in my wildest dreams did I think I'd get this lucky.

Now, if only I could get [lucky] . . . perhaps with the cowboy next door or the hot football coach in town.

Chapter 7

On the day I was born, the stars and planets aligned. Clouds parted and the sun shone bright, horns blaring while the angels sang out to all the universe, proclaiming that the most basic of bitches had arrived. Has it been a lot of pressure knowing this is the purpose I've been placed on this earth to fulfill? Of course, but it's my lot in life and I bravely face it every single day.

There's never been a seasonal latte I've shied away from or a style of Uggs I haven't owned. I know every Taylor Swift lyric ever written while also being a card-carrying member of the Beyhive, and a proud American Mixer who still occasionally weeps when I think of Little Mix. I can throw an amazing party with any theme and budget—my Alice in Discoland party was one for the history books—and this is part of why I was the go-to person for putting together events at the Book Nook. One of my best traits is my ability to romanticize absolutely anything. I enter every room knowing I'll be both the most basic and most extra person in attendance. I try to bring the same beautiful, chaotic energy to every aspect of my life, but after I lost my mom, it was easy to let the chaos overshadow the beauty.

To lose sight of the beauty entirely.

Only knowing my dad through a handful of pictures and stories told to me by those who loved him most, I've never known life without loss. The fragility of life has always danced in my periphery. The ghost of his presence acted as a constant, unspoken reminder to cherish each and every moment gifted to me.

I've lived my entire life closely acclimated to and acutely aware of death, but nothing—not the sickening realization it was coming sooner than I could've ever dreamt possible or the months spent watching . . . bracing—could've prepared me for the moment it came for my mom.

People—my therapist and Gabby—told me not to make this move.

They warned me time and time again that this house was a distraction. A weak attempt to run from grief that's impossible to escape. And while I'm a big enough person to admit they weren't completely wrong, I can't say they were completely right either. More than anything, this move has been about finding a safe, quiet space to tap back into the pieces of myself that grief ripped away from me and to bring the beautiful, chaotic energy back into my life . . .

Starting with my house.

I've been here for over a week, and it's time to get down to business so that it really feels like home.

"Are you sure you know what you're doing?" Gabby's big brown eyes narrow with skepticism and judgment as she watches me take off the final cabinet door in my kitchen over

FaceTime. "Didn't you say Hot Cowboy Neighbor knows a good handyman?"

"His name is Silas." I correct her even though I'm the one who trademarked Hot Cowboy Neighbor. "The handyman is his brother, and I will call if I need him. Which I don't."

"That's what you said when you were taking out the bathroom sink and the pipe exploded in your face."

"Excuse me." I drop the cabinet and put my hands on my hips, but I fear the impact is lost over the phone's screen. "Are you friend or foe? Why are you throwing my mistakes in my face?"

I mean, really! You flood a bathroom once and they never let you live it down.

"If I can't keep it real with you, then who can?" She asks the question I ask her routinely. I like it a lot less coming from her. "Just because I'm hundreds of miles away doesn't mean it's not still my job to make sure you're not acting before you think. I'm making sure you know what you're doing before you paint those cabinets because if you ruin them now, you're losing your time plus the money you're going to have to pay someone to fix or replace them."

I hate it when she's right.

"Who told you to be logical?"

"You sound like my students." She laughs. "And you know I'm always logical."

Now I'm the one laughing.

"Oh puh-lease! Was it logical when you triple-booked your Hinge dates and had them battle for your heart?"

"I was on a *Bachelorette* kick!" she says, like it's an actual defense and not a prime example of the point I'm making. "I wanted to know what it was like to have three men try to win and woo me without the pressure of being on national television."

If this was the only instance, I would let it lie, but there are hundreds, if not millions, of examples to choose from.

"What about the time you were working in the elementary school and your principal shot down your field trip to the zoo so you invited that animal keeper into your class without getting approval and then the snake got out?"

"Okay, yeah. That one was bad." *Bad* is an understatement. A student in the classroom where they found the snake was so freaked out, she had to start seeing the school counselor. Gabby was put on probation for the rest of the school year. "But that doesn't mean that the roles haven't reversed here and I'm not right."

"I appreciate your concern, but I'm very confident in my skills to accomplish this project. I've read ten different blog posts from Pinterest, and do you remember when I spent a weekend taking a DIY workshop at the rec center? We learned about refinishing cabinets!"

I was the only single non-mom in the class, and it was the most fun I've ever had. I won't admit it to Gabby, but we all met up for drinks after, and I learned more about their personal lives than I did refinishing. I need to call Ally. I wonder if she worked things out with her mother-in-law.

I watch Gabby throw her hands in the air out of the corner of my eye.

"Fine," she says. "But know that if it somehow manages to go astray, I do reserve the right to say I told you so loudly and often."

Considering I still bring up the zoo/classroom fiasco anytime I get the chance, I don't doubt this for a second.

"I would never deny you your God-given right as my best friend to mock my failures." I wedge the phone beneath my chin, and she gets a glorious view up my nostrils as I grab the cabinet and push open the door to my back porch with my foot. "But you're not—"

I lose track of what I was going to say when none other than Hot Cowboy Neighbor™ pulls the door wide open for me.

"I was fixing the fence and saw you bringing stuff outside. I figured the neighborly thing to do would be to come and help." He answers the question I didn't have time to ask. "If you want it, of course."

"Um, yeah." Heavy silence falls from my phone while I struggle to string words together as my speech returns. "That'd be nice."

He gestures to the cabinet door. "Can I carry that for you?"

I'm all for feminism. Huge fan. 10/10 stars. But when it comes to physical labor of any kind, I'm an even bigger fan of passing it off to the men. If I have to deal with a period and the patriarchy, they should have to deal with at least a moment of mild discomfort and strain their muscles to lift heavy things for me.

It's called equity.

"If you insist." I hand it over without so much as pretending to contemplate it, and the second I do, the screeching I assumed I'd hear moments ago finally comes.

"Oh my god!" Gabby's voice echoes into the great expanse of open fields and deep into my heart. "Is that—"

I know how that sentence ends, and there's no part of me that can allow her to say it in front of Silas.

"I have to go paint now!" I cut her off. "Talk to you later. Love you. Bye!"

I hit end before she can embarrass me and turn on Do Not Disturb after sending her immediate incoming call directly to voicemail.

"Someone from back home?" Silas asks with a knowing grin on his face.

Dammit.

One day I'll know how to play it cool.

"My best friend, Gabby." I pull my sunglasses from the top of my head and hope they can protect my eyes from the sun and Silas's smile—both equally liable to blind me. "Before I moved, we made a promise to have at least one FaceTime call a day. She's very invested in my home improvement projects and she likes to micromanage from the phone."

Micro-criticize is more accurate, but Silas doesn't need to know that.

"It's crazy what technology can do now." He walks beside me to the giant tarp where I've carefully displayed all my cabinet doors and gently places it on the open corner spot. "I had a friend move to Washington my sophomore year. We could only talk once a month because of long-distance fees."

"Even on your cell phone?" My grandma was from Chicago, and I still remember how happy she was when my mom gave her a cell phone. She sat on the couch for hours, calling her sister and all her friends back home. "I thought there were plans that included it."

"The cell service here was terrible until I was in college." He shakes his head. His honey eyes crinkle at the corners, flecks of gold winking beneath the sun. "It's why everyone around here still has a landline, especially the farther you get from town. There are still some companies we have to avoid because they drop more calls than they connect."

Cell coverage wasn't something I even considered in my move. Thank goodness my phone is still working.

"There's a rotary phone in the kitchen. I thought it was for decoration."

"I doubt that Mr. Monroe ever had a cell phone," he says. "That phone is probably the one thing in your house that doesn't need work."

Unfortunately, I doubt he's wrong.

I've had one too many surprises since I've started really looking around the house, and I have a feeling there are many more to come.

"So, what ended up happening with your friend who moved?" I ask. "Did you rekindle your friendship through Facebook and Instagram messages?"

The only thing I know about this man is nothing, but I can't miss the sadness that flashes in his eyes. The emotion looks so out of place on his perpetually happy face that I wish I could shove the words back in my mouth and choke on them.

"Uh, no." He clears his head and studies his boots. "We lost touch after a few months. Last I heard she was married and had a kid."

Interesting.

I have a million more follow-up questions, but I don't need to be a detective to figure out that he doesn't want to talk about it—about her—and as a person who would rather have all my teeth pulled than talk about my past, I get it.

"I'm sorry," I say, and I hope he can tell that I mean it. "It sounds like she was pretty special for you to still remember her so fondly."

"She was the best." His voice drips with sincerity. "Who knows, maybe someday our paths will cross again."

Silas is kind, gorgeous, and pretty much all the things anyone interested in a person of the male persuasion would look for in a partner. Hearing the longing in his voice when he talks about another woman should make me rage with jealousy. Instead, I feel nothing but deep sadness and hope that one day, they'll find each other again.

"I'm painting my kitchen." I forgo a smooth transition and inform him of something I'm sure he figured out on his own. "It's probably going to take me a century to finish. If you're free, I wouldn't mind the company or the help."

"I have the day to myself." He turns his attention back to me and aims a grateful smile my way. "Sanding cabinets with you sounds like the perfect way to spend it."

Not even the romance books I've pored over could prepare me for what it feels like for a man like Silas to look at me like this. It's as if the heavens have opened up and are shining upon me. A future spent lazing in the sun with him, turning the mundane into the romantic, flashes before my eyes. The possibilities are as glorious as they are endless, and it's too bad a faceless woman from his past has managed to encroach on my daydreams.

"I couldn't agree more."

Chapter 8

My skin is slick with sweat and my shoulders ache from the constant motion of sanding, priming, and painting my cabinets. It feels like we've been working for centuries, but the pile of yet-to-be-painted cabinets suggests otherwise. At least I have a good view though.

And I'm not talking about the landscape.

"Wow." Silas looks down at the cabinets we've managed to finish, his thick eyebrows damn near in his hairline. "It actually looks good."

Silas lost the button-up shirt he was wearing as soon as we got to work. His muscles flexed and strained beneath glittering bronze skin as the white tank top he's wearing became more and more transparent as time went on. It's a miracle I've been able to focus on the work at hand at all.

I shift the cowboy hat he sat on my head after I mentioned how bright the sun was and aim my most incredulous stare at him.

"Excuse me? Did you say *actually*?" I pretend to be only

slightly more offended than I really am. "Of course it looks great. I can't believe you ever questioned my vision."

"You're right. I'm sorry." He holds his hands up in front of him, veins running up his sinewy forearms. "I've just never seen a pink kitchen before. I didn't know what to expect."

That's fair. Even Gabby thought I was insane when I told her. I want this house to be like if Barbie were to buy a farmhouse, but even I can admit a pink kitchen is a lot. After searching endlessly through Pinterest and renovation TikTok, I narrowed my plan down to either pink cabinetry or all-pink appliances. In an ideal world, Silas would be helping me replace the fugly refrigerator with a brand-new bubblegum-pink one, but after looking at prices, I opted for a paint job instead. No budget in the world would've allowed me to spend that much money on a refrigerator.

"Well, besides the appeal of a maximalist kitchen, I hope you've also learned the very important lesson to never doubt me." I put the final touches of paint on the cabinet I'm working on and drop the roller onto the paint tray. "What do you think about taking a break? I need air-conditioning and something to drink."

Preferably something with copious amounts of vodka, but I haven't hit up the liquor store yet, and other than the half-empty (half-full?) bottle of bourbon, my supply is devastatingly nonexistent. I should also reapply my sunscreen. I can practically feel my skin wrinkling with sun damage.

"A break sounds good." He swipes his forearm across his forehead. I didn't know wiping sweat away could be sexy, but now I wish there was an option to watch in slow motion. "Should we bring the cabinets we finished inside?"

I don't want to do anything else that requires labor, but

I've only just met him and he's already witnessing the way I turn into a wilted, wet mess when I'm subjected to temperatures above eighty-five degrees. I can't make him aware of my laziness as well.

"Sure," I say. "I set up a drying station in the laundry room. We can put them in there."

By *set up*, I mean I laid a few tarps across the floor and over the new washer and dryer that I like to look at far more than I like to utilize.

I grab one of the cabinets that's been drying the longest and head toward the house without bothering to check if Silas is following. The heat of his gaze at my back rivals that of the pulsing sun. I really hope he's looking at my ass and not the sweat stain I'm sure is marring my paint-splattered T-shirt.

"Lucky for you, I went to the grocery store since you were last here," I say after we set the cabinets down and make our way back into the kitchen. "What would you like? I am a beverage girlie, so I have lots of options. Pop, tea, lemonade, coffee—iced or hot—water? Pick your hydration."

I pull open the refrigerator door and stare inside, trying to ignore the way he still manages to smell so good even after hours of sweating.

"Pop?" he repeats, and the teasing tone in his voice can't be missed. "Is that what they call Coke in Colorado?"

"No?" I shake my head, not understanding what's so funny. "We still call Coke, Coke, but pop is more than Coke. It's all the soft drinks."

"When you want *pop* here, you just ask for a Coke." He says this like it makes sense when, in fact, it does not. "Then they'll ask what kind of Coke you want and you'll tell them Dr Pepper or Sprite or whatever."

There are a lot of things I'm loving as a newcomer to the South. I'm all for *y'all*—mainly because even if it's not their original intention, it's a very gender-neutral and inclusive term. I love the way people say something sweet like *bless her heart* when they're really cursing a person to hell. I can even appreciate the way Texas natives devote at least 10 percent of their personalities to being Texan. But calling all pop Coke? No. I cannot, will not, accept it.

"But that's wrong. Coke isn't the genre, it's the artist. That's like if you wanted to listen to country music and said you want to turn on Shania Twain when you really want to listen to Tim McGraw."

"I don't know," he says, and his eyes dance with amusement. "I think renaming country music as Shania Twain is a great idea."

Well, he's got me there. I hate losing, but since he's looking this cute and complimenting my Canadian queen, I'll accept it this time. But *only* this time.

"Fine," I say. "But only because I love Shania. Now"—I gesture to his options—"would you like a *Coke*?"

"I'll have whatever you're having." His quiet chuckle fills my kitchen, and the warm sound makes the cabinet-less space feel like home. "Is the kitchen the first project you've done, or have you worked on anything else?"

I pull out the pitcher of sun tea I brewed yesterday and fill our glasses up to the brim.

"This is my second project." I hand him his glass before taking a sip from mine. "I worked on the bathroom over the weekend."

Attempted to work is a more accurate description of what was accomplished versus what I had planned. I wanted to paint the walls, replace the lighting, and swap the pedestal sink with the new vanity that was delivered. What I really did was cause a minor flood, nearly break my toe, and just manage to get the vanity installed before drowning myself in wine.

Small wins, am I right?

"Can I see?" he asks. "I mean, if you're comfortable—"

"Sure! There's not much to see, but my hair products are finally tucked away and not thrown all across the floor." I set my glass among the mess cluttering the counter and climb the creaky staircase to my room. "It's not much, but please pretend to be impressed."

I've tried to show Gabby, but I don't think she can get the full effect through the phone. I've been bursting for someone to be even a quarter as pleased with my work as I am. What can I say? Words of affirmation are my love language.

And gifts . . . and touch . . . and quality time.

This might be why I can only find boyfriends in my books. God forbid a girl have standards.

"Trust me," he says. "I won't have to pretend."

Gabby has called me delulu a time or two—or twenty—in the past, so maybe it's my imagination, but it feels like he might be talking about something other than my home improvement skills.

"That's a premature promise, but I appreciate it anyways." The heat rising in my face is getting harder to ignore. "Although, I'm pretty sure the flood I caused due to a minor pipe mishap might change your mind."

"Who hasn't flooded a bathroom or two before?" he asks. "I know you said you didn't need him, but if you change your mind or encounter a major pipe mishap, just say the word and I'll call my brother."

I walk into my bedroom, guiding him around the half-unpacked boxes I would've hidden and rushing him past the unmade bed I would've made if I'd known a cute guy would be in my room today.

"I appreciate that, but I think I can figure it out on my own." *Or at least that's what Pinterest and YouTube have convinced me.* "*Unless* it's an electrical issue, then I'll call right away."

Water is one thing but wires are another. I would very much like to not electrocute myself anytime soon . . . or ever.

"Does this house have a lot of electrical issues?" he asks.

Let's just say that when the list of issues from the inspection came back after I put in my offer, the price of the house dropped drastically. I think they thought it was going to scare me away, and if I was in any other mental state other than not well, it likely would have. But lucky for them, coming into a windfall while being a hot grieving mess and struggling to feel literally anything at all not only lowered my real estate standards, it heightened my desperation. They could've told me there was no roof and it still would've sounded better than staying in Denver.

"*A lot* is relative. It's an old house, so it has its fair share of problem areas." I push open the bathroom door and flip on the light switch, gesturing to the small space as if I'm welcoming him into a golden luxe bathroom of Versailles. "But lack of storage in this bathroom isn't one of them anymore."

"Wow!" His eyes go wide as he takes in the bright space. "This looks amazing."

He's overdoing it, but I appreciate his gusto.

"Amazing what basic organization can do, right?" The vanity isn't too special, but I didn't want anything to take away from the floral tiles and stained glass window. "I still have a lot to do, but I'm really happy with it."

"You should be; you did a really great job." He wanders deeper into the room to get a closer look at the claw-foot tub I love to look at but have yet to utilize, but pauses when the creaky floors groan beneath his feet. "Does it always sound like this?"

"For the most part," I say. "But the entire house makes noises. Isn't this just how old houses sound?"

I try to ignore the rising panic on his face.

"I think some noise is normal." The rickety floors groan louder with his every slow, measured step, and it doesn't stop even after he pulls me out of the bathroom. "But this—"

He doesn't finish the sentence.

And not because he's trying to drum up suspense or he loses his train of thought.

No. Nothing like that.

He stops talking because the floors stop groaning and begin to scream. A cloud of dust explodes from the ground just before the claw-foot tub I love so much falls through it.

"So . . ." I draw out the word, staring unseeing at the massive hole in the bathroom where a tub sat mere seconds ago. "It might be time for you to call your brother."

"Yeah, Luna," he says. "I think so too."

Chapter 9

Silas squeezes my hand in his and, in a reversal of roles, guides me through my house. I'm sure I would think it was sweet if I wasn't so busy freaking the fuck out. Every creak sounds like a bomb preparing to detonate, and now the charming soundtrack of my old house sounds more like the score from a horror movie. By the time I collapse on my couch, my watch vibrates on my wrist to alert me of my heightened heart rate.

"Hey." Silas holds his phone to his ear, but his concerned gaze stays trained on me. "No," he says, "you can't call back. I need you to head over to the Monroes' old place." The lines tighten on his face, and he clenches his jaw. I can't make out what the person on the other end is saying, but I don't need to hear to know they're pissing Silas off. "Jesus. Stop. This isn't some trick to get you to talk to Dad. The tub just fell through the damn ceiling and—"

The voice on the phone gets even louder, and I don't need to hear what's being said to know he's pissed off now too.

Wonderful. Having a hole in my floor isn't ideal, but neither is causing a fight between twin brothers.

"There's another bathroom." I try to stop him. "He's busy. He doesn't—"

Silas shakes his head and talks over me.

"That's the person who lives here. Wanna stop being a dick for a minute and come help her?" There's another long pause, but this time, whatever's said causes his shoulders to relax. "Thank you . . . yeah. See you soon."

He hits end on his phone and drops it onto the coffee table.

"Everything okay?" I ask after I've given him a minute to decompress. "Sorry that me and my house started a fight with you and your brother."

"Everything is fine and, trust me, that wasn't a fight." His full lips curve into a full smile, but for the first time since I've met him, it doesn't reach his eyes. "He's on his way. He just likes to give me a hard time."

I eye him skeptically. I've been dying to meet his brother, but I'm pretty sure the whole "good first impression" dream is shot, since it sounds like he's less than thrilled about having to come over. "Are you sure?"

"Positive," he says. "It's typical brother shit."

As an only child, I'm not familiar with sibling dynamics. Besides my friends growing up, the closest thing I had to draw on was my mom and uncle. And my uncle *sucks*. Although, to be fair, this has less to do with sibling dynamics and more to do with him being a raging, racist asshole. He pretty much cut my mom out of his life when she announced she was pregnant with me. But the joke was on him, because after that, my grandma practically cut him out of her life as well. There were a lot of things my grandma played about, but

I was not one of them. He's been trying to get in touch with me since I sold my grandma's house, but ever since he called me a selfish bitch before hanging up on me when I called to give him the funeral details for my mom (aka his sister), I haven't been too eager to take his calls.

Suffice it to say, it wasn't the most heartwarming example of sibling relationships.

"If you say so," I say. "Thank you for calling him."

"Your bathtub is in your laundry room." He reminds me of the unforgettable. "It was the least I could do."

If I have to find at least one bright spot in this, the tub somehow managed to miss not only my washer and dryer, but the cabinet doors we brought in were still leaning, unbothered and undisturbed, against the tarp.

"That might be true for you," I say. "But it means a lot to me."

He tips his head sideways and his eyes soften. "Luna—"

His phone vibrates on the table, and one word appears on the screen: Pops.

"Fuck," he mutters beneath his breath. "I have to take this, but I'll be right back."

He swipes the phone off the table and puts it to his ear as he disappears into my kitchen. I only hear his terse greeting before my back door slams shut behind him.

Without his gentle, concerned presence around, the unbothered facade I've been wearing melts like a Popsicle on the Fourth of July.

If I'm honest with myself, my mom was never the kind of mom you could count on. I don't think there was a single soccer season when she didn't forget at least one game. When I was a kid, I loved how childlike she seemed. She'd flitter in and out of rooms without purpose, the sound of her giggles the only thing as constant as the wineglass in her hand. It wasn't until I was older that I understood what was happening . . . that I realized her laughter was filled with sadness, not joy. I spent the majority of her last years taking care of her. Making sure she paid her bills, stocking the fridge with food that might possibly absorb the wine she was beginning to switch for vodka, rescheduling the doctors' appointments she canceled. Hiding the keys.

I'm used to shouldering my problems on my own. But even knowing she wasn't the kind of mom most people would think of, she was the only one I knew. And right now, I want more than anything to call her and hear her voice tell me everything is going to be okay. I need her to tell me I didn't make a mistake by selling the one place that ever really felt like home so I could move into a house that is quite literally crumbling beneath my feet.

I need my mom.

But she's gone.

My skin prickles as the cold reminder that I'm all alone in this world washes over me. I clench my eyes shut, hoping the tears that have been lodged in my throat for the last three months will finally fall, but they don't come.

They never come.

Instead, the anxiety always lurking in the back of my mind rears its ugly head and slithers its way down to my lungs, squeezing them so tight that I feel like I might suffocate. My vision grays as sharp pain ignites like fireworks shooting across my chest and wrapping around my back and down my arms.

"Pink couch, wood floors, white ceiling." I fight through labored breaths to name three things I can see like my last therapist told me to do. I wiggle my toes and twist my wrists and neck back and forth. I close my eyes while the fuzzy feeling in my brain starts to fade. The white noise filling my ears quiets until I can name three sounds. "Birds chirping. Air-conditioning buzzing. Gravel bouncing."

It's the last sound that tethers me back to the present.

My eyes shoot open just in time to hear the sound of an engine shutting off cut through the silence. A car door opens, and the driver doesn't have any qualms about slamming it shut. He's not happy to be here and he's making sure I know it.

Message received, Twin Jacobs.

Heavy footsteps draw closer, and I look around for Silas but he's nowhere to be found. A heavy knock rattles my front door, and just when I think another panic attack is imminent, icy numbness runs down my spine and a familiar mask slides back into place.

Thank god.

I think after my bathtub falling through the ceiling and experiencing the worst anxiety attack I've had in months, not melting down in front of Silas's brother is the least the universe could do for me. I know they say bad things come in threes, but if you look closer at the grand scheme of my life, I'm pretty sure I'm somewhere around number 3,791. It seems only fair that nothing else should happen to me for the rest of the night.

If not eternity.

My hand pauses above the doorknob, and I tuck an errant curl behind my ear. I take a deep breath, plastering on a smile I know looks real despite how it feels, and swing open the front door.

"Hi!" I say with false bravado. "It's so nice—"

A bulldog barrels past my legs, and my words lodge themselves in the back of my throat. My mind spins as I try to process what's happening and why, instead of staring into another set of honey eyes, I'm met with a pair of onyx ones.

"Tate? What are you doing here?"

Pieces from a million different puzzles fall into my head. A slow ache builds at the nape of my neck while I sort through them all.

He takes a step back and looks over my head, into my living room.

"Um, hi. Sorry," he says, and the confusion in his voice mirrors my own. "I thought you knew I was coming?"

I shake my head and open my mouth to tell him no, but before I can, everything falls into place.

I didn't see it at first.

I was so distracted by their differences, Tate's ebony skin to Silas's bronze, Silas's short fade to Tate's locs, Tate's stony demeanor to Silas's cheerful one, that I didn't see the similarities. The same slight slant to their eyes, the straight bridge of their noses, the strong line of their jaws. The self-assured way they stand. The quiet confidence that follows them into every room they enter.

It's unmistakable. I can't believe I missed it before.

"You're Silas's brother."

It's not a question, but he answers anyway.

"Yeah." He nods his head. "He told me you needed some help?"

Oh, I need help alright. I'm just not sure it's the kind either of the Jacobs twins can offer.

Chapter 10

"Sorry about that," Silas says. "My dad loses his mind if I send him to voicemail."

Silas is looking down at his phone when he finally walks back inside. He's so focused on whatever's on his screen that he doesn't even seem to notice Tate, *his freaking brother*, standing right beside me. While I, on the other hand, am hyperaware of both of them.

Silas and Tate are gorgeous on their own, but together? It should be illegal.

The door is closed and the air-conditioning is on, but heat still licks at my flushed skin. The Texas weather seems like child's play compared to the absolute hotness filling my living room. Need rushes through my veins as an all-consuming desire settles so deep in my stomach, I don't know if the feeling will ever fade . . . or if I want it to.

"We wouldn't want that, would we?" Tate asks. "Gotta keep the old man happy."

Silas's head snaps up and his gaze narrows on his brother. "When'd you get here?"

Duke catches wind of Silas, and his little body flails as his paws slip on the hardwood floors. His heavy breathing turns to snorts, and he runs across the room, torpedoing himself into Silas's legs.

"Hey, Duke." Silas bends over and gives Duke some well-deserved scratches. Duke licks his hand in approval. "You're such a good boy. Did you come to fix the floor?"

"Speaking of—" Tate turns to me without answering Silas's question. Talk about awkward. "What happened?"

I don't know what I expected of the Jacobs twins, but it's safe to say I assumed there'd be at least a modicum of affection between the two. Instead, they act more like strangers than two people who shared a womb. Weird energy rolls off Tate in waves, and the happy-go-lucky version of Silas that I've gotten to know is replaced with tension and hostility. If it weren't for Duke rolling round, so excited to see Silas, I might think they were completely estranged.

"Um, my bathtub." My eyes flitter between the two brothers. "It kinda sorta fell through the ceiling."

Silas tries to hide his laughter with a cough. Tate is less amused.

Tate's dark eyes narrow. "It *kinda sorta* fell through the ceiling?"

"Well . . . no." I worry my bottom lip. "It really, actually fell through the ceiling. It's in my laundry room now."

"Show me," Tate says.

"The laundry room or the bathroom?" I ask.

"The bathroom, Luna," he says. "Show me the bathroom where there's a hole instead of a bathtub."

"Yeah, that makes sense." I hurry toward the staircase. He's only been here for a few minutes and already sounds exasperated, so a little urgency on my part feels necessary. "It's this way."

"Hey." Silas puts a hand on my shoulder before I can make it out of the living room. "Are you okay with me heading out now that Tate's here? A couple of things I need to take care of popped up."

I was so consumed with my own issues, I didn't even stop and think that he had better places to go or things to do.

Selfish.

Just like my uncle said.

"Oh my god, of course. Go." Guilt rushes the words out. "I'm sorry I kept you for so long."

"You didn't. I wanted to be here," he says, his voice as soft as his smile. "I'll swing by tomorrow and check in."

"No, don't worry about it." I already owe him so much for his help today. The last thing I want is for him to feel obligated to come check on the mess next door. I know that feeling much too well to put it on someone else. "You don't need to do that."

"Yeah, you don't need to do that," Tate says. "Go handle the ranch or whatever Dad needs from you this time. I've got Luna covered."

"Like I said"—Silas ignores Tate and keeps his steady gaze trained on me—"I'll swing by tomorrow and check in."

I didn't think anything could distract me from their combined attractiveness, but I forgot to account for the power of pure and total awkwardness. Silas's smile never wavers and his tone remains the same, but the efforts are for naught. The hard lines, so out of place on his gentle face, are a dead giveaway for how he's really feeling.

And it's anything but happy.

Yikes.

"Then I'll be here," I acquiesce. "Thank you."

He nods and turns on a booted heel and walks out of the front door without so much as acknowledging Tate. The screen door slams shut behind him, and an uncomfortable silence hangs heavy in the air.

With Silas gone, Duke has gotten all the attention he needed and he finds a spot on the hardwood floor beneath the air-conditioning vent to plop down. His tongue hangs out of his mouth and his little body moves up and down with every laborious pant. It must be exhausting to be a puppy.

"So you two are close?" I joke, but surprising absolutely no one, it falls flat.

Even Duke looks embarrassed.

"Alrighty then!" I clap my hands together and infuse way more enthusiasm than necessary into my voice. If I wasn't still reeling from the discomfort of standing between Tate and Silas, I might have the wherewithal to feel shame. But that ship has long since sailed. "So, the bathroom?"

"Yeah," he says with the whisper of a smile that's barely perceptible on his stoic face. I worry I could get lost staring into his eyes and spend eternity inspecting his full lips trying to find it. "That'd be good."

I force myself to look away and rush to my rickety old stairs. Something about Tate's brooding presence is so much different than Silas's. I'm hyperaware of the way my heart races in my chest and my stomach twists into knots as his long legs follow effortlessly behind me. Everything about this man screams trouble, but that doesn't stop my body from craving something it's never had.

Something it never will have.

I hold open my bedroom door and gesture for the second hot man of the day to go inside.

"Just be careful," I say. "The entire house makes a lot of noise. I thought that was normal for an old house, but that was before the floor collapsed. I'm not so sure anymore."

Nothing like a bathtub-shaped hole to shake your confidence.

"The entire house?" he asks. "What did the inspection say?"

"The inspection? I'm not sure." My cheeks flame. I try to avoid his eyes as I push by him, but I don't get far. "The hole is right—"

Tate's large hand wraps around mine and he pulls me to a stop. "You did get an inspection, didn't you?"

"What? Of course I did!" I try to infuse as much indignation in my voice as possible, but it's hard to focus with the feel of his calloused palm resonating throughout my body and taking hold between my thighs.

"Luna, I'm going to ask again." He sniffs out my lie like some kind of bloodhound. His black eyes narrow and I squirm beneath his knowing gaze. "Did you get an inspection on this house before you bought it or not?"

"I did." I tell him the god's honest truth. "I just didn't pay much attention to what it said."

"Fuck. Okay." He sighs and drags his free hand across his face. "Show me the bathroom now. I'll call Patricia later."

"You will?" My eyebrows scrunch together. "Why?"

"Have you ever bought a house before?" he asks instead of answering.

"No, but—"

"So she knew you were a first-time buyer," he says, and I'm not sure I follow. "Did she go over the inspection list with you? Did she make sure you knew what you were getting yourself into before you bought the house that's been on the market for the better part of six years? A house that nobody in town would touch with a ten-foot pole because Mr. Monroe was always doing renovations but didn't believe in the government, so he never got permits before doing them?"

Oh.

Now I know where he's going with this, and fuck me with that ten-foot pole if it doesn't sound expensive.

Ignorance is bliss. Until it isn't.

"Maybe I should've paid attention to the inspection," I admit. "But this isn't on Patricia. She did her job. I was so ready to move that this place could've had no windows and a hole where the chimney should be and as long as I still could have a pink chicken coop, I would've signed on the dotted line."

Desperation and avoidance are funny motivators.

I didn't mean to give so much away, and I know the next question before he even asks it. His grip on my hand tightens, and I brace as I try to think of any reason for my hasty move that doesn't include trauma dumping my entire life story on him.

Turns out, my worry was for nothing.

"A pink chicken coop?" he asks instead. "That's what sold you?"

"It was really the air-conditioned shed," I say. "I was actually afraid of birds as a kid. I was convinced they were going to peck my eyes out. But I've been watching a lot of chicken content on TikTok and I've decided that not only am I not afraid of chickens, but I think I love them. I already have some names picked out. Kelly Cluckson, Henda Martell, and of course there will be Little Chix."

"Little Chix?"

"Yeah, you know, like Little Mix, but chickens," I explain. "Leigh-hen Pinnock, Jade Cluckwall, and Perrie Eggwards. If all goes well, I'll make them an Instagram account. The internet will love them."

There will also be Dolly Parton, but I couldn't come up with a pun for her. That's okay though because . . . well, she's Dolly.

"You know you're kind of a nut, right?" he asks.

I nod. "So I've been told a time or two."

His lips turn up at the corners, and at the sight of his smile, the rest of the world falls away. I ignore the way Silas smiles all the time and it never feel like this. I forget all about the great bathtub fiasco and the ever-growing to-do list I've yet to put a dent in. Victory courses through my veins, knowing I put that look on his face. The quiet noises of the house fade beneath the sound of our deepening breaths.

As if by magic, I drift closer to him. My skin prickles with awareness as I realize we're standing in the middle of my room and only a few boxes separate us from my bed. All it would take is one little step, and then . . .

"So where's the bathroom?" Tate drops my hand like it's on fire and takes a very pointed step away from me. "I should probably take a look at it so I can figure out what I'll need to fix it."

"Oh yeah. Good idea." I try to clear the embarrassment clogging my throat and I point to the half-opened door across the room. "It's right over there."

His only response is a nod of his head, and I follow behind him as he enters my own personal construction zone.

He hisses out a sharp breath. "Jesus Christ."

I haven't worked with many handymen before, but this seems like a bad sign.

"That bad?" I ask, and his angry eyes slice to me.

"There's a hole in the fucking floor where your bathtub was," he says. "So yeah, I'd say it's that bad."

Cool, cool.

"So how do we do this?" I ask. He might be kind of an asshole, but he's Silas's brother, and I don't think in a town this small, there's enough options to bother shopping around. "Do I sign a contract? Are you hourly? Should I pay up front?"

For some reason, this seems to make him more irritated than he was before.

I didn't think that was possible.

"I'll send you a contract tonight. You'll cover all the costs of the materials, and I'll bill you for my hours at the end, but Luna, this isn't going to be cheap," he says. "At first glance, I'm thinking this could run upward of ten thousand just on materials alone."

That's almost one-tenth of what I paid for the entire house.

My stomach hurts.

"Okay," I say, not because I want to, but because there's nothing else to say. "Get me the contract whenever you can, and I'll be sure to get it back to you as soon as possible."

"Thanks. I'll take a look around and see if I notice anything else," he says, turning his back on me. "I'll find you and update you when I'm done."

I don't wait for him to say anything else. I know when I've been dismissed. And although it's never happened in my own home, I don't need to be told twice.

I brave my way down the tenuous stairs and push through

my back door. The sun has settled high in the afternoon sky, and it's even hotter than it was before. My air-conditioning blows at my back, tempting me to wait it out inside, but I'd much rather put my anguish into finishing my cabinets over nursing my bruised ego on the couch. Distraction is my favorite coping mechanism.

Right below avoidance. Which I will absolutely be using the moment I see Tate again.

The cabinet doors I sanded with Silas are still laid out where I left them, but the paintbrushes and rollers have been wrapped in plastic and the loose paint I forgot about has been returned to the canister.

Silas.

I look over the fence, trying to spot the house nuzzled in the acres upon acres of Starlight Ridge Ranch before chancing a glance over my shoulder and trying to catch a glimpse of Tate through the stained glass window of my bathroom.

If I was smart, I'd forget all about Tate and never look back. I don't need to know him to recognize the unspoken ghosts he's fighting, and I have too many of my own to help him battle his. Too bad I've always been a slow learner.

I know I came to Celestial hoping for a cowboy romance of my own, but twins from the ranch next door? That's a trope too far even for me. I have a feeling that this plot twist can only end with me getting burned or—if recent history is any indicator at all—extremely hot and bothered.

Chapter 11

All I had to do was not.

I could've sat my ass at my apartment in Denver, gone to therapy, and pretended to be happy. I'd been doing it for years by that point, and other than the bone-crushing numbness that was slowly eating away at my spirit and soul, it was working out just fine for me.

But noooooo.

I had to turn my life upside down. I had to up and leave everything and everyone I knew in order to move to some small Texas town. And for what? To brush up on my knitting skills while a group of strangers talks about me like I'm not in the room?

Well . . . yeah.

And honestly? It's pretty freaking amazing.

"I don't know why she would buy the house in the first place," Esther says. "A fixer-upper? In this economy? Bless her heart, but it doesn't make much sense if you ask me."

Esther is a few years older than my grandma would be.

Bright red lipstick matches her flaming red hair that seems to be more of a warning than a style choice. The deep-set lines framing her eyes hint at a life well lived while the lines engraved on her forehead tell the story of a woman who is not one to suffer fools. She has a sharp tongue and a sharper sense of humor, and although I've only known her for a few hours, I already know I would die for her.

"Esther!" Millie's cheeks heat to the color of Esther's hair as she chastises her for the millionth time. "Could you please refrain from insulting Luna? You don't spend enough here to scare her away."

"Oh please." Esther shoos Millie away and waves her knitting needle more like a weapon than an innocent craft tool. "If I didn't think she could handle it, I'd wait until she left to talk about her like I do whenever I talk to those two fools opening that ridiculous juice bar next door. Luna might be from the city, but she's a tough one. She doesn't need you fighting her battles for her, Millicent Marie Dean."

Esther doesn't give the impression that she warms to new people or doles out compliments easily. I haven't lived in the South long enough to be sure that she's not insulting me, but even though her words were on the harsh side, the fondness in her tone allows me to err on the side of optimism. And for reasons I'm not sure I'm prepared to process, the approval of this older woman causes my heart to sing.

"Yeah, Millicent Marie Dean. I don't need you fighting my battles for me," I say, and my smile doubles in size when Millie's blue eyes shoot daggers at me. "But you know what would've been nice?"

She folds her arms in front of her chest and rolls her eyes. "What?"

"You telling me that Silas and Tate were brothers instead of letting me get blindsided in my own freaking living room," I say.

The attitude she was sporting only seconds ago evaporates into thin air.

"Oh . . ." She looks down, all of a sudden enraptured with the knitting square she's only looked at twice since class started. "That."

"Yeah," I mock. "*That.*"

Before moving to Celestial, I barely even took personal calls outside of my apartment, and I would've never dreamt of discussing my private life in such a public setting. But I guess there's freedom in everyone knowing your business at all times.

Katy-Anne gasps and her brown eyes nearly bulge out of her head. "You didn't tell her they were brothers?"

"No, Katy-Anne, she didn't. Not even when I stood in this very store, asking about Silas and Tate," I answer for Millie and take more pleasure than I should at her obvious discomfort. "And now I've been stuck at my house for the last two weeks while Tate works on my bathroom and Silas randomly checks in. It has not been fun."

That's not the total truth.

Getting to see Tate looking all hot in his jeans with a toolbox isn't exactly a hardship. Plus, Duke and I have started to become great friends. And it's absolutely not because I've been sneaking him the homemade dog biscuits I bake fresh for him each week.

Esther shakes her head and tsks her tongue, her silent judgment louder than words could ever be. Miss Margaret, on the other hand, is much more vocal about her feelings.

"Now, Millie," she says, her gentle voice thick with disapproval. "Why would you do such a thing? That doesn't sound like you."

Miss Margaret is the soft-spoken counterpart to Esther's hard edges. She carries herself with the grace of a dancer, so quiet and powerful that even the fine lines decorating her delicate mocha skin move with elegance. Her gray hair is pulled into a bun at the back of her head, showcasing the dainty diamond earrings that complement the wedding ring she's still wearing four years after her husband passed away. It only takes a minute of being in her presence to know that I would do anything to never disappoint her.

I have to assume it's also why her words seem to hit Millie the hardest.

"Okay, hold on. I'm not the bad guy here." Millie drops her knitting needles and square, needing full usage of both hands to defend herself. "We all know Celestial loves its gossip. Everyone in this room has had the experience of information being shared about them that isn't even remotely true, or worse, information that is true and we wanted to keep to ourselves. And still, nobody in this room has been the center of gossip more than the Jacobs brothers and more specifically Tate."

Her heated eyes dart from person to person, as if daring someone to disagree with her, and are met with the silent agreement of the room instead.

"That's what I thought," she says. "The gossip mill was running rampant like it always does when it comes to Tate. When I realized Luna didn't know the Jacobs family lore, I kept my mouth shut. I thought that for once, Tate and Silas could tell their story for themselves instead of someone else doing it for them. After everything that happened with Tate in . . . Never mind." She stops herself mid-sentence and focuses her attention on me instead. I don't know what she's about to say, but I do know I'm not going to love it. "They deserve that, and Luna, it might not feel like it, but so do you. I get that being new in a town like this can be hard. I'm sorry if you felt blindsided or like I set you up by keeping that information from you, because that was absolutely *not* my intention, but at the end of the day, I don't regret my decision and I'd do it all over again."

Well, fuck!

This was only fun when I had the upper hand.

"Fine." I deflate into the overstuffed chair and stab the needle through the yarn with much more force than necessary. It's bad enough to have to admit I'm wrong, but it's even worse to admit someone else is right. "I guess that was the right thing to do, and even though I don't want to, I respect your decision."

"Thank you very much, Luna. It's very mature of you to acknowledge your mistakes," Millie says to me before shifting her smug grin to everyone else in the room. "I hope you all learned a very valuable lesson here today and that in the future, should a situation like this ever arise again, you'll know better than to doubt me. As for apologies, I'll accept them in the form of lavender soy lattes or—"

"Oh, put a sock in it," Esther cuts her off. "The only apology you'll get from me is a sorry kick in the ass if you don't knock it off."

Like I said, I'd die for her.

"Geez, Esther." Millie picks up her knitting square. "No need for violence."

"Not if you stop with the nonsense, there's not," Esther says.

I try to swallow my laughter, but a very unladylike snort slips out, and Millie's glare slices straight through me. She opens her mouth to say something I can only assume is going to be laced with snark, but Katy-Anne beats her to it.

"So, Luna!" Katy-Anne says quickly, her Southern drawl sounding a bit thicker than it did before. "Other than a few more renovations than you planned for, how are you liking Celestial so far?"

"I'm loving it," I tell her honestly. "I don't know what I expected, but so far it's managed to exceed all my expectations."

Well, everything other than my bathtub falling through my ceiling, that is.

"I'm sure that has nothing at all to do with the handsome cowboy next door or the hot football coach in town, right?" Millie's eyes dance with mischief, and I wouldn't be surprised if she stuck her tongue out at me.

"I thought you said you didn't want to participate in the Celestial gossip mill." I repeat her words back to her, but instead of the intended effect I thought they'd have, her smirk turns into a full-blown grin.

"Nice try," she says. "But it's not gossip if we get it from the source."

I hate that her flawed logic makes perfect sense. I don't even have a chance to come up with an excuse before Miss Margaret aims her big expectant eyes at me. I couldn't live with myself if I disappointed her.

"Okay." I lean forward and drop my voice to a whisper. "But everyone has to promise that what happens in knitting circle, stays in knitting circle."

"Cross my heart, hope to die, stick a needle in my eye." Katy-Anne recites the old childhood pledge. It takes on a much darker meaning while wielding said knitting needle.

Everyone joins in.

Everyone except for Esther, that is.

"What?" she asks when the group turns expectantly toward her. "You're all overestimating how much I care and my desire to talk to other people. Both of which are close to zero."

"Oh please, don't try to play coy with me, Esther Briggs. You're just as bad as everyone else in this town." Miss Margaret purses her lips and rolls her eyes. "Don't think I forgot about the time you got Mary-Ellen kicked out of the church potluck or when you put flyers with pictures of Dan's Oldsmobile on every street corner and called the sheriff until the police darn near put a tail on the man."

My ears perk up. Church potluck drama is the exact level of petty drama that I love to hear. I knew Esther had it in her.

"Oh, don't you throw that in my face, Margaret. You know damn well that happened after three years of Mary-Ellen having her grandson drive to Dallas and buy that coconut cake she tried to pass off as her own. If she didn't want to get disqualified, she shouldn't have cheated." Esther's voice is steadily rising, and her face grows closer and closer to matching her hair with every impassioned word she says. "As for Dan, he was driving much too fast in residential areas. That wasn't gossip, that was a safety measure, and I'm sorry that I care about the pedestrians of Celestial. Next time I'll let them get mowed down by Dan's rusty heap of junk."

"He was only going a few miles over the speed limit and you know it," Miss Margaret says. I take her silence on cake scandal as confirmation that Mary-Ellen, who I have yet to meet, is indeed a dirty little scammer. "You were just mad that he got the car when he divorced Cheryl. You wanted to punish him."

"And?" Esther doesn't bother to deny it. "She spent her entire life supporting that jerk. She was too nice to fight him for what she deserved. Somebody had to do it for her."

Your honor, I love her.

"Sorry," I say to Margaret. "I've got to get behind Esther on these ones."

"Me too," Millie says. "If anything, Esther is the Robin Hood of gossip and the town needs her service."

"Thank you, girls." Esther leans back into her seat, looking mighty pleased with herself. "Now that I've been vindicated against Marge's outrageous claims, you may continue, Luna." She pauses for a minute, and a playful smile I didn't think her face was capable of producing tugs at the corners of her red lips. "Just be sure not to leave out the good details."

Miss Margaret throws her hand in the air and shouts, "See!"

Millie, Katy-Anne, and I burst into peals of laughter not long before Miss Margaret and Esther join in.

We laugh until we cry, all of us doubled over in the mismatched chairs, our knitting projects long forgotten. By the time we collect ourselves enough for me to regale them with the tale of two brothers and a bathtub, mascara marks stain my flushed cheeks, my stomach is sore from laughing so hard, and I realize belatedly that for the first time in months I'm not thinking of my mom or the house I sold. I'm not worried about tomorrow and what's going to go wrong. I'm not overthinking yesterday and what I could've done differently. I stop performing the could've, should've, would've song and dance altogether, and for once, I'm perfectly present.

It might not seem like much to anyone else, but it's everything to me.

Sitting in a craft store, surrounded by strangers, something inside of me shifts.

And I start to heal.

Chapter 12

It was such a perfect day, laughing with Millie at her store until the sun began to fall below the horizon, my hands cramping from holding the knitting needle and my cheeks aching from smiling. When the time came for me to climb into bed, I did it knowing that for once, I wouldn't have to fight to find sleep.

What a fool I was.

I look at my phone and watch the moment today ends and tomorrow begins. Crickets chirp in the distance, and the gentle breeze rustling the leaves on the trees punctuates another silent Celestial night. The melatonin I took two hours ago, hoping it would kick in despite months of experience telling me it won't, has yet to elicit even a single yawn. My legs itch as I grow restless in my bed. I throw the comforter off me and shift on the bed, hoping for what feels like the millionth time tonight that changing positions is the key to unlocking the night's sleep I so desperately need.

Shocker. It does not.

I reach for the Kindle on my nightstand and finish a chapter of my latest cowboy romance before unplugging my phone from the wall and typing out a quick "You up?" text to Gabby. I stare at the screen, willing those three glorious dots to appear or, even better, for her picture to light up my screen and my phone to vibrate in my palm. I must have used up all my good luck at the craft store, because after ten minutes of nothing, I'm forced to accept that while sleep eludes me, it has found my best friend.

I open my email for the first time in weeks, deleting without abandon until one familiar name catches my eye. Jack Brady, my jerk of an uncle.

Apparently, not answering his calls isn't enough to deter him and he's found another method. I guess tenacity that verges on the edge of obnoxious obsession is a family trait.

It's unnerving to know I have anything in common with a man I'm determined to hate.

My finger hovers over the innocuous subject line. How much damage could come from an email titled *Quick Question*? Knowing him? A lot.

I hit delete.

My mom is gone. My grandma is gone. There is nothing tying me to him, and I'm under no obligation to hear what he has to say. It's called boundaries . . . and not at all ignoring another one of my millions of problems.

I throw my phone to the side and toss and turn until resentment finally pushes me out of bed. Most nights, I drag my comforter down to my couch and stare at the TV until my retinas burn and my eyelids are too heavy to hold open. But tonight, my brain isn't the only thing that won't shut off. My feet tingle and my muscles twitch with energy I know will elude me in the morning. I use the flashlight on my phone to rummage through my drawers until I find a pair of shorts and a sports bra to throw on under the threadbare T-shirt I put on before bed. I slip on my tennis shoes and skip down the stairs without so much as even thinking about running a brush through my hair.

The sun is nothing but a memory this late, yet the warmth of the day still clings to the night air. Millions of stars dance overhead and the light of the moon casts shadows across the still, dark world surrounding me. Sleep might evade me, but in this moment, peace doesn't.

Gabby always calls me a grandma because I don't usually like driving at night, but without the other cars out, the black roads don't seem to faze me. By the time I approach the football stadium at the edge of town, I'm almost disappointed to see the yellow streetlights dotting the parking lot and illuminating the empty sidewalks. I park next to the front entrance, and the front gate I figured I'd have to climb over is wide open.

I can just add this to the ever-growing list of perks of living in a small town.

Even though the things that were never exactly easy breezy with Tate have grown significantly more awkward since our shared moment in my bathroom, I haven't given up my morning workouts alongside the football team. I hoped running this late would come with the added bonus of not accidentally catching his annoyed gaze and would be easier, but the stadium is eerily quiet without the sound of whistles blaring and teenage boys challenging me to a race. Keeping my pace isn't nearly as fun without someone jogging beside me and calling me Moon Girl.

My phone and headphones bounce inside the running fanny pack I found when I was unpacking my closet boxes. I let my thoughts run through my head uninterrupted until they finally go quiet under the hypnotic rhythm of my feet hitting the ground. Without the pressure of an audience, I have nobody to impress but myself and, unlike during my morning runs, I don't lose count of how many times I make it around the track.

Tonight I listen to my body. I push through deep breaths as my heart rate speeds up and my lungs begin to burn. I fight for every step. I don't let myself quit even after it gets hard . . . especially when it gets hard. I keep going until the anxiety that keeps me up at night drains from my body and my legs go heavy with fatigue.

I veer off the track and collapse onto the field. Exhaustion weighs down my body as my breathing slows and I sink deeper into the turf. The little rubber beads that always fill my shoes when I leave the stadium stick to my sweat-covered skin. I stare up at the night sky and attempt to count the millions of stars winking above me.

When I was a kid, there was one weekend I looked forward to every single year. For three days right after school started, my mom would clear her schedule—if she had a schedule to clear—and load up the trunk of her old Toyota with our sleeping bags and a tent that felt like the peak of luxury to my young brain, and we would go camping. We'd spend the drive up to Great Sand Dunes National Park singing at the top of our lungs and eating our way through bags and bags of peanut M&M'S and sour cream and onion Pringles. And when we finally arrived, I'd watch in awe as my strong, capable mom set up our campsite faster and more efficiently than any of the families around us.

Even the ones with dads.

We'd spend our days sledding down the sand dunes and playing in Medano Creek, splashing around and building sandcastles that were taller than me. When we were at our campsite, all the kids would end up hanging at our tent and my mom would transform into the Scout leader of the year. She'd pull out paint and glitter, showing everyone how to turn rocks into treasure and weeds into crowns. After they left, I'd tell her all about the adventures Grandma had taken me on over the summer and how I was liking school so far. She'd listen so intently—hanging on to my every word, laughing at all my jokes—that I'd be able to convince myself I was the most important person in the world.

Days were fun, but the nights were better.

The moment the sun began to set and dusk crept across the sky, the stars slowly coming out of hiding, my mom came alive. She looked to the skies with a clarity in her eyes and a pureness to her smile that I only witnessed on these trips. Some nights we'd stay at the campsite and look up at the stars over a blazing campfire, but if I was lucky, my mom would load up our backpacks earlier in the day and I'd know we were spending the night in the sand.

I trailed behind her, sand filling my shoes and sticking to my face, until she found the perfect spot to set up for the night deep in a valley of sand dunes. She'd always put up our tent, giving me the task of filling up bags with sand to use in place of stakes that had no use in the sand, but when the time came, we'd drag our sleeping bags over the sand and spend the night with an uninterrupted view of the sky.

"Do you see the Milky Way?" She pointed to the river of stars flowing in the sky, whispering as if her voice could chase the galaxy away. "Many cultures believe it connects Earth to the heavens. Your dad is on the other side, too far away to touch, close enough to feel, but always watching. Always sending signs. Whenever you see a shooting star, know that's him. Winking at you from where he sits just beyond the stars, telling you he's still there and that you're on the right path."

Those nights are carved so deeply in my soul that even though I'm lying on the plastic grass deep in Texas, I can see her lying beside me, pointing to the same stars I'm staring at now. It's as if, through the stars, she's right here.

Too far away to touch, but close enough to feel.

And I get so lost, searching for signs of my mom in the endless Celestial skies, that I don't even realize I'm not alone until he's right beside me.

My high-pitched scream slices through the peaceful quiet of the night. I scramble to get up, but my heavy limbs are too tired to move as fast as I need them to. Heat explodes in my bare legs as they scrape across the turf. I kick and swing a wild punch, only hitting air before remembering what I learned in my old boxing classes. I wind back and throw a loaded right cross followed by a mean left hook. My shadowy assailant groans, and a shot of adrenaline flows through my veins.

If I can't go out at a hundred and three playing bingo with my old-lady friends like I hoped, you better believe I'm not going down without a fight.

"Fuck! Luna!" a vaguely familiar voice shouts over the sound of my pulse pounding in my ears. "Chill, it's me!"

I stop fighting when recognition breaks through my panic.

"Tate?" I squint until my eyes adjust to the darkness and I can make out his large frame and telltale locs. "What are you doing out here?"

"That's what I was going to ask you." He rubs a hand across his chest, and even though I can't see the expression on his face, I know it's anything but happy.

But what's new?

"Whoa there, buddy," I say. "Are *you* mad at *me*?"

"Uh, yeah," he says, like I just snuck up on him and not the other way around. "What the hell were you thinking coming out here in the middle of the night all by yourself?"

"That's none of your business." My temper slides into place and I get the sudden urge to test my uppercut on him too. "Why don't you tell me why you're out here?"

"Because"—he raises his voice and gestures wildly to the locker rooms behind him—"I work here!"

Oh.

Well.

I guess that's a pretty good reason.

"This late?" I unzip my fanny pack and pull out my phone. "It's almost two o'clock in the morning."

"Yeah," he says. "I know."

I didn't know it was possible, but he sounds even more annoyed than usual. I turn on the flashlight and shine it on his face, which—rudely—is still hot when he's tired and angry.

"Shouldn't you be at home?"

As a newly appointed Texas high school football expert, I know the job is intense, but two in the morning seems excessive. Even Coach Taylor made it home to Tami for dinner most nights.

"The nights are long in the lead-up to the season," he says.

"You stay this late every night?"

"Not every night." He shrugs. "Once the season is underway, things will get better."

I'd think the opposite would be true, but since he's an actual coach and I just play one on TV, I'll take his word for it.

"When's your first game?" After my last week of working out with the boys, I'm practically a member of the team. I should probably know when we're playing. Plus, I'm a fantastic cheerleader—metaphorically, definitely not in the splits and cartwheel literal way—and they're obviously going to need my support. "Next time you come over, could you bring the schedule and roster?"

He narrows his eyes, and I add "suspicious" to the list of his hot facial expressions. "For what?"

"I need to mark the games on my calendar and know how many goody bags I need to make." From the look of practices, it's definitely over a hundred, but I need an exact number. "Include the coaches. I guess you guys deserve a cookie too. Which reminds me, am I allowed to bake cookies or do they have to be store-bought?"

"Whoa. Slow down." He holds his hands in front of his chest. "Booster club provides the boys with pregame and postgame meals, so you don't need to do that, and can we please get back to the subject at hand?"

"The subject at hand?"

"Jesus Christ." He growls. "Why are you running, by yourself, this late at night?"

"Or early in the morning, depending on how you look at it." I don't know why, but for some reason, I get a small thrill out of annoying him. Electricity fizzles through my veins for eliciting even an ounce of the feelings he brings out in me. "Maybe I'm just getting a head start on my day."

"An early start is why you spent the last hour and a half running like your life depended on it?" Sarcasm drips off every word. “I finished work thirty minutes ago, but I couldn’t leave because you looked like you were going to collapse long before you finally did.”

“I did not collapse.” I did. “I made the very conscious decision to lie down, ever so gracefully, on the field so I could look at the stars.”

“You—” He shakes his head and slow blinks. I’m afraid I might’ve broken him. “You were looking at the stars?”

I think the real question here is why is he not?

“Well, yeah.” I point to the blanket of stars overhead. “I mean, look at them.”

“I’m looking at you.” His fingers graze the bare skin just below the sleeve of my shirt as he brushes the rubber beads off my arm. “You’re covered in these.”

The air goes still.

“I know,” I whisper. “They’re in my hair too.”

My heart stutters in my chest and sparks leap from my skin. I don’t want to feel like this around him. I don’t want to feel the world start to slow each time he’s near or the gentle hum of excitement that washes over me whenever his eyes meet mine. I want to feel as unaffected by him as he seems to be by me. So unbothered by the sight of him that I don’t even know he’s around. If there is one Jacobs brother I should feel like this around, it should absolutely not be Tate.

I’m starting to realize that might not be possible.

“Why are you out here, Luna?” he tries again, his voice soft this time, and I hate how quickly I fold.

“I have a hard time sleeping.”

His eyebrows furrow, but this time he looks more concerned than annoyed. “All the time?”

“It didn’t used to be an issue. After my—” I stop myself.

Telling him I have insomnia is one thing; freely sharing my mom trauma is quite another. "It's been a few months. I'm sure I'll get over it soon, but I thought I'd try to exercise myself to sleep tonight."

"Did it work?"

"It might have," I say. "But then someone snuck up on me and scared me senseless."

He has the decency to look embarrassed, but not sorry.

"I was standing by the fence for a long time before I came over," he says. "I thought you saw me and were ignoring me like you do at practice."

Shit.

"I don't ignore you." I lie straight through my teeth.

He rolls his eyes, and the corner of his mouth pulls up into a very attractive, very infuriating smirk. "Sure you don't."

"I don't!" I repeat the lie with more conviction this time, but somehow, it's even less believable. "And I really didn't see you tonight. It was too dark, and I don't know if you noticed or not, but I was pretty focused on running. Also, you were watching me in the dark? Okay, stalker."

"I was trying to go home," he says. "Celestial is a safe town, but you never know who could be driving through or what could happen. If you couldn't see me standing right by the fence, you wouldn't have been able to see anyone else either."

I've watched enough crime procedurals to know he's not wrong. A shiver runs down my spine just thinking about it. "I guess, but—"

"Listen." He cuts me off with a shake of his head. "I'm here most nights, and the nights I'm not, I probably should be." He pulls my phone out of my hand and starts tapping away before I have the wherewithal to attempt to stop him. "Here's my number. If you ever want to come run late again, call or text me. I can come turn on the stadium lights and do some work so you're not alone and in the dark."

My legs go weak again, but it's not from overexertion this time.

"Thank you." I take my phone back, knowing I'll never take him up on it, but grateful that he offered. "That's really nice of you."

"It's not. Like I said, I'm always up here anyways and there's always more work to be done." He brushes off my thanks. "Plus, if anything happens to you at the stadium, it's just going to create a lot of paperwork on my end."

Tate doesn't strike me as the kind of guy who does something for the praise, and as I have a best friend who also hates receiving compliments, I know better than to push it any further.

"I wouldn't want that." I tuck my phone back in my fanny pack and pull out my keys. I don't know if I'm going to be able to sleep tonight, but I do know spending more time with Tate won't help my odds.

We walk to the parking lot in silence, and it's not until he hits a button on his keys that I even notice his pickup tucked away in the back of the parking lot.

"Are you okay to get home?" he asks.

It's only a twenty-minute drive to my house, and between the jump scare and his sweet offer I'm sure my brain will spend the next three to eight hours dissecting, I don't think I'm in any danger of dozing off.

"Yeah," I say. "I'll be fine."

He nods, but not even the darkness can mask his uncertainty. "I'm guessing you won't be at practice in the morning"—he assumes correctly—"but I'll be over in the afternoon to work on the bathroom if that's okay with you."

"Fine with me." I actually have some pretty exciting home improvement plans of my own tomorrow. "I'll see you then."

Instead of saying goodbye, he lifts his chin and turns on a heel without another word. I get into my car, and even though I'm probably good for the short drive home, I turn on my most upbeat playlist . . . just in case.

I roll down the windows, singing along with the radio as the wind hits me in the face. It's not until I turn into my long driveway and the car behind me does a U-turn in the middle of the empty highway that I realize it's the same truck I saw tucked in the back of the stadium parking lot.

And when I finally climb into my bed after a long, hot shower, the sleep that often evades me pulls me under right away.

But it's the dreams of dark eyes and a deep voice that give me the best night's sleep I've had in a long time.

Maybe forever.

Chapter 13

Time is a wily little sucker.

Its warped perception is always lurking nearby, mocking expectations and making a fool of my plans. Days I want to last a lifetime are gone in the blink of an eye while the ones I want to end stretch on for lifetimes. It's as if at any given moment, time could force a memory upon me from years ago like it happened yesterday before quickly ripping it away, stealing the details and leaving me with nothing more than a faded moment in time.

Seconds are moving agonizingly slowly today.

Tate usually gets here around noon when he comes over after practice, but it's already pushing two when I check my phone to see if he's called—he hasn't—and look out the front window to see if his truck's in my driveway—it's not. I know he said he'd be here to work on the bathroom today, but as the minutes turn into hours, I'm starting to think he's not coming.

I don't blame him.

You would think after one of the few decent night's sleep that I've had in months, I'd be feeling rested and at ease today, but you'd be wrong. I might've been too exhausted to think about what happened between me and Tate last night, but I woke up with enough energy to recount every single punch and agonize over every cringe-inducing detail from the track.

This also means that out of all the days he could've chosen, my uncle picked today to call me four times and send me two text messages. Worse yet, when I opened my email to see if I had any updates about a chandelier from a vintage shop in Dallas, I discovered three new emails from him as well. He's nothing if not persistent.

Thank god for the delete button and living in a home with more than enough to keep me distracted.

When I was a little girl, my grandma surprised me with a dollhouse for us to work on together. It was completely untouched and every surface was full of possibility. That's what my house feels like.

I wasn't expecting as much work as there is, but there's something so exciting about having the opportunity to turn this space into one that is so uniquely me, nobody will ever be able to walk in and wonder who lives here.

Besides the full—unexpected—bathroom renovation, I have at least three projects in every room of the house. I'm going for a cozy vintage maximalist vibe, and it's as hard to find inspiration as you would think. My Pinterest boards are filled with color and pattern, flowers and wallpaper replacing the white shiplap so many women my age love. Wallpaper samples cover my coffee table, paint swatches decorate each wall, and every tab on my phone is dedicated to rugs, obscure wall art, and vintage stores with shipping options.

And that's just inside my house.

I slide in the final shelf on the bookshelves I've spent all day assembling. When I first bought this house, I thought the shed in the backyard would be the perfect place for crafting, but after settling in and seeing the way the sun filtered in through the window in the evenings, I knew it was where my books deserved to live. A little library in my backyard where dreams are made while my imagination is fed.

The plush mint-and-coral rug is soft beneath my feet. The air-conditioning unit attached to the wall hums its quiet song as it keeps the space cool and I fall onto the emerald velvet love seat I tucked against the far wall. Small boxes filled with hundreds of pounds of books are stacked around the shed, begging to make their way to their new home inside my library. The hanging plants I picked up in town are sprawled across the floor until I pick out their final destination. Pieces of my vision are coming to life, and for the first time all day, Tate's onyx eyes aren't the first thing on my mind.

The power of books cannot be overstated.

I have big plans to rot on the love seat for the rest of the day, but when my stomach begins to growl, those plans change.

The banana bread I made yesterday is sitting next to the untouched jar of dog treats I made for Duke. I'm cutting my third piece of the day when the knock I've spent all day obsessing over finally comes.

"Luna?" Tate's deep voice echoes through my house as he lets himself and Duke inside. "Are you here?"

I'm sure he knows the answer, considering my car is parked outside and the door was unlocked, but I don't have time to respond before Duke barrels into the kitchen and gives away my location with his excited barks.

"Geez, snitch!" I whisper-yell at my favorite furry friend, but he's too cute for me to even pretend to be mad at him. I grab the container of dog treats off the counter and give him one before dropping down to the ground so he can get all the pets he deserves. Tate's boots appear in my periphery, and I keep talking to Duke like he's not there. "I'm sorry, you're not a snitch, are you? No, you're not, you're just the best boy!"

"Oh, I see how it is," Tate says. "So when Duke sneaks up on you, it's not a big deal, but when I do it? Uppercut to the jaw."

I knew I landed a few good punches, but thanks to the adrenaline, I had no idea where any of them landed. I'm not sure if you can die from embarrassment or not, but if you can? RIP me because I'm not sure I'll ever recover.

"Oh my god. I'm so sorry. Although, to be fair, it was a hook, not an uppercut." I tear my gaze away from Duke, preparing to beg Tate for his forgiveness until I catch a glimpse of the look on his stupid, hot face. "Wait . . . are you . . ." I narrow my eyes to make sure my mind's not playing tricks on me. "Are you laughing?"

"I'm sorry," he says through so much laughter that I can hardly understand him. "Are you breaking down the semantics of the punches you threw?"

"Details matter!" I push off the ground and try my hardest to cling to my anger, but it's so hard not to be distracted. I didn't think he was capable of producing this much laughter. "And you shouldn't laugh. I've spent all morning feeling awful about last night."

It's hard not to get lost in the awe of how much younger he looks with his eyes creased gently in the corners and his white teeth on display between his full, lush lips.

"I'm sorry," he says again, but this time it sounds like he

means it . . . at least a little bit. "But you shouldn't feel bad about what happened. Your reaction was fine. It was the being out there in the first place that was iffy."

"I know, I know." I roll my eyes, but the effectiveness is lost behind my smile. "Call you if I want to go running late at night again. Be safe. Blah blah blah."

"I'm so relieved my message of blah blah blah stuck with you."

His body is still shaking with laughter, and my hands itch at my sides to reach out and touch him, to know what he feels like when I'm not accidentally trying to fight him.

"It did." I shove my hands into my pockets. "Maybe you should consider picking up a side hustle as a motivational speaker."

"Yeah, I think I'll pass on that one." He shakes his head, and a shadow chases away the last bits of laughter from his face. "Between football, your house, and the other jobs I have around town, my hands are pretty full."

It was nice to see this other side of him. I was able to forget that he came here out of professional obligation, not pleasure.

"Of course, my bathroom is quite the project on its own," I say, belatedly noticing the boxes he brought into my kitchen. "I can't imagine how much you have on your plate."

His schedule is packed with football alone. The fact that he's able to squeeze in all the work my house needs is a minor miracle.

"Your bathroom is a lot, but if it's okay with you, I was thinking I could work on something else today."

There are endless repair options here, but the bathroom is the only thing I brought Tate in to do.

My eyebrows furrow. "You were?"

He nods. "I went to pick up a few things for the bathroom, but they're on back order for a few days. I figured we could work on your laundry room while we wait." He shifts back and forth on his feet and looks down to Duke. "If that's something you're even interested in. I don't even know if you'll like the stuff I grabbed."

He knows I'll like it. Unfortunately for him, he's been an unwilling participant to all the design choices I've made thus far. The look of shock and horror on his face when I asked him to help me choose between the strawberry print and the vintage floral tiles for my kitchen backsplash will live in my head forever. He might not understand me, but he knows me.

At least when it comes to my interior design taste.

I thought moving to a small town would be different; I just never could've known how different it would really be. No matter how hard he tries to deny it, Tate's a Celestial-bred boy through and through. I'm sure the grumpy mask he wears tricks some people, but I've witnessed Tate's generosity more times than I can count. Helping out his neighbors has probably been ingrained in him since the moment he entered this world.

I'm unsure of how to respond to such a kind gesture, and it takes me a moment to come up with something to say. "This is so nice of you, Tate, but I know how busy you are. I can't ask you to do this."

"You're not asking," he says. "I'm offering."

I spent so much of my life during the last few years putting what I needed aside for my mom that I don't even know how to respond. I know I'm not special, Tate would do this for anyone, but that knowledge doesn't stop my heart from slamming against my rib cage or the butterflies from wreaking havoc on my stomach.

"I know you are, but—"

"No, no buts." He shakes his head. "I talked to Patricia and she showed me the inspection. Someone should've stepped up and done something about this house a long time ago. Nobody did, and you ended up with a bathtub in your laundry room. You have to do a lot of work on this place, so you might as well learn to take the help where you can get it. Especially if you insist on doing those ridiculous 'hacks' you keep showing me."

Let's just say he hasn't been too impressed with the DIY accounts I follow.

I worry my bottom lip. "Are you sure?"

"I wouldn't have offered if I wasn't."

I take a deep breath once I realize he's not going to take no for an answer. "Okay," I say. "Thank you."

"See? Was that so hard?" he asks, a gentle smile tugging at the corner of his mouth that, while smaller than when he was laughing before, is no less beautiful. "Now come help me unload my truck. We're working on this together."

THE GOOD NEWS is that if nothing else, the washer and dryer I spent a fortune on double really well as a kitchen island if need be. The bad news is that for the next twenty-four to seventy-two hours, they're the newest fixture in my already crowded kitchen.

"Are you sure you don't want me to swing into town and grab something for dinner?" Tate eyes my new cutting board station with more suspicion than confidence. "I have most of the restaurants saved in my phone. It won't take me long to pick it up."

Duke is asleep by my feet. After demolishing my treat supply and getting us both yelled at by Tate, he wore himself out by chasing the squirrels around my backyard and barking at the cows that wandered closer to my fence than they ever had before. It was a lot of work for him, as evidenced by his deep snores vibrating through the floor.

"No," I tell him for the hundredth time. "After all the work you put in today, the least I can do is make dinner. And if you ask again, I'm going to start to think you're questioning my cooking skills and I'll be very offended."

"Whoa." He raises his mortar-covered hands up in surrender. "We wouldn't want that. I promise I won't bring it up again."

"Thank you," I say, returning my attention to mincing the garlic with my mortar-free hands. "That's all I ask."

I know Tate said I'd be helping him with my laundry room makeover, and I did . . . kind of. I put a lot of thought into picking which of the five options I wanted for the floors—one was plain white, two were patterned, and two were solid colors in the shape of hexagons. I considered allowing my laundry room to be white and simple, but I am who I am, and I went with the pink hexagon option instead. I lifted with my legs, not my back, and didn't complain once when hauling the boxes of tiles from his truck into my house. I listened intently to his every word and followed his directions down to the letter as I added water to the thin-set mortar and mixed it to the perfect consistency.

I was the perfect assistant . . . until it came time to actually lay the tiles.

It wasn't that I was bad as much as I was a hindrance. The

classes I took and the YouTube videos I watched provided me with the basics, but not the speed. We quickly came to the realization that I was much more helpful when I stayed out of his way. I pretended to protest for a few minutes before turning my attention to our dinner plans.

"So a handyman and a football coach? That's quite the combination," I call into the laundry room as I check to see if the water's boiling yet. "How'd you land on those two things?"

"I don't really know," Tate says. "It wasn't much of a decision, things just kind of worked out this way."

I add a pat of butter to my hot skillet and the most satisfying ASMR sounds fill my cluttered kitchen. "I mean, sure, I guess, but even if you land somewhere, you generally have to take a few planned steps to get there. Did you always want to be a football coach?"

"Nope."

I wait a minute for him to elaborate before repeating after him. "Nope?"

"Yeah," he says. "Nope."

Wow. Working with a real wordsmith here. I toss minced garlic into the pan and let it sauté until it's time to add in the asparagus and squash I bought at the farmers market while I try to think of something else to say.

"I'm surprised. Didn't Matt say you won state when you went to school here?" I think back to the day I found out he was the football coach. "He made it sound like you were really good. I'm sure you thought about wanting to keep playing football back then."

He turns on the saw and cuts through the last tile so it fits nice and snug in the corner of the room. "I guess."

I know Millie told me I should go to Tate with my questions

for him, but if these are his answers, I might have to resort to the town gossip tree after all. "Did you go to school for—"

"Jesus, what is this? If you have something to ask, just ask." He stands up and snaps, "I'm sure Silas filled you in on everything the first chance he had."

"I . . . I'm sorry?" I'm so taken aback by his response over my—admittedly terrible—attempt at small talk, I almost forget what I was talking about. "What does Silas have to do with you wanting to play football?"

Since Tate has started working on my house, I've barely seen Silas at all. He might like me, but not enough to risk spending any time around his brother. Sometimes he'll swing by on his horse, stopping at the fence to talk until I force him to come inside for a drink, but it's getting rarer and rarer lately.

Needless to say, when he does take the time to come by, Tate is the last thing we're talking about.

"You know what? I forgot I have something I need to do tonight." He avoids making eye contact with me and reaches into his pocket for his keys. "I'll come back and check on the tiles tomorrow."

The anger in his voice from seconds ago is gone. His words are so flat, so even, he doesn't even sound like himself.

It's worse than the anger.

I can't make sense of it, but I'd rather Tate feel anything for me than nothing at all.

I follow behind him, still trying to figure out what in the world just happened. "Um, okay." I watch him wake up Duke, unsure if asking him another question is going to piss him off again. Hoping it might. "Are you sure you don't want to stay for dinner? Feeding you is the least I can do after all the work you did."

I don't know what it says about me that I still want his company after this little show, but my pulse gets a little faster with every step he takes. I've gotten used to the way he looks at me like he's not sure if I'm being for real or trying to prank him. I was able to tell myself his little huffs of disbelief were actually out of amusement and signs that he was starting to warm toward me.

This feels different.

"Yeah, I'm good. Thanks," he calls over his shoulder, not even deigning me worthy of a last look. "I'll text you. We can reschedule."

His tone is so cold and devoid of emotion, it sends chills down my back. Even poor Duke looks confused as he follows slowly behind him.

This time, I don't respond. Not just because he's in his truck, his tires kicking up gravel as he screeches away before I can reach the door. No. It's because I have nothing to say. And even after the taillights of his truck have long disappeared into the dark of the night, I still don't know what the fuck just happened.

And after the way he ran out of here, I'm not sure I ever will.

It's a good thing I don't care. It might be one more thing keeping me up all night.

And now I have nowhere to run to.

Not even in my dreams.

Chapter 14

Tate hasn't shown up.

The tiles in my laundry have set, the walls I painted have dried, my washer and dryer are still in my kitchen, and he's nowhere to be found.

Well, this is only halfway true.

If I really want to see him, I know exactly where I can find him and the Celestial High School football program almost every morning. I write out twelve different texts all oscillating between profusely apologizing for whatever I did and calling him a jerk for running out and keeping me waiting. I never send them.

I can't stop trying to figure out what caused him to freak out the other night. My coffee turns cold as I examine every word I said to him and try to pinpoint what I could've said to have offended him so much. I try to convince myself that he wasn't lying and he really did forget he had something to do, but not even my best efforts will allow me to believe that.

His number taunts me from my phone, and my finger hovers over his contact. All it would take is one little tap, a quick conversation to clear everything up, but instead of doing what a mature person would do, I call Gabby and leave her a voicemail telling her everything I'm not saying to Tate.

Direct and thoughtful communication? Not in this farmhouse.

Luckily for me, my experience at avoidance is vaster than the land I live on. I've already organized my bookshelves and set aside a stack for Millie to come pick up—you can take the bookseller out of the bookstore, but you can't take the bookseller out of the girl—and strung twinkle lights around the shed, but as soon as I spot the two gallons of unopened paint, I know exactly how I'm going to distract myself this afternoon.

When I consulted the internet, it warned me not to paint outside when it's too hot, but considering the forecast isn't calling for the temperature to drop below triple digits in the next two weeks, I take my chances. I load the fresh roller brush with the newest shade of pastel pink I brought back from town and roll it down the splintered wood holding the chicken coop together. The brightness of the paint makes my problems seem dull. Every coat of paint takes me further and further away from my thoughts until the only thing I can think about is how great Little Chix and Kelly Cluckson are going to look strutting around their new home.

The tree keeping the chicken coop in the shade doesn't do much to protect me from the sun's ruthless rays. My hair is coiled tight at my nape, and my damp shirt clings to every curve I have. I drop the roller into the paint tray and drag my paint-speckled arm across my face, but it's too late. Sweat falls down my forehead, pulling the sunscreen I liberally applied with it as it sneaks behind my sunglasses and feels like acid flowing into my eyes.

“Fuck,” I hiss and clench my eyes shut.

I drop down to my haunches, trying not to rub my eyes as I feel around for the water bottle I, of course, can’t find. My eyes crack open just enough for more sunscreen to leak in until I finally spot the sticker-covered water bottle and snatch it off the ground.

My luck isn’t plentiful, but for once it’s on my side and the water bottle is still full when I pick it up. Cool water splashes over the rim as I twist off the lid with frantic hands. I don’t hesitate before pouring it over my face. There is a short reprieve from the heat as the water flows down the rest of my body. I blink the sunscreen out of my eyes, carefully dabbing the delicate skin around them with the fabric of my now-translucent shirt. The stinging begins to fade and relief sets in.

Just in time for the burn of embarrassment to take over.

“You alright over there?” a voice calls from the distance, and I don’t need to look to know it’s Silas.

I spin around so my back is to the fence and he doesn’t get a face full of boobs . . . or a longer view of them depending on how long he’s been standing there.

“Um, yeah,” I shout over my shoulder. “Sunscreen got in my eyes. I was just trying to rinse it out.”

I pull my shirt away from my body and shake it in the hot air, but no matter how fast I go, my nipples are still clearly visible. I always rolled my eyes and mumbled something about the patriarchy when my mom told me not to leave the house without a bra on, but it looks like on this one, very specific occasion, she was not wrong. If I listen close enough, I can almost hear her saying "I told you so" from the great beyond, the echoes of her laughter rustling the leaves overhead.

"Okay, skin care!" an unfamiliar female voice says. "I know they say Black don't crack, but anything is possible if you stand in this Texas sun for long enough."

I can hear Silas's sigh from all the way over here. "And skin cancer."

"Well, duh, that's a given," she says. "It's hard to have one without the other, and everyone knows that eternal youth lives where health, happiness, and little treats intersect."

I have no idea who this philosopher queen is, but I already love her.

Little treats are not only my biggest joy, but my most utilized motivator in life. There's not a situation I've ever encountered where a little treat isn't the answer. Meet a deadline? Little treat. Go to bed early? Little treat. Clear out your life possessions, sell your childhood home, and move to a different state? Little treat.

Works every time.

"What are you even talking about?" Silas asks. "Nobody needs—"

"She's right," I cut him off. "Putting on sunscreen was for my health, painting the coop pink was for my happiness, and I have ice cream in the freezer that's my little treat when I finish."

"See," she says. "I don't know why you still doubt me when I always end up being right."

I'm not looking, but I can almost guarantee that she's sticking out her tongue . . . and that this magical woman is his sister.

They bicker behind me until my curiosity beats out my

modesty. I fold my arms in front of my chest, grateful once more that I don't have much to hide, and turn to face the duo.

After seeing Silas and Tate, one could assume anyone sharing their genetics would be easy on the eyes. Not even a world as terrible as this would be so cruel as to let their sister grow up beside them and not at least be pretty. But even knowing what I know and guessing what I guessed, nothing could've prepared me for the reality of coming face-to-face with the Jacobs sister.

Even from a distance, it's easy to see that sitting astride a horse in a pair of light-wash jeans and a simple white tee with brown leather cowboy boots tucked into stirrups, the third Jacobs sibling is more stunning than I could have ever imagined. Her skin is a few shades darker than mine and glistens as if she's been dipped in gold. Strong, lean arms hold tight to the reins, and long braids flow over her shoulders and down her back. And rudely, the closer I get, the more beautiful she becomes.

The strong yet delicate lines of her bone structure accentuate every feature on her perfect face. Lashes so dark and thick they shouldn't be real frame the honey eyes she shares with Silas, and although she's not wearing a spec of makeup, not a pimple nor a wrinkle mars her flawless skin. A deep Cupid's bow cuts into full, pouty lips, and I wouldn't be surprised if plastic surgeons hang her photo on the wall as inspiration for all who enter.

The vibes are immaculate, and I honestly can't tell if I want to be her, want to be her best friend, or want to sleep with her. But no matter which I choose, one thing holds true: I am fully obsessed with her.

"You're like Cowgirl Barbie in real life and I'm a little intimidated by your overall"—I gesture wildly with one hand, trying my hardest to keep my chest covered with the other—"amazingness."

"Oh god." Silas groans from atop his horse. "Do not blow up her head any more than it already is. We won't survive it."

"Ignore him." She waves him off with a dismissive flick of the wrist. "Tell me more. What, exactly, do you find so amazing? Because I just got my hair done the other day and I wasn't sure how I felt about it."

"Here we go," Silas mumbles beneath his breath, but we both ignore him.

"Definitely the braids," I say. "You look like a mermaid who morphed into a magical, sparkly goddess who rides horses and slays men."

Wonder Woman who?

"Well, that's it. It's official." She leans back into the saddle and throws her hands in the air. "Someone alert the Celestial Whisper Network, Ciara Jacobs has a new favorite person in town and her name is . . ." She pauses and looks at me. "Wait, what's your name?"

"Luna Starr," I say and note the flash of skepticism that crosses her face. "My mom was kind of a nut. She was really into astrology, and when I found a town named Celestial, I thought it might be the perfect fit."

"Shut the fuck up. I love that," she says before resuming her earlier monologue. "Someone alert the Celestial Whisper Network that Luna Starr is my new favorite person in town!"

"I'm so sorry, Luna," Silas says to me. "She just moved back from Austin and insisted on coming out with me. I wish I could say she's never like this, but I wouldn't want to lie to you."

"Oh, whatever." Ciara rolls her eyes. "He's just mad because he probably wanted to impress you and I showed him up with my natural charm and charisma. I've been out here stealing my brother's girls since '96."

I can't tell if her saying Silas wanted to impress me is true or one more example of a little sister giving her big brother a hard time. Both are endearing, but my ego really hopes it's the former.

"Again, I'm sorry," he says. "To make up for my obnoxious sister, would you want to go on a ride with us? You've been over here for a while and you still haven't seen Starlight Ridge or met our horses."

Quiet hope and maybe even nerves replace the usual bravado in his confident voice. It's so sweet and I couldn't say no even if I wanted to . . . which I don't.

"I'd really like that," I say. "I just need to change fast, if that's okay."

"Of course." His bright smile turns megawatt and even Ciara looks giddy. "Take your time. Just make sure you wear long pants and closed-toe shoes."

"Jeans and boots." I mentally scan my closet for horse-friendly clothes. I won't look as cool and sexy as Ciara, but at least I have options. "Got it."

Excitement races through my veins like a bottle of shaken-up soda as I think of a day spent exploring Starlight Ridge Ranch. I turn around and skip past the half-painted chicken coop and up to my back door. I run up my stairs two at a time, peeling off my wet clothes and throwing them across the room without bothering to see where they land. I glance into my bathroom, and the unfinished floor spurs thoughts of Tate back into my mind.

Silas is literally sitting outside my house, on top of a horse, like the romance hero of my dreams. The last person I should be thinking of is Tate. The last thing I should want is to ride on the back of Tate's horse. It's like he's the hot, moody, asshole version of the annoying pop song stuck in your head. The more I try to forget about Tate, the deeper his tune burrows into my brain, his song playing on repeat in my mind.

If I had any sense whatsoever, I would shut this down right now.

Tate clearly isn't interested and I shouldn't be either.

If I was smart, I would take the hints he's not so subtly sending me and run straight into Silas's arms and never look back.

It's just too bad emotions don't listen to logic.

Chapter 15

As a Colorado native, it's been ingrained in me to care deeply about the environment. I always recycle what I can, I had a compost bin on my counter in Denver, and one of the reasons I'm so excited about my chickens is to have another way to prevent food waste. I stopped purchasing one-use water bottles over five years ago, and I'm working on reducing the amount of plastic I use on a daily basis. When I started working at the Book Nook and it was too close to my apartment to drive and too far to walk, I invested in a new bike and top-of-the-line helmet so I could cut down on my emissions and bike to work.

Gabby as my witness—thanks to the truly unhinged number of selfies I sent her of me standing in front of, next to, or on top of my bike, and in person, thanks to the one time I forced her to meet me at City Park for a test ride—not only were my intentions pure, so was my enthusiasm. I decked that bike out with every accessory you could imagine. I had a basket, a bell, a headlight just in case I stayed out too late one night, and even a personalized plate I ordered from Etsy.

What I also had, and did not account for, was a very sensitive vagina.

After a full month of trying out every seat cushion on the market, I still ended each day feeling like I'd been drop-kicked in my nether regions. I gave up my environmentally friendly hobby in lieu of an SUV with remote start, heated seats, and four-wheel drive, and my unsuccessful foray with a bike never crossed my mind again.

Until right now.

I tighten my arms around Silas's waist and readjust my hips behind him as Glory carries us around the ranch. There's an ache between my legs, but it's anything but pleasurable. I make a list of all the cowboy romance authors that might be receiving a strongly worded DM from me tonight for conveniently leaving this part of the experience out of their books. They're lucky they didn't lie about the scenery being beautiful.

When Silas told me how many acres the ranch was, I knew it was big. But knowing something and seeing it are two different things. I'm not sure there's any way I could've conceptualized how much land ten thousand acres actually was until Silas began to guide me through the trails and across the pastures of Starlight Ridge Ranch. There's something new at every turn. He introduces me to some of the ranch hands that we pass and shows me their living quarters deep into our ride. A creek I can't see from my house runs through the property along with countless ponds and watering holes for the more than one thousand cows roaming the ranch. I lost track of time ages ago and I still don't think I've seen more than a fraction of the property.

"This one is my favorite." Silas slows Glory to a stop next to another small pond. "A natural spring sits below it, so even when rain is scarce, this one never goes empty."

The entire property is a peaceful oasis, but I can see why this one would be his favorite. Weathered Adirondack chairs sit beside water that hasn't been muddied by the animals meandering about. Aging live oak trees drape overhead, long branches intertwining like the intricate design on a quilt made of shade. Cattle sit across the fence, vocalizing their displeasure with their lack of access to water while the others graze happily on the thick, lush grass.

"Do you come up here a lot?"

"As much as I can," he says. "It can be hard to get away. My dad said he was retiring, but all that's turned into is him getting more involved than ever before. I'm pretty sure he goes to bed thinking of new things to add to my schedule on top of the responsibilities I'm already committed to."

"Family can be a lot." I tell him something I'm sure every human walking the planet is acutely aware of. "I can't imagine working with them would make things easier."

Ciara hightailed it back to the main house soon after the tour started. She said she promised their mom she'd help with dinner, but despite her brilliant smile, I got the distinct impression there were other motives behind her quick departure.

"It's work," he says, "but it's more than that. Ranching is a way of life. It's baked into us from the moment we take our first breath. Hell, my mom says we're all attracted to chaos because she spent every pregnancy bouncing us around on horseback. We came out needing to ride."

Unlike when he mentioned his dad, his voice goes soft as he tells me about his mom. The respect and love he has for her is so apparent, so undeniably sweet, it nips at the ever-present sadness constantly nagging at the back of my brain.

It's been so long since I thought about my mom and felt more adoration than disappointment. I hope one day I'll feel that way again.

"Really?" I ask, shoving my feelings back into the little box where they belong. I'm not sure I ever want to unpack them, but I definitely don't want to do it with my arms wrapped around Silas on his family's ranch. "I didn't know you could ride when you're pregnant."

"My mom is a born and bred Texan, and I don't know if you've noticed," he says, "but the rules don't really apply when you're in Texas."

I have noticed.

"Yeah," I agree. "Texas definitely has rules of its own."

I'm still new, but from what I can tell, a few of them are: teased hair is imperative, cowboy boots are always appropriate footwear, insults should be so close to compliments that you can't tell them apart, and football is life.

"Now take Texas rules, multiply them by a hundred, and then you'll get close to what rules on the ranch are like," he says. "Starlight Ridge has been in our family for six generations. This place is how we make money but it's also our family's legacy. It's *our* legacy." The way he stresses the word cannot be ignored. I'm already pressed against his back, but I lean in closer. "To not only buy land in the 1800s, but to keep it all this time, through threats of violence and theft, through Reconstruction and depressions? It's more than an accomplishment; it's a testament. This land is our story. It's a connection to our history and resilience. Every acre we've added on, every head of cattle we've raised and horse we've trained is the promise of our future."

The unbridled passion and pride in his voice as he talks about his family history and the land we're riding on is contagious. The sun hasn't set and the temperature hasn't dropped, but chills race down my spine and up my arms.

"That's really beautiful." I see Starlight Ridge through a different lens as I look across the land surrounding us. "You're so lucky to have this."

Growing up in Denver with a white mom, every day was a fight to hold tight to my connection to my Blackness. It was reading books and joining clubs. It was doing my own research as a teenager to find a Black beauty salon and spending time at Gabby's house as often as I could. I can't imagine what it must've been like growing up here.

"I am," he says, but the way he says it, I'm not sure I believe him.

"Do you—"

His buzzing phone cuts me off.

"Sorry, hold that thought for just a second." He pulls his phone out of his pocket and his body goes tight beneath me when he looks at the screen. "Yeah." His clipped tone is miles away from the gentle, soft one he was just using with me. "Okay . . . yeah. We're on our way."

He hangs up without saying goodbye. Tension fills every line of his already taut body and permeates the still, hot ranch air. Silas is the happy-go-lucky Jacobs twin, and I'm not sure how to handle this version of him.

"Everything okay?" I ask.

He takes a moment to respond, and seconds turn into hours until his deep exhale cuts through the silence and his back relaxes into my front.

"Yeah, everything's fine. I'm sorry about that," he says. "How do you feel about checking out the main house?"

"The main house?" I ask. "There's more than one?"

He showed me the horse stables and two separate barns, one solely used for feed storage and the other for equipment, but other than the cabins where the ranch hands live, I didn't see any houses.

"Yeah," he says, and if it weren't for his body shaking in front of me, I wouldn't be able to tell he was laughing. "There's a few more than one."

A few more? Holy crap.

How big is this place?

WE DROPPED GLORY off in another set of stables, and Brandon, one of the ranch hands we met earlier, was there to greet us. Silas jumped off first and helped with my less-than-graceful attempt at getting off Glory before Brandon took her reins to get her settled for the night.

It was the perfect day with the perfect man. We were pressed close all day and it would've been easy for his hands to roam where they shouldn't, but he never so much as tried. He listened to everything I told him and answered every question I had—even the bad ones—with patience and kindness.

My stomach should be filled with butterflies and my heart should be pounding in my chest from just looking at him. I should be feeling like every romance heroine I've ever read about and dreaming of what a happily ever after with Silas would look like. What I shouldn't feel is like I spent the day with a really great friend, and I absolutely should not still be thinking about his stupid, infuriating brother.

But what I should feel and what I do feel are two different things, and I'm not exactly known for choosing the easy path in life.

The front steps to the "main house" are as impressive as the land they sit on. Rocking chairs line up on either side of the front door, flower pots exploding with blooms of every color sitting between them as ceiling fans—yes, multiple—spin overhead. Unlike my little white farmhouse, there are many modern, industrial touches that hint at this house being a newer build. Dark wood columns stand out against the light stone cladding climbing up the impressive two-story house. Wrought-iron frames the countless floor-to-ceiling windows, and it's as beautiful as it is intimidating.

Which is to say, very.

"So . . ." I drag out the word as I take in the home in front of me. "Ranching is a lucrative business, huh?"

"We do alright," he says with a shy smile, clearly underselling their success.

Because this isn't just a little bit of money.

This is wealth.

Before I can call him on his humility, the front door swings open and a woman who could be mistaken for Ciara's twin, if it weren't for the gray streaking her hair and gentle lines sprawling around her kind eyes, welcomes us with open arms and glasses of wine.

Bless this woman. The real way, not the passive-aggressive Texas way.

"You must be Luna." She pulls me inside and shoves the glass of wine into my hand. "I'm Pam. It's so nice to finally meet you."

"It's nice to meet you as well," I say. "You have a beautiful home."

I lift the glass to my lips, hoping the magical red liquid inside can help quell the sudden onslaught of nerves twisting my stomach into knots.

"Well, aren't you sweet?" She waves off my compliment with the practiced grace of a Southern beauty queen. "Not that I expected anything less. It's not often all three of my children agree on anything, but they've all had nothing but wonderful things to say about you."

Wine always makes me flushed, but it's her words that really cause my cheeks to heat. "Wow. That's nice to hear."

Of course I want to make a good impression on all my neighbors, but the knowledge that a certain one of her children thinks highly of me holds more weight than it should.

"And that's saying something, because Tate's an asshole." Ciara's voice cuts across the spacious living room. "You're either a saint or a witch with serious magic skills if you got him to say anything about you at all, let alone anything nice."

"Ciara!" Pam scolds. "Watch your mouth!"

"Sorry," Ciara says, but sounds remarkably not sorry. "But you know I'm right."

"Tate is not an a-hole," Pam defends. "He's just quiet and discerning—you know that. It takes him a while to trust people, and for good reason after what happened to him."

My ears perk immediately, and hope I don't want to feel blooms anew. Did someone hurt Tate? Did I misread his grumpy exterior? Could he really be a big, wounded softy who's just in need of love? It's a romance heroine's true catnip and the last thing I needed to know.

"Interesting rebrand, Mom," Ciara says in a way that makes me think Pam is going to regret this conversation. "So if we're calling it *quiet* and *discerning*, then does that mean you don't have a problem with Mrs. Stewart anymore?"

"How dare you. That wretched woman is nothing like your brother." Pam's almond-shaped eyes narrow to slivers. "She's sat in that front pew with her nose high in the air, cloaked in judgment, since high school. And she's not quiet, she's silent; there's a difference. The second those over-injected lips start flapping, she does nothing but bad-mouth every person who's ever crossed her miserable path."

I'm in the middle of making a mental note to never get on Pam's bad side when a man with an immaculately manicured beard and salt-and-pepper hair walks into the room. Weathered skin gives away years spent under the unforgiving Texas sun, and serious onyx eyes bear a stunning resemblance to Tate. His full lips are set in a firm line, but the second he catches a glimpse of Pam mid-rant, it transforms into an amused smile that's so full of love, it feels like I should look away.

"Who got her started on Janice again?" he asks. "You know she always gets like this about that poor woman."

"Calvin Malcolm Jacobs!" Pam slams her fists on her hips and turns her furious glare to him, but he doesn't so much as flinch. In fact, his smile gets even wider. "'That poor woman,' my behind. I'm not usually one to gossip in front of company, but you know darn well what that *poor woman* has done, and in this house, we don't empathize with the Devil."

Empathize with the Devil is a freaking bar. I've never

heard a more polite, more deadly read than that, and I'm not sure if I should fear or love Pam.

Both.

The answer is definitely both.

"Please." I hold my hands up in front of me. "Don't stop on my account. It sounds like this Miss Stewart woman deserves your wrath."

"Finally!" Pam throws her arms in the air. "Thank you, Luna. It's nice to have an ally in this house of traitors for once."

"I'm always on your side." Calvin crosses the room, and I can't help but notice the prominent limp to his walk. "But you also know how much I like it when you get worked up."

He sidles up next to his wife, and when I get a good look at them side by side, it's no wonder all three of their children are so striking. He drops his hand low on her back, and Pam yelps and swats at him, before rolling up on her tiptoes and touching her lips to his.

As an unrelated spectator, watching them together is adorable and life-affirming. For Ciara, on the other hand? Not so much.

"Ewwww." She groans and her beautiful face twists with disgust. "Aren't you too old to act like this?"

"Aren't you too old to pretend like you don't know exactly how you made your way into this world?" Calvin asks before kissing his wife one more time.

"Gross," Ciara says. "Have some shame."

"Sorry," Silas whispers in my ear. "They get like this sometimes."

"Nothing to apologize for." I tell him the truth. "You're lucky to have two parents who are still this enamored with each other."

My mom always told me tales about how my dad was the love of her life. She'd tell me that she would take a lifetime of heartache if it meant having the few amazing years they had together. I always thought it was the most beautiful sentiment in the entire world until I realized the devastation that came along with it. Now I wonder if she clung to her grief as a shield and used it as an excuse to never find happiness again.

"If you're done acting like teenagers," Ciara interrupts her parents, "maybe Dad could introduce himself to our guest instead of trying to make out with mom."

"I could do both." Calvin smirks at Ciara before planting one final kiss on a blushing Pam and turning to me. "Sorry about my children." He stretches out his arm and wraps a calloused hand around mine when I meet him to shake it. "Calvin Jacobs. Nice to meet you."

His skin feels like leather. It's rough, but worn and soft, and I get the impression his hands are capable of handling anything life throws at him.

"Nice to meet you, Mr. Jacobs," I say with my manners firmly in place. "I'm Luna Starr. I bought the farmhouse next door. Well, at least as close as next door can be out here."

"If you're in Celestial, you're a neighbor." He holds my hand in his, and his commanding presence turns welcoming. "Living in the Monroe farmhouse? That makes you family."

Tears that haven't fallen in months lodge in my throat and make it hard to speak. It's been years since I've felt like part of a family. The safety and comfort of mine died long before my mom did. The idea of family is as much a nightmare as it is a dream, as terrifying as it is beautiful.

"Thank you so much," I manage to choke out, only pulling my hand back when his grip loosens. "Your family has already been so kind and welcoming. I just met Ciara today, but Silas brought me a lovely welcome basket, and Tate is helping with some . . . unforeseen home repairs."

"You know how Mr. Monroe was always doing projects without permits or help?" Silas asks his dad, and Calvin nods in response. "The claw-foot tub in the bathroom he added on fell through the ceiling."

"Yeah, it wasn't great," I say, unsure of what to add on and hoping I don't have to explain the inspection report loaded with red flags that I ignored. I've never been scolded by a dad before, and Calvin gives off big lecture-dad energy. "Thankfully, Silas was there when it happened and called Tate. I know he's busy with work now that the football season is starting, but he's been coming over whenever his schedule allows."

I don't know what I said, but whatever it was causes the temperature in the room to drop and the tension to rise. Ciara and Silas look like they're holding their breath and bracing for an explosion. Pam aims wide, pleading eyes at her husband, who is visibly trying to keep a hold on his temper.

"It's generous of you to call what he does 'work,'" Calvin says, his tone dripping with disdain. "One of these days he'll realize football is a hobby, not a job, but until then, if you need more help, feel free to give me a call. I taught Tate everything he knows, and now that Silas is taking over the ranch, I have nothing but time on my hands."

"Nothing but time to micromanage," Ciara mock-whispers and alleviates the nervous energy filling the grand space. "Not that we're not grateful for all your helpful advice on every single aspect of our lives, right, Si?"

"I don't love anything more than Dad's nightly texts making sure I didn't forget to get the horses in the stable and ensure the gates are closed, even though I've been doing it for . . . ." He pauses and looks at his mom. "How old am I again?"

"You're thirty-six." Pam's eyebrows furrow together, and I note that her practically line-free skin is not due to Botox.

Some people have all the luck.

"Thanks, Mom," he says before turning his attention back to me. "Even after thirty-six years of doing it almost every single night."

"Nobody likes a smart-ass, son," Calvin growls, but there's no heat behind it. "I can't help that my family still needs me so much."

"Sure, honey." Pam wraps her arm around his thick waist. "You keep telling yourself that."

I take a sip of my wine as the energy in the room begins to mellow. I realize belatedly that not only is the wine delicious, but that after an afternoon of gulping water to stay hydrated, I really have to pee.

"Excuse me." I hate to pull the attention back to me, but now that my bladder has made itself known, it can't be ignored. "Where's the bathroom?"

Pam points to my right. "Straight down that hallway," she says. "The third door on the left."

I smile gratefully and place my glass on top of a coaster. "Thank you."

Their voices meld together with the sound of their laughter behind me as I follow her directions down the long, picture-lined hallway. I might've thought a house this large was too big to feel like a home, but I would've been wrong. Personal touches linger in every nook and cranny of the massive house. Framed children's artwork hangs on the walls between family portraits and casual snapshots, but one picture in particular stops me in my tracks.

There are huge bundles of orange and white balloons sitting on both sides of the family as they all huddle behind a table decked out with so much University of Texas paraphernalia, it looks like they robbed the school store. Pam is standing behind Tate, looking exactly as she did tonight, only she's sporting long layers and side bangs instead of the adorable bob she's rocking now, with Calvin standing tall at her side. A much smaller Ciara smiles huge at the camera with her braces gleaming. She's leaned into Tate's side, and his arm—not yet muscular, but still strong—is draped over her shoulders, holding her near. Silas stands to his right with one hand on Tate's shoulder and looks down at his twin with a look that can only be described as elation. Actually, other than his dad, who's wearing a cowboy hat instead of the UT baseball hat everyone else is wearing and whose smile looks like it pains him, the entire family shares matching expressions of joy with looks of pure, unbridled pride sprinkled in.

Everything about this picture is delightful, and as much as I try, I can't pull my eyes away from Tate.

The version of him captured in this picture is a stranger, but it's not his long, lanky build or his lack of locs that makes him unrecognizable.

No. Not it at all.

It's that I didn't know he could look so happy and carefree, and the Tate in this picture radiates so much joy, it practically oozes out of his pores. The heaviness clinging to him now is nowhere to be seen. His eyes crease from smiling, not weariness, and the guards so firmly in place nowadays haven't even begun to form. He has a smile that lights up the room, and I didn't have to be there to know that it rubbed off on anyone who was lucky enough to go near him.

What the hell happened?

Seeing him like this causes my heart to clench and break at the same damn time. What I wouldn't give to see him like this again. How I wish I was whole enough to have the energy to try and fix him.

If the past has taught me anything, though, it's that no matter how hard I try, I can't help someone who doesn't want it. I can't want better for someone than they want for themselves.

But, god, do I wish I could.

A loud knock at the front door spurs me back into motion, and I find the guest bathroom with no other detours. I hurry up and take care of business, only stopping to snap a picture of the soap so I can order some for myself when I get home. By the time I rejoin the group in the living room, someone new has arrived.

Two someones, actually.

I hear the telltale sound of Duke's nails running across the room before I see them.

I turn the corner to see Tate, who unfortunately looks better than ever in a collared shirt and dark-wash jeans, and he's standing next to a woman I've never seen before. She's as gorgeous as I'd expect the person Tate brings home to his family would be. Long hair hangs down her back in thick, shiny waves with not a strand out of place. She's got at least six inches on me, and where I'm built more like a power forward, she gives off Victoria's Secret model energy . . . and body.

I guess he wasn't lying when he said he had other things to

do. Seeing her beside him, the reasons he hasn't come back suddenly make a lot more sense.

"Oh, Tate. Hi." I run a hand over my messy hair, suddenly hyperaware of my makeup-less face and the smell of horses still lingering across my well-worn jeans and sweat-coated skin. "How are you?"

Instead of answering, his angry glare cuts from me over to Silas. "Really?" he asks, his displeasure at seeing me coming through loud and clear in that single word.

"Jesus, Tate." Silas raises a single eyebrow and meets him with a glare of his own. "I know this is how you treat everyone at this point, but have you ever tried not being a dick for just once?"

"Boys," Pam chides, but sadness comes through over the anger I think she intended. "Can we please not do this tonight? Not when we have guests."

Ciara's sympathetic eyes meet mine across the room, and it's too much for me to handle. I don't know what I was thinking, feeling as if I could fit in with a family like this. Pretending that I could belong.

"Actually," I say, trying not to fidget when all six sets of eyes turn to me, "I forgot that I have a packed day tomorrow. I should probably head home so I can prepare for the morning and be in bed early. I'm useless if I don't get a full night's sleep."

I'm a terrible liar and I crumble when faced with the barest hint of confrontation. I completely forget that Tate knows about my sleep trouble until I see his face mar with confusion.

"Anything I can help you with?" Silas asks.

So sweet. He's always so sweet. Why can't I feel for him the way I feel for Tate?

"Thank you for asking, but I'll be okay," I say.

Tate opens his mouth but snaps it shut when I beg with silent pleas for him to keep quiet. And considering he's made it abundantly clear that he's not happy to see me here, I don't know why he even cares. He should be thanking me.

Maybe I can get him to give me a discount on the bathroom if he ever comes back to finish it.

"Are you sure you have to leave now?" Pam asks, her Southern drawl more pronounced now than it's been all night. "I made dinner and you must be hungry."

I'm starving, and since I was out side all day, I didn't take anything out for dinner.

"You're so kind to offer, but I really should get home." My traitorous stomach growls, but luckily, nobody is close enough to hear. "Maybe we can plan for another night? I'll bring dessert."

Pam's smile softens and my throat tightens again. "I'd love that."

"Can I give you a ride back?" Calvin asks, and it's not until he speaks that I notice he's emitting the exact same vibes as Tate.

Yikes on a bike.

I'd rather take my chances with whatever predators lurk nearby.

"Thank you, but I'll be okay," I say. "It's nice to get some steps in without the sun beaming down on me."

"But—" Silas starts, but I shake my head and cut him off. I can't stand here and argue with their kindness all night.

"You've already done more than enough for me today," I say. "Enjoy your time with your family."

I can tell he wants to argue, but because he's Silas, he's too nice to do it.

"It was so wonderful meeting you all." I start walking backward, like prey trying to make its escape. "I'm sure I'll see you soon."

I pull open the heavy front door and everyone, minus Calvin and Tate, says their polite goodbyes before it slams shut behind me.

I search for the outside lights on my little farmhouse glowing bright in the night, and the moment I spot them, I take off running.

And as I cut through the long grass and climb over my fence, only two thoughts cross my mind: When will I see Tate again, and who in the hell was the woman with him?

Chapter 16

Moonlight spills in through my opened bedroom window. The muted silver light casts shadows where there usually aren't any and turns my ceiling into a map. I feel like a palm reader, tracking the lines and cracks above me, dissecting where they branch off as if they tell the story of the house. As if they are the key to knowing the love that's happened here, the lives that have been lived, and the stories still unfolding.

My story.

I hoped when I turned thirty, I'd have my entire life figured out, and in a way, I did. I had a great apartment in the ideal part of town, doing a job I absolutely adored. I had accomplished what everyone told me I needed to do in order to be considered a successful, mostly together adult. If everything kept going according to plan, it was going to pay off soon.

It's too bad life never seems to stick to the plan.

Looking back, I can't believe I didn't see the signs until it was too late, but sometimes it's hardest to see the thing that's right in front of you. Hindsight really is a bitch.

My mom might not have ever had it all together, but things always seemed to work out. I knew she loved her wine, but she was always quick to remind anyone who questioned her that drinking was "a pleasure, not a requirement." She could hold a job when she needed to—which, now that I'm an adult who sees things clearly, should have been all the time, not sporadically—and always put in a valiant, though ultimately unsuccessful, effort to make it to all my school and sporting events. But despite her flaky tendencies, I knew she meant well, and that knowledge was cemented the moment Grandma's health started declining. It was like something inside of her clicked. She jumped in with both feet to help and was on top of everything in a way I'd never seen before. She scheduled all the doctor's appointments, laid out the pills, and even though she was an awful cook, she'd still attempt to make dinner on the nights I couldn't make it over. She was responsible and steadfast, dependable when we really needed her to be. It was like she finally stepped into the person who had been hiding below the surface my entire life.

Then my grandma died.

At first I attributed it to the grief.

My grandma was the best person in the world, and with her gone, there was a gaping hole where she used to be. Without her smile, every day felt darker, and joy was an elusive commodity. My mom could barely manage to get out of bed; there was no chance she could make it to work. She was there for her mom, and now it was my turn to be there for mine.

Only now I know there's a fine line between helping and

enabling, and that once you've crossed it, it feels impossible to go back.

Her drinking stretched earlier into the days and turned into vodka as night came. What started with small loans turned into paying her bills. Bringing dinner turned into providing all the groceries. Being a shoulder to cry on turned into being expected to run to her the second she called. When I dared to tell her no, tearful pleas turned into weeklong guilt trips and manipulation. And because I was the only person she had, I would always go back and repeat the cycle all over again, hopeful that maybe that time would be the time she changed.

But the thing with addiction is that you can't love someone enough to make them sober. You can't make them change. All you can do is stand by, ready to put the pieces of the wreckage back together when things finally implode.

It's just that so often, there's no coming back from rock bottom. It's a lesson I should've learned from my dad—the lesson he died learning.

The sound of an engine and kicked-up gravel through my window pulls me from the thoughts I try to never lose myself in. I'm all too happy to jump out of bed to see who in their right mind would show up at my house this late at night.

I tiptoe down the stairs and lean into the living room, listening closely with my hand on my phone—just in case—when I catch a glimpse of the familiar shadow outside my front window. I hurry across the living room, flip on the porch light, and when I pull open the front door, an expectant Tate Jacobs is waiting on the other side.

"What are you doing here?" My voice is too loud after sitting in silence all night. "Do you know what time it is?"

I look over his shoulder, trying to see if the woman he was

with tonight is waiting for him, but the lights are off and I can't see into the cab of his truck.

"A little after midnight," he says. "But I had a feeling you'd be awake and probably hungry considering how fast you ran out of my parents' house."

"Not as fast as you were when you darted out of here the other night."

"I know," he says. "I really am sorry about how I acted." He holds up a glass container stuffed full of food that looks light-years better than the bowl of cereal I had before I tried to force myself to sleep. "Truce?"

"The way you left was pretty fucked-up." My stomach growls, but I need answers, not a half-assed apology, before I'm willing to call a truce. "I didn't ask for you to work on my laundry room. You ghosted me with my washer and dryer sitting in my kitchen. And I'm not sure if you're aware of this or not, but they don't tend to work well that way."

Not that I'm dying to do laundry, but that's not the point!

"You're right." He has the decency to look ashamed. "It was fucked-up and you didn't deserve that."

I eye him and the glass Tupperware with suspicion. "That's a little better."

"I have a proposition," he says when I don't move to take the food from him. "Why don't you go put on shoes while I put your washer and dryer back, then I'll explain what happened."

"What about your friend? I wouldn't want you to keep her waiting." I reach for the food, hating the way the jealousy I have no right to feel makes my stomach curdle.

"Oh no." He pulls the food away before I can grab it.

"What are you—"

"Nope." He turns me around and walks me back into my house. "First shoes, then you'll come with me and get the food."

"But what about—" I try again, to no avail.

"Go get some shoes on"—he looks down at my bare legs and his voice gets a little husky as he finishes—"and some pants. Then we'll talk."

Sheesh.

"Fine." I roll my eyes. "Bossy."

I kind of like it.

But only because he's going to feed me and not because I'm imagining all the ways he could boss me around in the bedroom. Absolutely not.

"I'm a football coach. It's my job to be bossy. Now go get dressed." He walks into the kitchen still holding my food hostage. "I'll be finished in five, so hurry. I know you can stay up all night, but the rest of us mere mortals need sleep."

Mere mortal? This guy? More like an infuriating Greek god.

But I keep that to myself and instead do as I'm told.

Just this once.

I TIGHTEN MY grip on the glass container as Tate's truck bounces across the bumpy grass field on Starlight Ridge Ranch. The windows are down, and warm night air hits me in the face, whipping around the strands of curls that fell out of my bun as I hurriedly got dressed to join Tate.

"Where are we going?" I look out into the darkness, but nothing is around.

"We're almost there," he says. "Just a little longer."

Patience is definitely a virtue I don't have, but I bite my tongue and pretend until the truck slows to a stop a couple of minutes later.

He turns off the engine, and darkness stretches around us for miles and miles. "We're here," he says.

"You know"—I look outside, trying to spot anything that gives me the slightest clue to where we are—"if you brought me all the way out here to murder me, I'm going to be super bummed."

Cereal cannot be my final meal.

"I would never murder you here." He opens his door and looks at me through the bright lights in the car. "My murder spot is somewhere else."

He winks before hopping out of the truck, and even though I was taught to know better, I open my door and follow after him.

"That wasn't very reassuring, you know," I say, but really, I never feel safer than I do with him at my side. "Maybe fewer murder jokes and more telling me why you brought me out here."

He unlatches the back of his truck and pulls out a folded blanket, tucking it and two pillows underneath his arm.

"This"—he pushes the tailgate closed with his hip—"is my favorite spot on the ranch. It's where I come to think and figure out game plans or where I come for space when I need to be alone. It's the one place in this world where I know I can set my mind at ease and just be. I thought you might need a place like that too."

My lungs freeze and my heart forgets how to beat, but the second it remembers, I fear it will only beat for him.

"Tate." I struggle to find words. "I don't . . . Thank you."

He either doesn't hear me or he ignores me—likely the latter—as he drapes the blanket on the ground and tosses the pillows on top of it.

He plops down, and even in the dark I can feel his expectant gaze on me. "Come on." He pats the spot beside him. "Eat, look at the stars, then we'll talk."

It's all the encouragement I need. I cross the space separating us and take off my shoes before sitting down. The worn, wool blanket is feather soft, and the thick grass feels like a cushion beneath us. I take off the lid to the food he packed for me, and he hands me a fork I didn't know he had.

"Thank you," I say again.

"You can stop saying that," he says. "I'm not sure if you figured this out about me or not, but I don't do things I don't want to do. You never have to thank me for doing something I want to do."

A million questions race through my head, but the moment between us feels too nice. I don't want to do anything that might ruin it.

"I can practically hear you thinking." His deep voice slices through the silence.

"What? No, it's . . ." I take a minute to figure out exactly what I want to say. "I just don't know why you brought me out here."

"I told you," he says. "I thought you needed—"

"No." I'm the one cutting him off this time. "I heard that, but why?"

"Why?" he repeats, confusion as heavy in his voice as the humidity in the air.

"Yes. *Why?* You freaked out and ran out of my house out of nowhere, then when you see me at your parents' house, you act like you're anything but happy to see me." I won't even mention the woman he was with. Yet. "So even though I appreciate this gesture, you'll have to forgive me if I don't understand what's going on here."

I'm not sure I have the right to ask him. I barely know him, and I spent the day hoping I could feel with his brother even a modicum of the spark I feel with him. But I can't sit next to him in the dark quiet of the night and not ask. Not when my feelings for him seem to grow every time I'm near him, no matter how much I wish they didn't.

"I was an asshole at your house. I'm not used to people around here asking me questions they don't already know the answer to. I thought you were fishing because people already told you the wrong and shitty version of my life. I made an assumption, took it out on you, and when I realized I was wrong, I was pretty fucking embarrassed." He rolls over and props himself up on his elbow, and suddenly I wish it was light out so I could see the corded muscles of his forearm flex under the weight of him. "You didn't deserve that and I'm sorry. As for tonight, well . . . that's harder. I don't know if you've heard anything about me and my family, but as much as I love them, I don't always love being around them. I'm never at my best when I'm with my dad and Silas."

"I did notice there was a little tension between you guys." Understatement of the century.

"Yeah." He lets out a humorless laugh, and my hands itch at my sides to hug him. "You could say there's 'a little tension.'"

As the president of the awkward family trauma club, I know better than to push. Now that I understand where he was coming from the other night and he offered a genuine apology, I'm happy to let him share what he's comfortable with while I busy myself shoving his mother's cooking into my mouth.

"Holy shit. This is amazing." I take a bite of the loaded mashed potatoes and groan. "Your mom is an artist."

"She does know her way around a kitchen and a potato," he says. "She says it's the only way she knows she can get all her kids back around her table, and she's not wrong."

"She's not." I take another not-so-ladylike bite, grateful for the cloak of darkness disguising my lack of table (blanket?) manners. "I might start showing up now too."

I am technically an orphan now. I wonder how adult adoption works?

I immediately scratch that idea. The last thing I'd ever want is for Tate to be my brother. Gross.

"She'd love that."

"Well, obviously. I'm a delight," I say. "Plus, your mom is great. She wouldn't even have to cook to lure me over."

He lies back down and stares at the sky. "She's the best."

I wait for him to continue on, and when he stays quiet, I follow his lead. I don't really understand what's happening between us, but thanks to his mom and Mother Nature, I have good food and a better view. There's not much else I could ask for.

Except . . .

"Was the woman you were with tonight your girlfriend?" I won't push the family stuff, but I have to know the answer to this.

He starts to cough and sits up straight. "What?"

"You know, at your parents' house." I shrug, attempting to go for casual and not like I've been obsessing over the beauty queen for the last six hours. "Is she your girlfriend?"

"Alessandra?" He says her name like a question.

Of course the tall, willowy woman with perfect hair and legs that went up to my waist is named Alessandra. I mean, really. It's got to be boring when everything about you is off the charts sexy. Get creative. Find a struggle.

"I don't know if that's her name," I say. "You didn't introduce us before I left."

"Before you ran?" He calls me out, which was—

"Rude and unnecessary." I contemplate lightly stabbing him with my fork before I think better of it. Running is my modus operandi, hence moving to Celestial in the first place. I might as well own it. "But yes, then."

His body shakes with laughter, and the raspy sound washes over me like whiskey, setting me at ease and winding me up all at once.

"Alessandra is not my girlfriend," he says. "She's not my type and I'm definitely not hers."

"Oh, I'm sorry. Not your type?" I set the almost-empty glass container down. I need both hands accessible in case I have to strangle him. "Do you have a problem with women who are physically flawless?"

She's probably smart and kind too. You don't have hair like that if you're rotten on the inside.

"It's not that," he says through laughter, and it's a struggle to focus on anything other than the rare sight of Tate Jacobs looking so carefree. "I've known Alessandra since she was little. She's actually visiting from your neck of the woods. She's at Colorado State getting her veterinary degree. I brought her by so she could talk to Dad and Silas about working at Starlight when she's finished."

Beautiful and saves animals? I wonder how it feels to be God's favorite.

"If you could just whisper one single flaw, it would do wonders for my mental health."

"We're not that close, so I couldn't tell you her flaws," he says, which is really just code for *everything I know about her is perfect.* "But what I do know is that whether or not she's my type is a moot point, since if she had her choice between the two of us, she'd be much more into you than me."

"Really?" I ask, even though, in my heart, this feels right.

Someone as smart, pretty, and seemingly kind as her shouldn't be subjected to the dumpster fire that is dating men.

I was right. Definitely God's favorite.

"She came out when she was in high school," he says. "I remember Ciara telling me."

I know I've enjoyed my time in Celestial, but it would be silly of me to pretend it isn't a small town in Texas. The chances are high that Alessandra was met with opposition, and that breaks my heart for her. She's obviously thriving and living her best life now, but the idea that the future vet could've been made to feel small because of standing tall in who she is makes me want to punch someone.

"People better have been nice to her." I defend the stranger against the villains of my imagination. "I've held grudges for less. What do we do in small towns? Should we go egg their houses? Tip their cows?"

"What the fuck?" he asks. "Did you watch every nineties' small-town movie before you moved here?"

I fold my arms and glare at him. "No."

Yes.

"I'm sure there are things I don't know, but if it makes you feel better, the only person I remember who was outwardly a dick to her was the pastor at a church in town," he says and that does not make me feel better. At all. "And he was basically chased out of Celestial after the fact."

I let out the breath I didn't know I was holding. "That does make me feel better."

It's one thing to feel welcomed in a town; it's another to be in a town that welcomes everyone. And as much as I hate to admit it, I'm also really relieved to know she's not his girlfriend.

I lay my head on the pillow he placed down for me. His head is right beside mine, and although I want to look at him, take in his perfect profile, and maybe—just maybe—catch him staring at me, too, I can't look away from the stars hovering overhead.

I search out the Milky Way just like I always do, straining my eyes and hoping for a wink from the Universe.

"I was happy to see you," Tate whispers into the dark of the night sky, his words hitting me like the shooting star I'm looking for.

"You were?" I don't know why I want to believe him, why I need this to be true, but I do.

"Yeah," he says. Our chests rise and fall in tandem, the sounds of our breaths melding together, harmonizing with the rustling grass and gentle breeze. "I was."

My fingers twitch at my side like a magnet being pulled to him. "No offense, but you had a pretty terrible way of showing it."

"I know. It's just that—" He pauses as if to gather his thoughts, and I have to pull my lips between my teeth in order to stay quiet while I wait. "I didn't want to be here."

I'm not sure what I thought he was going to say, but I know it wasn't that.

"What?" I move to sit up, but his hand holds me in place.

"No," he says. "That didn't come out right. I don't mean here, as in here with you." He stumbles over his words even as he tries to clarify them. I know it shouldn't, but for some reason, seeing him get all flustered makes him even more attractive. "I mean Celestial. I wasn't supposed to still be in Celestial."

Everything about Tate is a giant, noncommittal, walking red flag. The last thing I need, after he brought me to lie beneath the stars with him, is to know Pam was right and he's a wounded bird, in need of saving.

I should just let it be and not ask.

I absolutely should not ask.

I will NOT ask.

I ask.

"Where are you supposed to be?"

And the award for the biggest dummy goes to Luna Starr for her performance in *Seeking Out Emotionally Unavailable Men*, episode 78.

"I don't even know anymore. It's hard to explain. I love coaching and seeing these kids turn into young men. I even like doing home repairs. I'm good at it, and I like being the person people know they can depend on when they need something. It's . . ." He lets out a sigh that sounds like it comes from the bottom of his soul, and there's so much pain in it, I feel it deep inside me. "I didn't think this is where I'd be in my life. Sometimes it's easier to put that blame on other people than it is to deal with it myself."

"Woof." I peel my gaze away from him and stare unseeing at the stars above. "I can't tell if you're talking about yourself or attacking me."

"Attacking you?"

"I'm not sure if you know this or not," I say. "But leaving everything I knew, moving into a house sight unseen, and starting over at thirty wasn't exactly my childhood dream."

"Not even in a thriving metropolis like Celestial?" He rolls over and nudges my shoulder with his. It's the barest hint of contact and it twists my insides into knots.

"Shocking, I know." I hope he can't hear the nerves in my voice.

"Well, I'm glad you're here," he says. "And not just because you have my boys so hyped up to run laps every day that this is the best they've looked leading up to the season in years."

I couldn't stop my smile if I tried.

"It's been mutually beneficial. I might be an adult, but running in front of an audience made up of teenage boys has definitely increased my pace," I admit. "The last thing I need is for them to aim their brutal one-liners at me instead of Matt."

The pinpoint precision with which teenagers can locate your deepest insecurity and deliver a flawlessly executed burn should be examined in scientific studies. Like, you mean to tell me that you forgot a cleat at home for practice, but with one glance knew that joking about my ankles and kneecaps would cut the deepest? How?

"Matt loves it," he says. "You can't be a coach, an actual, good coach, if you can't handle a little ribbing from the boys. Coaches with precious egos are in it for themselves and shouldn't be out there in the first place."

He's still trying to sound light, but I can hear the change in his voice. When I look over, his shoulders have inched up toward his ears and his long fingers are curled into fists.

"Adults are usually the ones who ruin things for the kids." I want to reach out and grab his hand, but I keep mine tucked studiously at my side instead. "The kids are lucky to have you."

"I wouldn't go all the way to lucky," he says. "I do hope they know I want what's best for them."

I'm no more than a casual observer, but even I can see that the respect between the players and coaches is very much mutual. The boys love to give Tate a hard time, but when push comes to shove—or tackle—they latch on to every word that comes out of his mouth.

"They do."

He lifts his chin in response, almost as if doing any more to accept the compliment might physically pain him. Interesting.

A comfortable quiet falls between us. The warm breeze rustles the tall grass rising high around our blanket. Birds sleep while the bugs sing into the night, my muscles falling heavy as I listen to the quiet symphony between them.

My eyelids begin to droop, but I'm not ready to fall asleep. I'm not ready for this night to end.

"Can I ask you a question?"

He rolls to his side, looking at me through the dark night. "Anything."

"You don't have to answer if you don't want to." I preface the question with the permission I doubt he needs. "I know something happened with you, maybe with Silas, maybe your dad. We know people talk, but I'd rather just ask you now than hear it from someone else so we don't have a repeat of the other night."

I decide to leave out the part about Millie shaming me after refusing to share the gossip with me. He doesn't need to know about that.

"I really am surprised nobody told you." His earnest voice is devoid of the sarcasm I thought I'd hear. "I swear, people used to talk about me so much that I thought they'd add their version of my story to the town website."

"There's still a chance," I tell him. "The website looks like it hasn't been updated since 2007."

There was even a ticker on the bottom counting how many views the page had gotten. It was like taking a step back in technological time.

"I'm pretty sure Mr. Briglia put it up, so that tracks," he says. "He was an asshole and never wanted to share information or credit. He died, like, eleven years ago, and I wouldn't be surprised if he took the log-in information to his grave."

I want to laugh, but we are talking about another person's passing and that seems insensitive . . . even if the story of how he lived his life before his untimely death is, objectively, very funny. "Sounds like he left quite the legacy."

"That's one way to say it," he says before going quiet again.

I could kick myself for asking.

I don't know why I expected him to tell me more about his life than he already has. Sure, taking me out here was a nice gesture, but I can't make more of it than it really is. Despite his best efforts to convince the masses otherwise, Tate Jacobs is a nice guy. He saw that I was out of sorts tonight and he came to check on me. I think it's safe to say that what started with him being an acquaintance who was forced to spend time with me, thanks to my disaster of a house, has turned into a friendship. I should be satisfied with that. Wanting anything more would be greedy.

"The ranch has been in our family for six generations." His deep voice startles me out of my quiet reverie and my body goes stock-still. "The Jacobses were one of the first families to settle here. My great-great-great-grandma had a small inheritance. When she married, she trusted my great-great-great-grandpa to invest wisely and he did. He bought this land, and we've been fighting to not only keep it going but growing ever since."

"Silas told me some of the history earlier." Not the part about it being funded by a woman, though, which makes this entire operation that much more impressive. "Your family has done an amazing job."

"Yeah." He nods. "*They* have. But I haven't."

I feel my eyebrows scrunch together. "What do you mean?"

"I'm proud of my family and our history, but . . . fuck." He takes a breath and scrubs a hand down his frustrated face. "I don't know how to talk about this without sounding like a petulant asshole."

"Tate." I roll onto my side so I can look right at him. "I'm not sure if you're aware of this or not, but I'm a literal disaster. You're talking to a person who quit her job, ran away from home, and then immediately sunk thousands of dollars into a house without reading through the inspection. If there is anyone who can't judge you, it's me."

His soft chuckle washes over me like a cool shower on a hot day. My toes curl knowing I'm the reason for that beautiful sound coming out of his even more beautiful mouth.

"You aren't a disaster, but I appreciate you trying to make me feel better." He either lies or greatly underestimates me. "Starlight Ridge Ranch is the cornerstone of the community here. Everyone loves it, and they can't understand that while it's been my family's dream for over a century, it's never been mine."

The words tumble out of his mouth like he's admitting some dirty secret and not expressing a completely reasonable feeling anyone in his position might have, but once he gets started, he can't stop.

"I love this place, but I don't love the expectations. I don't love that my dad acts like I'm betraying my family for wanting something else or that he was offended by my success away from the ranch. I hate that Silas and I used to be inseparable but now I barely know him. I hate that in trying to prove I didn't need this place, I ruined everything."

He stops talking and I stop breathing. I don't know what to say or if there's even anything to say. I don't want to spook him if he wants to tell me more, but I can't let him lie less than a foot away from me and not do anything.

I scoot toward him, closing the space between us inch by inch. Slow enough that he could stop me, but not so slow that I talk myself out of it. His onyx eyes rival the endless night skies, but even with only the light of the moon glimmering down, I can still see them—feel them—on me.

I reach out a tentative hand, and when my pinky brushes against his, I feel like I'm thirteen again. It's the barest of touches, but I feel it in every corner of my body. The breath I was holding leaves me in a whoosh and my head starts to swim. His muscular arm slips behind my back, and with a tenderness I didn't know was possible for a man as big and tough as him, he tucks me into his side and links his other hand with mine.

The heat sticks to our skin, and trees in full bloom rustle nearby. Crickets chirp and Cygnus, my favorite summer constellation, winks in the clear sky. Reminders of summer are all around us, but under his touch, my body is springtime. Butterflies take flight in my stomach as goose bumps blossom across my skin and giddy vines climb my spine. Like after the longest winter, his hands have ushered in the warmth I forgot existed.

"I don't think you're wrong for wanting more." My voice is thick with want . . . with need. "And even if you're not where you thought you'd be, I'm glad you're here."

"Yeah," he whispers, so close to me that I can feel his breath against my skin. "For the first time in a long time, I'm glad I'm here too."

I look into his eyes, part of me wanting his mouth on me more than I want the sun to rise in the east, the other part of me desperate to etch this perfect moment into the deepest parts of my memory. Holding tight to the innocence of our hands tangled together and whispered secrets forever.

The growing ache between my legs might not appreciate it, but when Tate points to the Big Dipper, I know he feels the gravity of tonight too.

Just when I think I can't keep my eyes open any longer, it finally happens.

The shooting star flashes above me, like a quiet nod from my mom telling me that no matter how I got here, I'm exactly where I'm meant to me. And then, on a blanket atop a sea of grass, below an ocean of glittering stars, I drift to sleep in Tate's arms with no fear of tomorrow and the promise of days to come.

Chapter 17

"Is it always like this?" I shout to Millie over the steadily rising voices building around us and the current mix of pop, country, and hip-hop music blaring through the speakers overhead.

"This?" She looks at me like I might have a fever. "The night's barely started. The student section hasn't even gotten here yet."

It's not that football wasn't a big deal in Colorado . . . or at least, I think. It's just that my school's team sucked and we didn't have a college-equivalent stadium located right behind our school.

"I thought *Friday Night Lights* was an exaggeration." I look around the stadium slowly filling up with every face I've seen around town and ignore the curious, if not suspicious, glances being thrown my way. "But I'm starting to think they might've undersold it."

"Yeah." She nods her head, trying to take it in as if it's her first time like me. "Texans are serious about their football, but Celestial takes high school football to another level."

"I can see that."

I think it'd be impossible to miss.

Everyone is decked out in the school colors. Kids run around at the bottom of the bleachers in their matching Astro logo shirts dodging a group of little girls shaking their pom-poms with ribbons in their hair. People of all ages climb into the stands, schlepping up the steps with seats thrown over their shoulders and snacks in their hands. The team moms are impossible to miss and not only because of the cowbells so many of them are insistent on ringing. Beaded football earrings dangle from their ears, and the rhinestones glued to their sons' names on the backs of their T-shirts wink beneath the sun. The dads, though woefully less sparkly, are just as easy to spot all huddled in a circle with their hands shoved in their pockets, nervously shifting from foot to foot.

"Just wait till our rival game," Millie says, and the glee in her voice is both thrilling and unnerving. "Things get crazy."

"Are we good?" I ask, noting how desperately I want to include myself in this community. "I've seen the boys work out and I know they can run a mean ladder, but how are they in games?"

Growing up, I was competitive to a fault. My second grade teacher requested a parent meeting to discuss my "intensity around board games," and my mom almost pulled me out of soccer because I would get so upset if we lost, I'd cry for the entire weekend. Now, as an adult and a spectator who has been humbled by life, I'm much more laid back. Win or lose, I have goody bags in my trunk for the entire team.

That said, it's so much more fun to watch your team win, and for the sake of the boys I've grown so fond of, I really hope they don't stink.

"We're really good," she says. "We've always been decent, but ever since Tate came back and started coaching, we've been on the slow ascent to state. If the buzz around town is right, this could be the year we make it."

I try to focus on the topic at hand, but one mention of Tate and I'm right back on that blanket, waking up with the warmth of the sun beaming against my face, still wrapped tight in his strong arms.

"He seems like a great coach." I try to keep my voice light and unbothered despite the Godzilla-sized butterflies running amok inside my stomach. "Whenever I'm running while they practice, everyone always seems really happy even though they're working out in full pads in this heat."

That alone feels like an award-winning accomplishment.

"Tate knows what he's doing. He was, like, the best player in the state of Texas," she says. "Maybe even the country."

She says this so casually, I'm unsure I heard her correctly.

"In the country?" That has to be hyperbole.

"Yeah. I think he was projected to go in the first round of the draft before . . ." She pauses and her eyes widen like she just gave away the ending to the latest Marvel movie. "Never mind."

What in the world?

"Oh no—" I start to argue, but I don't get the chance, thanks to the marching band sitting in the section directly to our right choosing this moment to stand up and play. "Saved by the tuba!" I shout into her ear, ignoring the shit-eating grin that spreads across her deceptively angelic face.

The players are nowhere to be seen, but the field is bustling with activity. A group of ten men stand in the end zone, flanking the giant inflatable star they spent the last thirty minutes wrestling, and holding on to the straps keeping it in place for dear life. The cheerleaders are out in full force. Some of them are in the middle of the field, wowing the crowd with their acrobatics as others stand to the side, waving their pom-poms and chanting "Let's go, Astros," loud enough to be heard over the band, while the other set have created a tunnel of sorts coming from the inflatable star and onto the field and are marching in place.

"Remind me again," I yell to Millie, "why are there two sets of cheerleaders?"

"The ones in the hats and the cowboy boots aren't cheerleaders." She points to the group of girls in the cutest uniforms I've ever seen. They're all wearing matching white cowboy boots, purple cowboy hats dripping with sequins, and skirts covered in fringe. "That's the drill team. They're like the dance team."

"Do they sell their outfits in town?" I ask. "Because while I might not be rhythmically inclined, I do really need that hat and skirt."

Am I about ten years too old to wear this? Probably. Do I care? No.

I'm obsessed and nobody can stop me. This is the most Texas outfit I've ever seen, and I need it in my closet immediately.

"Good luck with that," she says. "I'm not saying the drill moms are sociopaths who would slash your tires and murder you in your sleep or anything, but what I am saying is gatekeeping is written into their code of conduct, and Abby Lee Miller looks like a teddy bear compared to Liza Smart."

I've heard a lot of names since I've moved, but that one isn't ringing a bell. "Liza Smart?"

"Liza Smart." She points to a woman standing against the

chain-link metal fence in a sequined Astros jersey with her last name written above the number 00.

Liza's back is to us, but even from this angle, she's giving pageant queen perfection. It only takes one glance to know she doesn't just abide by the old adage of the higher the hair, the closer to god, she lives it. Her long white hair is serving pageant queen realness. It's curled, teased, and pinned to perfection, and even from afar, it's clear that not a strand of hair is out of place. Her hands gesture wildly in front of her, with her long, purple-painted nails acting like a conductor's baton. Now that I'm tuned in, the unmistakable rasp that comes from smoking a pack a day carries over the crowd as she screams out step counts to the girls on the field.

"She seems intense," I say. "Complimentarily, of course."

"'Intense' is an understatement of epic proportions," Millie says. "She's been the drill team coach since before I was born. Rumor has it that she was engaged once, but her husband-to-be told her she'd need to take a step back from the team to focus on their home after they got married. She left him the same day. Nobody gets in between her and her girls. It's worked out well for her. I've lost count of how many championship titles she's led them to."

"Damn." If there's one thing I love most about living in a small town it's that even the things I might think are inconsequential have the best lore. There's a long, storied history about everything and everyone, and there's always someone close by willing to fill me in. "I respect and fear her."

She nods. "That pretty much encapsulates how the entirety of Celestial feels about her."

Before I can get Millie to give me the dirt on the cheer coach, the doors to the locker room swing open and the football coaches file onto the track. They all look equal parts adorable and determined in their matching polos, khaki pants, and baseball hats, and it's hard to tell who's who. Or, I should say, it's hard to tell who's who with the exception of one very tall, dark, and handsome head coach.

The moment he steps onto the track, it's like my body can sense him. My skin thrums with excitement and my body vibrates with recognition. It's almost like being pulled to him is simply a law of physics that cannot be denied or fought.

Not that I'm fighting.

"Oh, girl," Millie leans in and whisper-shouts into my ear. "If you don't think I won't be asking the second we leave this place about the way you're watching Tate, you're sorely mistaken."

Fuck. It would be so nice if my every emotion wasn't always broadcast across my face.

"There's not much to it," I lie, still unable to tear my gaze away from how well Tate's pants fit and how cute Duke looks trotting alongside him. "He's objectively very attractive and it's in my nature to appreciate beautiful things."

It's also in my nature to want to climb him like a tree and spend the rest of my nights tangled in his arms beneath the stars.

"You're a terrible liar and I will not be dissuaded," she says, but something catches her eye and her squirrel-like attention span proves her wrong. "Ciara!"

Somehow, Ciara hears Millie over all the noise. She waves back, zigzagging through the group of people huddled at the bottom of the bleachers and then taking the steps two at a time until she reaches us.

"Millie! Luna! I'm so glad you're here." She shimmies past

the other people in our row and wraps us in a giant hug. "I know I graduated forever ago, but this place still makes me sweat. I was worried the high school kids would call me a loser if they caught me sitting by myself."

"I'm pretty sure they might call you a lot of things"—goddess, supermodel, life goals, for example—"but I don't think loser would be one of them."

I don't understand much about the youth nowadays, but I don't need to, to know that not even they can deny the absolute perfection that is Ciara Jacobs.

"You're sweet, but trust me, nobody is above reproach in Celestial." She wiggles her way into the seat between Millie and me. "My high school years were anything but smooth sailing. If it weren't for Tate, I'd never come close to this place."

I'm not sure if knowing someone as perfect as Ciara also struggled as a teen makes me feel better or strips me of all hope, but I do relate to her even more. It'd be much easier to ignore my crush on Tate if I didn't like him or his wonderful family so much.

"Speaking of your brother . . ." Millie pauses, and my eyes practically leap out of my head. I try to stop her, but with Ciara sitting between us, I can't get to her in time. "Luna over here seems to have quite the eyes for him."

Ciara turns to face me, and I'm sure her shocked expression is a perfect mirror to my horrified one.

"Tate?" Ciara asks. "Not Silas?"

Crap. Of course she would think I was interested in Silas. The only time I met her, I was on the back of his horse and his guest in their parents' home. The same home where Tate was less than welcoming when he saw me.

"Well. I . . . it's—" I stumble over my words while I try to formulate an explanation that I can't find.

But then, for once, luck—not Millie, the traitor—is on my side. The band comes to a sudden halt and the announcer's voice bellows through the stadium speakers.

"Welcome to Lou Bridel Stadium, the home of your Celestial Astros!" The announcer gives room for applause before continuing on. "Tonight, the Astros will be battling the Northeast Spartans for victory in the first preseason game of the year. So get on your feet, Celestial! Here come your Astros!"

Other than me, Ciara, and Millie, not many people are sitting, but at the announcer's direction, we rise to our feet in time for the beginning notes of "Thunderstuck" by AC/DC to shake the bleacher floors.

The locker room doors swing open, and the moms that were huddled together suddenly appear on both sides of the doors, cheering on and high-fiving the boys as they walk toward the end zone. Five of the players—who I can safely assume are the captains—walk through the opening I didn't even notice at the bottom of the inflatable star. They stand in front of it, swaying to the beat as their voices steadily rise in perfect timing with AC/DC. A little boy wearing a Celestial jersey that's at least five sizes too big for him and carrying a flag with Celestial's mascot on it runs onto the field and hands it to one of the players before quickly scurrying back to the sideline.

"Thunder!" the entire stadium chants alongside the team until finally, the band joins, train horns blare from the opposite end zone, and the boys sprint onto the field.

I obviously came to the game prepared to enjoy myself and cheer for the team, but I wasn't expecting to buy into it as fast as I have. Goose bumps pepper my sweat-glistened arms, and I have to blink away the tears welling in my perpetually dry eyes. I haven't cried in months and there's no chance in hell a football game will be the thing that breaks the dam holding me together.

"I forgot how much fun these games are!" Ciara shouts and waves her long arms over her head to try and catch Tate's attention. "There's nothing like Friday night lights in Texas."

She's so not wrong.

"And here come the Northeast Spartans," the announcer says. His flat, bored tone is almost unrecognizable from the loud, enthusiastic voice we heard moments ago, and our sideline goes silent as the opposing team runs through an inflatable shaped like a football helmet. I'd feel bad for the other team, but their crowd is anything but small and their marching band plays them onto the field with as much fervor as ours.

Both teams line up on the sidelines with their helmets in hand, radiating enough nervous energy to power this town as they watch the color guard do their thing. The Spartans get to call the coin toss as the visiting team and opt to receive the ball in the first half.

"Smart choice," Millie says. "Once we get the ball, the game's already going to be over."

"Okay, cocky." I laugh, but I have a feeling she's right. If the way Tate and these boys have prepared for this season is an indicator of anything, it's that their opponents are in for one hell of a fight.

"Not cocky, confident. Tate has always been the most determined person I know," Ciara chimes in, and the way she says it, I get the feeling she's not talking about football anymore. "When he sets his mind to something, he doesn't lose."

"I get that feeling too," I say . . . also not talking about football.

Down on the field, the team is in a flurry. Each coach is huddled up with their position. Some players talk calmly while others jump up and down, slamming into one another like they're in mini mosh pits. Tate stands off to the side with Chance, the quarterback who's always polite but too focused to join in with the rest of the team when they're giving me a hard time at practice. There's an intensity moving between them that's not present in the rest of the team. They stand with their heads down, focused on the tablet in Tate's hands, until the special team units take their places on the field and the ref blows the whistle.

Girl bands might be my touchstone, but Taylor Swift is still part of my holy trinity and I absentmindedly hum "You Belong With Me" as the game begins.

As it turns out, all my nerves were for nothing. After Celestial scores the third unanswered touchdown of the game, I lose track of what's happening on the field altogether. The team is phenomenal, but it's Tate running up and down the sideline, shouting into the headset he's wearing, and celebrating with the team like he's seventeen again that's captured my full attention.

With every successful drive, the serious facade he wears fades like the setting sun, and by the end of the first half, he's transformed completely. It doesn't matter how far back we are on the bleachers, his smile is so big, so blinding, I swear I could see it from the moon. He trails behind the team as they make their way back to the locker room and throws his head back in laughter at something Matt says.

"I forgot he could even look like that," Ciara says almost wistfully, and I wonder if she meant to say it out loud.

"Like what?" I ask, my gaze still glued to Tate until he disappears behind the door.

Ciara swallows, her throat working as I wait for an answer, and just when I think she's not going to tell me, she whispers, "Happy."

The sadness in her voice is only masked by the obvious love she feels for her brother.

It's heartbreaking and beautiful and it causes something inside me to shift.

I know it's a fool's errand, but standing beneath the Friday night lights, surrounded by a town that adores him no matter what he might think, I make it my mission to see this version of Tate so often people forget he was ever the brooding, grumpy football coach.

And maybe, if I'm lucky, one of the reasons behind his smile will be me.

Chapter 18

I started dating my first boyfriend in sixth grade.

By dating, I mean I waved at him in the hallway and ran away while my friends teased me mercilessly. I think we maybe had four conversations in total, not a single one lasting longer than three minutes, and still, when we broke up after eight days, I thought the world was over.

I didn't get my next boyfriend until my sophomore year of high school. That relationship lasted six months and covered the span of two school dances. Pictures of me with my back pressed to Jayden's front while wearing glittery dresses I found in the juniors' department at Macy's were still framed in my grandma's house before I sold it. There was one more high school boyfriend, one college boyfriend (in between countless situationships), and a few relationships that ventured pretty far beyond their dating app origins.

All that is to say that while I might be new to Celestial, I'm not new to this particular rodeo. Outside of being a very vulnerable and emotional prepubescent girl, I'm pretty chill when it comes to dating. My therapist said I created walls to prevent myself from ending up like my mom. She might not have been completely off the mark, but when it really came down to it, there was always too much going on in my own life to ever understand the appeal or find the time to chase a man. Plus, I couldn't live with myself if I was the reason behind a mediocre man gaining even an ounce of audacity.

They don't call me a girl's girl for nothing.

Not even in my wildest dreams did I ever think I would engage in groupie behavior, but if it somehow came down to that, I thought it'd be kind of glamorous. Maybe I'd follow a band across the country or camp out in a fancy bar near whatever professional sports team was rolling through town. I'd think it would've been anything other than camping out in the empty parking lot behind a high school stadium in a small Texas town.

Oh, how the mighty have fallen.

Millie and Ciara left before the game officially ended, but long after it was over. The final score was something like seventy-something to three. It got so painful to watch that by the third quarter, all our starters were sitting on the sideline and I was almost cheering for the other team. They couldn't make it into the end zone, but at least it wasn't a shutout.

Not that I would dare say that to the Celestial fans.

The bright streetlights illuminate the cups and wrappers littering the parking lot that cleared out almost an hour ago. I've told myself to go home approximately a million times, yet here I sit, alone in a parking lot left with nothing but my thoughts and bad decisions.

I know I shouldn't, but I swipe open my phone and pull up my emails again. Most of them are spam and reminders of the shopping carts I've left hanging—*sorry to be a tease, Pottery Barn, but I'm never going to complete the checkout*—but there's one subject line that stands out above the rest: YOU CAN'T IGNORE ME FOREVER!

At least you can't say my uncle is discreet.

I usually hit delete and go on with my day. He spent my entire life ignoring my existence, and it seems only fair that I return the favor. But lately, something has changed. His efforts to contact me are not only becoming more frequent, but there's been a shift in the intensity that doesn't just make me curious, it makes me nervous. And even though I'm tempted to send it to the trash where it belongs, not knowing is going to make it worse.

So I do the last thing I want and open it instead.

From: Jack Brady
Subject: YOU CAN'T IGNORE ME FOREVER!

Luna,

As I'm sure you're aware, I have been trying to get in touch with you for months. I know you are your mother's daughter and I shouldn't be disappointed, but for some reason I can't explain, I expected better of you.

Not only did you steal my house, I've found out that you somehow managed to be the lone recipient of all the bank accounts she had, including the money she inherited from my dad. A man you never met and who would've been just as disgusted by your mother's relationship as I was. I'm sure he's rolling around in his grave knowing his only son is struggling while some little girl he never met is out blowing his hard-earned money.

As you know, elder abuse is a very serious allegation and the authorities take matters like this very seriously. Your mother took advantage of my mom's kindness for years. She drained her physically, emotionally, and then you swooped in and drained her financially. You are both leeches who have to steal from others because you're incapable of building anything for yourself. You manipulated my mom into thinking I was the bad guy and then tricked her into trusting you, but you can't trick me.

I know you're going ignore this email like you've ignored the rest, but if you were smart, you'd see that I'm giving you a favor that you don't deserve. My lawyers tell me I have an airtight case against you, but I'm offering you the chance to handle this now and out of court. The faster you resolve this, the faster I can go back to pretending you don't exist.

You have one more opportunity to give me what's mine, but please know my patience is beginning to run thin. If I don't hear back from you soon, this is going to get real ugly. And trust me when I tell you, you don't want that.

You know how to reach me.

Jack

By the time I get to the end of his bonkers fucking email, my hands are shaking so hard, I almost drop my phone. But it's not from the fear I know he intended; it's out of pure, unadulterated rage. This little man, who my grandma removed from her life years ago, has the gall to think he can harass me into handing over money he has no right to have?

Absolutely the fuck not.

I don't need to know Jack to know he's a bully. He thinks

I'm the same sad girl who called him crying all those months ago. He doesn't know that I do home repairs and ride horses or that I've found a community who welcomed me in and caught the attention of the most fascinating man I've ever met. He doesn't know I'm not the one.

But he's about to find out.

I hit reply and my fingers fly across my phone before my brain can catch up.

From: Luna Starr
Subject: Re: YOU CAN'T IGNORE ME FOREVER!

Jack,

I was trying to take the high road by ignoring your ridiculous, bordering on harassing emails, but now that I see you have mistaken silence for something else, it's time to clear things up once and for all.

When my grandma, your mother, was sick and in and out of the hospital with one problem after the other, how often did you go visit her? How many times did you even bother to call her on the phone? Maybe even send her one of these emails you seem so fond of writing? When she was alive? Where the fuck were you? I don't know where you were, but I know you weren't ever by her side because I was.

She has been gone for almost four years now. If you ever thought you were entitled to anything of hers, the time to come forward was years ago. I can only assume you didn't because you knew my mom, the same sister whose funeral you didn't even attend, would have laughed in your face for even trying.

My grandma was the purest, most wonderful soul I've ever known. She taught me everything I know about not being a nice person, but a kind one. She showed me what it meant to be there for others and love people even when it's hard. She also didn't allow anyone to treat her or the people she loved like shit. Which, I can imagine, is why she wanted absolutely nothing to do with you. It's also probably why, in all the legal documents she signed, she made me, not you, the sole recipient of everything she left behind. I can't help but think that the reason she did that is because I would give it all away if it meant more time with her and you would throw her to the wolves if you thought you could make a penny.

You were right when you said this could get ugly. I would hate for all the people you know to discover what a terrible person you are and how after neglecting your sick mother for years, you're now harassing the niece you cut out of your life because I'm Black. Call me a leech if you want, but you're the true parasite here.

You know how to reach me, but please, for your sake, don't.

Wishing you the life you deserve,
Luna

I hit send before I can think better of it. The soft *swoosh* confirming the email was delivered sounds more like a bomb inside my car, which is fitting considering I'm pretty sure I just declared war. Realization of what I've done starts to set. My stomach turns and my pulse speeds up, but it's anticipation, not regret, rising beneath my skin. I've spent my entire life running from confrontation only to realize at the grand old age of thirty I might love it . . . just not enough to hear from Jack again. Before he even has a chance to respond, I scroll through my phone and block his email and his phone number.

May he never know peace again.

Laughter bubbles at the back of my throat, and when I can't hold it in any longer, I double over, laughing until my cheeks ache. The entire situation is so dark and so ridiculous that, as soon as I think I'm finished, another round of the giggles slams into me. I can't remember the last time I've laughed this hard. Would it be nice if the cause was about anything other than my asshole uncle? Of course. But I've had too many losses to ignore the wins when they're handed to me. I get so lost in the absolute absurdity that is my life, I forget where I am and, more importantly, who I'm waiting for, until it's too late.

A large hand on my window turns my laughs into screams and sends my newly discovered bravado spiraling into the atmosphere . . . along with my phone.

"Luna? Shit. I'm sorry." Tate leans in to get a closer look at me through my dust-covered window, but not even a film of filth could hide the concern written across his gorgeous face. "Are you okay? Wait . . . are you laughing or crying?"

If my heart was already going one million miles an hour, the sound of his voice sends it racing to two million. I open the window, and the sound of Duke's excited snorts glides inside my car along with the muggy night air.

"I was laughing, then I was screaming, and now I'm attempting to talk to you."

One day I'll go an entire conversation with him without being a weirdo, but it's not today.

"Laughing, huh? What was so funny?" he asks, and for one terrible, impulsive moment, I almost tell him the truth.

"A random email," I say as if a half lie doesn't count. "I don't think it was even that funny. It was a long day and I might be a little slaphappy."

At least that part is true. I spent all morning wallpapering Gabby's room and met up with Millie for a pregame cocktail. The football game was fun, but my energy is beginning to teeter on empty.

"Then what are you still doing out here?" A loc falls in front of his face. My fingers itch to reach out and tuck it behind his ear. "Are you okay to drive or do you want me and Duke to give you a ride?"

If I wasn't busy trying to come up with a reason that doesn't make me sound like a stalker, I might melt into a puddle. This man has no right to be this hot *and* this sweet.

"Oh no, that's okay. Thank you for offering, but I just, you know . . . I wanted to tell you good game. Say hi to Duke." Duke's snorts turn into impatient whines when he hears his name, and his little nails tap-dance on the pavement. I lean my head out the window and wave to him. "Hi, Duke."

Good game? Say hi to Duke?

I waited in an empty parking lot for over an hour to tell him *good game* and wave to his dog? It probably would've been a good idea to think of what I was going to say to him at some point over the last hour.

I blame my uncle.

"That's nice of you, but I didn't really do anything." His voice is thick with skepticism, but he's too kind to call out my very obvious lie. Again. "The boys did all the hard work."

"Oh my god! I almost forgot!" He reminds me of one of the actual reasons I had to be here. I hit the button to open my trunk and jump out of my car. "I made something for the boys."

Duke bumps into my legs and demands his well-deserved scratches for being the very best football dog tonight. I happily oblige.

"Were you the goodest boy?" I ask him. "I think you need a jersey like your teammates, don't you?"

My sewing skills are average at best, but now that I'm picturing Duke in an Astros jersey, nothing will stop me.

"Luna." Tate calls my name and his eyebrows are furrowed in that way they always are when we're together. "You made something for the boys?"

I stand up, trying my hardest to avoid Duke's disappointed puppy eyes.

"I said that I would. We've been preparing for tonight for the last month and a half. What kind of training partner slash honorary teammate would I be if I didn't help celebrate them for their first game?" I grab Tate's hand and pull him to the back of my car to show him the trunkful of goody bags I assembled for the team. "I made one for everyone on the roster, plus the coaches, and then I added an extra ten in case I messed up the math somehow. It should be enough, but if anyone is left out, you have strict orders to let me know right away and I'll bring more up to the school, stat."

He grabs one of the bags and starts rummaging inside.

"These must've cost a fortune." He unwraps one of the protein bars I stuck inside and takes a giant bite out of it. "These are really nice. You didn't need to do this."

"Duh." I roll my eyes. "I didn't need to, I wanted to, and I had a lot of fun putting them together. I didn't know if they could have home-baked items, but if you give me the go-ahead, they'll be even better after the next game."

When I wasn't scrolling Pinterest for more home decor ideas and chicken tips for beginners, I was looking for athlete-approved snacks to give the boys. I found so many that I had to start a new board to organize them all. I already bought the ingredients for a few of them because even if I can't bring them to the school, I'm making them for myself. There's nothing I love more than a treat I can trick my mind into believing is actually good for me. It's like when I pat myself on the back for ordering a low-calorie Diet Coke over a regular Coke when really I know it's just as bad, if not worse, for me.

"When it comes to special treatment for student athletes in Texas, there are no rules," he says, furthering my belief that *Friday Night Lights* was more fact than fiction. "I don't know what the official rule is, but I know the team moms have made things for the team before."

I'm not a mom or even the teeniest bit related to the team, but my ears perk up and my interest is immediately piqued.

"Team mom?" I repeat, already concocting a plan to infiltrate the group. "What do they do, and do they need an extra set of hands?"

"Oh no." He shakes his head and holds up his hands like he's warding off evil spirits. "Trust me when I tell you that you don't want anything to do with them. They're always the source of some kind of drama. The only group worse than them is the fucking booster club." He shivers at the mention of the innocuous group. "I know how to handle a team full of teenagers and a wrench, but I don't think I'll ever know how to deal with those people."

Tate might not outwardly like most people, but he's never

given me the impression of someone who talks crap about people who don't deserve it. If he's cautioning me away from the booster club, it's probably in my best interest to heed his warning.

"No team mom, friends of the team, or booster club memberships for me." I close the trunk. "Got it."

"Good choice." He leans against my car and bites back his smile. It's almost as if the joy he felt on the field has seeped into him off of it.

"All my choices are good."

"If I wasn't in the process of fixing your bathroom because you didn't read the inspection, I might believe that," he says. "But I am, so I know they're questionable at best."

A small breeze brushes against my legs and wafts his cologne in my direction. Nobody should smell that good after standing outside—running and jumping—for as long as he did.

"First of all, rude." I fold my arms in front of my chest. I hope it looks like I'm annoyed and not like I'm hiding my nipples that have gone hard beneath my tank top. "Second of all, the floor technically needed to be fixed whether I lived there or not. If you think about it, I should be heralded as a hero for saving some nice, innocent Celestial native from falling through the ceiling. And last, are you ever going to tell me how much I owe you?"

He said he would get me an estimate when he first came to inspect the damage, but he's more than halfway finished and I've yet to see a single bill or receipt.

"Okay, hold on. I need to make sure I don't miss anything," he says. "So, one, I'm sorry. I'd never want you to think I'm being rude . . . to you. Two, you're right. I'll reach out to the principal and see if we can honor you as the local hero you are before one of the games. And three, maybe, but unlikely."

"Excuse me." My jaw falls to the ground as I struggle to process what's happening. "Are you . . . are you teasing me?"

"Teasing you? Who would do such a thing?"

Other than the jerky version of him that ran out of my house and gave me attitude at his parents' house, I like Tate in all his forms.

I like him brooding and moody. I like him focused and determined. I really, really like him when he's soft and gentle, lying on a blanket and stargazing with me. But without a doubt, Tate carefree, happy, and teasing is by far the very best.

"You would and you do." I try to pout but my heart's not in it. It's too busy falling deeper for the man in front of me. "At least I can count on Duke to defend me. Right, buddy?"

Duke looks up from the spot he's claimed on the pavement and grunts his agreement.

"That's not fair," Tate says. "You've bribed him for his loyalty. He's always on your side."

I shrug and bend down to pet an uninterested Duke. "Sorry, Coach. That sounds like a you problem."

"I guess I can't blame him too much," he says, and I don't know if it's my imagination, but I swear his voice drops an octave. "I'd take your side over mine too."

"I'm glad you're a big enough person to admit that." My husky voice cuts through the now-empty parking lot, and I'm suddenly very aware that we're all alone.

Again.

His eyes darken beneath the amber glow of the streetlight and the air goes still.

"I always thought being by myself at the ranch was the only thing that could bring me peace." His voice is barely above a whisper. "But I'm starting to think I was wrong. That you might be my peace too."

The earth shifts and time stops. Constellations shine brighter above us, as if his quiet admission shifted the planets and moved the stars. His presence swirls around me like a drug, and I breathe him in until I'm high off him. I feel lightheaded. The air is too thick. It's too much.

It could never be enough.

The space between us closes. I reach for his hand, and the touch alone is enough to set me at ease and on fire at the same time. His long fingers wrap around mine. He pulls me closer, so close that I'm sure he can feeling my heart beating out of my chest.

"Tate—" I say, but the sentence falls away.

What am I supposed to say to him? That I want him? That I'm afraid if this happens between us that I'll need him? That I'm terrified to need anyone ever again?

But because this is Tate, I don't have to say anything.

He lowers his head until his mouth is hovering over mine and I can't tell where his breathing begins and mine ends. "I know," he says. "I know."

It feels like we stay like this for centuries, suspended in the before, living in the possibilities. I know I should walk away. It's the smart thing to do. But standing in front of him, reveling in his touch, I have a feeling the promise of Tate is greater than the risk of the heartbreak he's sure to bring.

Shutting down all thoughts and acting only on instinct, I roll onto my toes and touch my mouth to his.

I don't know how a man so big and tough can be this gentle.

His lips are soft, but the kiss is softer. It's painstakingly sweet and so perfect I could cry.

And it's not enough.

Thankfully, Tate feels the same.

Faster than the lightning racing down my spine and between my legs, Tate tangles his strong fingers in my unruly mass of curls and pulls my head back so that he's the only thing I can see.

"If you don't want this, I need you to tell me now," he says between heavy breathing. "I've tried so hard not to let you under my skin, but you've embedded yourself so deep, that if I get another taste of you, I know I'll never be able to work you out of my system."

He's giving me an out.

I should take it, let us both go on with our lives. Life has already burned me, and the last thing I need is to play with fire again.

It's just too bad Texas has taught me to love the heat.

"Promise?" I ask instead.

He doesn't ask again.

His calloused hands dip beneath my tank and his mouth crashes to mine.

It's not gentle.

Neither of us have it in us to pretend this is anything other than what it is, to act as if every second spent together before this wasn't decadent torture leading to this exact moment. That we weren't inevitable. My toes curl in my shoes, and need pools between my thighs. I taste like desperation in his mouth.

He tastes like wonder in mine.

It's like this is my first ever kiss, like I've known his touch for a lifetime. Every single emotion I've fought to suppress pours out of me. His teeth nip my bottom lip, and our tongues twist together in unspoken promises. My nervous system turns to static beneath his touch. Electricity shoots through my veins, and sparks ignite in my heart.

It's the best kiss of my entire life, and when it ends, I feel the loss down to my soul.

"Wow." He effectively sums up how I feel in a single word. "That was . . ."

He stops and I know why. There are no words to describe what that was.

"I know," I finish for him this time. "It was."

"Now that we sorted that out," he says before stealing one more quick kiss. "Have you eaten yet?"

It's such a simple question, and after what just happened between us, it shouldn't be enough to make my heart skip a beat or twist my stomach into a million and one knots.

But it does.

"I had some popcorn at the game, but I could go for dinner." I try to sound unbothered and have *some chill* as the kids would say, but not even an asteroid could wipe the smile off my face. "What about you?"

"I could eat," he says, but when his gaze focuses on my mouth, I get the distinct impression that he's not talking about food anymore.

Lucky for him, I'd be thrilled with either.

Chapter 19

I love going out in Celestial. It has the dreamiest little downtown. Everything is so quaint and magical that it feels like stepping out of the real world and onto the set of a Hallmark movie. The moment I drove through it for the first time, I knew there wasn't a place in the entire world that I would like more.

But that was before I pulled into the driveway of the unassuming bungalow right on the outskirts of town.

"So this is where *the* Tate Jacobs lives," I say. "It's nice."

He waves off my compliment. "It's not much, but it works. The stadium is close and there's a good-sized yard for Duke. I like it."

I look around the space that is somehow exactly and nothing like I expected. The walls are cream and the wide plank hardwood floors are spotless. A gray sectional is pushed against the wall in the corner of the room, topped with pillows I'm sure Ciara or Pam were behind, and one corner is filled with noticeably less aesthetic pillows and a throw blanket covered with fur. Duke's spot. The handsome coffee table houses the only clutter in the room, and I don't have to look closely to know it's all pages of his playbook and notes on the team. His walls are blank except for one lone canvas picture of him standing on the sideline with three Astros players, all their heads thrown back laughing, their joy shining bright even though the picture is black-and-white.

I wonder what his bedroom looks like . . .

"Well, it's only fair that you finally invited me over." I take off my shoes and set my purse on the corner of the couch. "You've only been to my house a million times. It's about time you let me see yours."

He crosses the living room to turn on the light in the kitchen, and from what I can see, there doesn't look to be any more personality present in there than in here.

"I know, and I'm sorry. I was worried you wouldn't like it." He starts pulling box after box out of the bag of take-out food he ordered. "Not only are my cabinets not pink, but my bathtub hasn't fallen through the ceiling, and I know how much you like that."

I'm walking toward him, but at his words, my steps freeze. Duke wiggles around at my feet and whines, not understanding why I stopped.

"Hold on, Duke," I whisper, and crouch down to my favorite puppy as I give him a quick belly rub. "Your dad just told a joke, and I didn't know he knew how to do that."

"Ha ha." Tate grabs two plates and some forks out of his cabinets. He moves easily through the space, and it's clear that while he might not like to cook, he loves to be at home. "I'm actually hilarious—you just haven't paid close enough attention to realize it yet."

He's wrong. When it comes to him, I notice everything.

I lean against the opening to the kitchen. "Aw, yes, the ever-elusive straight man who has to tell women he's funny. I think I've heard of this before."

He throws his head back and laughs. The sound fills every nook and cranny of the empty house, and all of a sudden it feels like a home. It feels like a gift anytime I hear Tate laugh, but here, standing barefoot in his kitchen with him as he pulls take-out boxes out of a bag only for the two of us? It's euphoric. I can almost feel the sound of his raspy chuckle as it bounds across my skin and takes root some place much, much deeper. I want to run across the kitchen and pull his mouth to mine, absorbing the sound of his laughter until it lives in me.

"You're right. I'm sorry." His smile is bright and unguarded. He holds his hand up in front of him in the Scout's honor gesture. "I might not always be funny, but I solemnly swear that I will never mansplain."

Funny and charming in one night? This isn't going to end well for me. After the kiss in the parking lot and now standing in his home, I'm in serious danger of falling. And falling hard.

"You know just what to say to get the ladies going." I'm going for sarcastic, but it comes out sincere. Heat rushes up my cheeks, and I try to change the subject. "Thank you for dinner, by the way. This looks great."

"I can't believe you haven't been to Sandy's yet. Best Southern food in Celestial. Maybe even Texas." He pulls out a chair and gestures for me to sit. How he manages to be terse, chivalrous, and playful at the same time is one of life's great mysteries. It will never cease to amaze me. "I'm glad I get to be the one who you try it with for the first time."

I know he's only talking about the food, but warmth curls

through me as I think about all the firsts we've already had and how many could come if we play our cards right. The past has told me not to plan for the future, but when I'm with him, I can't help it. It's a thought I should keep to myself, but for once, I don't want to be shy about what I'm thinking.

Add that to the list of firsts.

"You were my first Texas football game too," I tell him, and when I'm rewarded with the way his onyx eyes turn molten, I keep going. "And the first person to take me stargazing on a blanket in a wide-open field. You were the first stranger to talk to me at a bar in Celestial and the first person to sneak up on me and scare me at the track. You're so many of my firsts, and I don't think I'm any of yours."

It's too much.

I know it's too much.

"I'm a pretty good first," he says. "That doesn't sound too bad."

He turns away and walks to the fridge before I can respond, and I can only imagine what's going through his head. That was way too deep, way too fast, and I'm sure he's already plotting how to get me out of his house as soon as he can.

Stupid, Luna. So stupid.

"Can I get you something to drink?" he asks, interrupting my inner doomscroll. "I don't have as many options as you, but there's Dr Pepper, some Gatorade, and one Diet Coke Ciara left when she came over to annoy me the other day."

I force a smile on my face and try to ignore the sinking feeling in my stomach. I push away thoughts of what might be and try to focus on what is, which means for at least this very moment, sitting with the man I really, really like and eating dinner with him.

"Diet Coke, please," I say, grateful none of my inner turmoil is evident in my voice. "And if you see Ciara before I do, please thank her for saving me from having to drink Dr Pepper."

"Hey!" He reaches into the fridge and grabs me the Coke. "Not again with the Dr Pepper slander. You don't know what you're missing."

I make sure to keep the drinks he likes on hand since he's over at my house so often. It's just such a shame that the one he seems to love is disgusting.

"I do know what I'm missing, because I drank it when I was a kid," I remind him. "Before I developed taste and standards."

His lips curl up in a crooked smile I might like more than his big, wide-open one.

"So now that you're older," he says, handing me the pop and taking the seat in front of me, "what are your standards like?"

"Now I drink pop that has zero calories, a weird aftertaste, and so many chemicals that if I drink enough of it, I might not need to be embalmed when I die." I crack open the pop can and stare at him over the top as I take a sip. "Like an adult."

He laughs again, and this time, I can't watch because I'm too busy doing it with him.

"You were wrong, by the way," he says once we've stopped laughing and fallen into a comfortable silence while we eat.

"Impossible. No, I wasn't," I say before I realize I have no idea what he's even talking about. "Wrong about what?"

"I've never taken anyone to my spot at Starlight before. I've never kissed anyone in the parking lot after a game. I've never looked forward to going to work each day, knowing I'm going to see the beautiful woman who's going to bring me a Dr Pepper even though she hates it and make me laugh when I least expect it. I've never introduced anyone to my team or brought them to my house. So you were wrong," he says again. He puts his fork down on the table and stares at me with something I don't recognize, but immediately love, burning behind molten lava eyes. "You are my first for a lot of things too."

The food is delicious, but it's hard to maintain an appetite when your heart is blocking your throat.

"I'm not hungry anymore." I push my plate to the side, picking off one last piece of chicken to give to an expectant Duke who hasn't left my feet. "Your couch looks pretty comfortable though. How about we come up with another first and make out on it?"

I don't have to ask twice.

Eventually, after kissing with my back pressed against the wall in the kitchen and then the living room . . . and then the other living room wall, we finally make it to the couch. And after we finish kissing and watching a show while Tate fills me in on the locker room antics the boys got up to last week, I fall asleep with my head on his shoulder and Duke's head on my lap, and out of all the firsts of the night, I think that one is my favorite.

Chapter 20

I open my front door before Millie turns off her car.

"Welcome to my humble abode!" I open my arms wide and yell from the porch. "Who's ready to paint the town pink?"

And by town, I mean the chicken coop. Obviously.

"I am!" Millie hops out of her car and pulls open the back door to reveal tote bags full of craft supplies. "This is going to be the best day ever!"

Ciara doesn't share in our enthusiasm.

"You two are out of your minds," she says. "How did I let you talk me into this?"

It wasn't hard.

"If you want, I'd be happy to bring you back over to your parents' house." Millie slings a tote bag over each shoulder. "Otherwise, I suggest you turn that frown upside down and get excited to work on the chicken hammock I have planned for you."

"Fuck." Ciara groans. "I'm sorry I've been acting like a bitch. I'm still adjusting to being back at home and I'm irritated about some things over at Starlight, but I'll get my act together."

"Don't worry about it. We all have those days." I meet them on the driveway and grab a bag from Millie. "If it makes you feel better, there are two curated stacks of romance novels with your names on them in my library, a cooler filled to the brim with premade cocktails in the backyard, and if you're hungry, I might have gone a little overboard with the spread I put together. There's a salad, sandwiches, an antipasto and fruit tray, and more goodies and sweet treats than your heart could desire."

Ciara pops up from grabbing the bags that migrated to the passenger side floor and looks at us over the roof of Millie's car. "Did someone just say *sweet treats*?" she asks, and a smile pulls at the corners of her mouth for the first time since she arrived.

Sheesh.

These Jacobs siblings are so touchy.

"I did," I tell her. "And they're really good ones too."

Not to brag or anything, but my baking skills are top-notch.

"Did you make those raspberry lemon cookies you brought to knitting circle last time?" Millie asks. "I swear, I dreamt about them for a week."

I nod my head and Millie squeals. "I tried out a new recipe too. Four words for you." I draw it out, looking between my two sugar-addicted friends: "Peach. Cobbler. Cheesecake. Bars."

There was a box of peaches on sale when I went grocery shopping, and it was such a good deal, I couldn't resist. I just had no idea how many peaches came in a box. I feel like I've been eating them for days, and I still have half the box left.

"That's it. What are you both waiting for?" Ciara's chipper, singsong voice is a far cry from the grumpy goddess of two minutes ago as she rushes past me with a bag in each hand. "We have a coop to paint and goodies to eat. Move it, ladies!"

"It actually makes total sense that dessert would be the key to unlocking Ciara's motivation," Millie says to me as we trail behind Ciara.

A little treat is effective in every situation, but even though my skills in the kitchen are wonderful, that doesn't just apply to me. "It does?"

"Of course," Millie says, and it's only then that I catch the mischievous glint shining in her blue eyes. "Just add her to the list of Jacobs siblings obsessed with tasting your goodies."

I gasp and somehow manage to choke on the humid air. I knew whatever she said was going to be out of pocket, but I could've never predicted that.

Ciara drops the bags she was holding and skids to a halt. Her long braids go flying as she spins around to face Millie.

"Number one," she says, pointing an angry finger between the two of us. "How dare you?"

"Hey! This is all Millie." I hold my free hand up in surrender. "All I did was try to make you something delicious to eat. I'm innocent here."

Millie shoots me her dirtiest look, but the joke's on her because between her pink and purple hair and the Powerpuff Girls shirt she's wearing today, she still just looks adorable.

"You're right, Luna. You didn't deserve that," Ciara says. "This is Millie's fight, and I'm sorry I pointed a loaded finger gun at you."

"Apology accepted." I step away from Millie and stand by Ciara's side.

"Traitor," Millie hisses beneath her breath.

I don't even attempt to argue with her. Add this to the list of reasons why I could never go to war. I'm not taking a bullet—literally or metaphorically—for anybody. Not even someone who is providing me with free labor and discounted craft goods.

"Now that that's sorted, where was I? Oh yes." Ciara holds up two fingers. "Number two, no jokes that even allude to Luna's goodies. Gross."

"Hey!" *How did I just catch another stray?*

"Oh yeah. Sorry, Luna," Ciara says, before adding on a very half-hearted "no offense."

"A little late for that, don't you think?" I ask, ignoring the way Millie sticks her tongue at me when Ciara isn't looking. "Why don't you go ahead and holster those puppies. Your aim is a little too wild for my liking."

"That's fair." Ciara tucks her left hand in her pocket and turns to me. "Permission from the court to use one hand for this last point?"

I nod. "You may proceed."

"Number three!" Ciara shouts, holding up three fingers for all to see, and if nothing else, I appreciate her commitment to the bit. "As a designated representative of all Ciaras around the world and on behalf of *the* Ciara Princess Harris Wilson, it must be known that Ciaras don't want the goodies, we *are* the goodies."

An important distinction and an impassioned speech. Impressive.

"Great," Millie says, clearly not as amused with the situation as I am. "Are we finished now?"

Ciara pretends to think about it for a second.

"We are," she says, scooping up the bags she dropped on

the ground. "Thank you for still being my friend and letting me go off the rails every now and again."

"Of course." Millie opens my screen door and we follow her inside. "Plus, now that I was so forgiving, you won't be able to—" Millie's sentence comes to a stop as suddenly as her steps.

"What happened?" I ask, narrowly avoiding slamming into her back. "Are you okay?"

She doesn't answer.

"Luna." She says my name instead. "Why are there chickens in your living room?"

Oh.

"So about that . . ." I drop the tote bag filled with craft supplies next to my door and move beside the plastic bin filled with chicks. "Ciara, Millie, meet my ladies! And maybe let's start with finishing the chicken coop."

PINK PAINT IS splattered across my face and my hands, and sweat is falling down my neck. I'm going to need three Advils and the longest shower ever to alleviate the pain in my shoulders, and still, I've never been happier.

Fluffy white clouds dance in the bright blue sky above us. I managed to have the perfect amount to drink so I don't feel drunk, but I'm not quite sober, and my stomach hurts from laughing. The cows over at Starlight Ridge have ventured closer to my property, their gentle mooing and curious stares critique our work as we put the final coat of paint on the chicken coop.

When I bought this house, these were the days I dreamt about, and nothing could make it any better.

Except for maybe one certain person.

"So, that was fun and all." Millie grabs a drink out of the cooler and joins Ciara and me on the blanket I laid in the shade. "But now that our work is finished, is it finally time to gossip?"

"Oh." Ciara perks up. "I'm always up for that. I don't feel like I was in Austin for that long, but so much changed while I was gone and I can't keep up."

"I thought you didn't like to participate in the rumor mill," I say, even though I, too, would love some gossip.

Ciara snorts beside me. "She told you that? They used to call her Rumor Millie because she always knew everything about everyone."

"I've grown. I'm trying to be better." Millie's cheeks are bright red, but they've been that way for hours . . . despite me offering her sunscreen twice. "But this doesn't count, because I want to gossip about Luna and Tate."

"Well, that's not exciting." Ciara picks up one of the books I loaned her and takes a closer look at the cover. "I'm pretty sure that after the way they were watching each other at the game, the entire town figured out that something is going on between them."

"We were not watching each other!" I say a little too loud for it to sound believable. "I mean, sure, I saw him, but he's the coach and we were at a football game. It would have been impossible not to."

Plus, his butt looked really cute in his slacks, and at the end of the day, I'm just a girl.

"Girl. You do know we have eyes, right? The only time you weren't looking for him on the sideline was when he was in the locker room," Millie says, like she's a detective laying out her case. "Then you stayed when the rest of us headed out.

And no offense, but I have a hard time believing you like high school football that much."

The only problem with living in a small town is that there's nowhere to hide. Everyone sees everything no matter where you are.

Including my house.

But I try anyways.

I get off the blanket and grab the hammer and disco ball sitting close by and retreat to the chicken coop, or, as Ciara has affectionately dubbed it, the Pink Chicken Club.

"It was my first Texas football game. I wanted to stay," I say once the gate has closed behind me. "Plus, somebody had to stick around. The other team looked so sad when everyone started to leave early."

"The other team looked sad because they were losing by, like, a hundred. Not because the strangers on the opposing team's bleachers were leaving," Millie says. "But nice try though."

"And none of that changes the fact that we all saw Tate turning around after damn near every single play to make sure you hadn't left," Ciara says. "I've known that man my entire life and I've never seen him so obvious. He was smoother in middle school."

"Seriously," Millie cosigns Ciara's observation, oblivious to the way my mind is on the verge of combusting. "I don't think I've ever even seen him so much as glance at the crowd before that game."

I drag the stool we used to paint the outside of the coop inside their little house and step on top so I can reach the ceiling. "He did not do that."

I would've noticed because I actually *was* staring at him all night.

"Are you trying to gaslight us?" Ciara asks.

"He even smiled at you!" Millie shouts like my mom would after she had to explain a math problem to me for the umpteenth time. "Tate doesn't smile!"

"He does too," I say, accidentally hitting the nail attaching the disco ball string to the ceiling a little too hard. "You just have to pay closer attention."

I can't help but feel defensive when it comes to Tate. If I close my eyes, I can still feel his lips against mine and hear his throaty chuckle as he filled me in on the locker room antics the boys pulled after their victory. There was a lightness to him that I'd never seen, and I can't help but feel protective over it.

"Oh yeah." Ciara's laughter drifts into the coop. "You're never beating the allegations now."

I try to find something else to keep me busy inside the chicken coop, but Millie already hung the curtains and Ciara tacked up the hammock she made. The disco ball was the final touch, and now that it's up, I'm left defenseless against the two women I voluntarily invited over to my house. This is why I should've kept to myself when I moved. I have nobody to blame but myself.

I latch the door behind me and grab another drink that I shouldn't have, but think I need, before I rejoin them in the shade. "What allegations?"

Ciara and Millie share a look, and something unspoken passes between them. If I thought I didn't want to know before, I'm positive I don't want to know now.

"It's nothing," Ciara says. "I have a question though."

"Okay." I nod, a little nervous about whatever she's about to say. "Shoot."

"I love seeing this side of Tate, and it's been so nice to see him start coming back into himself, but . . ." She pauses, and my stomach falls to my feet. "Was there not something going on with you and Silas? I didn't know after the ride around the ranch and all."

"You went on a ride with Silas?" Millie asks, but she sounds more offended that I didn't tell her than curious about said ride. "When was this?"

"A couple of nights before the game." I look to Ciara for confirmation. "Right?"

"Yeah, Wednesday," Ciara says. "I was showing Silas some of my ideas for the ranch when we saw her starting to paint that"—she eyes my coop, still unsure about the color—"and Silas came to say hi and introduce me. Then Luna hopped on the back of his horse and he took her on a tour around the ranch."

Millie looks like her eyes are about to pop out of her head, and the niggling little seed of guilt and doubt in the back of my mind takes root. I'm sure to everyone on the outside, if there were a choice to be had between Tate and Silas, Silas would be the obvious answer. And I don't think they're wrong. He's just not the right answer for me.

"Silas is so nice. He's sweet and generous and has been there for me since the day I arrived. He's literally a romance hero come to life. If I had half a brain, I would've asked him to move in with me the second he showed up on my doorstep. But something always felt a little off?" I pull my sunglasses off the top of my head and slide them over my face. "Not in a bad way or anything, but in a way where I got the feeling we were never going to be more than friends. Then I got to know Tate better and he's just . . ." I try to think of how to explain what I have with Tate. The way my skin burns whenever he's near and my heart aches when he's not. How the world stops and the heavens open when he smiles and I know it's only for me. The way his mouth on mine alters my brain chemistry. "Tate is special."

I want to tell them about our night beneath the stars and our first kiss in the parking lot. I want to tell them about sharing takeout in his living room while Duke snored with his head on my lap. I want to tell them everything . . . but I want to keep it for myself more. I want to relish in every first, filing them away like hidden treasures only we know how to find, before we allow the very well-meaning voices of Celestial in.

"Tate *is* special." Ciara reaches for my hand and her face goes soft. "He's got a tough exterior, but I can't tell you how happy I am that you've breached it and found what I've known he's been hiding for years."

"He's pretty great," I say before voicing the worry I've been too afraid to give life to. "But do you think Silas is going to hate me for this?"

And not because I think he's going to be upset I'm not dating him, but because the guy I am dating happens to be his twin brother who—it must be said—he doesn't seem to like all that much. I know Millie was joking when she called me a traitor earlier, but maybe she wasn't too far off.

"No." Ciara shakes her head. "Silas isn't that guy. He and Tate have their own issues, but he would never put that on you, and I don't think you're wrong about the friend thing either. Everyone thinks I'm crazy, but nobody can convince me he isn't still stuck on his old girlfriend."

Millie's mouth falls open and she goes pale . . . or paler. "Palmer?"

Ciara nods. "To this day, if I mention her name, he leaves the room. I don't know if he'll ever get over her."

"Wait." I wade in between the two women who may as well be speaking in code. "What am I missing here? Who's Palmer and why do we think he's not over her?"

"Palmer was Silas's first girlfriend," Millie says. "They were, like, couple goals before couple goals were a thing."

"I swear they started dating in, like, kindergarten or something ridiculous. Some of my earliest memories are of playing with Palmer and Silas on the swing set in our backyard while my mom and Mrs. Dorothy drank coffee and gossiped," Ciara says. "He made my mom keep Ring Pops stocked in the pantry and he brought her one every week so all the other boys knew she was his."

A little alpha hero in the making. The scene Ciara paints is so sweet, I could weep knowing it doesn't end with Silas living happily ever after with the girl he's loved since kindergarten.

"Why'd they break up?" I ask.

"She moved," Ciara tells me. "Her dad got a job in Washington that paid more than anything he could ever make in Celestial. They stayed friends for a little while, but it wasn't as easy to stay in touch with someone back then. Silas started looking at schools out there, but after Tate made it clear that he had no interest in taking over the ranch, he changed course. Went to College Station and majored in agricultural science instead."

"Wait, did you say Washington?" Something about this feels so familiar, and I search my memory trying to remember where I've heard this. "Oh my god," I say when I finally remember. "Silas told me about her!"

"He did?" Ciara looks like she's about to jump out of her skin. "He never talks about her."

"I mean, he didn't mention her by name or anything." It feels like it was so long ago. I try to think of exactly what he said. "He mentioned he had a friend that moved to Washington and they lost contact soon after she moved. I think he said she's married with a kid now."

It was sad when he told me then; it's devastating now.

"I want to shake him sometimes." Ciara clearly does not share my sympathy for her brother. "He never wanted to take over the ranch, but god forbid he ever stops playing the dutiful son."

"He never wanted the ranch?" I would've never guessed after the way he waxed poetic about Starlight Ridge when he showed me around. He seemed so proud to take charge and carry on his family legacy.

"God, no." Ciara laughs, but there's no humor behind it. "He wanted to be an architect. He basically designed my parents' house in high school. But instead of doing that, he'd rather martyr himself for a lifetime so that Dad will be proud of him and he can hold on to this bullshit wedge he created with Tate."

You only have to be around Tate and Silas once to know something isn't right in the water. They try to play nice for everyone around them, but tension practically vibrates off them.

"Yeah," I say instead of asking for every sordid detail she's willing to share. "I've noticed something is a little off between them but haven't wanted to ask what it's about."

"There's no answer because it's not about anything." Ciara doesn't even try to hide her hurt or frustration, although I can't tell which feeling is more prevalent. "Dad got into an accident on the ranch not long after Tate and Silas went to college. It was bad, and as much as he wanted everything to go back to the way it was when he recovered, it couldn't. So he took control the only way he knew how and tried to force Tate and Silas to come back home and take over. Tate, rightfully, refused. Silas didn't, and now he takes his regret out on Tate because he's pissed he didn't have it in him to do the same. It's a tale as old as time, another Jacobs man sacrificing everything in the name of legacy."

"That sucks." It more than sucks, and there's something heartbreakingly ironic that the thing that's supposed to represent their family is what's ripping them apart.

"It doesn't suck. It's fucking stupid." Fire laces her voice and burns the hurt into ashes. If I didn't know better, I'd think she might start breathing fire. "I know I was too young when it first happened, but I wanted to run the ranch! They could've hired some extra hands to help out until I could take over. Silas could've run off to wherever the fuck he wanted to do whatever the fuck he wanted. I would've happily stayed here my entire life, living for Starlight Ridge, but god forbid a person with a vagina be in charge."

"Damn." It's not often that I'm at a loss for words, but I am now.

"It's why I was in such a bad mood when I first got here," she says. "The only reason I moved back home is because Silas promised I could have some more responsibility around Starlight. Implement some of my ideas, get to the point where even if he won't step down, we're working together. But now every time I suggest anything, Dad says no, and Silas is still too much of a people pleaser to tell him to fuck off."

"I'm sorry, Ciara." I know my words don't mean much, but they're all I have. "I hope your dad realizes how lucky he is to have someone as smart and dedicated as you at home."

"Well, fuck!" Millie cries out and stomps her foot. "I thought we were just going to paint and get drunk. I wouldn't have brought up gossiping if I thought it would lead to me feeling bad for you and your brothers! I hate feeling bad for men, especially when they're as hot as Silas and Tate."

"Ew. Gross." Ciara scrunches her face and makes a gagging sound. "Don't call them hot."

"They're hot. You're hot. Even your parents are hot." I tell her something there's no way she's not already aware of. "It's a blessing and a curse, but you have to learn to live with it."

"If that ever gets too hard and you want to switch places"—Millie, who is also hot, bumps her shoulder into Ciara's arm—"I'll gladly bear that cross for you."

Ciara rolls her eyes. "You're such a good friend."

"Selfless, really," Millie says, nestling her head in Ciara's chest. "Just like Silas."

Ciara tenses up and Millie bursts out laughing.

Me? My time in the sun is up.

"Alright, you beautiful, selfless people, what do you think about taking this party inside?" I grab the empty tray that was once covered in dessert and tuck it under my arm. "I need to check on Little Chix. Dolly Parton was picking on Kelly Cluckson last time I checked, and I can't have the girls fighting."

"I would personally love to go inside and pet your chicks," Millie says. "But only if you name one of the ones you haven't named yet Tanya Clucker."

Dammit. It was right there!

"I can't believe I left Tanya Tucker out," I say, disappointed and disgusted with myself. "Of course that will be their name."

"When they are old enough to move into the Pink Chicken Club, I'll make sure to ride Beyonc-hay over to meet them," Ciara says. "They'll love each other."

"You have a horse named Beyonc-hay?" I ask, more in love with Ciara Jacobs than I ever thought possible. "How was this not information Silas gave to me on the tour?"

"Because boys shouldn't be in charge of ranches," she says. "If I was in charge, introducing you to her and Hay-Z would have been the first thing on the schedule."

Beyonc-hay and Hay-Z?

Oh yeah. These are my people.

I know I might have been running away from my problems when I decided to move to Celestial, but as I walk inside my adorable house to my adorable chickens, I can't believe I didn't know this was what I was running to. I can't help but think that no matter what happened in the past, I'm beyond lucky that it led me to this small Texas town where I found great friends and a boy who could steal my heart.

If he hasn't already.

Chapter 21

Tanya Clucker and Henda Martell have become the natural leaders of my pack.

"Be nice to Jade Cluckwall." I hold Henda's soft little body in my hands and look into the sweet, beady eyes. "You're sisters now. You have to take care of each other, not bully them for front spot at the water trough."

She chirps twice and I take that as confirmation that my point got through and set her back down in the bin. I check to make sure the brooder at the back is working so they stay nice and warm in my over-air-conditioned house, and I'm topping off their food when the sound of paws scrambling over gravel pulls my attention to my front porch.

Duke's labored snorts come long before Tate knocks on the door. I swing open the door and drop down to my haunches to welcome another one of my favorite pet friends into my home.

"Duke!" I hold my arms out wide as the wiggly little potato leaps into my arms—well, as much as a bulldog can leap—

and covers my face in kisses. "Are you excited to see me or are you tricking me for treats?"

"Excuse me." Tate joins us and his voice sends shivers running down my back. "Duke is a gentleman. He would never use a woman for her treats."

"You're right," I say to Tate, but keep my eyes on one very excited puppy . . . who absolutely just wants a treat. "I'm so sorry, Duke. You deserve a treat for my awful accusation, don't you? Because you're the best boy ever!"

I don't know if it's the word or my overly excited, high-pitched voice, but his paws slide back and forth on the hardwood floor like he's winding up and then *boom*! Like a shot, he's off, running straight through my living room, past my bucket of chicks, and into my kitchen, no doubt coming to a halting stop next to the freezer where I've been storing his treats.

"A cute little genius."

"Of course he is," Tate says. "He learned everything he knows from me."

I almost make a joke about going to the bathroom outside, but stop myself. Barely.

"You both are pretty slobbery." I wink and turn my back on Tate to join Duke in the kitchen. I open the freezer and pull out the glass container filled to the brim with bone-shaped treats. "Now these are a new recipe, but I think you're really going to like them. They're peanut butter cookies, but instead of water, I used bone broth for added nutrients and flavor. On top is a coconut oil peanut butter drizzle, and they're nice and cold to cool you off from the awful Texas heat your dad subjects you to with his open windows."

I hold my hand down, and ever so gently, he takes the treat

from my hand like the little angel puppy he is. Then he chomps it down in a single bite.

"I think he likes it!"

Tate is leaning against the doorframe of my kitchen. His strong arms are folded in front of his solid chest, but the smile on his face is anything but hard. It's almost impossible to believe that the man standing in front of me is the same grumpy stranger people warned me about.

"He's a dog, Luna. Of course he likes it." His smirk reaches his onyx eyes. My knees wobble a little at the sight. "But I'm sure he likes them even more because you're the one who made them for him."

"That's sweet." I close the container so I can put the treats back in the freezer before Duke tricks me into giving him one—or five—more and cross the kitchen to Tate. "Are you laying on the charm extra thick because you know I spent yesterday getting day drunk with your sister and Millie and you're afraid they spilled all your secrets?"

"I'm always sweet and I don't have secrets," he lies through his straight, perfect teeth. He doesn't even flinch, and I don't know if I should be impressed or concerned. "And sorry for asking, but is day drunk different than night drunk?"

I know he's trying to change the subject, and normally, I wouldn't take the bait. But since this particular subject includes me harnessing the power of margarita-fueled bravery to set in motion a plan that has a very high likelihood of exploding in my face, I allow it to slide.

"Absolutely. Night drunk is for dancing, kissing strangers, and making friends with girls in bathrooms." I don't know if I'm breaking girl code by filling him in on the intricacies of girls' nights out, but he avoids talking to the majority of people, so I figure our secret is safe with him. "Whereas day drinking is for gossiping with your friends, eating snacks, lounging around, and sharing your favorite TikToks."

He frowns and his eyebrows scrunch together. "But can't you do all the day drinking things at nighttime? Why does the time of day matter?"

Boys are so cute when they're confused.

"You can and it doesn't." I know it's pointless, but I try to explain anyway. "Time is a social construct, but vibes are a law of nature. The categories and the ability to do one or the other is not dependent on whether the sun is out or not."

"I still don't understand, but I'm going to take your word for it." He shakes his head, and the sound of his laugh washes over me as he pushes off the doorframe.

"Good choice," I say. "Some things aren't meant to be understood."

He moves closer to me, and his smile fades as his finger grazes the bridge of my nose. "You got sunburned."

I don't know if it's the gentleness of his touch or the quiet concern in his voice that does it, but I melt into him. "I know," I say. "I got a little lackadaisical after our third round of margaritas, but you should see Millie. She looked like a lobster. We tried to take her to the emergency room, but she wouldn't listen to us. Your sister ended up spending the night at Millie's to make sure she didn't blister to death overnight."

Growing up with an Irish mother and grandmother who never tanned a day in their entire lives, I've seen bad sunburns before, but nothing quite like Millie's as we finished the final touches of the chicken coop. Between the hangover

I know she had to have thanks to my superb mixologist skills and her scorched skin, I have a feeling she had to call in for backup at the Artist Alchemy today.

"I don't know what it's going to take for her to learn her lesson." Tate shakes his head and rolls his eyes, sounding more exasperated than compassionate for my pale friend. "This happens to Millie at least once a year."

I couldn't keep the shock out of my voice if I tried. "She's burned like this before?"

I only need the slightest bit of discomfort or inconvenience to never do something again. I threw up after going on an upside-down roller coaster when I was thirteen, and I haven't set foot on another one since. Don't even remind me of the time Gabby convinced me peppermint schnapps in my hot chocolate was a good idea. As delicious as it was in the moment, you couldn't pay me to touch the stuff after the hell I paid the next morning.

"Oh yeah." He nods his head, and his long dreads bounce around his face. "At least once a year, sometimes more. If I remember right, I'm pretty sure she ended up in the hospital from sun poisoning one year."

"I'm glad you told me. Now that I know, I won't allow it to happen again."

I make a mental note to stock up on sunscreen and to research the best dermatologists in and around Celestial.

"Many people have tried," he says. "But if I had to put my money on one person to succeed, it'd be you."

Other people don't have years of codependent experience trying to keep their mom sober. This is a cakewalk compared to that. I'll have sunscreen at the ready from now until eternity. Millie's skin is going to be so grateful.

"Thank you." I rest my hands on his chest and push onto my toes. "Your faith in me means the world."

I tilt my chin up and he meets me in the middle, touching his mouth to mine. Not that making out with him in the football stadium parking lot wasn't the epitome of my sports romance dreams coming true, but there's something about the casual ease of kissing Tate, standing barefoot in my kitchen while Duke pants at our feet, that makes my heart constrict. The pressure and awkwardness I carry with me, the insecurities that linger in the back of my mind, all disappear when I'm around him. His strong, steadfast presence grounds me in a way I've never experienced before.

It's amazing and terrifying. I'm afraid if I hold on too tight, I might push him away, but if I don't hold on tight enough, I risk letting him slip through my fingers.

"You're easy to believe in," he says, coming back in for another kiss and soothing my irrational fears. "Your house, on the other hand, has been harder to come around on."

"Your feelings and concerns are valid, but look how cute it is already!" I gesture around my kitchen. The pink cabinets came out better than I hoped, and the crystal knobs I attached are the crowning jewel. "It's going to be your greatest achievement yet when it's finished."

"If it's ever finished," he grumbles, the corners of his mouth fighting a grin. "This place is the song that never ends."

Today is finally the day we're bringing the new claw-foot tub into the bathroom and the renovation to a close. The guest bathroom I've been using is fine, but I can't wait to soak in the bathtub like I dreamt about when I bought this house.

The renovation probably would've been finished much faster if it weren't for the approximately million and one side quests that have popped up along the way. Not only did he fix my laundry room, there were also the minor electrical issues he fixed by rewiring the "fucking nightmare" Mr. Monroe jury-rigged. Then there were the stairs he insisted had to be addressed. Apparently, some of the noises I thought came with living in an old house were actually alarm bells. I tried to argue that it was fine; between football and his other clients around town, I didn't want to pile more onto his schedule. But then he said that if I didn't let him look at them, it would be me, not the bathtub, falling through the floor. And since falling through the floor is something I'd very much like to avoid, I decided to listen to his advice. Four steps had to be replaced.

And that's not including all the "fun" projects I roped him into whenever he was gearing up to head home for the day. He installed a new ceiling fan in my living room and a chandelier that looks like it's made out of vintage teacups above my kitchen table. Then there was the time he hung up the curtains Miss Margaret surprised me with and supervised while I swapped the old kitchen sink faucet for the fancy gold one I got for a steal on eBay. Thankfully, I learned my lesson when I flooded the bathroom and it went off without a hitch. He doesn't know it yet, but a massive order of wallpaper will be arriving next week, and he gets to be my assistant.

But no matter how much extra work I pile on him, other than our initial agreement, he always manages to avoid talking finances with me.

"You do know that eventually, you're going to have to let me pay you for everything you've done around this house."

"I don't know what you're talking about," he says. "You already paid."

"No I didn't," I remind him. "I paid for the supplies and materials when you first started, but you still haven't given me an invoice that includes labor costs or receipts for the things you've bought since."

"And I'm not going to," he says, and I can tell he's gearing up to launch an ironclad defense. "I've been doing this in my spare time, and even before I found out what a good kisser you are, you were my family's neighbor. I already get enough shit from them. I'd never hear the end of it if I charged you for this."

It's not that I'm dying to spend money, but he's being ridiculous.

"This is Celestial. Everyone considers everyone a neighbor. You couldn't make a living if this is how you handled all your clients."

"Maybe," he says. His dark eyes turn molten, and he flattens his hand against the curve of my back. "But you're not all my clients."

I exhale a shaky breath. "Then what am I?"

He stares down at me, and the intensity in his eyes stretches seconds into an eternity.

"What are you?" he asks, and his voice is thick with meaning I can't quite decipher as he pulls me closer to him. "You're the woman who came into town, sat at a bar, and without warning, upended my entire life with a single smile."

His words hit me so hard, I forget how to breathe.

I forget about my past, and the future ceases to exist. I forget all my fears and worries and reasons we shouldn't be. For one wondrous moment, I forget about everything except the man standing in front of me and how it feels to be wrapped in his arms with his mouth on mine.

And I get so lost in this moment, with my fingers tangled in his locs as I get drunk off his taste, my body shaking as need unfurls into the deepest parts of me, that I forget all about what I had planned until it's too late.

Much, much too late.

Chapter 22

"Hello?" a voice calls out from the living room, and the door slams shut. "I'm here."

Tate's head jerks back and his body tenses beneath my fingers. "Luna—"

"Did I forget to tell you?"

"Luna."

"I thought I told you." I try to play it cool even though I'm feeling so uncool, like flames are licking at my feet. "It's not a big deal. I just figured you might need help moving the bathtub upstairs."

You know how they say the road to hell is paved with good intentions? Well, ladies, gentlemen, theys, and thems, welcome to hell.

"Hey, you know you have chicks in your living room? Most people do that in the laundry room." Silas walks into the kitchen and the smile falls off his face the second his eyes land on his brother. "Tate."

Tate nods his chin. "Silas."

"Hi! Thank you so much for coming!" My voice is about five octaves too high, but it does nothing to detract from the irritation vibrating off the brothers. "I'm no help when it comes to physical labor, so I really appreciate it and so does Tate. Right, Tate?"

Is this overstepping of the most egregious form? Who's to say? But what else was I supposed to do? It felt like a crime to sit idly by while these *literal twin brothers* let their relationship continue to erode over what I really think is just a big miscommunication. The codependent fixer in me had to try something.

"I have it covered." Tate doesn't even attempt to play along. If there was a way to discreetly kick him, I would. "You can go back to the ranch. I'm sure Dad has something for you to do."

"Here we go." Silas's kind eyes go hard and his mouth is set in a firm line instead of the easy smile always gracing his handsome face. "Couldn't even say hi before you started, huh?"

Tate shrugs his broad shoulders. "I don't see the point in pretending, but then again, I've never been as good at the bullshit as you are."

Silas takes a step toward Tate. "You're such an—"

"Whoa there, big fellas." I slide in between them. My kitchen seems much too small and fragile for the three of us all of a sudden. I can practically feel the anger radiating off Tate behind me, and Silas doesn't seem much happier. "How about everyone take a deep breath and calm down for a second?"

I was really hopeful we could solve this problem with words, not fists, but maybe, just maybe, it wasn't the brightest idea in the world to invite these giant, feuding men into my house without anyone else to help break them up if—and more likely, when—they came to blows.

You live and you learn, I guess.

"I'm sorry, Luna." Embarrassment crosses Silas's face, and he deflates in front of me. "I shouldn't have come. I knew this was going to happen."

"Then why did you come?" Tate asks. "What was the point of this? Why do you insist on always doing shit you know you don't want to fucking do?"

Silas's jaw goes hard, and for a moment, I don't think he's going to answer.

"Someone has to do the shit nobody else wants to do," he finally says. "Not everyone can run off and forget about everyone else. Not everyone can ignore their responsibilities to chase every single selfish fucking whim that crosses their mind."

Thanks to Ciara filling me in on some of the history, I know they're not talking about my house anymore. Tate pulls me until my back is flush against his front and his fingertips dig into my hips, like touching me is the only thing keeping him from losing the final grip on his temper.

"You don't think it's selfish to blame all your problems on someone else?" Tate's voice cracks and my heart breaks. "That it isn't fucked up that you're happy to throw away all your other relationships instead of owning that you might've made the wrong decision, but it was still yours to make?"

"You act like I had a choice," Silas shoots back, his voice pure steel. "I made the only decision you left me with."

It's clear that both of these men are so deeply hurt by each other. Pain leaps off them with such ferocity that it almost knocks me to my knees. The love they have for each other is so loud. I can hear it fighting to break free, but it's been buried beneath too much anger for much too long.

When crafting this plan, it probably would've been a good idea to mind my own business and not do it at all. Then, after making the well-meaning but misguided decision to go through with it, I should've spent some time researching mediation techniques. I'm not at all qualified for this, but it's too late to turn back now.

"My mom died!" I yell out with no preamble or plan, and the energy in the room comes to a screeching halt. "That's why I moved here. She died and it was bad. It was bad before she died. She was . . ." I've avoided talking about this for so long that even when I need them, the words won't come. "Our relationship wasn't what I wanted it to be. It was toxic."

Tate and Silas both turn to face me. I can feel their eyes on me, but I can't bring myself to meet their gazes. I can't stomach seeing the looks of pity, or worse, disgust, staring back at me.

"You only have one mom, and she only had me. She sacrificed everything. It was my duty as her daughter to stand by her or else she'd be all alone." The well-meaning words I've heard so many times over the years come tumbling out, and my face burns with the shame I thought I'd learned to live with. "It didn't matter that the last three years were like living in hell. Nobody cared that I had to sit by, watching as her pale skin turned yellow and she disappeared with every passing day. Nobody cared that she had become such a stranger to me that when she died, the first thing I felt wasn't sadness, it was relief."

I feel like I'm going to throw up. It's been months since she's been gone, but the guilt at vocalizing the secret I was prepared to keep forever is so strong, I nearly choke.

"Luna." Tate's whispered voice in my ear is like a comfort I don't deserve. "I'm so sorry."

I turn away from him, accidentally looking up and catching a glimpse of Silas's soft, concerned eyes watching me as if I'm about to break.

"No." I shake my head and try to infuse my voice with strength I don't quite feel. "I'm not telling you this because I want you to feel sorry for me."

"We don't—" Silas starts, but I cut him off.

If I don't get this out now, I never will.

"The only reason I'm telling you this is so that you know I'm not one of those people who thinks you have to forgive someone because they're family. I should have gone non-contact with my mom years ago, and I regret that I didn't every single day. If I had stepped away, maybe she would've stepped up and learned to take care of herself, or maybe she wouldn't have and things would've ended the same. Just like if my dad would've, he might still be alive. But either way, I wouldn't have had to watch. I wouldn't be sorting through so much anger and resentment that it keeps me up all night. Nobody deserves a place in your life if they don't respect you and your boundaries, and toxic is toxic whether you share genetics or not." My voice is shaking, and I don't know how they're going to receive this, but I've come too far to stop now. I steel my spine with determination and meet their worried gazes head-on. "But that's not what I see here."

Tate's fingers flex into my hips, and he hisses out a sharp breath at the exact same time as Silas.

"It might be hard to tell, considering how we ended up here, but I know it's not my place to meddle. I'm new. I wasn't around to witness everything that happened between you two, but maybe that's why I seem to be the only person who sees how much you care about each other," I say, and when neither of them yell at me or run away, it's all the encouragement I need to keep going. "I'll never know the full scope of what happened between the two of you, but Ciara did fill me in on some of it. You can both tell me to go to hell, although, actually? Please don't. I don't employ the dead mom card often, but I'm feeling very emotionally raw, and that might send me over the edge. You can yell at me later."

"We aren't going to yell at you, Luna," Silas says, and Tate nods his head in agreement.

I think it might be the first time I've ever seen them agree on anything. My plan might be working!

"Thank you," I say and get back on track. "I could be wrong, but I don't think you guys are mad at each other. I think you're mad at your dad, maybe even your mom, and as a person who's been forced to deal with very uncomfortable feelings about a parent, I think it's easier for you to take your anger out on each other instead of them."

My labored breathing cuts through the heavy silence hanging in the air as I wait for them to say something. Silas's eyes drift over my head, and I watch in adept fascination as a thousand thoughts cross his face and millions of unspoken words pass between him and Tate. It's like after years of being offline, their twin connection has finally found its signal.

"Fuck." Tate's hoarse voice is thick with emotion.

"Yeah." Silas nods. "That pretty much sums up my feelings too."

It's not an undying pledge of their love or a solemn vow to never be angry with each other ever again, but it's a start. I'll take it.

"Ciara's going to hold it over our heads for the next twenty years if we figure this out, isn't she?" Tate poses it as a question, but everyone in the room knows it's a fact.

The corners of Silas's mouth tip upward, and the knots I

didn't even know were in my stomach start to loosen. "She's going to be insufferable."

If I hadn't already pushed every limit known to mankind, I'd consider mentioning what Ciara told me about wanting to work Starlight Ridge, but I have, so I keep my mouth closed, and revel in my hard-earned victory instead.

"Listen," Tate says, and there's a weariness in his voice I haven't heard before. "I know we have a lot to talk about, but I want you to know that I'm sorry about the ranch, and I appreciate you for doing it."

That twin connection flickers again, and something passes between them that I'll never know.

"Thank you," Silas says. "When the time comes for us to talk to dad, you can pay me back by going first."

"Bet." Tate laughs and slaps Silas's hand before pulling him in for that bro hug all men seem programmed with. "I can do that."

"Well!" I clap my hands together, very pleased with not only the progress they've made, but myself. "Now that all that's out of the way, what do you think about the two of you using your big, strong muscles to carry my bathtub up the stairs?"

Silas rolls his shoulders and stretches his arms. "I was kind of hoping you forgot about that part."

"Why?" Tate asks. "Afraid your big brother is going to show you up?"

"You're two minutes older than me," Silas says, and the way he does it tells me this isn't the first time they've had this argument. "That hardly means you're *bigger* than me."

"Maybe," Tate says. "But these two inches I have on you do."

"Luna!" Silas turns and looks at me with what I think is

supposed to be a serious expression on his face. "Your boyfriend is being mean to me."

If the dirty looks I'm getting from more than a few women here tell me anything, it's that not everyone wants me to feel like a real Celestialian. I appreciate the gesture, though.

"Am not." There's a sparkle in Tate's onyx eyes when he looks at me. "Don't listen to him. I'm stating facts, and facts aren't mean."

"The brotherly ribbing is cute and all, but don't you both have something to do that's a little more important right now?" I try to sound annoyed, but it's a colossal failure. I'm too busy trying to ignore the giddy feeling rising from my toes after hearing Silas call me Tate's girlfriend and Tate not object.

"Sorry," they say at the same time, and then, when they finally get to work, they do it laughing.

I've learned enough about pipes and bathtubs to know it's best if I stay out of their way. The only thing I'll do is slow them down, and the faster they work, the faster I can get to soak in the bath salts I've been dying to use. But every so often, when my curiosity gets the best of me, I peek around the corner and catch a glimpse of Tate's smile as he works side by side with his brother. It's perfect.

Later that night, long after they're gone and my fingers have turned into prunes from soaking in the bathtub that is every bit as wonderful as I dreamt it would be, I can't help but think that maybe, despite my historically horrendous luck, I finally hit the lottery.

A man who's gorgeous and knows how to fix a pipe? The only thing that could make him any better is if he knows how to lay it. And if by some miracle my luck continues in this way, hopefully I'll discover he delivers on that promise too.

Chapter 23

When Tate told me he planned a surprise date night for me, I envisioned the most romantic night of my entire life complete with candles, champagne, and the whole nine yards. It might sound over-the-top, but to be fair, these are the expectations he set up for himself. What else was I supposed to think when, before I even thought we were friends, he brought me to his favorite spot to look at the stars and I fell asleep wrapped in his arms? He set the bar high, not me.

"This is getting out of hand," I yell over the live band who has moved on to the next song on their list of the men of country's greatest hits. "It's just disrespectful at this point. Not even a single Reba or Dolly song? Where have you taken me? This is sacrilegious."

I did not allow Millie and Ciara to force me into blister-inducing cowboy boots and denim shorts that make my thighs chafe for these mediocre-ass men to disrespect some of the most important voices in country music.

"You're not a real Celestialian until you've made it to the

Whiskey Rose," he shouts back. "If anyone was going to make it official with you, I wanted it to be me."

If the dirty looks I'm getting from more than a few women here tell me anything, it's that not everyone wants me to feel like a real Celestialian. I appreciate the gesture, though.

"I want to think that's sweet, but thanks to this set list, it kinda feels like a punishment." Not to mention the fact that despite the ceiling fans spinning overhead and the air-conditioning pouring through vents, my legs are sticking to the vinyl barstools and beads of sweat are dripping down the back of my neck. "If you hadn't already fixed my entire house for me, I might say you owe me."

When it comes to my experiences with nightlife, they are neither vast, nor endless. I've never been a big fan of clubs, and before tonight, I'd never set foot in a honky-tonk. But even though I have little to no expertise in this realm, the Whiskey Rose is exactly how I would've pictured it to be.

Multicolored Christmas lights hang from the ceiling, and an almost whimsical glow reflects from the sticky film coating every surface in the building. Neon beer signs hang on every wall, and mismatched chairs surround the beat-up tables sporadically placed all around the bar. The dance floor is packed with familiar and new faces line dancing their hearts away to the musical—and man-centric—stylings of the Dusty Cowboys, who, although they seem to hate women vocalists, are very talented with their respective instruments.

"Don't worry, they only play until ten," he reassures me. "As soon as they're off the stage, I'll be sure you get your fill of the Chicks, Shania, and Dolly."

"Don't forget Reba."

The corners of Tate's mouth tip upward, and even with the

live ruckus blaring through the speakers, I can still hear the gasps of Celestial residents all around us at the sight of his smile. I see it so often now, I forgot it's a rare sighting for everyone else.

"A single mom who works two jobs? I could never forget about her," he says, ignoring the curious eyes that have been staring at us all night. "I'm thinking 'Fancy.'"

And just like that, Tate gets even hotter.

I take a sip of the whiskey soda I resorted to when I realized they didn't have a drink menu or sparkling rosé, but it does nothing to quench the thirst I'm suddenly feeling. "'Fancy' is always a good choice."

"It is—"

"Tate Jacobs!" a high-pitched, slightly slurred voice shouts from somewhere in the packed bar. "Well, as I live and breathe. What have we done for Celestial's golden boy to grace us with his presence tonight?"

Ever since Tate's reunion with Silas, it's like the pressure valve has been released. Things aren't perfect (yet), and they aren't calling each other to hang out all the time (yet), but the tension in his shoulders has loosened. His smiles come and go much more often, and his little dimple has even made an appearance a time or two. It's like he's a new person. But the moment the tall blonde sidles up beside us, the old Tate falls back into place so fast, my neck hurts from the whiplash of it all.

"Kayleigh." His mouth is set in a straight line, and his eyes turn to stone when he says her name.

"Kayleigh? Really? I don't see you in ages and that's all you have to say to me?" She slaps his arm and leaves her bony hand resting on his bicep. "I know Mrs. Pam taught you better manners than that."

His mom? Touching him was already bad enough, and now she's talking about his mom? I don't think so. Protective, possibly jealous, instincts I can't remember ever feeling before rear their ugly heads and push me off my stool.

"Hi!" I knock her hand away and shoulder in between them until my back is flush against Tate's chest. "I'm Luna."

"The woman who bought the Monroe house." She eyes me up and down, and her bright pageant smile does nothing to detract from the disgust in her eyes. "I've heard so much about you."

"That's so funny," I say, but in the way where it's obvious that I don't find it funny at all. "You gotta love the Celestial Whisper Network, but I feel bad! I haven't heard anything about you. It's Katie, right?"

I'm not laughing, but if Tate's body shaking behind me is anything to go by, he is.

And she is not happy about it.

"It's Kayleigh, actually." She corrects me, the smile on her face faltering so quickly that if I blinked, I'd miss it.

"Oh my goodness." I wave around to the crowded bar, making sure my smile looks every bit as authentic as hers. "I'm so sorry, it's just so loud in here. It's impossible to hear."

"The Whiskey Rose is always like this," she says. "But we never see Tate here anymore, not like we did in the good old days at least. Right, Tate?"

I recognized her dirty game the second I clocked her rhinestone-encrusted hoop earrings and spiked stiletto heels on the dirty, uneven floors. But just because I don't like her game doesn't mean I'm above playing it . . . at least for a second or two.

"Tate used to come here a lot?" I ask her before aiming my

attention at a now grimacing Tate. "Does that mean you've been holding back your line dancing skills?"

After one particularly brutal experience line dancing in my third grade gym class, I never had a desire to do it again. But, if it means I get to piss off Kayleigh and watch Tate shake his cute butt in one fell swoop, then get me on that dance floor stat!

"I'm not holding anything back from you." Tate drops his hands to my hips and hooks a finger through the belt loop on my shorts. "I haven't danced since college."

Kayleigh's blue eyes laser focus on his hand at my hip.

"Don't let him trick you. He was so good at these dances." Kayleigh tries to play it cool, but her beet-red cheeks are impossible to miss even beneath the neon glow of the bar signs all around us. "And I would know since I'm the one who taught him."

"Really?" I know I shouldn't egg her on, but I can't stop myself. "You have to tell me more!"

Tate's fingers bite into my skin and a victorious twinkle sparkles in her eyes.

"I don't think—" Tate starts, but Kayleigh bulldozes right over him.

"He was the captain of the football team, and I was the captain of the Celestial Belles," she says, losing me as fast as she got me.

"The Celestial Belles?"

"*The* Celestial Belles," she repeats, bringing an affronted hand to her chest. "The national championship–winning Celestial Belles, led by the incomparable Liza Smart for three decades."

"Oh!" The name rings a bell from my first football game. "The fancy cheerleaders with the fringe and the hats!"

"We are not cheerleaders." Disdain drips from her tone, and she sounds much more offended now than when I called her Katie. "Belles are dancers."

"Sorry, we only had cheerleaders in Colorado. I'm still learning all the intricacies of Friday night lights," I apologize, even though I'm not sure why she's so upset. Cheerleading is a sport! And I would know. I binge-watched both seasons of *Cheer* and I know every word to *Bring It On*. "But dancers or cheerleaders, they were all amazing."

All the drama and ceremony happening around the game was more entertaining than the game itself, and both the cheerleaders and the dancers contributed to that.

Don't even get me started on the band.

"Oh well, I did hear you're a Northerner, so I guess that makes sense. But back to the story," she says, and at this point, I don't know if she's trying to be a bitch or if she's being sincere. "As the captain of the Belles, I was assigned to teach the captain of the football team a line dance to perform at the Celestival." She looks over my shoulder at Tate like he's the prize she's still working hard to win. "But I would've taught him anyway. We were high school sweethearts, right, Tate?"

No amount of music or chatter could hide the deep sigh that seems to come from the very base of Tate's soul. "We dated in high school, Kayleigh, not a minute after. We weren't high school sweethearts."

I get the feeling that he's had this exact conversation with her countless times in the past, and judging by the dismissive wave of her hand, he'll continue to have it many times in the future.

"Semantics." She winks and I fight back my ever-growing ick. "And who's to say things can't change in the future?"

"Me," he says without a hint of remorse. "I'm to say."

"All I'm saying is you can't predict the future." She tosses her long blond hair over her shoulder, and her smile doubles in size. "You have to remember how much fun we had together. And now that we're both back in Celestial, it could be nice to see where things stand between us."

As the person standing between them, I can tell her firsthand that things between them feel bad. Awkward and bad.

"We were kids. Of course we had fun, but we've been back in Celestial for years and nothing has happened." He pulls me closer and touches his soft lips to my cheek. "I'm seeing Luna now. I'm not interested in revisiting the past."

I knew Silas had said something in passing, but we haven't talked about the status of our relationship. As much as I try to tell myself he's just saying this to push Kayleigh away, I know Tate would never compromise my feelings to get to her. My heart practically leaps out of my chest, and hope I didn't know I would ever feel about a man races through my veins.

"Oh . . . you're . . . oh!" Her face crumbles as she stutters over her words. "I didn't know. I'm so sorry. Wow! Tate, in a relationship again. Who would've thought?"

His arms cage me in as the heat of his breath grazes the side of my face. "Not me, that's for sure."

"Well, congratulations," she says. "I know coming back home wasn't something you were thrilled about, but I'm glad it's working out in the end."

The challenge behind her eyes fades, and the bitchy luster of her perfect smile dims. She remembers to check her posture a second too late, and her shoulders fall under the weight of a crestfallen heart. The jealousy I felt only moments ago morphs into sympathy. She might be unpleasant, and this conversation has been nothing short of painful, but to have Tate, even for a second, and lose him? I can't help but feel sorry for her.

If that happened to me, I'd be mad fifteen years later too.

"It was nice meeting you," I say, and surprisingly, it's only a half lie. "Maybe I'll see you around sometime?"

"It's Celestial. I'm sure you will." Her smile wavers before she walks away, and she looks so much younger without the catty slant to her eyes.

"Was it just me," I begin once she's gone, "or was that incredibly awkward?"

"It wasn't just you." He turns me around so we're face-to-face and so close, our noses touch. "Now you can see why all my orders are to-go and I like to stay inside more often than not."

"I can imagine that it gets old fast."

"You'd imagine right," he says. "I was over it the first time it happened . . . twelve years ago. It doesn't matter how much time has passed; something like this always happens. Someone is always standing nearby, waiting to remind me of the past."

The band onstage takes a bow and says their farewell for the night. Sweat-covered cowboys and cowgirls pour into the bar area, eager to rehydrate with whiskey and beer after a busy night of line dancing just in time for Kacey Musgraves's crisp voice to fall out of the speakers.

I intertwine our fingers together, pulling Tate with me as I start walking backward. "If they're always watching, then the least we could do is give them a show."

I expect him to fight me on this and pull me back to the bar, but his onyx eyes warm and his hand tightens around mine as we walk onto the now-empty dance floor.

The hush that falls over the Whiskey Rose is deafening, and my skin burns with the heat of all the gazes glued to us. My cowboy boots clack against the hardwood floors as he pulls me closer and drops his arms around my waist. We sway together, his eyes never leaving mine, as Kacey makes him promise not to be too good to be true.

I've never loved being the center of attention, but wrapped in Tate's arms, everyone around us falls away and it's just me and Tate in the middle of the room. One song turns into another, and eventually, people stop staring and join in. Their quiet chatter blends with the country voices floating through the speakers, but my attention never leaves Tate.

His hand settles on the curve of my back like it was designed to be there. "I don't think I've danced like this since high school."

"I'm not sure I even did this in high school." I loved the idea of a coming-of-age romance moment as much as anyone, but reality never quite lived up to the hype for me.

Until now.

"Probably for the best," he says. "Kayleigh did teach me to dance, but she left out the part where I missed a count and almost broke her toe."

"Ouch." I shudder at the thought. I saw the pictures of Tate in high school in his parents' house—he was far from scrawny. "That does alter the story a little bit though."

Not that I blame her. A clunky teenage boy not paying attention and stepping on your toes isn't nearly as much fun as the romantic tale she tried to weave.

"That's how all the stories in Celestial feel. So close to the truth that you can't be sure what's real and what's not. At least this time she spun it in my favor."

He's hinted at the gossip in Celestial more than once, and I've been around long enough to hear whispers here and there. Before everything happened between us, I didn't want to pry and I definitely didn't want to push. But now? Now I feel safe enough to ask him the questions that have been skirting around my brain for the last few weeks.

I only hope he feels safe enough to answer.

"What happened?" I ask. "I know your family are basically the local celebrities around here, but there's something different about the way people look at you compared to Silas."

His muscles go taut and his jaw clenches, but his eyes go soft. It's as if his mind is at odds with his body, and I can see his brain working and feel his heart beating. I'm waiting to see which side wins as the beginning chords of the next song play and Garth Brooks's familiar voice drifts over the room in the way only his voice can, and all of a sudden, I forget what I asked and why I asked it in the first place.

The tricky thing about grief is, even in the best-case scenario—if there is such a thing—it's not a straight line. Some days are good, some are bad, and a lot of them are both. The line goes up and down and back up again until eventually, the lows aren't as low and highs are even higher. The problem for me isn't that the line has been too low or even that it's moved too slow; it's that there hasn't been a line at all.

My grief has been so elusive, so fleeting, I've spent months trying to capture the dark cloud hovering overhead. I've prayed for the skies to open and rain down the emotions that have evaded me for so long. Like if maybe the numbness began to wear off and I could feel anything at all, I might finally be able to move forward. Not just run away.

I've been waiting for the moment it would finally come. I

just didn't think the storm would roll in when I had blistered feet, a whiskey-clouded mind, and the full attention of a good man.

"Hey," he says, and the concern in that one little word is the only thing louder than the song forcing its way into my soul. "Are you alright?"

I nod my head and hold on to him tighter.

"I'm okay, I'm okay," I repeat, unsure who I'm trying to convince, myself or Tate. "I'll be okay. It's just . . ."

It's just that when you're used to feeling nothing, even a hint of emotion has the power to knock you off-balance, and right now, I've lost my equilibrium altogether.

His eyes narrow and he watches me closely. "Just what?"

"My mom." Those two words alone cause my chest to go tight. My head swims with every sharp, labored breath, and the tears that have long run dry nip at my sinuses. "She loved this song."

Realization crosses his face and chases away all thoughts of rumors and secrets. His hand leaves my back, and before I can even process what's happening, the humid night air is filling my lungs and noise from the honky-tonk is muffled behind us. I didn't finish the single drink I ordered, but it's like my feet aren't connected to my brain. After I stumble the second time, Tate takes over so that I'm in his arms and my offending feet are no longer on the ground. His pace doesn't slow, and his boots kick up the loose gravel of the packed parking lot until we reach his truck in the very last row.

He opens the door for me and makes quick work of setting me on the passenger seat. "Seat belt, baby," he whispers before touching his mouth to mine. "I'll have you home soon."

Maybe it's because he asked so nicely or maybe it's because

the lump in my throat hasn't fully dissipated yet, but for once, I forgo giving him a hard time and do what he asks.

I reach for my seat belt with shaky hands. "Thank you."

He leans in and tucks a stray curl behind my ear. "You never have to thank me for this," he says.

If there's anything I should thank him for, it is this, but he closes my door before I can tell him he's wrong.

Tate hurries to the driver's side and the engine rumbles to life beneath me as he throws the truck into gear. He pulls out of the parking lot, and songs that I hear, but don't listen to, play on the radio while Tate makes his way through the quiet streets.

I roll down the windows the moment Celestial fades away and the empty highway spreads out in front of us. The warm breeze dances against my skin and rustles my curls. Stars wink and the moon shines above us, nothing but the bright headlights cutting through the heavy, dark night. I close my eyes and push away the grief I'm not ready to feel, searching for the numbness to come back. And just as my heart rate slows and my breathing returns to normal, Tate's raspy voice turns my attention back to him.

"When we get back to your place, I want to tell you."

I sit up and look at him, but it's hard to tell what he's thinking under the glow of his dashboard. "Tell me what?"

"Everything," he says. "I want you to know everything."

Chapter 24

By the time Tate turns into my driveway and parks in his normal spot, my palms are slick with sweat. My heart hammers against my chest so violently I'm sure my rib cage is going to splinter. Every piece of calm I've collected over the years flew straight out the window, shattering across the empty highway, the moment he said he wanted to talk.

I know this is my fault. I have nobody to blame but myself. I'm the one who poked and prodded and asked all the questions, but now that he's ready to talk, I don't know if I'm prepared to listen.

Guessing what happened to him is one thing. Knowing is another.

I watch the clock and beg time to slow down. I plead with it to allow me extra time to live in the before, but it doesn't listen.

It never listens.

It just keeps on ticking, dragging me into the after no matter how much I kick and scream.

"Do you want anything to drink?" I walk to my kitchen and open the fridge. My voice sounds surprisingly steady. "I did a beverage restock in town this morning and they had that blackberry Dr Pepper you like."

He grabs a can off the shelf and cracks it open. "I need to stop drinking this stuff, but I can't say no."

I knew there'd be some cultural differences when I moved to Texas. I just had no idea one of them would be the Texas natives' love of Dr Pepper. The number of moms I saw at the morning football practices casually sipping cans of Diet Dr Pepper will never not be shocking to me. I've questioned Tate's love of the overly sweet pop more times than I can count, but it seems to be his only vice. He's obsessed with the stuff.

"You already know I don't get it." I ignore the wine I really want to uncork for whatever the conversation ahead has in store for me and reach for a grapefruit sparkling water instead. "But I guess if you have to pick one thing to be addicted to, flavored Dr Pepper is one of the better options."

"If you give it a chance, I know you'll like it." He tries to convince me . . . again. "The fifth graders take a trip to the Dr Pepper Museum every year. I'll ask around and see who we have to talk to so we can tag along. You're only one well-planned field trip away from understanding what all the hype is about."

I laugh and the bubbles from my sparkling water burn my nose.

"I think I'd need new taste buds to appreciate it like you do." I tell him the unfortunate truth. "I am curious about this museum though. I heard it's haunted."

I'm not sure if I believe in ghosts, but this makes sense to me. If there was one pop that might be flavored by evil spirits, it'd be Dr Pepper . . .

And maybe Mountain Dew.

"The only thing haunting this stuff is deliciousness. But if that's what it's going to take to get you to become a believer, I'll go with it."

"Well, the great news for you is that if the presentation is good, I can be convinced of most things pretty easily."

It's actually a problem.

I banned myself from watching documentaries unless I dedicate an equal, if not greater, amount of time researching the other side. Gabby stopped allowing me to go to group events without her after the third time she prevented me from joining Petunia Lemon, a multilevel marketing skin-care company that is now out of business on account of it being a scam. I think her biggest fear of me moving away wasn't that I'd forget about her, but that I'd return to her a few months later as a full-blown boss babe. Or a cult member.

Unfortunately, both were valid concerns.

"I'll be sure to keep that in mind." Tate sets the can on the counter and takes my hand in his, but when he smiles, I can't help but notice that it doesn't reach his eyes. "Come sit on the couch with me?"

As much as I'd love to stand in my kitchen, laughing about everything and nothing at all, pretending that I'm fine and he's fine, I know my time is up. All I can do now is look on the bright side and hope for the best. I might not know what his past entails or the secrets he's kept, but at least I'm still fairly certain he's not a serial killer.

"Yeah." I nod and follow behind him.

We sit down on the couch together like we have so many times in the past. I tuck my legs beneath me on my side, and he drapes the throw blanket I always snuggle under over my lap before he falls onto his side and stretches his long legs in front of him. It's a familiar scene, but my feelings are new and I hope they aren't written all over my face.

"I know I said I'd tell you about me, but I want to make sure you're okay first. I know you don't love to talk about your mom, and I don't want to push anything." He reaches across the couch and laces his fingers through mine. The warmth of his skin immediately sets my nerves at ease. "But if you ever need anything, I'm here."

My heart stutters in my chest, and I tighten my hold on his hand.

"I'm okay," I tell him, and I don't think it's a lie. "My mom used to love 'The Dance.' I hadn't heard that song in a long time, and it sparked some feelings I didn't expect."

And now that I've gotten a taste of the emotions I thought I wanted to feel, I'll gladly avoid them for the rest of forever, if possible.

"I don't want to brag, but I have been told by multiple people that I'm much better at listening than talking." He says it like a joke, but I have a feeling he's serious. "So as long as you're sure."

Am I sure that I don't want to talk about the way my mom used to play that song on repeat for a week at a time on her and my dad's anniversary, my dad's birthday, and the day he died every single year?

"Positive," I reassure him. "I've already trauma dumped on you once, and I wouldn't want you to think I'm selfish. Tonight is your time to shine."

It's not that I enjoy hearing other people's trauma—I wish everyone had lives filled with rainbows and sprinkles—I just don't want to think about mine.

"You're such a giver," he says, shifting uncomfortably on the couch. "Thanks so much."

"You don't have to do this. I don't ever want you to feel like you're obligated to tell me anything you don't want to share." I grab the remote off the table and put it on his lap. "That new thriller everyone has been talking about is streaming on Netflix. We could watch that instead."

Would I love it if he felt safe enough to confide in me? Of course, but I'd hate it if he felt like I was forcing him to discuss something he wasn't ready to. He can keep his secrets forever if he needs to. I just don't know how long I'd be willing to pursue something with him if he did.

No matter how hot, kind, and helpful he might be.

"No." He shakes his head, and his locs fall in front of his face. "It's not that. I want to tell you. I don't . . ." He looks at the ceiling like he might find the words he's looking for up there. "I don't know where to start. Everyone has always told their own version of my story. I'm not sure I've ever told it myself."

I'd joke about the Celestial gossip tree, but the hurt and insecurity that flashes in his eyes is anything but funny.

"It would be awful to have my entire community talking about me the way you've had to deal with." I inch across the couch until the fabric of his soft denim jeans is pressed against the bare skin of my thigh. "Start wherever you want. Nobody else's story matters. I only want to hear what you have to say . . . unless you're going to tell me you're married with kids. It would really suck to find out I was a mistress."

His full lips tip up at the corners and amusement dances in his dark eyes. "I'm not married and I don't have any kids."

"Look at that," I say. "The perfect start. What else do you want me to know about you?"

I wish I was more prepared for this conversation, but in what I'm sure will only come as a surprise to 0.0001 percent of the female population across the world—and likely the universe—this is the first time a man has ever offered me answers *and* honesty about his life. The entire situation feels so fragile. I'm afraid one wrong word or sudden movement could send him running back home.

Letting him lead the conversation feels like the safest bet.

His foot taps relentlessly on my rug-covered floors, and his hand twitches in mine. "I know you did your little mastermind thing to get me and Silas talking again, but did you ever hear what happened to pull us apart?"

I've tried to avoid it, but it's impossible to live here and not hear rumblings about the Jacobs brothers.

"A little bit, but not much. The only person who really talked about you two in front of me was Ciara, and she was more venting than gossiping. I would've told her to stop, but since she's your sister and my friend," I say, though the latter is said more out of hope than fact, "I had to let her talk."

Girl code is the most serious code of them all. I really like Tate, but I will never put my good standing as a top-tier girl's girl in jeopardy over a boy . . . no matter how hot and grumpy and secretly sweet and caring he is.

"That's good," he says. "At least Ciara knows the real story. It's everyone else who walks around making things up and then repeating it like it's fact that gets to me." He pauses and his jaw tightens. "Someone said I moved back because I was in trouble with the law and Celestial has the only police department that would look the other way. I think it was added to my Wikipedia page."

"I know it's the least pertinent bit of information out of everything you said, and I'm so sorry for asking, but did you just say that you have a Wikipedia page?"

He eyes me suspiciously. "You didn't know that?"

I shake my head. "Millie told me not to google you, and she might be tiny, but she's scary." God forbid she found out I ignored her. She owns a craft store. Crossing her could mean waking up to a glittered deer head in bed. "Although, now that I'm getting my information from the source, I might be able to peruse the inter-webs for tidbits about you at my leisure."

"Yeah," he says. "Maybe don't do that."

"I'll consider it, but you have to tell me the goods if you want me to make any promises." I regret the joke the instant it leaves my mouth. "Kidding! I'm kidding!" I repeat a little louder the second time. "That was a joke. A really bad joke, but a joke nonetheless. I won't google you."

I am curious about what pictures I'd find, but if I ever get that desperate, I'll just hop the fence and ask his mom to pull out some photo albums.

"It's okay, I was messing with you," he says. "You can look me up. Some of the stuff on there isn't great, but I don't really mind that. It's the stuff that people say around town that bothers me the most."

"Really?" I feel like I would care more about what the entire world could see over what a few people in a small town might say about me. "Like what?"

"God. So many things." He scrubs a hand over his face. "I

can't even tell you how many stories are out there about what happened between me and Silas. I heard that I stole his girlfriend and that he was the one who tanked my football career out of revenge. One of my old players told me he heard I burned down the stables on the ranch because my dad banned me from riding. That's total bullshit for a ton of reasons, the main one being I quit riding as soon as I got to high school."

"Hold on, hold on, hold on." I grab his arm and cut him off again. "What do you mean when you say you quit riding? Does that mean you used to ride?"

"Luna, focus," he says through a throaty chuckle, and the couch vibrates with laughter. "We're going to be here all night if you keep asking about all the unimportant details."

First of all, does he think I'll complain if he's here all night? Secondly, 'unimportant'?

Is he insane?

I just found out the hot handyman / football coach might actually be a hot handyman / football coach / cowboy! This is the most important detail of all!

"Yeah, yeah. Sure, whatever. I promise I'll get back on track in just a moment." I brush him off, needing this information more than my next breath. "But first, I'm going to need you to explain to me, in great detail, what you riding used to entail."

"You know you're ridiculous, right?" he asks, but I don't deem that question worthy of an answer. I stare at him, not blinking once—my obscure party trick—until he breaks. "Fine!" He throws his hands in the air. "Silas and I did barrel racing and tie-down roping until middle school. Happy?"

"I have no idea what any of those words mean, but I still

love hearing them." My insides tingle and my imagination goes wild. "Why'd you quit?"

He shrugs. "I liked riding on the ranch, but rodeo wasn't really my thing. Dad insisted we all try—you know, family legacy and all that. I bided my time until I could quit and play football. Silas was better than me and stuck with it a little longer, but Ciara was honestly the best."

"Duh. Obviously, she was the best." I remember Ciara telling me how overlooked she felt at home, and my heart breaks knowing that she not only wanted to work the ranch, but had the skills to do it too. Part of me wants to mention it to Tate, but I decide to keep my mouth shut . . . for now at least. "Boys drool and girls rule and all that jazz."

"Silly me, how could I forget?" He rolls his eyes, and it looks so out of place on his stoic face that I have to fight back the laughter bubbling up in my chest. "Do you have any more rodeo questions?"

Only a million.

"One more and a request."

"What's the request?"

"It's not much." At least not compared to the many requests he's attended to inside my house. "Next time you come over here, could you take me for a ride around Starlight Ridge? I'd love to see you ride and to have you show me the rest of your favorite places while I'm on the back of your horse."

"I'd love that." His face goes soft, and I feel the look between my legs. "What's your other question?"

"You said you quit riding in high school, but that you quit rodeo in middle school." I repeat his words back to him. "They were different?"

His flinch is almost imperceptible.

Almost.

"Dad knew rodeo wasn't for me, and Mom hated every second we were out there. If he gave us a hard time about that, he would've had a lot more to answer for than he was willing. Riding though . . ." He pauses and chews over his next words. "He never thought I'd stop riding. It was expected. Not optional."

"But you made it optional?"

"You know I played football, right?"

"Yeah," I say. "Tate Jacobs was the best quarterback in Celestial. That's one thing about you that seems to be pretty indisputable across the board."

"It wasn't only Celestial," he says, and my ears perk up even more. "I was the top-ranked quarterback in the country."

"In the country? Like the entirety of the United States of America?"

"Probably in other countries too," he says, modesty taking a back seat to confidence. "But they weren't scouting other places, so I can't be sure."

Well, damn.

I knew he was good from the way everyone fawns over him when he touches the football field and from Millie's slip about him being NFL-worthy. But I thought she was trying to hype him up to seem even more impressive to me than he already was . . . not that he needed any help with that.

"No wonder everyone is so happy that you're back to coach." I state the obvious, still unsure how it's connected to him riding at home. "But what does that have to do with riding?"

"College coaches started reaching out to me before I started high school. By the time I was a junior, I had something like thirty college offers. Coaches were tripping over themselves to get me to commit to their school." He says this without pride or boasting, just as fact. "They were bending over backward to give me whatever I wanted, but there was one thing they all agreed on. If I wanted an offer, I had to promise to stop riding. It was too risky to have their incoming QB1 on the back of a horse."

"So you had to choose between football and the ranch?" I ask as pieces of this convoluted puzzle start to fall into place.

"Football is everything in Texas, but for my dad, Starlight is," he says. "He didn't think I'd choose anything over the ranch and was inconsolable when I did. Didn't talk to me for a month and held a grudge for longer. Mom had to threaten him before he would come to my signing ceremony."

I remember the picture hanging on the hallway wall of his parents' house and how strange I thought it was that his dad looked so unhappy next to his smiling family.

"I'm so sorry, Tate." I squeeze his hand in mine. "That really sucks."

"It does," he says. "I thought he'd get over it once I got to college. I mean, most of my teammates' parents would've died to give their kids what I had. A full ride to one of the top universities doing what I love? Why would he be mad? But he was. He was pissed I'd put my own wants above the family legacy, and he was going to do what he could to punish me for it."

"Punish you? What do you mean?"

I'm having a hard time understanding. My mom made too many bad decisions for me to ever judge anyone else's parents, but as bad as it got with my mom in the end, I can't imagine a world where she would've punished me for going to college.

"Back when I was in college, it wasn't like it is now. There were no NIL deals. Name, image, and likeness wasn't a thing. You couldn't get paid for playing college sports, and you were so busy with your football schedule that it was impossible to have a job outside of school. He used that against me," he says. "He cut me off and told me if I didn't want to ride or work at the ranch, I couldn't expect to benefit from it.

"My dad's a good man, but he's also a stubborn asshole, and for better or worse, the apple didn't fall far from the tree. If he didn't want to support me, I didn't want his support either." He turns his head away, but I can still see the lines of regret on his handsome profile. "My mom tried to mediate things between us. She'd send me checks. I'd send them back. He'd leave the room when she called, and I'd only call when I knew he'd be gone. I loved him and Starlight Ridge, but I was going to show him that I didn't need them. I was going to prove that I would be fine on my own. And for a while, I was."

I'm the kind of person that fast-forwards to the end of a show if there's even a hint of suspense. I won't watch or read anything with a cliff-hanger until the sequel is released. I hate being stressed in fictional situations, and I hate it even more as Tate talks. My stomach turns knowing he's still at odds with his dad.

"I don't like this." I shrink into the couch. "I want it all to work out and I hate that I know it hasn't."

"It's not a pretty story," he says. "Things were already bad. Then my dad got hurt and it got worse. He wanted me to come back, take over Starlight. He said football was a game, the ranch was life. It was legacy. It was fucking stupid.

"I was a freshman and I was already starting and setting records. All the things I'd dreamt about were coming true, and my dad, of all people, was the person trying to ruin it."

Hurt twists across his handsome face like this happened yesterday and not almost fifteen years ago. "Looking back, all I had to do was keep my head down and focus on the end goal. Play ball like I always had and let the pieces fall into place. But I was young and stupid and had way too much fucking pride for my own good. I wanted to prove I didn't need him and that I was better off without him."

I go still and my lungs turn to ice. I don't know what comes next, but I know it's not good.

"These schools make millions off our names. They were selling jerseys with my name on the back and leveraging my name to bring in more donations while I was sitting there, trying to figure out if I could afford groceries. What I did might've been against the rules, but if you ask me, the rules were bullshit." It doesn't matter that this happened years ago; it still affects him today. Fire laces his words, and frustration colors his tone. "So when someone approached me with an opportunity, I didn't hesitate before saying yes."

"What was the opportunity?" I ask, but I don't need to know the answer to know whatever it was brought more strife than anything else.

"They gave me some things to sign. It started with some jerseys and footballs for a few hundred dollars," he says, and it sounds innocent enough. "The more they sent, the more I signed, the more I made. Then, the bigger my name became, the more they wanted. It wasn't long until they were flying me out during the offseason, putting me in hotel suites, and paying me more money than I could've imagined at twenty. And all I had to do was sign autographs and shake some hands."

Call me an idiot, but I don't see the problem here. If schools can make so much money off their athletes, then shouldn't they be able to profit from their work as well? "That wasn't allowed?"

He shakes his head. "Not even a little bit."

"That's bullshit."

"It was," he says. "And what sucked even more was that an agent who was interested in representing me fed into it. He loaned me a car after I gave mine back to my dad and would fly Silas and Ciara to all my away games. He gave me all sorts of things I never asked for, but was too young and naive to refuse, and then, the moment I decided to go with another agent, he reported me to the NCAA and tanked my entire career. I lost my scholarship, we had our wins and championship titles revoked, and even though I was slated to go in the first round of the draft, I ended up not going at all."

I try to swallow down my horrified gasp, but I fail miserably. I feel like I want to throw up, cry, and punch something all at the same time.

"Holy shit," I whisper, unable to come up with anything even slightly eloquent to say. "That's so fucked-up, Tate."

If I ever find that agent, I'll . . . Well, I don't know what I'll do yet, but I do know I'll spend every night of the foreseeable future plotting my revenge.

"It was a long time ago." He echoes the same adage I use whenever I talk about my dad. "It was horrible when it happened, and then when I came home, it was worse. My dad still wasn't speaking to me, and I was this town screwup who everyone thought threw away their family for fame. Then, as the icing on the shit cake, a rumor started going around that Silas was the one who turned me in. I knew it wasn't true, but it doesn't mean that didn't add to the already fucked-up dynamics we had."

I think about how bad things got between me and my mom. The thought of people knowing and then making up stories to add to it is almost too much to bear.

"You didn't deserve that. Neither of you did."

"Silas didn't," he says. "Still not sure about me."

Silas and Tate are such good men, and my time in Celestial wouldn't be the same without them. I hate that they lost so many years together. I hate even more that Tate has been walking around with this cloud of shame hanging over him.

"No, do not do that." I turn to face him fully. "That rule was stupid, and even if it wasn't, nothing you did was worth a lifetime of punishment. You were a kid who did something you came to regret? So have ninety-nine percent of people. Big freaking whoop."

He tries to look away, but I'm done with it.

I'm done with us hiding from each other. I'm done pretending I don't want Tate to know me inside and out. I'm done pretending I haven't thought about his mouth on mine every single moment since the first time he kissed me. I'm done pretending I don't dream about his hands on me and what it would feel like to explore every square inch of Tate Jacobs and have him do the same to me.

"Look at me." I pull my hand from his and climb onto his lap. "We all make mistakes, and do you know what?"

I take his face in my hands and stare into his eyes that hold more mystery and magic than the night skies above.

"What?" His voice is quiet, timid even. The softness at direct odds with the growing hardness beneath me.

"Knowing you're not completely perfect only makes me like you more."

His mouth tips up in the corner, smugness somehow making him even hotter as his hands find my hips. "You like me?"

My mouth draws closer to his as I whisper, "A little bit."

"Interesting," he says. "Because I like you a lot."

I shift my hips over him, and my breathing turns into a moan.

"Oh, thank god. I feel the exact same way." I graze my lips against his. "What do you think about moving this party to my room?"

"I couldn't think of anything better."

And then, before I even know what's happening, I'm in Tate's arms and my house flies by in a blur as he runs through my living room and up the stairs. He kicks in my door with so much force, I think he might have to add replacing it to his to-do list . . .

Right after me.

Chapter 25

Tate throws me on my bed, and my comforter feels like a cloud. His hands feel like heaven.

"Do you know what it was like to work in your bathroom, staring out into your bedroom?" He climbs over me, his strong arms caging me beneath him. "What it's been like to walk past your bed and imagine you in it, day in and day out for the last month?"

"Tell me," I whisper, my voice hoarse with need.

My fingers itch to touch him, and for once, I don't stop myself. I've been craving this man's touch since the moment I laid eyes on him, and I don't think I can wait a moment longer. I push my hands underneath his shirt, and he hisses out a breath of air as they glide across his abs. His smooth skin is like silk beneath my touch, and I wonder if he's that soft everywhere.

"Torture." He drops his mouth down and nips at the shell of my ear, soothing the sting with his tongue before he whispers, "I drive home picturing you wearing those fucking dresses and the way they cling to your body. How soft your skin looks when it glistens in the sun. Every night I fall asleep thinking about what it would feel like to wrap your long curls around my fingers. I dream about pulling you to me and not letting go until you come apart beneath me."

Shivers run down my spine as flames burn hot in my stomach.

"Is that so?" I drag my fingernails down his back and pull him toward me, pushing my hips into his. I nearly unravel when I feel his arousal between my legs. "Then what are you waiting for?"

"Well then," he says. His hand moves to the back of my head, and his long fingers twist my curls until I can feel the gentle ache between my thighs. "Don't mind if I do."

Moonlight pours in through my open window beside my bed and bathes Tate in the faint silver glow. From this close, I can see the moment his restraint snaps and the man he's been hiding from the world steps out of the shadows. His jaw sets with determination and his grin turns devilish. The need I feel reflected in his liquid black eyes is the last thing I see before his mouth is on mine.

His soft lips claim mine, gentle, yet demanding as our tongues twist together. He swallows my groans as I drink him in, getting drunk off his taste. I kiss him like I've never been kissed before, biting his full lips while I claw at his back, but it's not enough.

I don't know if it could ever be enough with him.

"Jesus, Luna." He pants against me. "You're everything I've dreamt about. Everything I never thought I'd find."

My mouth goes dry. My already racing heart combusts in

my chest and the pieces scatter in the night, rearranging themselves until my heart only beats for Tate.

"Tate, I—" I start but he cuts me off with a kiss. The lingering taste of the bourbon he had earlier melts into my mouth and mixes with lust, concocting the most intoxicating cocktail.

"Not yet," he whispers, and his gruff voice sends shock waves through my veins. "We'll talk later. Now is the time for play."

Even if I wanted to argue with him, I couldn't. Not when he steals my ability to speak with a single touch.

His grip tightens in my hair. He pulls my head back to expose my neck and doesn't wait a moment before dropping his mouth to the sensitive skin that has a direct dial to my nipples. My back arches as he bites down, nipping and sucking—marking me—until our heavy breathing is the only thing that can be heard in the quiet of this perfect Texas night. I thrust my hips toward his, needing the pressure of his groin against mine and too desperate to pretend to have decorum.

"Please." I claw at his back. "I need more."

My head is swimming and the room is spinning and I don't recognize my own voice. I'm not usually this forward, but I'm too desperate to feel him *everywhere* to pretend otherwise. Too overcome by wanton desire to let embarrassment deter me from the thing my body is crying out for.

His locs brush against my skin and I'm wound so tight that even that light touch is enough to send goose bumps racing up my arms. I don't remember the last time I was with another man, but even if I did, the point would be moot because nobody has ever made me feel the way Tate has.

"We'll get there." He peppers kisses down my neck and across my chest, leaving a trail of scorched skin in his wake. "I need to commit every second of this to my memory. The next time I fall asleep without you beside me, I want to remember the way you looked spread out beneath me. I want to see the way your curls are fanned out across the pillow." He lets go of my hair and grabs the hem of my shirt, pulling it over my head in one swift move. "I want to remember the way your flushed skin looks under the glow of the moon. I want to remember the sounds you make when you're too overwhelmed to talk. The sounds you make when I touch you here . . ." He slides down the cup of my bra and rolls my already hardened nipple between his fingers. I arch off the bed and into his hands, a needy whimper falling from my mouth as my breathing turns frantic. Chills dance across my skin and beads of sweat form behind my neck.

"Tate." His name is a plea, but I don't know for what. All I know is if he stops touching me, I might die. "Please."

"Shhhhh," he whispers. "I've got you."

I don't have a chance to process what he says before his mouth closes around my nipple and his hands drift down to unbutton my shorts. My eyes snap shut and my head pushes into the mattress. I squirm beneath his expert touch, needing more even though it's already too much.

His hot skin is a sharp contrast to the cool air-conditioning blowing down on us. His taste lingers and my mouth waters for more. My loud breathing is overwhelming yet sounds a million miles away at the same time. All my senses are on overload, but when his hands slip into the stiff denim shorts I somehow let Millie convince me were a good idea, time freezes and the entire world goes black.

"Fuck, Luna. You're so wet." His deep groan brings me back

to earth as his hand moves against the thin cotton separating him from where I need him the most. "This is all for me?"

It's a statement. A question . . .

A knowing.

I nod in the darkness, my words trapped behind the moans struggling to get out. Under his touch, I come apart like I've never done before. It's as if Tate—and only Tate—holds the key to my body and he's unlocked something inside of me I didn't know existed.

"I want to hear you say it." His hoarse whisper vibrates across my skin before his mouth lavishes my other breast. "I want to hear that you want me as much as I want you. That I'm not the only one fantasizing about getting lost inside you. I want to hear you say you're mine."

My heart beats so hard it bruises. The sound of my pulse radiates in my ears, drowning out the rest of the room as his words echo in my mind. *Say you're mine.* My nerves are set aflutter at the rightness of those words, at how much I want them— No. How much I need them to be true.

"I'm yours." The words are ripped from the back of my throat—the bottom of my soul—and they extinguish the final embers of Tate's self-control.

The loud rip of my underwear cuts through the room, and Tate's mouth replaces his hands between my legs. As competent as he is with his hands, they have nothing on his mouth. He leaves no part of me untouched, his tongue teasing at first, soft and gentle, his quiet hums of appreciation making my toes curl until he's had enough.

I can barely process what's happening as the first waves of my orgasm lap against the base of my spine. His mouth finds my clit and he latches on, sucking and nipping until I'm shaking. My hands fly into his hair, twisting his long locs around my fingers, unsure if I want to pull him closer or push him away.

It's too much. Too fast. Too hard.

Too good.

Pressure builds deep in my stomach. Electricity splinters into every ounce of my being until my skin is alight with sparks and only a single match could set the world on fire.

"Tate—" I cry out, but I don't get any further.

He thrusts two fingers deep inside of me, curling them to hit *the spot* and sucking my swollen clit into his mouth at the very same time.

I don't stand a chance.

I explode around him and the world disappears. The stars I gaze at every night appear behind my eyelids as wave after wave of pleasure slams into me. He continues to work me with reckless abandon and rips another orgasm from me the second the first one ends. A sharp cry claws from the back of my throat, and I hold on to him tighter, positive that I must be levitating.

Pinpricks cover my entire body when Tate's mouth finally disappears and I drift back down to earth. My lungs fill with fire as I try to draw in a breath. Sweat glistens across my naked skin.

"You're perfect. So fucking perfect," Tate says against my mouth, his lips still wet with my taste. "I could spend every day eating you, feeling you come around my fingers."

Nobody has ever talked to me like this, and I can't believe how much I like it. Wetness pools between my legs, and even though I'm still tender from my last two orgasms, I already want more. I feel empty, and there's only one thing that can fill me up.

"I need you inside of me." I twist at the fabric of the shirt he's still somehow wearing. "Now."

"Bossy." A cocky smile pulls at the corner of his competent mouth, but that's all he says before his shirt is on the floor next to a pile of my discarded clothes. "But I think I can do that for you."

He stands up at the side of the bed and his hard body is all I see as he pulls a foil wrapper out of his wallet. Strong hands, the whisper of which can still be felt deep inside of me, make quick work of his pants. He pulls them down with his underwear until he stands naked in front of me, like the portrait of a god. Brown skin still glistens in the dark of my room, the shadows only making the muscles all over his body even more evident. His abs flex above the deep V of his hips pointing to the most impressive cock I've ever seen standing long and thick between his powerful thighs. My legs squeeze together involuntarily, and my stomach knots with anticipation knowing that soon, I'll know every inch of this perfect man.

"You can't look at me like that," he says as he rolls the condom down to the base.

I force my eyes to meet his. "Look at you like what?"

He climbs back onto the bed and brings his mouth back to mine, kissing me gently despite the fire raging between us.

"Like you'll never be happy again until you feel every inch of me buried deep inside of you." He positions himself at my entrance. "Like you want me to live inside of you, making you come over and over again until the day I die."

I suck in a sharp inhale of breath and my body quivers as I wait for him to push into me.

He lowers himself until the tip of his cock rubs against my

clit. Everything is still so sensitive that even that is enough to have me jerking beneath him.

"Is that what you want?" he asks again.

I'm too aroused to contemplate my words, too needy to care about anything other than feeling Tate so deep inside of me that I forget where he ends and I begin.

"It's not what I want." I thrust my hips upward. "It's what I need."

Firm hands latch on to my hips, and he kisses me softly, a wicked glint in his eyes as he whispers, "Hold on."

I don't have time to follow directions.

He thrusts inside of me in one smooth motion, and I levitate off the bed. Colors explode behind my eyes and the world freezes. My moans turn into screams as he works me like a fucking fiddle. Moving inside of me with expert precision, deep and hard, slow and gentle, then back again. Building me up and letting me down until I can't think straight. All I can do is feel.

And I want to feel all of him.

"Please," I moan over our frantic breathing. "Harder."

He slows down.

"I didn't hear you." The subtle strain in his voice is the only indicator that he's just as close as I am. "How do you want it?"

"Harder, Tate." I claw at his thighs. "Faster. Harder."

"Why didn't you say so?"

He pulls out and flips me onto my stomach. Pulling me to my knees and wrapping my curls around his fist, he locks me exactly where he wants me before he slams back into me exactly how I need him.

The sound of our skin slapping together echoes throughout my room. Tendrils of another impossible orgasm begin to wind around my spine, anchoring me to Tate as he thrusts into me over and over again, never slowing or tiring.

“That’s it, Luna,” he groans out, sliding his hand from my hip to between my thighs and pinching my clit. “Come for me.”

I don’t have a choice but to obey. I thought the first two orgasms were incredible, but they were simply an appetizer to what he’s serving now. My insides clutch him tight as I ripple around him. I scream out, half cry, half moan, as white light explodes behind my eyes. The blinding orgasm rips the world from beneath me and catapults me straight to the heavens, and pleasure reverberates throughout every inch of my body. My limbs give out, and I collapse onto the mattress a moment before I register Tate’s weight pushing down on top of me, his breathing ragged from his own release. He traces my spine with kisses as we slowly drift back down to earth.

“Wow,” I say once I regain my ability to speak. “That was . . .”

Otherworldly? Life changing? The best sex I’ve ever had in my entire life?

“Yeah,” he says, wrapping his arms around me and pulling me to his side. “It was.”

He touches his lips to the top of my forehead and keeps them there as his breathing evens out. I lie awake beside him, waiting for the onslaught of thoughts that find me every night. But instead, wrapped in the comfort of Tate’s arms, sated and blissful, sleep pulls me under without a fight.

And the only thing to find me are dreams of Tate and an impossible future that all of a sudden is so close I can almost taste it.

Chapter 26

September passes by in a blink and somehow, October seems to be moving just as fast.

I guess that's what happens when you're having fun. It's amazing what good sex, a new bathtub, and no more triple-digit days can do for a person's overall happiness.

"Shut the fuck up!" Gabby chirps like the chicken she's holding. "I knew you said Celestial was great, but this place is freaking euphoric."

Her plane landed this afternoon, and it's been a marathon of giggles and gossip from the moment she leapt into my arms at the baggage carousel. I'm pretty sure onlookers thought she was my lover, and we were too enthralled in shrill laughter to correct them. Plus, if there's one person left on this planet who I've loved the longest, it is, without question, Gabrielle Jenea Owens. She might not be my lover, but she has my heart and that's enough.

"You can admit that you thought I was lying." I nudge her with my shoulder.

I could hear the worried disbelief in her voice every time we talked on the phone. I knew she thought I was overcompensating and trying to convince myself the rash move I made wasn't a mistake. But for once, she was wrong.

"Fine," she huffs, and even though I can't see her face, I know she's rolling her eyes. "But can you blame me? An idyllic farmhouse in a mysteriously inclusive small Texas town? Nobody would believe that shit."

She sets Leigh-hen Pinnock back on the ground and Gabby scurries off to be with Henda Martell and her Little Chix sisters who are pecking away at the frozen-fruit ice cubes I dropped in the water bowls around the chicken coop.

Dolly Parton and Kelly Cluckson have gone off on their own.

"I don't know how idyllic the house was when the bathtub fell through the ceiling." I remind her of my less-than-glamorous experiences over the last few months. "Or when I got locked out during the thunderstorm."

That was actually terrifying. I thought Colorado had numbed me to extreme weather, but flash floods have nothing on Texas thunderstorms. I damn near passed out when I saw the clouds begin to circle overhead. Thankfully, I had my library shed to hide out in, but it felt less than sturdy when the thunder caused the floor to shake and the strong winds rattled the windows. No matter how hard I tried to focus, I don't think I retained a single word I read that day. I did, however, find new books for Ciara and Millie. They'd been on my back for weeks to re-up their reading materials, so at least that was a win.

Needless to say, I now keep a key hidden beneath a painted rock leading to the chicken coop.

"The bathtub that yielded a hot handyman slash football

coach slash cowboy?" She's clearly up to date on his many titles. What kind of friend would I be if I left her in the cold about such important details? "I'm not sure that counts as anything other than a disastrous meet-cute."

"Heavy on the disaster." I loved that bathtub. I love my new one more, but still. It was very upsetting in the moment. "Plus, I had already met Tate, so I'm not sure it would technically be considered a meet-cute."

"I don't care what your romance books say. This is real life, and here, I make the rules, and I say it's a meet-cute. But now that you brought him up," she says, knowing damn well she's the one who mentioned him, "when am I going to get to meet the man of our dreams?"

My pulse kick-starts, and the giddy little butterflies that take flight every time I think of Tate wreak havoc on my stomach.

"The game starts at seven." I look down at my watch and calculate how long until I can feast my eyes on my favorite man all over again. We haven't spent a day apart since our night together, and it's still not enough. My house is too empty without him and too quiet without Duke. In a matter of months, they've imprinted themselves so deeply into my life that I can't imagine it without them. "We should probably head over in an hour though. Friday nights are the only time there's anything resembling traffic in Celestial. Tate said it might be even worse since it's the homecoming game and some of the streets are shut down for the carnival tomorrow."

"Is the hot cowboy brother going to be there?" she asks, horny mischief gleaming in her eyes. "I wouldn't mind a little vacation fling."

"Is it a fling when he's my next-door neighbor?" I ask. "I

barely made it out of the Jacobs brothers' mess unscathed. We can't push our luck. I'm going to need you to switch your target."

"Selfish." She pouts as I lock up the chicken coop behind us. "I didn't think you'd turn into a hot-guy gatekeeper."

Her hurtful, inaccurate words stop me in my tracks.

"Excuse me?" I spin around and point an unpolished nail in her face. "I would never gatekeep hotness from you and you know it. I'm the one who hooked you up with the owner of that brewery I liked, remember?" She went out with him three times before deciding that the way he chewed gum gave her the ick and blocked him. I couldn't go back to the brewery again without him glaring at me from behind the bar. "And don't forget about Jackson. He was hot and you kicked him to the curb after he told you he was a Chiefs fan."

"Fuck the Chiefs," she spits out with the fervor only a die-hard Broncos fan could. "He clearly had terrible taste. What would it do to my reputation if I was seen with him?"

She proves my point for me.

"I understand. You're too gorgeous, brilliant, and wonderful not to have the highest of standards. Silas is an A-plus guy, but he's still stuck on his ex, and neither of us wants that for you. Not even for a vacation fling," I say before Dante, one of Tate's equally hot, but less complicated coaches pops into my mind. "There are some single coaches who will lose their minds when they see you. We can scout the bench when we get to the game."

She narrows a perfectly lined eye at me. "Are they also cowboys?"

"Probably." I shrug. "There's a rodeo at the festival tomorrow. We can cross-reference who rides while we're there."

She considers this for a second before giving in and extending her manicured hand. "Deal."

We shake three times, kiss our thumbs, and smash them together like we have since middle school.

"Good, now that that's settled, we have more pressing matters to discuss." I hold open the back door for her, and we kick off our shoes as soon as we step inside. "Do you want to pregame for old times' sake? Ciara said she'd drive as long as you told her three mildly embarrassing childhood stories about me."

Considering I have about 4,972 horribly mortifying stories she could've asked for, this was an easy yes. I would've told her anyway if she just asked. This honestly worked out in my favor because I was able to negotiate the caveat that in return for my friend's compliance, Ciara must agree to share at least one, but preferably two, adorable tales of the Jacobs children's time in the rodeo circuit. Pictures were encouraged.

Tate rolled his eyes when he heard about our deal and not because he's tight-lipped about how adorable he looked in his cowboy hat, but because since our night together, he answers any question I have. He's told me multiple stories about the time his horse almost stepped on him or when Silas got his second concussion in a month. It's just that when Tate relays his time as a junior cowboy, he states facts. When Ciara tells us, she waxes poetic. He's a great coach, but when it comes to his storytelling abilities, he lacks the same lyrical nuance his sister was just born with.

"We're spending our night surrounded by teenagers. Of course I want to pregame." She takes a seat on the kitchen stool she helped me pick out. "I am really excited to see a high school football game in Texas though. The Coach Taylor fan in me has been freaking out all week."

I pull out the pitcher of pineapple margaritas I made under Millie's close supervision. Apparently, the only beverage that Texans are as serious about as Dr Pepper are margaritas, which is something I can actually get behind.

"You're going to love it." I grab a glass from my pink cabinets that bring me as much joy now as the day I painted them. "It's a whole production. Nothing like our games growing up."

Nobody does Friday night lights like Texas. I can't believe I went my entire high school experience without extravagant band performances for halftime, inflatable tunnels, and multiple sets of cheerleaders.

"I'm sure." She takes the glass from my hand, and her eyes damn near roll to the back of her head after she takes her first sip. "Holy shit!"

"I know." I try to muster up a kernel of decorum and not gulp mine down. "Fresh-squeezed pineapple juice and limes. Life changer."

"You know what else is a life changer?" She leans forward and her smile softens. It's a familiar look, and my eyes mist over before she can tell me. "You taking your happiness into your own hands. I know I thought this was crazy and impulsive, but you were right. I miss you like hell in Denver, and that will never change, but I'm so proud of you for fighting for yourself when it would've been just as easy to fold."

This is why I decided to wait until the very last minute to put on makeup. I'm a dry well of emotions unless it comes to her. She knows the precise way to knock me in my feels.

"You know how much I love hearing you say I'm right," I say once I've blinked my tears away without letting a single one fall. "But to be fair, now that I've been here for a while and I don't see my home renovations coming to an end anytime soon, I have to agree that packing up and moving to a house sight unseen was not my most level-headed decision."

"Level-headed? Maybe not," she says. "But go big or go home, you know?"

I do.

Because as I look around my house that's already crammed with memories I've made with new—and now old—friends, I realize that when I moved to Celestial I might've gone big, but I also found home.

At least I hope so.

Chapter 27

Holy shit!" Gabby cries over the excited crowd. "I know you said he was hot, but I didn't think he was obscene! It almost hurts to look at him. And his dog in the football jersey? I can't."

I follow her line of sight down to the sideline and feast my eyes on Tate. He's huddled up with the quarterback, and Duke is sitting at his heels, all his little puppy rolls hidden beneath the jersey I made him. The offense is about to take the field again after the defense forced the opposing team to another three and out—a term that, as the coach's girlfriend, I now know. The game is almost over and we're up by thirty-five, but by the serious expressions on Tate's and Brandon's faces, they aren't going to lose focus until the game is over and they've secured the end goal.

Securing the end goal—I've learned, thanks to many late nights, early mornings, and bouts of afternoon delight—is something Tate takes very seriously.

"I told you so," I say over the squishy feeling in my stomach. "I'm pretty sure he's the hottest guy I've ever met."

And somehow, he's all mine.

Ciara groans beside us. "Please stop calling my brother hot."

"Why?" Gabby asks. "You're related to him, so by calling him hot, we're also saying it about you. If your brothers are ever complimented, you're allowed to take ownership of it. If it's an insult, though, then clearly you're your own person and shared genetic links don't mean much anyways. It's sibling math."

As an only child, I cannot relate, but I can absolutely agree.

"Sounds right to me." I cosign Gabby's logic and so does Millie.

"Thank you," Millie says. "I've been trying to explain this to Ciara for years. Maybe you'll get it to sink into her gorgeous, thick skull."

"A thick skull is something else she has in common with Tate," Silas chimes in from his seat behind us. "Which, unlike being undeniably good-looking, is a trait I don't share with either one of those two knuckleheads."

Of course sweet, wholesome, undeniably good-looking Silas Jacobs would only be able to come up with the term *knuckleheads* when insulting his siblings.

Things between Silas and Tate have been coming along slowly but surely. Silas has started riding Glory over to my fence line more often when he knows Tate is over. Sometimes he'll even come in for lunch. Tonight is the first football game he's come to in years, and according to Millie, it's been the talk of the town.

Things with their dad, on the other hand, are still the same, but I'm hoping that changes soon too.

"What?" Gabby whirls around on the cowboy boots she bought for her trip. "Who says that anymore?"

"Silas is a nerd. Ignore him." Ciara brushes him off. "What we really need to focus on is our plan for the Celestival. Mom asked me to judge the pie competition, and you already know I'm not getting on a single ride that arrived via U-Haul, but other than that, I'm open."

"Luna said there'd be a rodeo," Gabby says. "As a Celestial tourist, watching a man in a cowboy hat and Levi's ride a horse and/or a bull is imperative to my overall health and happiness."

"I'm so glad your flair for the dramatics has faded since I left." I laugh. "I want to go to the rodeo, too, and I really want to check out the award-winning produce."

I've been planning my future garden since I moved in. My history with plants is less than optimal, and I think seeing gigantic strawberries and zucchini would be really inspirational.

Ciara opens up the notes app in her phone and starts writing them down. "So pies, rodeos, and ribbon ceremonies. That's a good start."

"I can't believe the person taking notes on the Celestival called me a nerd," Silas teases as the other team calls their final time-out.

"You're a nerd. I'm organized," Ciara doubles down. "There's a clear difference."

She's not wrong, and I, for one, appreciate her attention to detail.

Thanks to the easy, breezy way of living in Celestial, other than football games, I haven't had to navigate a crowd in months. I get overwhelmed very easily, and knowing we have a game plan for the day has set the nerves I didn't even know I had at ease.

"Speaking of nerds," Millie pipes in, "I finished the books you gave me. I've loved my time in romantasy, but I think I'm feeling romantic suspense for my next order. Maybe a couple of rom-coms thrown in there if you have any."

"If I have any? How dare you." She can question a lot of things in my life, but my book collection isn't one of them. "Give me a few days and I'll have a new stack ready for next week."

"You're the best! I have Tuesday off. I'll swap my books out then," Millie says. "If they didn't already have a new tenant lined up for the building next to the Artist Alchemy, I'd tell you to open a bookstore. Celestial needs your services!"

I loved my job at the Book Nook, and even though my little shed doesn't have the same inventory of a bookstore, I've had so much fun turning my new friends into romance lovers. Opening my own shop would be a dream, but it's probably better that I focus on my house before I bring even more chaos into my life.

"Maybe one day," I say as the game clock winds down to zero.

Everyone still in the stadium rises to their feet as the boys line up to shake hands. This was an expected win, but excitement still buzzes like a live wire as they add another win to their undefeated record. Tate has been trying to play it cool, but whenever the subject of the team comes up, he can't hide the pride that lights up his face.

"Oh my god." Gabby claps her hands together and bounces on her boot-clad toes. "Does this mean it's finally time for me to meet Tate?"

Those latent butterflies take flight again, and the dreamy

smile that I've been wearing damn near nonstop the last month tugs at my mouth.

"It does," I say. "Just remember, the embarrassing stories were for Ciara and Millie only. If you tell Tate about the time I didn't realize Jell-O shots were alcoholic beverages and not a light snack, I will send you back to Denver expeditiously."

I was throwing up red for two days. My mom thought I was going to die until I told her about the copious amount of strawberry Jell-O I had the day before. Whoever decided to add alcohol to a classic childhood snack should get a serious talking-to.

She wipes her smile off her face and holds up three fingers. "Scout's honor."

"You weren't a Scout," I remind her. We joined Girl Scouts together and quit after a week.

"The intent is there all the same." She shrugs. "My lips are sealed until I pen my maid-of-honor speech for your wedding."

The thought of having a boyfriend was a foreign concept until recently. Marriage feels so far away and so massive that I could pass out just thinking about it.

And I almost do.

The stadium lights go blurry and my head swims. "My wedding? I haven't known him long enough to even think about that." I grab on to the metal railing splitting the bleacher stairs. "Let's add marriage to the list of banned topics for this weekend."

"Fine." She pouts while the rest of our group snickers. "But only because I've missed you."

"Thank you," I say, and my vision clears as my panic recedes. "If I would've realized that distance was the key to you going easy on me, I might've moved earlier."

"Please." She rolls her eyes. "I'm the only thing from back home that you miss."

I bump my shoulder against hers as we weave through the crowd of parents waiting for their athletes to come out. "Cocky," I say, but she tells no lies.

Colorado was the only home I'd ever known, and I was sure I would miss it when I left.

But I don't.

Of course there are small things, like the restaurant I used to get a breakfast burrito from every weekend and the Ruffly Rose, the adorable flower shop where I'd go to treat myself to fresh flowers once a month. But the big things? Like the way my heart beats slower and my breathing comes easier? I'm not sure there's a place on earth that could compete with Celestial.

Celestial feels like that old pair of jeans that you'll never throw away. It's soft, worn, fits like a glove, and the frayed bits add character that you couldn't find in any store. I can't believe I spent so much of my life not knowing I could feel so peaceful and happy. I hate the reason I moved here, and I wish more than anything that my time with my mom had a different ending, but I'm grateful that she gave me this gift and I hope more than anything that I don't ruin it.

"How was your first Texas Friday night lights experience?" Millie asks Gabby when we reach the locker room. "Did it live up to your expectations?"

"Highly surpassed," Gabby says. "I still can't believe this is the production you all have for high school games. I've been to colleges that weren't as impressive. Both on the field talent and off. I still need to find out where those other cheerleaders get their boots."

"They aren't cheerleaders!" Millie, Ciara, and I all shout in unison.

"The Belles are dancers, not cheerleaders," I correct, looking over my shoulder to make sure no dance moms heard Gabby. There are supervillains and horror movie monsters who aren't as scary as they are. I'd rather take my chances with Michael Myers over the Celestial Belles parents and enthusiasts.

Talk about chilling.

Confusion mars her gorgeous face, and her eyebrows knit together. "But they were both on the side of the field with pom-poms and cheering for the team. Does that not make them cheerleaders?"

"You would think so." Fear rings out in Millie's whispered voice. "But we don't make the rules, and don't let the name trick you: The Belles are willing to throw down anyplace, anytime."

"I called them cheerleaders with style my freshman year, and the next morning, the acre just inside the gate to Starlight Ridge was coated in instant mashed potatoes," Ciara says. "I spent an entire week putting up a makeshift fence so the cows didn't eat them. My dad almost pressed charges, but not even he's brave enough to go against Liza Smart and her horde of miniature terrorists."

"Are you being serious?" Gabby stares at us, slack-jawed. "You're messing with me."

"I joke about a lot of things," Millie says. "But the Belles are not one of them. You're leaving soon, so you might make it away unscathed. The rest of us are at their mercy."

The locker room door swings open and we all jump at the sudden movement.

"Fucking hell, Tate!" Ciara scolds like he could've known

we were all on edge. “Didn’t Mom teach you not to slam the door?”

“I didn’t mean to.” He looks confused as he takes in our looks of terror. “Are y’all okay?”

I don’t know about everyone else, but now that Tate’s here, I’ve never been better.

“Yeah”—I close the distance between us—“we were just telling Gabby about the Belles and how they are absolutely not cheerleaders.”

He shivers. “Oh god. Please don’t let Liza hear you say that.” His grip tightens on my hips. “The new booster club board won’t stop harassing me and demanding meetings that should be emails, and Mrs. Conklin reached out this afternoon about having new kitchen cabinets installed. I don’t have it in me to deal with Liza coming at me too.”

“Mrs. Conklin?” Millie repeats. “Didn’t she just redo her kitchen last year?”

“Yeah,” Tate says. “So you can see why having Liza strong-arm me into asking Joan to earmark money for new Belles uniforms is the last thing I need.”

Joan Wilson is the athletic director at Celestial High School. This, according to Tate, is a big deal because when it comes to most high schools in Texas, the athletic director is almost always the football coach. Taking the position would havc earned him an extra fifty to one hundred thousand dollars a year. He said two million dollars wouldn’t have been worth the stress of dealing with all the other coaches, countless parents, and district politics.

But even though he doesn’t hold the official title, football is still at the top of the athletic food chain. And Liza Smart, who has been working the system for thirty years, knows exactly who to go to when she needs a little extra power on her side.

"We're in the clear," Silas says. "I heard one of the moms say they were leaving as soon as the game ended to finish their float for the parade tomorrow."

"I never thought I'd say this, but thank god for the Belles' obsession with winning the best float," Tate says, and all the native Celestial residents share a laugh.

I don't love not being in on the jokes, but when it comes to the Belles, I'm happy to sit this one out.

"Now that we don't have to put you in hiding, I have someone for you to meet." I point to my best friend, who is staring at Tate with the open appreciation of a human with great taste. "Tate, this is my best friend, Gabby. Gabby, this is my . . . um, Tate. This is Tate."

I stumble over my words, realizing a little too late that even though Tate feels like my boyfriend, we haven't had that conversation yet.

"Nice to meet you, Luna's Tate," Gabby teases. "I've heard so much about you."

That's it. Back to Denver she goes. She's dead to me.

"Nice to finally meet you, Gabby." Tate extends his hand and drops his voice to a conspiratorial whisper. "You should know that My Luna has done nothing but sing your praises. I hope you like your room. She about killed herself putting up that wallpaper."

I wish this was hyperbole, but it's not. I fell off a ladder. It wasn't great, but thankfully the extremely tall, handsome handyman I'm sleeping with offered to take it over for me.

And by offered, I mean he has banned me from ladders until the end of time and I didn't argue.

"I'm obsessed," Gabby says. "I can't believe it's the same house she showed me in the pictures."

"None of us can," Ciara says beneath her breath, and Millie lands an elbow in her waist.

"Ha ha. Very funny. Let's all laugh at the girl who had an impeccable vision the rest of you couldn't muster up." I try to defend my rash and irresponsible actions, but I don't know why I bother. They all have a trump card that will always beat my excuses.

"I'm sorry." Gabby angles her body like she couldn't hear me. "Was the bathtub falling through the ceiling part of the vision we couldn't see, or are you talking about something different?"

And there it is.

"That was an added bonus," I say.

Gabby puts her hand on my forehead. "Are you feeling okay? How are extensive home renovations a bonus?"

"It's not obvious?" I point at Tate. "How else was I going to trick him into spending time with me?"

"Touché!" Gabby says, but I barely hear her before Tate pulls me into his side and touches his lips to mine.

Since our night at the Whiskey Rose, we haven't shied away from physical affection. Whenever he's around, we find ways to touch each other and sneak a kiss—or more—in. It's just that usually, we're alone in one of our houses or at the track after hours, not out in the crowded parking lot after a football game. I didn't take Tate as someone who'd be up for public displays of affection, but I'm into it.

"Trick me? You must've missed the part where I was gone the second I spotted you across that crowded bar in July." His black eyes go soft and his words flow like warm honey into my veins. "I might not have known who you were, but I knew you were mine."

Kissing me in front of our friends and a declaration of his feelings at the same damn time? I don't know how to process this. My hands fist around the loose fabric of his shirt, and the ability to speak escapes me, but it doesn't matter because he keeps talking.

"I'm still pissed Patricia let you buy that death trap, but selfishly, I'm glad you did," he says, his voice dropping to a whisper. "I thought my life was over when I moved back home. Now I have a future in front of me that I didn't even think was possible and a girlfriend by my side who makes me happier than I've ever been before. Even when she makes me wallpaper her bathroom ceiling."

"But the ceiling looks really cute." I choke out the words, refusing to cry no matter how much my previously defunct tear glands want me to. "And just to be sure I heard you right, you did say girlfriend, correct?"

Because if I misheard him, as the kids say, I will crash out.

"I did," he says, apprehension creeping into his tone. "If that's what you want. No pressure."

Confident Tate is hot. Competent football coach is hotter. But nervous, wants-to-be-my-boyfriend Tate is one hundred percent the hottest.

"Yeah." I nod my head and try to play it cool, but I'm pretty sure the smile about to split my face in two gives me away. "I think I'd be good with that."

"Girl!" Gabby punches me in the arm with too much force to be considered playful. "Now is not the time to be coy! You better tell this man you want him."

"You, hush!" I glare at my best friend (for now), too prideful to give her the satisfaction of rubbing my arm that is definitely bruising. "You're going to scare him away."

"If that house didn't scare him away, then there's no chance I will," Gabby says. "Plus, I'm a goddamn delight, and he might've just met me, but he knows it too. Right, Tate?"

It's more of a threat than a genuine question, but Tate, forever the good sport, plays along.

"Of course," he says, and his smile is brighter than I've ever seen it.

"Okay," Ciara cuts in, clearly sick of our bullshit. "This has been adorably disgusting, but Tate's coaches keep peeking out the door and are too scared of his grumpy ass to interrupt. Plus, if we don't get to the Whiskey Rose soon, they're going to be out of dollar shots."

"Dollar shots?" Gabby's ears perk up. "Why didn't you lead with that? Will there also be cowboys?"

"The night before the Starlight Stampede?" Ciara's laugh lacks any humor. "That's all that will be there."

"Alright then! Time to move it!" Gabby claps. "The first person to the car can get the super exclusive story about Luna after prom, and trust me, folks, it's a doozy."

Motherfu—

"After prom, huh?" Tate turns me to face him. "I think you're going to have to tell me about that one."

I roll up onto my tiptoes, incapable of standing this close to him for this long without kissing him. "Maybe in one to two business years if you're patient."

He smiles against my mouth. "I think I can wait that long."

"Alright, lovebird." Millie pulls my arm. "Say goodbye to your boyfriend so he can get back to work. You'll see him soon."

My boyfriend?

I think I can get used to that.

"Bye, boyfriend." I wave over my shoulder as Millie—who's deceptively strong for her size—drags me toward the car. "Call me when you're finished here."

"Later, girlfriend," he says back, and I swear I see a blush graze his cheeks. "Don't let Ciara and Silas get you into too much trouble."

"It's the other way around and you know it," Silas shouts back, and the poor guy really seems to be regretting his decision to tag along tonight.

But right now, he's the only one.

Surrounded by all my friends, my boyfriend standing behind me, I can't bring myself to regret a damn thing.

"Ciara wins!" Gabby shouts when the two of them reach the car. "Now let me tell you, the year was 2014 . . ."

Except maybe I regret letting Gabby spill my secrets.

Chapter 28

Tate couldn't make it to the Whiskey Rose.

He usually goes over game film the morning after a game, but thanks to the parade kicking off the Celestival, he had to stay late with the other coaches to go over film and other football things that I'm not privy to. I'm no Tami Taylor.

Yet.

I missed falling asleep next to him, but even though my bed is big, once Millie and Ciara decided the night called for a sleepover, there wasn't enough room for him anyways. Plus, it made it even better when he swung by in the morning with donuts, kolaches, and a gallon of iced coffee from the Donuterie. I know some women like it when men shower them with diamonds, but I'd choose carbs and caffeine every time.

It was the perfect fuel for the meticulously chaotic day Ciara had in store for us.

"Where are we going next?" I adjust my grip on the bags I've acquired during our shopping portion of the day. "I might have to make a pit stop at the car soon to drop these off."

I've heard about the Celestival since before I moved to Celestial and approximately thrice a day since I've arrived. The people of this town have a lot of pride, and it was evident in the way they discussed their annual festival. In fact, they put so much effort into selling the Celestival and the Starlight Stampede that I began to think there was no way it could live up to its expectations.

But once again, the people of Celestial have proven me wrong. If I thought this town was like a Hallmark movie before, I had no idea what was coming for me.

The entirety of downtown has been shut down. Every road in and out of town has been closed to make way for the parade route and the food trucks that have traveled in from near and far. Small vendors, both local and not, have booths and tents lining the sidewalks, selling everything from homemade jam—I got strawberry jalapeño and a peach bacon jam I was not convinced of until they gave me a free sample . . . then I bought three jars—handcrafted jewelry, hand-drawn maps, vintage T-shirts, refurbished furniture, and custom trucker hats. It reminded me so much of the craft fairs that I went to with my grandma that I had to step away for a moment and take a few deep breaths.

"Same," Gabby says. "If I keep this pace, I might need to find a new suitcase before I head back home."

Attending the Celestival for almost the entirety of their lives, Ciara and Millie have shown a little more self-restraint than me and Gabby. My normally frugal friend has flashed her credit card more today than in the last five years combined.

"It's really important to support small businesses in times like these," she'd say after every purchase. "It's called being a global citizen and good neighbor."

I don't think it was either of those, but I wasn't going to stop her. If I was going to spend seventy-five dollars on the quilted makeup bag Miss Margaret sewed and the pillowcases Esther made for the Artist Alchemy's booth, it was only fair that she also splurged on the quilted tote bag Katy-Anne made. They were so happy that we bought their goods, I think I'm going to be in Esther's good graces for at least a week . . . maybe even two. I'm not above buying people's affection. When I saw Esther's rare but sparkling smile, I almost cleared out her stock. The only reason I didn't was because Millie jumped in to remind me to leave enough products for the rest of the customers.

But don't you worry, I'll be back tomorrow.

"A pit stop is a good idea." Ciara looks closer at the note in her phone. "After shopping we have games, and you'll need all hands available for that."

"Agreed," Millie says. "I'm the reigning ring-toss champ, and I don't want to hear any of your excuses when I kick your asses."

"Intense much?" I ask even though I once almost broke my ankle after some random dude in a bar challenged me to an obstacle race.

"Don't look at me." Ciara holds up her hands in surrender. "I'm just trying to win a goldfish."

We take a quick detour to find Millie's car in the merchants' parking lot. She has a parking pass, thanks to the Artist Alchemy booth that she's sworn up and down she'll be working tomorrow. My shoulders cry with relief once I'm free of my bags, and my fingers itch to beat Millie in the carnival games. It's not my best trait, but she woke up the competitive monster that lives inside of me.

We navigate the crowded streets filled with residents and visitors alike, and my stomach warms with pride for my new town. Little kids run by with ice cream cones dripping down their hands and rainbow-shaped cotton candy bigger than their heads. Adults follow closely behind them, their inner children shining while they delight in their treats and the company of strangers.

The game portion of the carnival is set around the town square. Every athletic team, club, and miscellaneous Celestial High School group partnered with a local business to come up with a booth for the Celestival. There are games and baking stands, tarot card readers and sketch artists, and even a competitive improv booth courtesy of the drama club.

You can tell how much effort everyone put into their booths, and I'm pretty sure I could wander around for hours, going to visit every single one. But, if I'm being honest, there's one specific booth I'm looking forward to seeing the most.

"Moon Girl!" The sound of my nickname rises above the crowd in a perfectly imperfect blend of teenage boy voices.

"Did they just call you Moon Girl?" Gabby asks, and like the best friend she is, I can tell she's prepared to be extremely offended on my behalf.

"They did, but I love it," I say. "I don't think I'll ever understand teenage boys"—nor do I want to—"but from what I do know, this is their way of expressing that I'm their favorite."

And after all the laps I've run with them and goody bags I've provided, it's a position I've earned.

"Okay," she says, still sounding skeptical. "If you like it, then I love it."

"Don't worry." I grab her hand and start pulling her in the

direction of the group of football players waving their hands over their heads to get our attention. "You'll see when you meet them."

I'm sure it comes to a shock to no one, but the football team's booth has prime real estate front and center at the top of the square. They partnered with Big Score Sports, the one and only sporting goods store in Celestial, for an expected, but no less delightful, football toss booth. The boys put in a ton of effort painting the tire targets they decided would look much cooler than the inflatable game Tate was going to order, coming up with the rules, and deciding on the prizes. I'm so excited to finally see the fruits of their labor.

Little boys in Astros gear run around their booth, playing with the foam footballs they won from the game, and high-fiving the players. A few extra adorable ones even ask some of the players to sign their shirts, a request that the team is all too happy to oblige. Tate is at the back of the booth talking to one of his coaches, but the moment he sees me a soft smile touches his lips and he winks before turning his attention back to his conversation.

"Moon Girl finally made it!" Aiden, who has maintained his position as one of my favorites, yells when he sees me. "And she brought a moon friend!"

"I'm Gabby, but you can call me Galaxy Girl," Gabby says, and Aiden's smile triples.

Dammit.

Galaxy Girl is way cooler than Moon Girl.

"Alright. Enough already." I toss the latest bag I've acquired on the booth and pull my arms across my chest in a big show to stretch. "Introductions have been made. Are we going to keep talking or are you ready for me to show you how to really throw a football?"

"Nice try," Landon, one of the most prolific shit-talkers on the team, says as he hands me the football. "Girls can't throw. Look how small your hands are. You can barely even hold the ball."

You'd think at the big age of thirty and after spending more time than I'd care to admit kicking these boys' butts whenever they challenge me to a race, I'd be skilled in ignoring their ruthless taunts. But I'm not, and because of that, I do what any irrational, un-levelheaded adult would do.

I pick up the gauntlet and throw it right back at them.

"So that's how you want to play this? Don't think that just because you're undefeated, which, congratulations, I'm so proud of you boys"—I fall out of character for a minute before snapping back in—"doesn't mean I won't kick all your high school butts in a football toss any day of the week."

"Oh no." Tate enters the conversation, and he looks so handsome in his official Celestial football polo and his mass of locs piled high on top of his head, I almost forget I'm too busy trash-talking and get distracted. "Please tell me you didn't challenge her to a game? I thought I told you the rules when you showed up for your shift."

I'm not surprised Tate created a rule centered around me. Not only was he a first-hand witness to the many household projects I made a million times worse all in the name of my pride, but he was also the one carrying me off the track when I got a little too cocky and challenged Devin—the wide receiver and state championship sprinter—to a 400-meter race.

"Do you hear that?" I ask Landon, pointing to Tate. "Sounds like someone is scared I'm going to show up his team."

The boys are too cool to giggle, but they do let out a few manly chuckles and, let me tell you, there is not a greater high than making teenagers laugh with you instead of at you.

"Dang, Coach T!" Aiden, never one to shy away from stirring the pot, says. "You're gonna let your girl do you like that? She must not know 'bout you!"

"Don't you worry, I know all about Tate Jacobs and his iron arm." I take off my sunglasses and hand them to Gabby, who's watching this scene play out with conflicting expressions of exasperation and amusement. "But *you* must not know about *me*."

"Oh my god. Someone has to go against her," Gabby says, no doubt having flashbacks to the time I almost got thrown out of a pool hall in college. "She won't stop until she wins."

"And don't even think of going easy on me." I narrow my eyes at all the boys lining up for the challenge. "When I crush you, I want to know I did it while you were at your best."

"ARE YOU GOING to walk around with that thing all night long?" Ciara eyes the gigantic stuffed cow I picked out after winning ten straight matches in the football toss. "We can go put it in the car if you want."

"And deprive the people from realizing they're in the presence of a champion?" I adjust the cow on my hip. It's growing heavier by the minute, but I won't let a silly thing like physical discomfort hold me back. "I don't think so."

"If you insist," she says, and I can't read her mind, but if I could, I'm pretty sure she'd be screaming that she thinks I'm nuts. "I left the schedule open before the Starlight Stampede.

We can either do rides first and eat after or eat first and do rides later."

"It's up to you," I say. "You're the Celestival expert. I'm just happy to be here."

My phone vibrates in my purse, and I grab it, hoping to see Tate's name on the screen. Instead, I almost throw it across the crowd when I see the missed call and voicemail notification from the lawyer's office that helped me work through my mom's and grandma's wills and the sale of the house. I haven't heard from them in months, and my stomach falls into my feet thinking about what they could possibly be calling me about or, worse, who.

But before my brain can begin to conjure up one worst-case scenario after another, a pair of strong hands wraps around my waist and pulls me out of the panic spiral before it even begins.

"I say rides now," Tate answers with the easy decisiveness that's always eluded me. "I just walked by them and the lines are practically nonexistent."

He pulls the cow out of my arms, relieving me of its weight, and touches his mouth to mine. It's short, but heartachingly sweet, and I feel the eyes of the entire town watching. My stomach does cartwheels. His touch is much more thrilling than any of these rides could ever be.

I drop my phone back in my purse and thread my fingers through his. I'll figure out what the lawyers want tomorrow. Today is for the Celestival.

"You're finished with the booth?"

He nods. "Shift change. Dante took over for me," he says to me before turning his attention to Gabby. "He told me to tell you he's excited to hang out if you're still interested."

"I am!" Gabby screams into the crowd. "I definitely am."

Playing it cool has never been one of her strengths. For better or worse, Gabby wears her heart on her sleeve.

Tate's body bounces with silent laughter at my side. "Cool," he says. "I'll let him know to meet us at the food tent after the Stampede."

"Okay then," Ciara cuts back in. "Now that we have all that decided, I'm going to hang out over here while you go risk your lives on those rusted machines of death."

"Drama queen." Millie tsks. "If you ate too much pie during your judging segments, just say that."

To say that Ciara took her job as a pie tester seriously would be an understatement. She was never satisfied with one bite, and by the end of the competition, her bronze skin had turned olive and everyone thought she was going to blow. I think it's the only reason Pam didn't throttle her when Ciara ranked her blueberry pie in second place.

"Laugh if you want, but my stomach comes secondary to the obvious safety issues of climbing onto a Ferris wheel that was in San Antonio yesterday," Ciara defends herself. "It's Six Flags or nothing for me."

"A ride stopped working when she was a kid," Tate explains to the newcomers—that is, me and Gabby. "She hasn't set foot on a Celestival ride since."

"It didn't just *stop working*," she shoots back. "I was hanging upside down for fifty minutes! I couldn't eat more than crackers or walk in a straight line for a week!"

My excitement for the rides fades.

"Um . . ." I look up at Tate. "Maybe we should stick with the rides that keep us right side up."

"That's what I thought." Ciara sticks her tongue out at Millie. "Some risks can't be avoided, but spinning upside down on a ride held together with rusted nails, duct tape, and a prayer isn't one of them."

We follow Ciara to the bench in front of the Tilt-A-Whirl and load her up with my stuffed cow and the rest of our goodies before putting our lives in the hands of disinterested ride operators.

Gabby and Millie team up, ignore all of Ciara's warnings, and head directly to the Helix 360, a horrifying ride where you're basically tossed into a cage and spun upside down over and over again. Tate and I opt for the slightly less thrilling Viking Pirate Ship that swings but doesn't go upside down.

"I don't remember the last time I've been on a ride." I bounce from toe to toe as my nerves start to assault me. "I used to go to Elitch Gardens all the time as a kid."

"Elitch Gardens?"

"It's an amusement park in Denver. I think it was bought by Six Flags at one point, but don't quote me," I tell him. "It was the best. There were so many rides, and it had the best water park. I don't know why I stopped going or when the roller coasters stopped being thrilling and became terrifying."

Growing up sucks for so many reasons. I wish I could go back and view the unknown with wonder instead of fear. I hate that I let life steal that from me, but if my move to Celestial has done anything, it's pushed against my belief that I have to know all the answers. Maybe now I can embrace the magic of adventures again.

"Probably when the news started being delivered to your phone. It's hard to remain unscathed when we're constantly inundated with the worst of the worst."

"You're not wrong. Do you think I should swap out my iPhone for an old Nokia?"

I remember thinking my mom's brick of a phone was so cool. The world was much simpler when you had to text with numbers and the only thing to do on your phone was to play *Snake*.

"Or you could turn off the notifications," he offers like the rational king he is.

The ride slows to a stop in front of us, and people flow off of it as the attendant opens the gate and checks our wristbands. I grab Tate's hand and pull him to the last row of the boat before the rest of our group can take all the best spots. A couple that I don't recognize slides in beside us. After months of learning everyone's names, it's been so strange to see so many new people hanging around. Now I know what it must've been like for everyone when I arrived.

"Arms up," a deadpan voice on a speaker says, and we all follow directions as the lap bar falls across our thighs.

My stomach turns as last-minute regrets chase away my excitement, but when I look at Tate, it's all forgotten. There's a mischievous glint in his eyes that makes him look younger and—impossibly—more handsome than ever, and he's looking at me with the same smile I see before we go to bed each night. My toes curl in the tennis shoes Ciara pressured me to wear as I realize that lust might be the only thing more potent than fear.

"Ready?" Tate asks.

With him by my side? There's only one answer. "Always."

Chapter 29

A very strong, very particular smell assaults our senses when we enter the arena for the Starlight Stampede. It's a strong mixture of livestock, leather, fear, and adrenaline.

It's impossible to decipher which is the most potent.

"Where'd Tate go again?" Gabby asks as we follow Ciara to our seats. "Is he going to make it back in time for the rodeo?"

"I'm not sure." I try to ignore the niggling disappointment that's been gnawing away at me since he made his abrupt exit after our third whirl on the Ferris wheel. "One of the coaches called and said they needed him back at the booth for something. He said he'd try to join us here later, but you never know with football."

You'd think he was an on-call emergency room doctor with the hours he works and how many fires he's constantly putting out. I knew football was important in Celestial, but nothing could've prepared me for the amount of calls he's always fielding. Add in the home emergencies around town and I don't know how he manages to keep his head and his schedule straight.

"Oh my goodness! If it isn't my favorite girls in the whole world." Pam stands from her seat in the front row and gives me, Gabby, and Millie all hugs before narrowing her eyes on Ciara. "I see you brought my traitorous daughter with you."

"If I knew you only asked me to judge the pie contest so I'd rig it in your favor, I would've said no," Ciara growls, and I try to swallow the laughter bubbling at the back of my throat.

"I didn't want you to rig it. I wanted you to be fair," Pam snaps back. "There's no way Darla's basic strawberry pie was better than my bourbon blueberry pie. She didn't even grow her own strawberries, for goodness' sake."

"I hate bourbon!" Ciara throws her hand in the air. "What did you expect?"

"You hate bourbon?" Pam's perfectly arched eyebrows come together. "I thought that was Tate."

"No, Mom. It's me." Ciara's hands curl into fists, and I just know she's grasping at the fraying strands of her self-control. "Silas took me out for my twenty-first birthday and fed me so many shots that I was never able to go near the stuff again."

"Oh. Well then." Pam sits back down, her line-free skin flushing red under the harsh overhead lights. "I'll remember that for next year."

Ciara looks like she's about a millisecond away from her head exploding.

"Mrs. Jacobs, did I thank you yet for letting us sit with you?" I ask, hoping to draw her attention away from her daughter. "These are great seats. You must've had to get here so early to save them."

Pam waves me off. "Oh, sweetheart, no. Do I look like a

woman who's desperate to sit in the front row at the rodeo?" Her twinkly laughter fills the musk-scented air around us. "Starlight Ridge is the largest sponsor of the Starlight Stampede, hence the name. These seats are one of the many useless perks of shoveling money over. We've been sitting here for the last thirty-odd years."

"Thirty years is a long time." Literally my entire life! "You must be so proud that your family plays such an important part in Celestial."

"Thank you for noticing." Calvin's voice booms loud in the enclosed space, and curious heads turn from all directions to see what the commotion is all about. "If you could convince that hardheaded boyfriend of yours of the same thing, I'd appreciate it greatly."

"I don't know how many times I have to tell you, Dad." Silas slides into the open seat at the end of the row and saves me from what could've been the most uncomfortable situation of the night. "Ciara and Tate both share the same hard heads. Nothing can get through to them."

"Just Ciara and Tate?" Pam scoffs and turns wide eyes toward her son. "That's a long-held Jacobs family trait, and don't think you're not included. I'm the only person in our house with any sense."

"You're the worst out of all of us!" Silas, Calvin, and Ciara all shout in unison.

"Well, I never." Pam gasps and holds an offended hand to her chest before turning her attention to me. "You cook, clean, and raise an entire family, and this is how they treat you. I hope you treat your mother better than these three treat me."

A look of panic chases away Silas's easy smile. "Why don't we leave Luna out of this?"

"Nonsense." Pam waves him off, either not hearing the warning in Silas's tone or ignoring it completely. "She's our neighbor and your brother's girlfriend. Luna doesn't need to be left out of anything. In fact, when her mom comes to town, I'll be sure to make my second-place bourbon blueberry pie for her and I'll tell her all about how much nicer her daughter is to me than my own flesh and blood."

Everything Pam is saying is so kind that if I wasn't so focused on the growing look of horror taking over Silas's face, I'd want to permanently store her words in my brain.

I can feel Gabby's concerned gaze on the side of my face. She reaches for my hand, and the familiar touch of her quiet comfort wraps around me like an old quilt.

I squeeze her hand and try to keep my smile from wavering. "That's so kind of you, but it won't be necessary."

"Of course it is," she says, completely unaware of the shift in the air.

"Mom—"

"Oh, will you stop, Silas?" She swats away Silas's efforts like it's one of the flies buzzing around the arena. "It's going to happen. How else is she going to know Luna is being taken care of? A mother needs to know these things."

My dry eyes burn in the humid tent as Pam's well-meaning words slice through my weakened guards. My mom cared about a lot of things the last few years. She cared about how much money I could loan her and how fast I gave it to her. She cared about the liquor store down the street keeping her favorite brand of vodka in stock. She cared about twisting my words until I never questioned her again. What she did not care about, though, was whether or not anyone cared for me.

But that is a truth simply too ugly for someone as beautiful as Pamela Jacobs to hear and I can't let my darkness rub off on her pure soul.

"She would've been so grateful for how you and your family have welcomed me in," I say to her, and the lie glides effortlessly off my tongue as old habits slip into place. "But she passed away earlier this year, so that won't be necessary."

"Oh my . . . I'm so sorry." Her face falls, embarrassment and sadness crossing her delicate features. "What about your dad? Will he be coming down?"

The inappropriate urge to laugh builds low in my stomach.

"Um . . . well." I fight back the instinct to resort to dark humor and struggle to think of a way to give her this information in the gentlest of terms. "He actually passed away too."

That, apparently, was not it.

"Oh, sweet heavens." The color drains from her face and her eyes well with unshed tears. "I'm so sorry!"

"No, no, it's okay." I wave off her sympathy. "He passed away a long time ago, and you've already done more than you know to help after my mom."

As a society, we're pretty terrible at discussing grief altogether. Death comes for us all, and yet it feels like the most taboo topic of all. There's so much nobody warns you about in the aftermath of the loss of a loved one, but one of the things nobody ever mentions is how much of your time is spent reassuring other people. It's a skill I harnessed a long time ago. Not many kids had a dead parent in elementary school, and if adults aren't equipped to handle this conversation, let me tell you, neither are children. I should be used to it by now, but it never ceases to take me by surprise when it happens.

I'm gearing up to recite the usual platitudes I tell other

people when they hear about my past, but then Pam's long, elegant fingers wrap around my wrist.

"Honey," Pam whispers, "it's not okay and that is okay."

The sincerity in her words throws me for a loop. A funny feeling I don't recognize tugs at my heart as I try to come up with something, anything, to say.

"Celestial, Texas!" A loud voice that sounds suspiciously close to the person who narrates the football games explodes from the speakers and grants me the mercy I've learned not to expect. "Welcome to the thirty-fourth annual Starlight Stampede! If you're ready for a night full of some of the most talented up-and-coming cowboys and cowgirls in the rodeo game, then get on your feet and make some noise!"

Lights flash and the metal steps rattle beneath my feet as everyone in the packed stadium follows his directions. People hoot and holler, clapping and stomping until the gates at the rear of the stadium push open and two women, decked out head to toe in bright pink, barrel out of the back. They race around the arena, one waving the American flag, the other holding the Texas flag, and while I'm not sure I've self-identified as patriotic in quite some time, it is thrilling to watch. And even better, all conversations of my dead parents are long forgotten, trampled beneath the manicured hooves of meticulously groomed horses.

We all stay on our feet through the national anthem and something the announcer calls "The Cowboy's Prayer" only taking our seats when the music starts to play again and our pink queens bid their farewell. But the reprieve is short-lived before the announcer makes himself known again and introduces the first event.

"I hope y'all are saddled in steady because, boy oh boy, do

we have a treat for you on night one of the Starlight Stampede." There's more twang in his voice than at the football games, and I appreciate his commitment to the bit. "We've got tie-down roping up first, followed by bareback riding, and then do we have a surprise for you to kick off barrel racing."

"Oh! A surprise." I look at all the Jacobses, assuming one of them must know something, considering the part they play in the rodeo, but they're all wearing matching looks of confusion.

"Don't ask me," Ciara says. "I'm never on the inside of rodeo goings-on."

Calvin looks equally out of the loop. "I sign a check. That's the full extent of my participation, and I like it that way."

It's not that I hate waiting, I just really love feeling special enough to know what others don't. It's why I'm so good at keeping secrets. The more people who know, the less exciting it is.

"Getting us started in the tie-down roping, we have Laramie Walker," the announcer says, and a group of very scantily dressed girls on the opposite side of the stadium burst into cheers.

"Buckle bunnies." Ciara answers my unspoken question. "They're groupies, but for cowboys."

"Interesting." I strain my eyes to try to get a better view of their outfits and long curly hair hidden beneath sparkly cowboy hats. "As a feminist, I try to support women's rights and wrongs, but I'm having a really hard time understanding the appeal of being this excited for anyone named Laramie."

I had a terrible experience visiting a friend at the University of Wyoming. Just the thought of that windy little valley sends shivers down my spine, but who am I to yuck another person's yum? I love a woman who knows what she wants, and if they like it, then more power to them.

At the other end of the arena, a group of men gather around the cage where one guy sitting atop a horse holds the reins in one hand, a lasso in the other, *and* has something in his mouth.

"What's tie-down roping?" Gabby leans over the railing to get a better look at what's happening. "Does he have something in his mouth?"

"Yeah," Calvin says. "That's piggin' string. The ropers use it to—"

A buzzer cuts through the excited chatter before he can answer and we get to witness firsthand exactly what tie-down ropers do and how piggin' string is used.

A side gate I didn't notice until it's raised opens and an adorable calf sprints out of the corral followed closely by a very determined Laramie. Excitement flees my best friend's face and trepidation quickly rushes in as she watches Laramie launch his lasso right around the sweet baby cow's neck. She latches on to my hand and we let out matching horrified gasps as Laramie leaps off his horse and sprints to the calf. He doesn't miss a beat before picking the cow up, slamming him on his back, and using the piggin' string to tie three of his legs together.

The crowd goes wild, but I feel like I might be sick.

And if the forlorn expression on Gabby's face is anything to go by, I'm not alone.

"Fifteen point seven seconds. A season record for Laramie! That's one heck of a way to start off the rodeo, and with a time like that, he's sure to give the rest of the cowboys a run for their money. And speaking of money," the announcer says, and Silas and Ciara slink down into their seats, "the Starlight

Stampede would like to welcome Calvin and Pamela Jacobs tonight. Without their support, this rodeo wouldn't be possible."

Calvin and Pam stand up and wave with the ease of practiced politicians as polite applause surrounds us.

I know they told me they sponsor the event, but hearing and seeing are two different things. They're so down to earth, it's easy to forget not only how much they have, but how important their family is to the community. Who they are and what they've accomplished was created from generation after generation working to build a legacy and provide for family they'd never meet.

It's a hell of a difference from the pocket change I fell into thanks to dysfunctional family trauma the well-to-do Jacobs family could never even dream of.

I have to quiet the voice inside my head telling me I'm not good enough for them. Telling me to leave them alone before I drag them down to my level.

"This is never not mortifying," Ciara says through clenched teeth and a forced grin as she waves to the onlookers.

"Just smile and wave, Ci," Silas says. "Smile and wave."

"Mortifying?" Pam asks once the rodeo has commenced and all eyes are off her. "How? They aren't looking at you."

"Damn, Mom." Ciara's mouth falls open and Gabby giggles beside me. "That was harsh."

"If you think that was harsh, then you didn't spend enough time with your grandmother." Pam takes her cowboy hat off and dabs at her hairline with the paisley handkerchief she pulled out of her purse. "That woman would have you in tears. I was the inventor of gentle parenting compared to her."

Whatever response Ciara was gearing up to say dies on her

tongue. Ciara isn't one to back down, so this leads me to believe that Pam isn't exaggerating about their matriarch. It's comforting to know not even the regal Jacobs family has it all together, but I'm sure their problems pale in comparison to the absolute mess that consumed my life for years before I moved to Celestial. I can't help but feel like every onlooker is trying to figure out how a fraud like me infiltrated the perfect Jacobs family, their stares warning me not to let the stain of my past tarnish their royal family.

The rest of the rodeo flies by in a blur of cringing and gasps and heart-stopping terror. I can't believe I ever thought football seemed dangerous before watching this. Tie-down roping was the worst—I still wince thinking about the way they tossed those calves—but bareback riding was terrifying. I spent the entire hour convinced I was going to witness somebody's death.

"So you're telling me people do this for fun?" I ask Calvin. "Like, you saw this and thought, 'Absolutely, yes. I'd love nothing more than to tempt death by teasing a mammal that outweighs me by a thousand pounds'?"

"It's the closest I've ever been to god," he says, quickly amending his declaration when Pam's heated glare hits him. "After marrying Pam and raising my kids, of course."

Pam rolls her eyes. "Of course."

"See, the thing about rodeoing is that it's not about being perfect, because it's not up to you. You see that beauty?" Calvin leans toward me and points to the horse in the corral. "Once you're on the back of a horse or bull, it's all about surrender. It doesn't matter what's going on in the world or if you're having problems at home. If you bring that to your horse, they'll sense it and then you're done for. It's the one place on this earth where the only thing that matters is you and your horse."

My lens of this rodeo has been one of brutality and horror, but now as I watch the next man buck into the arena, I try to see it through Calvin's eyes. There's a reverence. A connection to nature and through it, to self. You still couldn't pay me a million dollars to do it, but I have a little more appreciation for those who do.

"I see it," I say. "Thank you, Mr. Jacobs."

He wraps an arm around my shoulder and pulls me into his side. A small smile softens his hardened face, and for the first time, I see the resemblance to Tate that goes much deeper than appearances.

"You're welcome, Luna," he says. "I know Pam is usually the one who leads the welcome wagon at Starlight Ridge Ranch, but I hope you know that despite what those pain in the rear kids of mine try to tell you about me, I'm always around if you need help."

I don't know if it's emotional residue from my earlier conversation with Pam, but something about the sincerity in his voice takes aim at my resolve to stay out of things between him and his children and smashes it to pieces.

"How 'bout them cowboys, Celestial? Let's give one more round of applause for all the contestants who came out to put on a show for us tonight." The announcer leaves room for cheers and whoops of excitement. "Now, if you thought that was something, then just you wait. Because for the first time in almost twenty years, the two-time junior barrel racing champion, former Mr. Texas Football Player of the Year, our hometown hero, Tate Jacobs, is returning to the arena!"

The ground rattles and my ears ring. You would think by

how loud they scream it was announced that Elvis had returned to life and was gracing the crowd with a performance. Everyone is on their feet and clapping their hands.

Everyone, that is, except our little group nestled safely in the confines of the Jacobses' exclusive seats.

Silas breaks the silence. "Did they just say Tate?" he asks. "As in my brother Tate? Our Tate?"

Hope flashes across Calvin's face before he fights it back. "It couldn't be."

But he's wrong.

Because it is.

Like something out of my deepest fantasies, the back gates open and Tate charges out on horseback looking every bit the romance hero of my dreams.

Seeing Tate inside the arena might be a surprise, but seeing that he doesn't exactly fit the mold like the other riders is not. Of course, if Tate was going to return to the arena, he was going to do it his way. And we should all be very thankful.

I know I am.

His long locs hang from beneath his black cowboy hat, bouncing around his chiseled face as the horse he's riding speeds into the arena. The white tee he's wearing molds to his hard body, and his brown skin shimmers under the lights. He races toward the first barrel, and just when it looks like his horse might run right past it, I watch his horse slow and his shoulders lift higher. Tate holds tight to the reins, not faltering once as he makes a sharp right around the barrel and sends a cloud of dirt flying into the air. He explodes out of the turn and races to the next barrel with as much control and confidence as every other cowboy who set foot in the Starlight Stampede before him. His posture never changes, his focus never falls, and when he completes the cloverleaf pattern around the barrel and gallops across the timer line, he finishes with the third-fastest time of the night.

It's a fever dream.

I don't even realize I'm holding my breath until he disappears from the arena. Oxygen crashes into my lungs, and the fire that always seems to burn when Tate is near blooms hot and heavy in my core. My thighs clench together, and I'm afraid if I stand up, my legs might give out from beneath me.

"Holy shit," Gabby breathes out beside me. "Luna . . ."

She doesn't need to expand. "I know."

I totally get those buckle bunnies now.

Calvin is sitting right beside me, and I try to push away the thoughts of all the things I want to do to Tate while he's wearing that cowboy hat, but it's a lost cause.

"Millie asked if I wanted to see her place tonight. I was thinking maybe I'd spend the night with her and we can all meet back up in the morning for breakfast?" Gabby, bless her, suggests.

"No," I say, but my heart's not in it. It's too busy tripping over the man who just trotted away on the back of a horse. "You don't have to do that."

"I know I don't have to, but . . ." She leans in closer and drops her voice to a whisper. "You're out of your mind if you think I would ever deprive you of an uninterrupted night with your man after he turned into *a freaking cowboy* for you."

I love her for offering, but she flew down to Texas to be with me. I would never want her to think I'm casting her to the side or that I didn't want to spend time with her.

"I'm not sure. I don't want you to—"

She cuts me off. "I'm sure and I want to. I won't hear another word about it," she says. "Now go get your man."

She doesn't have to tell me again.

I say goodbye to Millie and Ciara with promises to meet up for breakfast tomorrow, and after I give Pam a quick hug and one last thank-you for the night, I hurry away pretending I didn't see the knowing smile that crossed her face.

The rodeo has a few events left, but there's only one cowboy I want to see when I walk out of the stadium exit.

Scraps of trash and spilled popcorn cover the pathway leading toward the back of the arena, but I feel like I'm walking on sunshine. Being with Tate is like stepping outside after a winter of cold and darkness and feeling the sun wash across your skin. It's like he harnesses the power to brighten my day with a single glance and the ability to turn my world upside down with a touch. I can't believe that after the best day, spent with so many people I love, I get to end it next to a man who never fails to go above and beyond to show me how much he cares.

I feel utterly undeserving, but that doesn't stop me from breaking into a full-fledged sprint so I can be in his arms as soon as possible.

It's just too bad that shadows roll in as fast as the light.

"Luna!" someone calls from behind me. "Luna," they say again, but closer this time, something vaguely familiar about the sound of their voice. "Is that you?"

I'm so busy trying to remember where I've heard his voice that when I turn around and see his face, I'm too surprised to realize what's happening. And for a few blissful seconds, time is my friend, holding me back in a moment where I was happy.

Where the pieces of the fragile life I only just began to put together had yet to come crashing to the ground.

But time doesn't wait forever.

The peace was nice while I had it. How silly of me to think it would last.

"Jack?"

Chapter 30

The man standing in front of me is a far cry from the version I saw in the pictures growing up, and I'm almost more surprised that I recognize Jack than I am to see him here.

Time has not treated him well.

"You're a hard person to track down, Luna Starr." Jack's voice cuts through the night like a bullet. "You'd think a name like that would make you a little easier to find."

He forces his thin lips into a smile, but it does nothing to set my nerves at ease.

If anything, it makes them worse.

"Well, usually when a person isn't easy to find, that means they don't want to be found," I say, proud of how steady my voice sounds. "Most people take that as a hint. You should try it."

"Gotta admit, though, I did laugh when I found out you ended up in a town named Celestial," he says as if he didn't hear me at all, but the flush of red blooming across his sallow skin gives him away. "I mean, really, what are the chances?"

Jack takes one step closer and then another, until the

space between us disappears. I knew he wasn't doing well before, but it's even more noticeable this close up. The smells of the rodeo fade beneath the sharp tang of body odor and faint scent of whiskey coming off Jack in waves. My stomach turns. He's got at least a hundred pounds and five inches on me, but I know what game he's trying to play, and I refuse to step back.

"What are you doing here?" I finally ask.

"What do you mean? Can't an uncle come and visit his favorite niece?"

My temper spikes and quiets my fears.

"Cut the crap, Jack. I made it very clear in my last email that I had nothing to say to you. So I'll ask you one more time and one more time only." I pause, not losing eye contact with him once, and say as slowly as I can, "What are you doing here?"

He does not like this.

"You think I cared about your little email?" The mask he was wearing crumbles and rage simmers behind his yellow eyes. "I don't give a fuck what you said. I care about what's mine."

His voice vibrates with the same angry, hysterical lilt I heard from my mom on her very worst nights, and his hands curl into fists at his sides. I should be scared of the way his knuckles are turning white or that his pinpoint pupils are from something much stronger than alcohol.

And I am scared, terrified, actually, but not because of Jack.

Or not totally, at least.

Just over Jack's shoulder, Aiden, my favorite football player, steps through the arena exit with a group of his friends and then, instead of turning left with them, I watch as he heads straight in my direction.

"Moon Girl!" He calls my name before I can think of a way to subtly caution him away. I don't know what Jack's capable of, but I don't want Aiden anywhere near when I find out. "Did you see Coach T on that horse? I didn't even know he could do that! Did he—" He stops talking the second he comes from behind Jack, and the smile I've never seen leave his face is replaced by an expression I don't like at all. "Are you okay, Miss Starr?"

It's the first time he's ever called me by my real name.

"I'm okay," I say, but it's hard to talk over the lump in my throat. "Why don't you go catch up with your friends?"

He doesn't listen.

"My man," he says to Jack. "Why don't you go ahead and take a step back? You're a little too close and she doesn't look like she likes it much."

Yeah.

Definitely my favorite football player.

"It's okay, Aiden—" I start before Jack cuts me off.

"Do I look like someone who listens to kids like you?" Jack snaps. "This has nothing to do with you."

Jack might weigh more than Aiden, but Aiden has two inches on him, and the weight he does carry is muscle. Jack might be trying to act tough, but I can see straight through the bravado in his voice. He's scared and he's getting more agitated by the second.

And that makes him even more dangerous.

I need Aiden to get away from here and fast.

"Aiden, I'm okay, really. This is my uncle." I step in between him and Jack and try to force him to listen, but Aiden's eyes never stop looking over the top of my head. "I'll be alright, but I really need you to leave." Any grip I had on my composure has disappeared, and my mouth goes dry with panic.

"Now, Aiden," I say, my voice breaking from the barely concealed panic turning my blood cold. "Leave now."

His eyes finally come down to mine, and I watch the moment understanding passes over his face. He doesn't say a word, but he does what I asked and turns to leave. I almost fall to the ground as relief shoots through my legs like needles.

Too close. That was much too close.

The announcer's voice has been muffled inside the arena, but all of a sudden it's much too loud and his words informing the crowd that the rodeo is coming to an end come through crystal clear.

"Why don't we take this somewhere else?" I suggest to my uncle, ignoring the warnings from every self-defense class I've ever taken not to go to a second location with your attacker. But at this point I'll take whatever he has coming as long as there's no collateral damage. "We can go someplace quiet and figure this out."

I don't know what there is to figure out—he was left out of the will and I wasn't—but desperation is one hell of a motivator, and if writing a check is what it will take to get him away, then that's what I'll do.

"No." He shakes his head. "I've waited long enough. I want to talk now."

A slow trickle of people leaving the rodeo starts to flow through the exit, and no matter how hard I'm trying to keep it together, panic is rising inside of me like a tide. The subtle tremor in my hands is spreading up my arms and the sharp pang in my chest makes it hard to breathe.

"Okay. That's okay." I try to think of another plan, hoping my smile doesn't look as unhinged as it feels as people begin to walk by. "I think there might be some tables around here somewhere. Would that work?"

"That's fine." There's a glint in his eyes when he nods. He felt the shift. For the first time, he knows he has the upper hand.

It doesn't last long.

I scan an open corridor for a table or a quiet corner where we can hide, but I find Tate with Aiden at his side instead. I don't know if I'm relieved to see him or not, and I don't have time to figure it out, because the second we lock eyes, he's on the move.

His long legs make quick work of the distance separating us. His face is thunder, but the storm brewing in his dark eyes is deadly.

"Are you okay?" he asks as soon as he reaches me, but his onyx eyes never deviate from my uncle.

No. Not even a little bit. I've never been worse.

"I'm fine." I try to keep my voice even when all I want to do is scream and, if I'm lucky, finally cry. "This is my uncle, Jack Brady."

Uncle Jack eyes Tate up and down and makes it clear he's not impressed with what he sees. "Who are you?"

Tate's shoulders tense at the distaste in Jack's voice, but he remains silent.

"This is my boyfriend." I don't give him a name. He doesn't deserve to know it.

"He shouldn't be here." Jack runs a hand through his thinning gray hair and peels his gaze from Tate back to me. "This is a family matter."

"A family matter?" I repeat, making sure I heard him right the first time.

"Yeah," he snaps. "Family. You know, like me and you. Not this asshole I've never seen before."

Jack crosses his weak arms across his puffed-out chest. I know he's balancing on the edge of lunacy and I need to take him seriously, but for some reason, him trying to look intimidating is the only thing funnier than him pretending like he's ever acted like we're family before this moment. And I can't help it.

I start to laugh.

Not just a small, cute little giggle that I can pretend is a cough either.

No.

It's the from the tips of your toes to the top of your head, doubled over, can't breathe, and will feel it in the morning kind of laughter. And every time I think I've gotten it under control, I take one look at the deep frown lines on Jack's cherry-red face and I start all over again.

"You think this is funny?" he asks, and I can't tell if it's the first time he's asked or the tenth.

"Do I find you ambushing me at a rodeo and demanding that I talk to you funny? No, not really," I manage to say without falling into another fit of giggles. "But you saying something is a family matter to me, the person who you ignored my entire life and then called a selfish bitch when I called to tell you your sister died? Well, that's pretty hilarious."

Out of the corner of my eye, I notice that the trickle of people leaving the rodeo turned into a steady stream sometime while I was laughing, but I'm too focused on the way Tate has turned to stone beside me to give them much attention. If the vibes were bad before, they're straight-up rancid now.

Tate doesn't say a word, but he doesn't need to. He's as still as a statue at my side, his taut muscles wound so tight that the slightest breeze could set him off.

It's just that, in this case, the breeze has a name. Jack Brady.

Who, by the way, is still fucking talking.

"You're still going on about that? Get over it already." Jack's face turns as red as the flag he personifies. "I hadn't talked to her in years. I don't know what you expected from me."

"Oh, I don't know." I pretend to think about it while I gather what's left of my self-control. "Your only niece calls to tell you that your only sister has died and that even if you've never spoken before, you're the only family she has left now. I didn't expect tears, but some human decency or a little compassion would've been nice. I would've even been fine with a 'bummer.' Anything other than what you did actually."

He nods long and slow. "I get it now, but I think you forgot one thing," he says, but the way he says it, I know to brace. "Your mom was a fucking liar who spent years poisoning my mom against me. You wanted me to say 'bummer,' but I couldn't find it in me. You want to know the truth? Lisa was a lying, selfish bitch, and the world is better without her. The day you called to tell me was one of the best days of my life."

I know Jack is delusional enough to think the house that was legally and rightfully given to me was his. I've read enough of his emails to know he's not a fan of me. I'd have to have even a minuscule amount of respect for him to care. He's a small loser of a man, and I have more respect for the dirt on the bottom of my shoes than I do for him.

Nothing he says could faze me, except, it turns out, for one little thing.

"Don't say her name." I haven't heard my mom's name said

aloud in months, and hearing it come out of his mouth feels like a punch in the face. Pain ricochets up my arms and straight through my heart as the protectiveness I'd thought I lost long ago rushes to the surface so violently that if it weren't for Tate's hand at my back, it would've knocked me over.

"She was my sister," he snarls. "I can say whatever I want to say about Lis—"

I shove a finger in his face and cut him off before he can finish. "Don't you dare say her fucking name." Acid strong enough to corrode metal drips from my voice. "You have no idea what she went through or who she was. You weren't there after my dad died. You weren't at the hospital with her when she never left Grandma's side. You weren't there for any of it. You lost the right to say her name years ago."

My vision narrows beneath a red haze. I'm so focused on the man in front of me that I don't realize Tate isn't the only person at my back anymore. Jack's eyes drift over my shoulder, and for a moment, I think I see fear, but it happens so fast, I can't be sure.

"You think I don't know who she was because I wasn't there? You don't have to be an engineer to know a train wreck when you see one, sweetheart," he sneers, his decaying teeth a far cry from the bright smile in the pictures that hung in my grandma's house. "And if you were by her side during all this, what does that say about you?"

His words are a dart laced with poison, and he hits me with pinpoint precision. I rock back on my heels, unable to argue with the truth.

"You don't know what you're talking about."

"I don't?" he asks, cruel satisfaction lurking behind his malicious smirk. "That's where you're wrong, because I know exactly what I'm talking about. Lisa was a walking disaster for as long as I can remember. She relied on everyone around her for her entire life, and my mom catered to her bullshit until it finally killed her. She was a user, a thief, and, when she wasn't hiding who she was to try to get something out of someone, a fucking bitch. Which is the only reason I'm not shocked the apple didn't fall far from the bitch tree."

I can practically feel the color drain from my face as horrified gasps erupt at my back. The anger rolling off Tate hits me like a wave and the restraint he was clinging on to finally snaps.

"That's enough." He steps in front of me and is immediately flanked by Silas and Mr. Jacobs. The three of them tower over my uncle like a trio of dark knights. "It's time for you to leave."

"Who the fuck are you to tell me what to do?" Jack tries to sound tough, but the tremor in his voice gives him away. "Last I knew, this was a free country and I can be wherever the hell I want to be."

"Then last you knew was wrong," Tate says. "Because if you think you're going to come to my town and talk like you've lost your fucking mind to any woman, let alone mine, you don't know where the hell you are."

"I thought Texas was the land of free speech," Jack says.

It's an unwelcome reminder that while he's never been the sharpest tool in the shed, he was always the loudest idiot in the room, and we share genetics.

"Free speech doesn't mean no consequences," Tate says, and Calvin tightens his grip on his son. "Keep talking and I'd be happy to show them to you."

"Is that a threat?"

"No," Tate says, and I can see the vein in his neck throb. "It's a promise."

Jack steps forward, but before he can say anything, Silas slides in front of him and holds a hand up to stop him from coming closer.

"I don't know who you are, and honestly, I don't care. You don't seem worth our time," Silas says. "What I can tell you is that in Celestial, we protect our own, and Luna? She's ours. You can make the wrong decision if you want, but you should know nobody will come running to your rescue if you do."

"You're all crazy if you think she's worth doing all this for. Just wait and see—she's exactly like her addict mother, and if you're not careful, Luna will put you in an early grave just like her mom did to her dad." He steps to the side and strains his neck so that he's only looking at me as he shouts his final parting line. "And if you think I'm not getting every cent from *my* mom's house, you've got something else coming."

I'm not often prideful, but I can't let this asshole get the last word. I muster up all the strength I have left and shout at his retreating back, "I'd love to see you try." My voice echoes against the metal bleachers and empty booths, but he doesn't look back. "I look forward to it."

A massive crowd still mills around. Strangers stare with morbid curiosity, their expressions dripping with disdain as hushed whispers rise above the deafening silence beating against my eardrums, but it's Gabby who rushes to my side.

"What the hell was that?" Her beautiful face twists with concern I thought I'd seen the last of. "Are you okay?"

"That"—I point to Jack's retreating back—"was my uncle Jack."

She's heard about him before. "Fuck," she whispers.

"Yeah," I say. "You've got that right."

The cool breeze blows across my heated skin, and my teeth start to chatter as the reality of what just happened starts to set in. Gabby walks in front of me, blocking me from the view of curious bystanders all the way to the car. Pam drapes her arm over my shoulder, Ciara holds my hand, and humiliation claws at my throat as this perfect family is forced to face this walk of shame because, no matter how hard I try not to, I inevitably ruin everything I touch. Pam and Ciara try to distract me during the walk to the car, but I don't hear a single word they say. I can't hear anything at all over the unwelcome thoughts flooding my brain.

And as the realization starts to settle deep into my bones and the numbness I thought I'd escaped wraps around my body, I look up at the night sky, and there, in all its blazing glory, is the wink from the Universe I've been waiting for.

A message from my mom.

But this time it's not telling me I'm in the right place, it's reminding me of who I am. I'm not meant to have forever. My uncle might be an asshole, but there was truth in his words. I am my mother's daughter and where we go, destruction follows.

I thought I could run to Celestial for my fresh start, but I was wrong.

You can't run from what you are.

And I do not belong here.

Chapter 31

Tate brings me and Gabby home after the Celestival, and for the first time ever, I don't invite him inside.

He comes in anyways.

"Can you give us a minute?" I ask Gabby.

My voice is unrecognizable to my own ears, and I'm sure Gabby doesn't miss the exhaustion in my tone. She chews on her bottom lip for a minute, and I start to worry she's not going to leave when she finally nods her head.

"Sure," she says. "You know where to find me if you need me."

She touches Tate's shoulder on the way out with a sadness in her eyes that tells me she knows exactly what's coming next.

There's a bottle of wine calling my name. I grab a glass out of the pink cabinets I wasn't able to enjoy for nearly long enough.

"Do you want something to drink?" I offer Tate once I hear the door to Gabby's room close. "There's enough wine to share, but there's Dr Pepper in the fridge if you want that instead."

He doesn't answer.

He closes the space between us and pulls the wineglass from my hands. He sets it on the counter beside the bottle that will likely be gone by morning and pulls me so tight to his chest, he almost squeezes the resolve out of me.

Almost.

I allow myself to rest my head on his chest, indulging in these final moments, hoping I can remember the sound of his heart beating beneath my ear, the smell of his cologne, and the safety I know I'll never find outside of his arms.

"Are you okay?" his deep voice whispers into the top of my head. My heart breaks a little more, knowing I have to let all of this go. Knowing he deserves better. "What can I do for you?"

I squeeze my eyes closed and give him the answer I know he'll never accept. "Nothing."

He shakes his head. "There's something I can do," he says. "We just haven't thought of it yet."

Part of me wants to draw this out forever, but I know what will happen if I do. I will turn everything that is good, bad. Leaving him with the familiar scars the Starr women leave behind.

And Tate Jacobs is too good of a man for me to allow that to happen.

I look up at him, and the expression on his face is so sweet, so tender, it knocks the wind out of me. I hope I don't forget that either.

"Come sit with me?" I ask.

He nods and follows behind me to the couch, never dropping my hand. Never losing my touch.

"I'm gonna hang out here tonight," he says. "Silas followed your uncle and made sure he left town. I don't think he'll be back, but I want to be here on the off chance he chooses to make the wrong decision."

I didn't know Silas followed him. One more person getting roped into my mess.

The blast zone of my life is endless.

I have to get this over with before someone else gets hit with shrapnel.

"Do you remember our first night at the Whiskey Rose?" I ask.

"Of course." A lazy smile tugs on the corner of his mouth. "I don't think I'll ever forget that night."

"Not that." My thighs clench together, and I fight to stay focused. This is already hard enough. The last thing I need is to be distracted by thoughts of his mouth on mine. Thoughts of how it will never be there again. "Before we left. Do you remember what happened on the dance floor?"

He pauses and thinks for a second before it comes back to him.

"Yeah, I think." He nods. "Wasn't there a song that came on that reminded you of your mom? You said she really liked it?"

Of course he remembers. Nobody has ever made me feel more cared for than this man, and it makes me hate Jack, and myself, even more.

"That was true, it just wasn't the entire truth." I fight the urge to pick at my fingernails or look at the floor, anything to avoid having to look into his eyes as I say what I have to say. "You know how they say smells bring memories? That night it was like that, but with sound. Does that make sense?"

"I think so."

"That song . . . I hadn't heard it in so long, but when I was growing up it was a staple in my house. There were three weeks a year that my mom would pull out that CD and play 'The Dance' on a loop for a week straight."

"Three weeks?"

"A week for her and my dad's anniversary, a week for my dad's birthday, and"—I inhale, pushing against the emotions trying to creep back in—"a week for the day he died. The day he died driving to pick my mom up because she'd had too much wine. Again."

"Jesus, Luna," he whispers into my messy curls. "I'm so sorry."

Tate's arm flexes around my shoulders, and I scoot farther away. I can't feel it anymore.

Not when the comfort of his arms no longer belongs to me.

"It was hard," I tell him, ignoring the flicker of hurt that passes over his face. "She missed him so much, and even though I don't remember him, his presence was such a big part of my life. Her grief was overwhelming. Her guilt was all-consuming, but never enough to make her stop."

I close my eyes, and for a moment I can see my mom so clearly, it nearly knocks my breath away.

She's younger.

Her cheeks are still full. Her skin is bright and unlined, the effects of the wineglass in her hand yet to be seen. Her long legs are tucked beneath her in the ivory chair in the corner of the living room, her delicate neck bent down, as if she's trying to fold into herself. Grease weighs down her beautiful wavy hair. It hangs like a heavy curtain over her face.

Garth's voice is playing so loud from the stereo beside her she doesn't notice I've come into the room until I call her name. I don't remember where we were going or why I needed her, but I do remember the panic I felt when she turned to me with tear-stained cheeks. I remember thinking, even though she was sad, how beautiful she looked and the way her blue eyes turned electric rimmed in red. I remember making myself believe her when she wiped away the stray tears and told me she was okay through a shaky smile.

I remember that if I ever bothered to look close enough, I would've seen the bone-aching sadness that lingered beneath the stunning facade she tried her hardest to keep up. It's a look I know so well.

It's the look I see reflected back in my own face.

Maybe if I took the time to look closer, I would've known she'd broken years before the mask finally cracked.

"She never got over losing him." The quiet admission slices through me like a million hot knives. "I don't think I ever knew her happy."

I don't think I'll ever be happy.

I leave the quiet part unsaid.

"What do you mean?" Tate asks after a few moments.

"I mean that I'm a mess." The admission feels like a literal blow to my chest. "For the last five years, I've been so mad at my mom that I failed to realize it turned me into her. The house, the chickens." *The relationship*. "It was all a distraction. It was all a fake. It was all a lie."

"It wasn't a lie and it damn sure wasn't fake." His shoulders draw back as understanding dawns on the gorgeous face that I'll no doubt spend the rest of my life dreaming about. "I've been here. I've seen it all. You can try to lie to yourself, but you can't lie to me."

"You saw what I wanted you to see." I tell him the truth I

never wanted to say out loud. "That's the thing with me, Tate. I'm just like my mom. You'll never know what's real because neither do I. We hide, we lie, and we run, but it's never enough to prevent our mess from spilling onto everyone we love, and I can't do that to you. You deserve so much better than anything I can give you."

"No, you don't have to do this. You don't have to run anymore and you never have to hide from me." His gruff voice cuts through the peaceful quiet night that only a person like me can ruin. "Don't do this, Luna."

He says my name like a prayer, and it puts the final crack in my already breaking heart.

"There's nothing to do," I tell him and watch as the shadows that disappeared from his face fall right back into place. "It's already done."

"So what's the plan here?" There's a sharpness to his voice that I've never heard before, not even in the beginning. "You're just going to live next door to my family you insisted I make up with and ignore me for the rest of your life? Expect me to pretend none of this ever existed between us?"

I'm sure he thinks the anger will be harder for me to hear, but I welcome it in.

Anger he can get over. Heartbreak is much harder, and I'll gladly take that burden from him. I hope he will hate me as much as I hate myself.

"No." I squeeze my eyes shut and I wish I could cry. I wish I could give him the tears he deserves. But I can't. So I give him the only thing I can provide: the space to move on without me. I can't stay. "I'm moving back to Denver and selling the house."

He doesn't say anything else.

The full lips I know I'll dream about until my dying days flatten into a straight line and the eyes I sought comfort in turn to ice, their daggers taking aim straight through my already broken heart.

And as he walks out of my door and out of my life, without so much as a glance backward, I close my eyes and whisper to the skies, hoping that somebody up there can hear my wish.

Give him the person he deserves. Give him somebody better than me.

I'm not meant for a life filled with happiness and love, but Tate is.

He might not understand now, but one day he will. He deserves the world and when he finds it, I know he'll thank me for this.

In the end, this pain will all be worth it.

For him.

Chapter 32

I already knew Gabby was lying when she said she loved a road trip, but it's confirmed during our drive back to Denver.

The forty-eight hours after Tate walked out my door stretched for an eternity and passed by in a blink. Ciara promised to take care of Little Chix and the rest of my ladies, even vowing to leave the chicken coop painted until I came to my senses and moved back.

She didn't realize this was me coming to my senses.

Patricia was thrilled to put the house back up for sale. Apparently, the housing market in Celestial isn't what one would call "booming," and the renovations I'd done on the house, as niche as they were, still included bringing a bathroom up to code and fixing the wiring. She assured me that both of those things meant the house would move light-years faster than it did when she sold it to me.

I hope she sells it fast.

I hope she never sells it at all.

And now that I'm officially homeless until I sign a lease for an apartment in Denver, I'm Gabby's newest houseguest and, unfortunately, the target of a barrage of worried glances and concerned questions. I'm so grateful that I've managed to not destroy one relationship with a person who loves me, but I need her to stop looking at me like I'm going to break.

In better news, however, apparently when you have copies of text messages, emails, undeleted voicemails, and witnesses to a person stalking and harassing you, the courts can work pretty fast. I didn't even have to wait a week before my restraining order against Jack was granted.

I still haven't talked to Tate, but I know he was one of the people who vouched for me.

I lie back on Gabby's couch—that I'm definitely going to have to replace after rotting on it for so long—and glance at the growing number of unread messages on my phone. There are lots from Ciara and Millie, some from Miss Margaret and Esther filling me in on the gossip I've missed at knitting, and then, the ones I try to avoid the most, a few from Tate. I miss him so much that it physically hurts. The steady throb that's been nagging at the base of my neck since he walked out of my door becomes more noticeable as my finger hovers above his name on my phone. Maybe if I give in and open his message, it will be enough to finally give me some relief.

Just one text couldn't hurt . . .

The front door slams open and the frames hanging on the entryway wall rattle precariously as Gabby storms inside.

"Enough!" She throws her tote on the console table and kicks her shoes across the room with the dramatic flair only

Gabby could pull off. "I love you. I'm always here for you. But it's almost been a month and it's time for you to get your ass up and sort through your life."

Sheesh.

I know I said I wanted her to stop looking at me like I was going to break, but this feels a little extreme, no?

"Whoa there, killer." I sit up, ignoring the way my matted hair feels at the back of my head. "I am sorting through life. I told you I have apartment tours scheduled for Monday, and Drew said I can have my job back at the Book Nook the second I'm ready."

You would think moving back home would be easier than leaving, but the opposite has been true. Reminders of my old life lurk behind every corner, but even though everything is familiar, nothing feels the same. The food at my favorite restaurant doesn't taste as good. The stores I loved to shop at feel outdated and dull. I was only gone for a few months, and yet, it feels like lifetimes have passed.

The only place that hasn't disappointed is Gabby's couch and it seems like I might be losing that soon too.

"Either you think I don't know you or you think I'm an idiot." She twists her hair into a bun on the top of her head and shoves me to the side so she can sit down next to me. "Neither option is great."

"First of all, I don't think either of those two things." I turn to face her and tuck my legs crisscross applesauce. "Second, what is happening? I don't understand what you're even talking about. I thought we had a plan and things were moving along nicely."

Fuck.

Did I manage to ruin the last remaining relationship in my life? I knew my welcome was wearing thin.

"We did," she says. "But that plan's not working for me anymore. You can't stay here."

My stomach falls to my feet and dread claws at the back of my throat. I should've known better than to think Gabby and I could escape this without destroying everything. "What? I didn't—"

"You did and you're full of shit." She cuts me off before I even have the opportunity to be full of shit. "You think you have me fooled into thinking you're okay. You think I don't hear the constant buzzing of messages on your phone from all the people who, whether you want to admit it or not, care about you and are worried. You think you can ignore this, but I'm not going to let you."

The lump in my throat from fear goes away, but it's quickly replaced by years' worth of unshed tears. "Gabby—"

"No!" she says. "The time for that is over. So now you're going to sit and listen to me, and then, when I'm done, you're going to get your ass back to Celestial and go talk to Tate, because I love you too much to let you shut him out."

I'd try to wiggle my way out of this, but it's too late. She's using her teacher voice and there's no changing her mind when she pulls that out. "Fine," I say. "You can talk, but I'm not too sure about the Celestial part."

"I don't care if you're sure about it," she says. "I'm getting your ass back down to that cute freaking house you poured yourself into for months, even if it means taking another week off work and suffering through another road trip."

"So we're going to play it like that?" I try to sound annoyed, but her aggressive love hit me right in the heart and has left me feeling exposed and defenseless.

"Yeah." She sits across from me and folds her arms across her chest. "We're going to play it exactly like that."

Well, fuck.

What do I say to that?

"Fine." I pout. "Then I guess we're talking."

I hate losing, but for some reason, this feels like it might turn into a win.

"I know you've been trying to pretend like that scene that happened with Jack didn't affect you," she says, and I hold my breath. I don't know why, but I was not expecting her to go back to this. "You keep acting like you had some big 'aha moment' when really, I was there. I saw the look on your face when he brought up your mom, and I can't ignore the fact that your smile hasn't reached your eyes once in the entire time since you've been back."

"Who notices all that?" I ask. "Are you a teacher or a super spy?"

Get a best friend, they said. *It will be fun,* they said. The liars.

"Neither," she says. "I'm your best friend who's let you get away with too much because I've been too worried about you to give you the tough love you needed."

If Gabby thinks she's treated me with kid gloves, I'm not sure I'm ready for her real talk.

"Fine, I'm ready." I take a deep breath and brace. "Give it to me."

"I did you a disservice after your mom died." The words rush out of her in a single breath. "I should've said something when you sold your house and moved, but I thought a fresh start might be what you needed."

"I thought it was what I needed too," I say. "I couldn't stay in that house."

Ghosts hid on every street corner, painful memories inside every store. Leaving my house became a herculean task, and staying inside added to the growing depression I didn't know how to address.

"I know that now," she says. "But you didn't even try. You just ran away and buried yourself beneath home renovation projects and chickens and now you're doing it all over again. Coming back to Denver won't change anything. Diving back into selling books and throwing events and whatever else you come up with to distract you won't help. You think that this is you dealing with your grief, when in reality, I don't think you've even scratched the surface of what the last few years did to you."

She's not wrong, but she's also not right.

I don't think I've dealt with my grief, but I have managed it, and that's more than I could ask for at this point. "Gabby—"

"No, please." She holds up a hand and her voice cracks. "Please let me get this out."

Her chestnut eyes gloss over with unshed tears, and my already shattered heart crumbles to dust.

"Okay," I say, even though I'm not sure I'm ready for what she's going to say next.

"You know how much I love your mom. Still, to this day, I love her. I still have the card she gave me for my sixteenth birthday," she says, and an impossible smile tugs at my mouth at the memory I forgot. "The time she took us to the Sand

Dunes will forever be one of the best weekends of my life. She was so much fun, and I always loved when she would come around and I could laugh with her all over again."

Every labored breath feels like a knife to my chest, and I hold tight to the pain. It's so much easier to feel than the emotions threatening to rip me to shreds.

"She loved you too."

"I know she did," she says, and the tears welling in her eyes start to fall. "But I also know that the Lisa who died is not the Lisa I loved, and I know that even before she disappeared, the Lisa I loved was never without her flaws."

My eyes burn and I squeeze them shut, willing a tear to fall like they are falling for Gabby. "I—"

"No," she says. "I know that you told me some of the things she put you through, but I'm your best friend. Do you really think I didn't know that even when she was dragging you through the mud, you were still protecting her? Do you think I couldn't see the shadows that eclipsed your light as you hid the secrets that were never yours to begin with? I let you have that because I knew you needed to do what you felt was necessary to protect her while she was here, but she's gone now. It's time to unburden yourself of the heavy load that's been wearing you down to nothing."

I love Gabby. I know how blessed, favored, and lucky I am to have someone who has seen me through almost every stage of my life by my side. But, fuck, it really is impossible to hide anything from her.

"I didn't mean to hide it from you," I choke out through the tears that still *won't fucking fall*. "I didn't want to taint the way you thought about her."

She leans across the couch and clasps my hands in hers.

"I know. I don't blame you for not telling me everything. Even though she hurt you, you still loved her. And as someone who's been lucky enough to receive your love, I know how much you give to us. I know how hard you are on yourself. Which is why, right here, right now, I'm giving you permission . . . No," she corrects herself, "I'm demanding that you let it go. I'm demanding that you acknowledge that even though you went above and beyond for your mom, you can't save somebody who doesn't want to be saved. I'm demanding that you accept that it's okay to be relieved that she's gone and you no longer have to worry about whether she's safe or getting in the car drunk. I'm demanding that you acknowledge that you're her daughter while knowing you're nothing like her. You're allowed to mourn the woman you loved while being angry at the person who died. You can hold both, and I hope, for your sake, you finally do."

Her tearstained cheeks flush, and if I didn't feel like I was about to pass out, I'd tell her how unfair it is that she's a pretty crier on top of every other wonderful thing about her.

"You know, it's kind of rude to attack your houseguest like this." It still hurts to breathe, but something comes loose in my chest. "But I guess I'm glad you did."

"Damn straight you are." She swipes away the tears rolling down her face like streams of glitter. "Now you're going to get your cute butt together and back to Celestial, because I'm not letting you run. Not again."

And as if conjured by the magic of a best friend determined to keep me from self-destructing (for a second time), my phone starts to ring.

A Texas number I don't recognize is on the screen.

"Hello?" I answer.

"Luna, hi!" Patricia's heavy Southern drawl rolls through the phone. "I'm having some issues with my phone, so I'm sorry to call you from a different number, but I just had to let you know the great news. We have a buyer for your home!" she says, and for what feels like the millionth time over the last month, by heart falls to my feet. "But there is just one small problem."

"There is?" I ask, scared to feel hope.

"I'm going to need you back in Celestial for this to go through," she says. "Is there any way you could be here by Monday?"

I think of the apartment tours I have planned and the lunch meeting with Drew.

I'll cancel them all.

"Of course," I say. "I'll see you then."

And when I hang up, the sadness has fled from Gabby's eyes, not a trace of concern lingering on her face as she reaches across the couch and pulls me in for a hug.

"I love you, Gabby," I whisper as I hold her tight. "I hope you know that."

"I do," she says, pulling away to look right into my eyes. "I also know I'm not the only person who should hear those words from you."

She's not wrong.

I only hope Tate wants to listen.

Chapter 33

I've been in Celestial for two days, and it's surreal how happy I am to be back.

With summer behind us, crisp autumn air welcomed me home with open arms. I wandered around the downtown streets and browsed the farmers market for groceries. I met up with Millie for dinner, and her guilt trip only lasted for about twenty minutes before she accepted my apology and filled me in on the latest town gossip—apparently, the couple opening the juice bar in the storefront next to the Artist Alchemy backed out at the last second and now everyone is scrambling to figure out what to do next. I settled back into my house and took the world's longest bath in my hard-fought-for bathtub. I checked in on Little Chix and my girls and tidied up their coop.

I've done so much. I have not, however, seen Tate.

Although, it must be said, it's not from a lack of trying on my part.

The texts that I sent him before I came home are still

sitting, unanswered, in my phone. A half-written paragraph that I'll no doubt read and rewrite approximately fifty more times before I ultimately delete it is sitting in the text box below it. I've driven past his house once and the football field twice. I even sat at the bar at Crumb and Crust, nursing a glass of wine for about an hour longer than is socially acceptable, willing Tate to come in like he had on my very first night in town. I'm desperate to see his gorgeous face again. To see the way his onyx eyes go soft when they land on me. To hear the way his deep voice says my name like a prayer. It's all I want, but the more time that passes, the more I begin to realize it might not happen. I'm ready to come back, to try again, but that doesn't mean he will be.

It sucks, but I'm still going to stay. I'm no longer running from what I fear. Been there, done that. I'm going to spend the rest of my life running recklessly into everything and everyone that I love.

Even if it really fucking hurts.

"I'm so sorry my client is late, Miss Starr." Patricia checks her watch again. "They told me they'd be free to meet at three."

The conference room in Moonlight Realty is exactly as I pictured it to be. Patricia has forgone the clean lines and modern aesthetic my real estate office in Denver went with in favor of a more modern rustic look. A giant iron logo is attached to the shiplap wall. An old metal milk container has been repurposed as a vase, and vintage frames hold prints of houses they've sold.

Joanna Gaines would be proud.

"It's not a problem. I don't have anywhere to be." I take a sip from the Moonlight Realty–branded water bottle she handed me when I walked in the door. "But since we're waiting, I do have one question."

Her pink-painted lips spread into a genuine smile, and she leans toward the table. "Of course," she says. "I'm happy to answer any of your questions."

"Is it normal for a meeting like this to happen?" I fidget with the plastic bottle cap. "Do buyers usually want to meet the previous owner?"

Thanks to all the rookie mistakes I made purchasing my house here, I'm sure it was abundantly clear to anyone paying attention that I was a first-time homebuyer. When it comes to selling a house, though, I'm slightly more experienced. I know every situation is different, but when I put my grandma's house on the market, nothing even similar to this happened. I didn't ask the name of the family who moved in, and they didn't ask about me. We worked through our Realtors, signed the paperwork, and went our separate ways. When it came to my house in Celestial, well, the house had been empty for so long that meeting with the previous owners wasn't even in the realm of possibilities.

"Not often," she says. "But to be fair, I haven't sold many houses that had acquired such"—she pauses, most likely trying to come up with a more delicate way of saying my house was a complete shithole—"extensive upgrades and renovations. I think they just want a detailed list of what was done and to know more about what you had left to do. Easy, really."

"Oh, okay. Easy," I say. "Thank you."

Easy, I repeat. *This is easy.*

I run through the list in my head. I repainted the walls and repaired the stairs. The bathroom attached to the primary bedroom is brand-new, claw-foot tub and all. Fresh paint, bold wallpaper, and new light fixtures abound. The lace curtains Miss Margaret made for me frame the new windows in the living room. Pink kitchen cabinets and gold knobs might be a bit of a hard sell, but if the buyer has vision—and taste—it shouldn't be too hard to get them on board.

The list of what I've done isn't too bad; it's the things I had left to do that are harder.

Sure, I wanted to replace the air-conditioning unit, and the gutters were running on their last legs, but it's the dinner parties I had yet to host that haunt me the most. The late nights sitting on my porch next to Tate . . . the early mornings waking up with him by my side. The life we would build together.

I close my eyes and try to finish the list, picturing someone else completing it, but I can't. Because it's mine.

The person joining us today doesn't need to come at all, because I won't be selling.

"Patricia." My voice shakes when I say her name. She's been sweet enough, but I'm sure she won't be thrilled when I tell her there's not a commission to be made anymore. "I don't think—"

"Oh, good!" She claps her hands together and jumps from the table. "They texted me and they're walking in now."

"Okay, but—" I try again, but Patricia is a woman on a mission. She's gone from the room before I can say another word.

She leaves to go meet the new buyer in the front, and I square my shoulders as I wait. I know how hard it is to find a house that you love. The thought of being the person to rip it away from them makes my stomach turn, but this isn't about a house for me anymore.

After years of searching, I finally found my home.

I hear Patricia's loud Southern drawl as she approaches, but I can't make out the voice of who she's with.

She refused to give me a name—something about client confidentiality—but with how small Celestial is, I know there's a good chance I'll recognize the person I have to break this news to.

I brace as the door swings open, but nothing could have prepared me for who I see next.

"Tate?" The entire world falls away the moment a pair of onyx eyes lock on to mine. "What are you doing here?"

The air is too heavy to breathe. His scent infiltrates the room, and my body recognizes him instantly. My lungs struggle to inflate and my heart hammers in my chest.

I've been miserable in the month since I've seen him last. My hair is still recovering from weeks of not combing it. I've gone through more concealer than ever before attempting to disguise the dark circles under my eyes and stress pimples.

Tate has never looked better.

"Luna." He nods tersely and takes the seat across the conference table from me. "Nice to see you again."

All the warmth I knew and loved is missing from his eyes. The gentleness gone from his voice. It's him, but it's not.

Fire rages in my sinuses, and for the first time since I can remember, my eyes well with tears. Worst. Timing. Ever.

"It's you?" My voice breaks, but I don't hate the way it sounds. I couldn't cry the last time I saw him, but even if he doesn't feel the same way anymore, I want him to know I still care. That I love him. Even if I'll never get the chance to tell him. "You're the one who's buying my house?"

I guess this is one way to make sure he never has to see me

in Celestial again. Though I have to imagine there are more cost-efficient options.

He nods, his hard features and cool expression not giving anything away.

"Okay then." Patricia shifts uncomfortably in her seat. "Now that both parties are here, we can get started."

I shake my head. "Can I have a moment with Tate alone first?"

Patricia's eyes fly between me and Tate, and her hands fidget nervously with the stack of papers sitting in front of her.

"Umm . . ." Her gaze settles on Tate, and her shoulders relax when he tips his head up slightly. "Sure, you take as long as you need. I'll be just outside."

She stands up slowly and, much to her credit, keeps her steps even instead of running out of the room like I'm sure she wants to. The door closes behind her, and I wait until the sound of her heels clicking against the tile begins to fade. My pulse skyrockets with every second that passes. I try to keep my expression as blank as the one Tate is wearing, but if I were to look down, I'm sure I'd see crescent-shaped cuts from my fingernails digging into my hands.

I've been waiting to see him for days—weeks, if I'm being honest—and now that I'm finally alone with him, I need whatever I say to him to be profound. Meaningful.

Instead, all I say is, "Hi."

The word is barely a whisper, but somehow the single syllable gives away every bit of anxiety, fear, and regret gnawing away inside of me.

His jaw goes tight. "Hi."

My body goes taut with the urge to run, but for once, my

heart is louder. And it's telling me that even if he can't forgive me, I owe it to both of us to let him know how I feel.

"I was prepared to tell the buyer no." I start in the middle of the conversation. "I was going to tell them good luck on finding another home and apologize to Patricia for wasting her time, but the farmhouse is mine. I was going to say no," I repeat. "But I won't say no to you. Not again."

He sits up straighter, and it's the only hint he gives that he's heard me at all. Good thing I don't need him to say anything in order for me to get my feelings off my chest. I tuck my hands in my lap, send up a silent plea that this won't end in total disaster, take a deep breath, and then I let it all out.

All of it.

"I don't know what I was looking for when I moved here. I thought I was coming for a fresh start. A chance to forget all my problems with the help of a new town and a few home improvement projects. I hoped for a few new friends and a cute cowboy or two to look at and thought that would be enough. Anything other than the constant grief of home would've been fine." He's still not giving me anything, and I force myself to hold his gaze as I say this next part: "Then I met you and all thoughts of *fine* vanished because you made everything better than I ever thought it could be.

"You snuck into my life and turned the dial so that my world was so full, so bright, I couldn't even remember what *fine* felt like. It was like you cracked me in half and everything I'd been burying for years came tumbling out. My joy ran deeper, my laughter was louder, my love was stronger. I felt safe enough to feel again, but after years of being numb, I forgot that pain and fear weren't things I needed to run from.

The second things got scary, I did what I've done my entire life. I was stuck with that pain and I was the cause of yet another mess, but I thought if I left, at least you would be free of it all."

"I never said I wanted to be free of it." His deep voice cuts across the room like a shot, and my body recoils at the sound of it. "You made a decision for me without thinking to ask what I wanted."

My heart is in my throat, and I'm afraid the words I have to say won't have enough room to come out.

"I know. I was wrong." Tears sting my eyes and regret pricks at my skin. "I wish I could take it back, but I can't. All I can do is tell you how sorry I am and, if you let me, I promise I won't run again. I promise that I'll stay."

Something flashes in his onyx eyes, but it's gone almost as fast as it came. His full lips are still pulled into a straight line, and even after I've said everything I wanted to say, I'm still not sure if he heard me. Or worse, if he did and he just doesn't care anymore.

He stands up and my heart leaps. For one wonderful moment, I think he might come to me. But instead, he turns his back to me, opens the door, and calls for Patricia to come back.

Patricia joins us in the room again, and my head swims as I try to keep my breathing measured. I don't know if I want to scream, throw up, or both. Both, actually.

Definitely both.

I can tell Patricia is uncomfortable as she takes her seat, but ever the professional, she paints on a smile and ignores the silent stream of tears falling down my face.

"So." She grabs a sheet of paper and looks it over, her eyes studiously trained away from me. "It looks like before Mr. Jacobs puts an official offer on the house, he has a few concerns to go over with Miss Starr. Is that correct?"

"Not concerns," Tate says. "More like conditions."

I didn't think my heart could sink any further, but it does.

"Okay." I nod, swiping away my tears. I knew things could end up this way. It's time for me to deal with the consequences of my own stupid actions. Have I mentioned how much I hate being a freaking adult? "I'm ready. Whatever you want."

"Great," he says. "I'm glad we're on the same page."

He reaches into his pocket and pulls out his phone. Seconds turn into centuries as he taps on his screen, and I wait to hear what he says next.

"Number one." He looks up from his phone, and if I wasn't so distracted by dread, I might've noticed the way his full lips turn up at the corner and his onyx eyes have gone soft. "In order for me to go through with this purchase, it must be understood by all parties involved that not a single item inside the house should change. Not the pink cabinets in the kitchen, the loud floral wallpaper, or even the ridiculous Pink Chicken Club in the back."

I forget how to breathe as a tendril of hope, that stupid little feeling I know damn well not to trust, starts to unfurl from somewhere deep inside of me.

"Two." He puts the phone down on the table in front of him and looks directly into my eyes. "If updates are to be made, they must be done entirely of Miss Starr's volition. Every design decision must be attributed to the countless Pinterest boards, TikTok videos, and Instagram posts she has made me watch to understand her 'vision' for the house."

"Tate." His name comes out as a sob, and not even I can tell if it's from laughing or crying. I don't need a mirror to tell me I'm a snotty, blubbering mess. "I—"

"No." He shakes his head. "I'm not done yet."

The fear that I've misread this comes rushing back. I'm going to need a massage from the emotional whiplash of it all.

"This one is the most important, so I really need to make sure you're listening." He stands up, and before I can even register what's happening, his long legs have made quick work of the small space and he's standing right in front of me. The smell of his cologne wraps around me, and my fingers itch to reach out and touch him. "Number three. Ms. Starr is the only person who can ever live in this house again. It's her home. It's where she belongs. And if, on the off chance she were to ever be in need of company and has the patience to deal with a bulldog and an occasionally grumpy football coach who loves her, she might allow them to move in too."

I lost control of my tears eons ago. They fall with abandon as my hope crescendos and visions of a future with Tate at my side flash before my eyes.

"You were going to buy my house for me?" I reach for him, and when his strong hand wraps around mine, my heart begins to soar. I've missed everything about him, but I might have missed his touch—and the way it makes me feel so alive—most of all. "You know that's crazy, right?"

It is, but it's also beautiful and romantic and every good thing I never imagined I could have in my life.

"Maybe." He shrugs, pulling me until the only thing separating us is the fabric of our shirts that I can't wait to rip off. "But when it comes to you, Luna Starr, there's nothing I'm not willing to do. Do you know why?"

The answer dances on the tip of his tongue, the implications and the promise almost too impossibly big for me to say . . . let alone believe. But if the man in front of me has proven one thing, it's that anything is possible. Especially when it comes to him.

I take a deep breath and gather the courage to say what I know deep down in my bones is true.

"Because you love me?"

"Yeah," he says. "Because I love you."

"What luck." I wrap my arms around his neck and pull his face to mine. "Because I love you too."

I don't know Patricia's stance on public displays of affection, but I couldn't make myself care even if I tried. Tate Jacobs loves me and I love him too. I've loved him from the moment I lay beside him, staring at the stars, but dreaming about him. Now, tucked in the back office of Moonlight Realty with Tate's mouth on mine, in the little town of Celestial, Texas, I've just been handed the entire world.

Epilogue

The bell over the front door rings, and Millie barges in holding a teetering tower of boxes.

"Hey, neighbor!" Millie says. "I know you're busy, but I come bearing gifts."

"You know I'm never too busy for you or presents." I slide the book I was filing into its spot and climb off the ladder to greet my friend and fellow business owner. "What'd you bring this time?"

"More of the same." She sets the boxes on the ground and starts to flip them open. "More pillows for your reading chairs, a few embroidery hoops to hang on the wall, and . . ." She pauses for added effect before pulling something out of the box. "Your bookish quilt!"

If my house is maximalist chic, then the Ethereal Shelf is cozy calmness at its very best. Twinkle lights hang from the ceiling, and chestnut bookshelves and tables filled with books cover the intimate space. Lush, cozy chairs are nuzzled in the back of the store for readers to sit and relax or for book clubs to laugh as they discuss their latest read. I open next week, and now, with this quilt to hang on the wall over the reading nook, it feels more real than ever before.

"Oh my god." I take it from her and spread it across the checkout counter. My eyes gloss over as I absorb the intricate details of the book spines on the quilted shelves. "I don't care what you say—you're going to have to let me pay you for this."

She holds her hands in the air and takes a step away. "That's sounds like a problem for you to solve," she says. "This is a gift from knitting circle, and if you want to argue about it, you're going to have to take that up with Miss Margaret and Esther."

"It's probably best you just say thank you then." Tate comes out of the stock room and Duke runs across the room to say hello to Millie. "The last time you tried to go against those two, they made you feel so guilty that you ended up getting roped into making three pies and a cake for the elementary school bake sale."

That did happen. I spent a week obsessively testing recipes until I had four that I thought would meet Esther and Miss Margaret's standards. They did and they sold out so fast that I am now on speed dial for every charity bake sale in town, which, considering how small Celestial is, is a surprisingly high number.

"You're not wrong." I look at the beautiful quilt one more time. I can only imagine how much time and energy went into creating such a masterpiece. "It just doesn't feel right to take something like this and not pay them back somehow."

Tate wraps his hand around mine and pulls me into his hard chest.

"What makes you think they want you to pay them back?"

His onyx eyes are soft, and the smile that's almost always on his face these days is gentle. "You're one of us now, and in Celestial, we show up for one another. You being here, opening this store, is more than enough."

"Remember when you were grumpy all the time, Tate?" Millie says as she rubs Duke's belly. "I'm still not used to this lovey-dovey version of you."

"You'll get there one day," he says to her, but looks to me. "I don't plan on it changing anytime soon."

Lucky for me, neither do I.

"Speaking of changing"—I remember the text I got from Ciara earlier—"your mom wants to know if we can go over for dinner tomorrow instead of tonight. I guess your dad is forcing Silas to ride up north for some kind of cow convention."

Where things with Tate and Silas are better than ever, tensions between Silas and Calvin are higher than ever. Things have gotten so intense that Pamela has started coming over to my house during the day to get away from them. I'm still hoping things will change, but I'm taking Tate's lead and sitting this one out.

"I don't think cow conventions are a thing." Tate's smile widens just like I hoped it would. "But as long as you're free, so am I. Unless you want to stay home and—"

"Lalalala!" Millie sticks her fingers in her ears and turns to leave. "You two are disgusting. I'll be next door if you need me when this love fest ends."

"Sucker," Tate whispers as the bell above the front door rings again. "She makes it so easy."

"So easy to what?" I ask.

He doesn't answer . . . at least not with words.

He leans down, and when his full lips touch mine, the store filled with love stories disappears as my happily ever after sharpens into focus. And as I lose myself under his touch, I can't help but think how lucky I am that this isn't a perfect ending, but the most beautiful beginning.

Acknowledgments

Kristine Swartz, thank you for still being on this journey with me. I am so grateful to have walked this journey with you by my side. Thank you for always listening to whatever crazy idea I'm thinking of next and not immediately telling me to delete whatever pop culture references I've planted into this book. I couldn't do this without your patience, guidance, and support, and I can't wait to stay in Celestial with you for a little while longer.

Kimberly Whalen, thank you, thank you, thank you, for being the best advocate and agent I could've ever asked for. The way you have stood by me, listening when I needed it the most, has meant absolutely everything to me. I am so thankful you were willing to take a chance on me and my books. I'm so lucky to have you on my side.

To the amazing team at Berkley, thank you for making this book happen. You are the dream team, and I still pinch myself that my books have found a home with you. Your support means the world, and I can't wait to see what this small-town romance can do, thanks to you.

To booksellers and librarians everywhere, thank you. The work that you do is more important now than ever before. Thank you for sharing your joy and knowledge with readers everywhere and fighting to get books into the hands of readers. The world can be a dark place, but it's brighter thanks to the love you give.

When my family made the decision to move to Texas, other than hot summer (and fall) days, intense football seasons under the Friday night lights, and learning how to navigate the many, many highways, I wasn't sure what to expect. We'd moved plenty of times before and I had a hard time believing this move would be much different. I couldn't have been more wrong. Moving to Texas, I finally found the community I'd been praying for. GPJ, Grandma Frankie, Denise, Herman, Frannie, Junior, Mercedes, Stephan, Santi, Ayrin, Ace, Tee, and Karter. Being this close to you has been the gift I never knew I needed. Watching my kids grow up with you has been the greatest blessing. Carolyn, Dipa, Liz, thank you for making the school that shall not be named tolerable. We have the best boys, and I'm grateful that a semester turned into a lifetime. Lindsay Van Meter, making friends as an adult isn't always easy, but I feel like I've known you all my life. Thank you for raising the best girls and loving Ellis the way you do. Jocelyn Williams, where do I even start? It felt like fate brought our families together. From lunch dates to football games, I'm so thankful for our time spent together. Now please mentor me in being an adult. I really need you. Lol!

One of my favorite things to write about in my books are the female friendships my characters always find. It's one of the most important things in my books because it's one of the most important things in my life. I have been spoiled beyond belief with the most amazing friends a person could ever ask for. Abby, Taylor, Brittany, Lin, Tav, Natalie, Suzanne, Meredith, Ali, Mel, Sarah, Rosie, Andie, Tarah, Amber, Phoebe, Jennifer, Sophie, and Rachel: You inspire me and motivate me to be better every day. I'm so lucky to have friends as brilliant and as talented as you are.

Lindsay and Maxym: I wish I had the words to say what you mean to me. Our cult is my favorite, and I love you both.

Mom, Grandma, and Grandpa, you better be having fun up there because I don't know if you've seen what's happening earthside, but it's not so great down here. Rude that you all left so soon. I miss and love you more than I ever thought possible.

Derrick, I don't know when you'll read this, but it feels important to tell you that just yesterday, you walked in on me sitting on our bed and crying. When you asked what was wrong, I couldn't tell you because I honestly didn't know myself. But you got me out of bed, showed me your facility, and took me to lunch at a restaurant we've been wanting to try. We had the best time, which didn't come as a surprise because I always have the best time when I'm with you. Thank you for loving me and for standing by my side since 2003. I can't wait to see what comes next. I love you.

DJ, Harlow, Dash, and Ellis, I love you all so much. I don't know what I did to deserve the best kids ever, but I'm forever thankful that I get to call you mine. You are everything good in the world and the reason for every smile. Getting to watch you grow up has been the honor of a lifetime. I'm so proud of you and the amazing humans you are. You are the lights of my life and being your mom is the best thing that has ever happened to me.

Thank you, readers, for picking up this book and going on this journey with me. We've been at this for a while now and I will never take this for granted. None of this would be possible without you, and I'm forever grateful.

And lastly, to Little Mix. I'm really loving the solo eras, but remember, you said this was a hiatus. Don't let Little Chix down.

Keep reading for a preview of Alexa Martin's

INTERCEPTED,

available now!

Chapter 1

For the first three years, it's fun being a pro football player's girlfriend.

"Marlee, let me see your hand! Did Chris propose yet?" Amber asks.

I'm in year ten.

"Still naked." I wiggle my fingers in front of her the same way I did last week and the week before that . . . and the week before that. #HeDidntPutARingOnIt

Sometimes, I like to hashtag my life. #CheaperThan-Therapy

I sip my margarita. "When it happens, I promise to let you know." *Or, you know, keep asking every time you see me.*

"Marlee." Courtney sighs. She stands at the head of the table clutching a glitter-coated gavel. "We made exceptions for you to join the Lady Mustangs. Try to acknowledge that and save your little side conversation until we've finished."

"Sorry, Court." Every time I call her Court, she strains her Botoxed forehead and glares in my direction, so obviously, it's the only thing I call her. Well, sometimes I call her bitch, but she doesn't know about that.

"As I was saying, the annual Lady Mustangs Fashion Show is in three weeks. Everyone *must* attend the next meeting so we can discuss the outfits for you and your husbands."

I catch her eye again. She raises her chin, and her fat-injected lips form an actual smile.

"Oh, I'm sorry. In your case, Marlee, you and your *boyfriend*."

See? What a bitch.

"Thanks for the clarification, Court, but I understood." My fingernails dig into my palm as I fight the urge to ask if one of her husband's girlfriends will be joining the festivities.

"I didn't want you to feel like you were being excluded."

Hmm . . . including me by pointing out my differences. Makes so much sense. I don't know if she's trying to convince herself, me, or the rest of the Mustang wives, but she isn't succeeding with anybody.

"You're so thoughtful," I return with an equal amount of authenticity.

Courtney is the president (how obnoxious) of the Lady Mustangs, the charitable organization consisting of the wives and girlfriend (singular) of the Denver Mustangs. We get together every Wednesday during the season to plan different events to benefit the community. There is an unspoken rule—each woman only gets one season to lead—but surprising nobody at all, Courtney didn't think the rules applied to her. This is her fourth year as president. Her husband, Kevin Matthews, is our quarterback, but her head is bigger than his. And that's saying a lot. There are football players and then there are quarterbacks—which are an entirely different breed. Courtney has also made it her mission during her reign of terror to put me in my place, a spot well below her. She doesn't seem to realize I'm fresh out of fucks to give.

"As I was saying, now that the season has arrived, everyone needs to be here every week. No excuses." She looks toward me again.

So I've missed some meetings, sue me. But, unlike Courtney, I have an actual job that includes more than lunching. We also live in the day and age of email, something that seems to evade her.

"Remember what we always say? We work hard to inspire our husbands' on-field success with our off-field dedication, support, and achievements."

Vomit.

Honestly, besides the constant pressure to prove I'll be the best football wife ever, the only reason I keep coming to these awful things is because it gives me an excuse to drink in the early afternoon. I focus on the Colorado sun shining down on our rooftop patio table as I sip my oversized margarita, listening to the music as it switches between seventies pop and nineties hip-hop—until Courtney's shrill voice pulls my attention back to her.

"Is there anything else that needs to be discussed today?" Courtney asks. After a quick glance around the table confirms there's nothing else to be said, the gavel slams into the table and glitter explodes off of it, covering the table, plates, and floor.

Fantastic.

Like the waitstaff needed more of a reason to hate us

beyond the ten separate checks, no dressing/no flavor orders, and the three women who sent their meals back because they spotted a carb.

Whenever these meetings end, the switch flips from good deeds to gossip central.

"Can I have a chip?" Naomi says. "Salad is so stupid. Why don't you ever tell me not to order one?" She draws my attention away from the brewing gossip storm as she reaches to my plate without waiting for an answer. Not that she needs one, she does this every week. And every week she still orders a salad—like the calories don't count if I'm the one who orders them. #WhoNeedsScience

"What if I was going to say no?"

"Were you?" She crunches into the chip in a manner so un-Lady-Mustang-like, I'm surprised Courtney doesn't slam down the gavel again to reprimand her.

"No, you can have the rest, I'm done. Playing nice while Power Trip Barbie threw her jabs stole my appetite."

I love Naomi. She has never questioned the authenticity of my relationship because of my lack of a gaudy diamond decorating my left hand. She's the first to call me to get together when the guys are out of town. She also doesn't partake in the hype some of the other women do when it comes to the faux fame of being an athlete's wife.

"Don't mind Courtney. She's just pissed they're bringing in another quarterback, and Kevin's reign as leader supreme is coming to an end . . . not surprising considering how he played during preseason." She doesn't even finish the sentence before she's grabbing the untouched taco still on my plate.

"Wait. What? When did that happen?" I ask.

"They announced it this morning. How do you not know

these things? As a wide receiver, this affects Chris more than anyone else, except for Kevin." Her eyes never meet mine, and if I didn't know better, I would've thought she was whispering sweet nothings to a taco.

"The season started. Chris isn't around to tell me these things, and I don't have ESPN alerts sent to my phone like the rest of you freaks. Who'd they get?"

Instead of an answer, all I get is one flawless, manicured finger in my face while another points toward her mouth as she chews what was left of my lunch. Rolling my eyes to the heavens, I try to gather patience while she takes an eternity to swallow and chase it down with her watery Diet Coke.

"Gavin Pope—he was the Bears quarterback," she says with shrug.

She's all nonchalant while I, on the other hand, contemplate grabbing my chest and calling 911. My heart is racing so fast, I'm afraid I'm seconds away from keeling over. The sunshine now feels like a heat lamp, and my straightened hair against the back of my neck starts to curl.

"Holy shit. Are you okay? You just turned white."

"Actually, I'm feeling a little queasy. I think I drank my margarita too fast." I'm well accustomed to explaining away my distress around the wicked wives, and sitting by Naomi, hearing the one name I work overtime to avoid, is no different. "I think I'm going to head out, rest a little before Chris gets home."

"Good, go and feel better. Call me later if you need anything." Naomi's watchful gaze follows my shaky movements as I put enough money on the table to cover my bill and offer a small apology for the glitter they'll no doubt be cleaning for the next six months.

"I will, thank you." I give Naomi a hug, shout a quick goodbye to our table, and get the hell out of dodge.

The problem with a rooftop patio is there's no quick escape.

How is this my life? I know Lady Luck has never been too fond of me, but it's just cruel that out of all the quarterbacks and all the teams, Gavin Pope ends up on the Mustangs.

Halfway down the stairs, my knees are knocking so hard I have to stop and let the wall support me. My breathing won't slow, and I'm dizzy from all of the scenarios spinning in my head.

"Are you okay, ma'am?" an unexpected voice calls from behind me. I jump back and hit my head against the sports memorabilia–covered walls. One of the pictures crashes down, landing at my feet. I bend to pick it up and my shaking hands almost drop it twice before my nerves calm enough to look at it.

I forget where I am. Instead of a restaurant in a Denver suburb, I'm back in that Chicago high-rise. The guy I'd just had the hottest night of my life with—the one who told me he was an investment banker—has framed pictures of himself in his apartment. But instead of a suit, Gavin Pope wears a Bears hat with the NFL commissioner's arm draped over his shoulders.

"Ma'am?" The waiter's voice startles me back to the present.

I shake the memories of the Chicago police officers staring at my tight dress, smudged mascara, and just-been-fucked hair as I ran out of the high-rise and focus on the picture frame in my hands. It's not Gavin. Instead, it's my boyfriend, both feet in the air, football locked tight in his outstretched arms.

"I'm fine. Thank you." I hand him the frame, and then I'm running again. I don't stop until I'm sitting in my car. But once I'm inside my Prius, the news hits me all over again.

Gavin Pope.

Here.

Like a tsunami, each memory of that night hits me like another wave. His eyes as he watched me undress. *Crash*. My tongue dancing against his. *Crash*. The way he took me to the edge of euphoria over and over and over again. *Crash. Crash. Crash*. I'm drowning with the sinking realization that all of my hard work to bury every panty-dropping, toe-curling memory of that night was for nothing.

Not only did fate decide it'd be fun to remind me of him, it threw him right smack-dab in the center of my life. I mean, it's not like the quarterback holds the wide receivers' careers in their hands or anything. How could this possibly go wrong?

I guess it depends on whether Gavin Pope even remembers who I am.

Chapter 2

Chris and I live in what I fondly refer to as the seventh circle of hell—oddly enough, that's located in Denver.

We are both native Denverites; we met in high school, and somehow, Chris lucked out by being drafted by the Mustangs and never being traded. In the NFL, getting to play at all is odds defying. And staying on the same team for more than five seasons is a damn miracle.

With Chris's awesome income, the money I get from my freelance design jobs, and no kids, we should be living the high life. Denver is the coolest city with the most eclectic, vibrant mix of people. But we don't live in an industrial condo downtown or a historical bungalow in Washington Park.

No, no, no. Chris and I—just the two of us—live in eight thousand square feet of obnoxious marble and crystal covered extravagance in the gated community of all gated communities with all the other Mustang starters in #TheLandWhere-HighSchoolNeverEnds.

I grew up middle class. Chris grew up loaded. His dad is

still the most sought after plastic surgeon in Colorado—a common topic between the other wives and I. And to this day, I still have no idea who the hell Chris is trying to impress. I guess showing your daddy you're a big boy includes ugly chandeliers and gold leafed wallpaper.

After hearing about Gavin's arrival, I knew Chris was going to be upset. And because I'm such a wonderful girlfriend, I made him my world famous red velvet cake to help ease the pain. I absolutely did not make it in an effort to eat my own feelings. And the extra bowl of cream cheese frosting hidden in the back of the fridge isn't for that either. Sweet decadent denial.

"Fuck Coach Jacobs!" Chris's entrances tend to have a flair for theatrics, but he has outdone himself this time. His deep voice echoes off the gallery art–lined walls. His heavy feet against the white marble causes them to rattle. But the crowning glory on this manly display of fury is the way he launches his workout bag across the kitchen the moment he sees me. Almost as if in slow motion, I watch his Nike bag soar over the island into my favorite teal cake stand holding my beautiful, iced to perfection, world famous red velvet cake. Both fall to the floor with a frosting-padded thud.

"What the hell, Chris?" I walk over and start picking out cream cheese–covered ceramic. I'm contemplating whether or not to still eat the parts of the cake that didn't directly touch the floor when Chris starts yelling again.

"Are you really more worried about a fucking cake than me right now?"

Well . . . yes.

"Of course not. It's just a mess, and I don't want either of us to cut our feet." Lies.

Bye, cake. I'll miss you.

I stand up to look at him and when I do, I realize leaving the cake for later is for the best. Chris's normally mocha complexion has a cherry hue to it, and his full lips are pulled into a thin, straight line. If I didn't know him better, I'd think he's about to cry. "Holy shit. Are you okay?"

"No, I'm not fucking okay! That piece of shit Jacobs brought in another quarterback. Fucking Gavin Pope. Even the guy's fuckin' name is pretentious." His eyes are focused on the coffered ceiling and his hands never stop roaming his not-quite-bald head.

In all my time knowing him, I've never seen him so worked up over football.

"Kevin and I were solid. I was his receiver. With him throwing me the ball, this was going to be my biggest contract year yet. And that rat, son of a bitch, knew it. He doesn't want to fuckin' pay me, and he thought bringing in some pretty boy was going to stop me. Fuck that. He's got another thing coming."

"I thought Pope was supposed to be good?" Not like I'd know, or that I've looked up his stats once a week, every week for the last four years or anything.

"It's not about him being fucking good, Marlee!" His attention snaps toward me. It seems he didn't appreciate that little tidbit. "Do you listen when I talk to you?"

"First of all, yes, I do listen. Second, check yourself. I get you're pissed and taking it out on Nike bags and innocent, baked-with-love cakes, but you will not take it out on me. I'm not Jacobs, I didn't make this trade. I want to help you, but not if you're acting like I'm the enemy here." #99Problems-ButChrisAintOne

"Fuck. I'm sorry," Chris says. He looks properly chastised,

and resisting the urge to dust the dirt off my shoulder is almost too much for me to handle. "This was going to be our year, baby. I was going to be the number one receiver in the league; we were going to fly to Hawaii so I could play in the all-star game. I was going to get the franchise tag and the contract we've always dreamed of so we could start our family the right way—on top. Now Jacobs is putting it all at risk."

I hate the way the dormant butterflies always take flight the second Chris mentions starting a family. If he was waiting for money, he could have proposed six years ago. But instead, every year passed without an engagement and another item added to his pre-marriage bucket list. But at last, Chris is nearing the end of his list. Plus, a few weeks ago, one of my rings went missing, and when I asked him about it, he got all jittery and nervous. I've wanted to be Mrs. Chris Alexander since I was sixteen and now, nearly eleven years later, the time is almost here.

"What can I do? There has to be something we can do to keep you in your number one spot." Stepping over the long-forgotten mess on the floor, I make my way around the kitchen island (or, more accurately, the kitchen continent) to Chris and wrap my arms around him. I've always loved how when I hug him, my head rests right above his heart.

"There is something you could do. I invited the wide receivers over next Tuesday. It'd be great if you make dinner."

"Of course. Should I make Nonna's lasagna? Is TK coming? He loved it last time." Between the circles he's drawing on my back and the rhythmic thumping of his heart beneath my ear, I'm at a serious risk of falling asleep in this kitchen.

"Sure, but make double because I invited Kevin and Gavin too."

I pull back from Chris so quickly, you would've thought he told me Jeffery Dahmer was coming for dinner. Even though . . . Gavin has eaten me before.

Dammit.

Don't go there now, Marlee!

"Gavin? Why would you invite him? Weren't you just complaining because he's on the team?" I try to cover my reaction with confusion. The last thing I need is for Chris to catch a whiff of what Gavin's name does to me.

"I don't want him on the team, but he's here and the best thing I can do now is try to butter him up. Feed him some food, play some poker, try to bond with the guy. I need him to want to throw to me. So can you do it?"

I can't.

I cannot cook dinner for Gavin Pope in the home I share with Chris. Granted, my one night with him happened during the break Chris wanted . . . okay, he'd pretty much dumped me, but still. Aren't there rules about this kind of thing?

"I have a few projects, but their deadlines aren't for a couple of weeks. I'd love to do this for you. I gotta do my part to support Team Alexander."

"That's why I love you—you always put the team first." His lips crash into mine and when he pulls away, the anger he walked in with is nowhere to be found. Chris's smile is so bright, the contrast between his brown skin and freakishly white teeth nearly causes me to squint.

"You know me—they don't call me Marlee 'Team Player' Harper for no reason." And if they knew what Gavin and I did, they'd be calling me that for a whole lot of other reasons. "Speaking of, I gotta feed my man. Do you want me to make you a plate?"

"No thanks, babe. I'm gonna head back to the facility. I left early because I was pissed about Pope, but since you calmed me down, I'm gonna finish watching film. First regular season game's this weekend. I have to be ready now more than ever. You don't mind, do you?"

"Nope. Go do your superstar prep. I'll clean up here and knock out some work." I roll onto my tippy toes and kiss his chin at the same time my palm stings from slapping his ass.

"I'm not sure how long this will take, so don't wait up."

Fine with me. I have an entire Tupperware filled with cream cheese frosting, an unopened bottle of wine, and unwelcome feelings to avoid.

"Okay, but try not to burn yourself out too early in the week," I call to his back as he's walking out of the kitchen.

"Always looking out for me. Bye, babe!" I barely hear the words before the rattling of the art alerts me he's gone, and the only sounds left are the alarms bells in my head.

Holy shit.

I'm going to see Gavin Pope again.

Photo by Kristie Chadwick

ALEXA MARTIN is a writer and stay-at-home mom. A Nashville transplant, she's intent on instilling a deep love and respect for the great Dolly Parton in her four children and husband. The Playbook series was inspired by the eight years she spent as an NFL wife and her love of all things pop culture, sparkles, leggings, and wine. When she's not repeating herself to her kids, you can find her catching up on whatever Real Housewives franchise is currently airing or filling up her Etsy cart with items she doesn't need.

VISIT ALEXA MARTIN ONLINE

AlexaMartin.com

AlexaMartinBooks

AlexaMBooks